A Song of Swords

Book 3 Whill of Agora
(Legends of Agora)

Michael James Ploof

ISBN: 1492214981
ISBN-13: 9781492214984

Agora
Volnoss
Hornhollow
Sidnell
Orenden
Shierdon
The Twin Lakes
Fendale
Fennamoore
Brindon
Belldon
Bearadon
Cavanar
Eldalon
Brenahime
Brinn
Breggard
Opalmist
Ky'Dren Pass
Orington
Kell Torey
Sherna
Dy'kore
Devandes
Tren
Ry'Del
Thendor Plains
Do'adore
Senteal
Turell
Fendora Island
Burning Mountain
Eldon Island
Hentaro
Locknar
Heldon
Harrow
Horton
Orensteel
Nordon Sea
Ebony Mountains
Orindale
Uthen-Arden
Gulf of Arden
Cerushia
Drakkar
Isladon
Shoreshell
Del'Oradon
Del'Harred
Elladrindellia
Indello
Pearlton

Other Books by Michael James Ploof

Legends of Agora

Whill of Agora

A Quest of Kings

The Sock Gnome Chronicles

Billy Coatbutton and the Wheel of Destiny

Billy Coatbutton and the Ring of Sockchild

This book is dedicated to you, the reader.
Thank you for following Whill this far.

CHAPTER ONE
Elladrindellia at Long Last

Whill walked out of the gathering place with the whole of the elven assembly following him. Outside, along with the crowd, Aurora and Azzeal waited. Avriel had flown up and over the twisted vine walls of the living half-dome. She now landed not far to Whill's right.

His voice had been enhanced by the power of the sword Adromida, and his words had been heard by all within the city, and all came. Droves of elves young and old came rushing toward the gathering place at the city's center. Whill climbed atop Avriel and stood upon his saddle. He raised his arms to the crowd to be seen.

"It is he…"

"It is Whill of Agora."

"We are saved!"

"The prophecy has come true!"

The crowd erupted in a clamor of proclamations and announcements of divine glory. Will stood proud atop Avriel's back, awed at how much like humans they seemed.

"What should I say?" he asked Avriel.

"Little," she answered. "Your legend speaks for you; do not tarnish their fancy with too many words.

Will nodded his agreement, glad to have her at his side at such a time. He smiled at Aurora, who beamed back like the rest of them, though she towered head and shoulders above any elf, aside from one which had shown up in bear form.

"It is true, then?" asked a female elf with hair the color of dark moss. "You have found the sword of the great seer Adimorda, you have come to learn our ways, and you are…the savior?"

Will gulped in answer and Kellallea's words played in his head: *The prophecy is a lie; you are just a cog in a wheel of Eadon's design.*

Will panicked. Had they heard his thoughts? Was he projecting? Even now, just thinking about it made his paranoia worse. His head spun and his vision swam and he wavered upon his saddle. From on high he surveyed the crowd. Some looked on expectantly, others sobbed. Many bowed or fell to their knees, others jumped and cheered and kissed those around them. Few wore faces of skepticism; of the few that did, one was the face of Azzeal.

"Remember the garden, Whill." Avriel's voice swooped down and caught him before he passed out. To distract from Whill's state, Avriel breathed a great shooting jet of fire from her maw. Then her mind spoke to all who would listen, and her growls accentuated her words.

"It is true, as I am the daughter of Araveal, daughter of Verelus, given forfeit life anew within the body of a white dragon. I am Avriel, and he—he is the chosen one. Whill of Agora, named by Adimorda in his most far-reaching prophecy. Whill of Agora, wielder of the great power of the blade of Adimorda—the blade which no elf may wield," she reminded any who might forget.

"And she." A white claw like a sword pointed at Aurora, who froze on the spot as all turned to regard her. "This beauty of the north is Aurora Snowfell. She is of our company and named elf-friend. Many others of our company will join here soon, King Roakore of the Mountains Ro'Sar among them. We have had a grand adventure, and the tales shall be told. But for now our Whill must rest and make preparation—"

"Please, Lady Avriel! We would hear the One speak, if but a word," begged a female elf and many murmured in agreement.

The crowd hushed and waited in perfect silence for Whill to speak. Avriel crooked her neck around to look at him. Her eyes searched his but she offered no guidance. Whill cleared his throat, and to him the sound echoed in the silent anticipation.

"I am Whill of Agora," he shouted.

"The blade!" yelled a male elf. "We would lay eyes upon the blade of legend!"

Whill unsheathed his sword and raised it high. From it blinding light poured forth and outshone the light of day.

"I have found the blade Adromida! With it I shall vanquish the enemy, and once again bring peace to Agora!"

The crowd erupted in cheers as he sheathed the blade of legend. Avriel wasted no time. She leapt from the ground and flew off with Whill, the cheers and shouts of the crowd following them to the outskirts of the city.

"To where do we fly?" Whill asked over the wind.

"I would see my brother," Avriel replied. "You did well back there."

He scoffed at that. "I wasn't prepared to be worshipped like a god. I expected elves to act less…"

"Human?" she offered.

"I suppose," said Whill.

They circled the house of healing in which Zerafin and Avriel's bodies lay. Whill sensed overwhelming trepidation from Avriel; he guessed that she did not want to see her soulless body. He gave her time and together they circled until the dragon took a deep long breath and ascended to the balcony overlooking one of the Thousand Falls' channels.

From the cliffs beyond the water poured into rivers which flowed calmly through the city and surrounding land. Everywhere about the land were arched foot-bridges of vine and stone. Mist from the falls bathed the land with life-giving vapor. Trees grew to new heights here, unlike anything to be found within Agora. Even the native flora and fauna grew larger within the city's borders. The house of healing was a wide (and at the moment roofless) dome; from living vines hung silk curtains, now open. Around the sick beds stood a half a dozen elves, hands locked and voices humming. The healers were dressed in brilliant white robes, and upon their heads sat what looked to be gemmed crowns that glowed softly. Their deep voices chanted in unison for the sick. As Whill and Avriel approached, they broke the circle and stepped aside. Many bowed to the two, offering their condolences.

Whill stroked the head of Avriel's comatose elven body which lay next to Zerafin's tortured form. Many elves tended to them, some working to keep Avriel's body alive, others holding Zerafin's rotting curse from consuming his body. The Elf prince was not lucid but suffered feverish sleep and often thrashed in his throws of agony.

An elf approached with four hand maidens in tow, by the look of her he guessed that she was the Queen of Elladrindellia. She wore long flowing robes of sunrise orange and a simple silver crown upon her head. Whill stood and looked to Avriel for guidance, she however did not see him, like the others she was watching as her mother strode into the house. She walked right up to Whill with a wide smile and took his hands in hers.

"Whill, it is good to see you again."

"Queen Araveal, I am pleased to meet you, though I do not remember the first time." Whill replied.

"It was long ago, you were young. On behalf of all elves of Elladrindellia I welcome you to the elven lands, that which your ancestor gifted us with centuries ago," said the Queen.

She looked to the sword and then to her children's sleeping forms. Whill looked to them also and cringed to see how the rot ate away at Zerafin's skin.

"I can help, with the sword…"

"You are not strong enough to attempt to counter Eadon's spell." Queen Araveal argued.

"Then I can lend the power of Adromida to one who can," he begged, hating to see Zerafin suffer so.

"Perhaps, once the spell is deciphered. It is a powerful and complex spell. Our greatest spell crafters have yet to fully understand it. Any interference now could mean the death of my son. It cannot be attempted as of yet."

Whill new her to be right, he could not hope to unravel Eadon's spell. He resigned himself to the hope that the spell crafters would soon figure it out. They sat in silence near to the running river with Avriel in dragon form close by.

After a time Whill turned to the queen and was about to ask the question that had been on his mind for some time. But before he could ask she spoke.

"You would ask why we did not keep you here as an infant, to be raised with knowledge of your lineage."

Whill waited for the explanation. He could see the worry on the queen's face as she gazed upon her children's sleeping forms.

"It was decided by Abram and I that you would be safer if you were kept secret. This is the first place that Eadon would think to look, and we were not sure of spies in our midst. Therefore you were taken far away, and few were privy to the knowledge of your whereabouts. But know that I have always watched over you from afar."

Whill smiled back at her though he did not quite agree with the long ago decision. Kellallea came to mind, and her claims that the prophecy was a lie. He still did not know what to think of it.

"When we took the gate to Drindellia, and spoke to the ancient Kellallea, she told me that the prophecy was a lie."

"Yes I know." said the queen. "Avriel and I have spoken about it."

Whill was surprised by her calm demeanor in the face of such a possibility. "Do you believe it?"

She answered without hesitation. "I don't know. It would explain many things. What do you believe?"

Whill let out a sigh. "I know that Kellallea believed it."

She repeated the question. "What do you believe?"

"I do not know, but my heart tells me that it is true. I am nothing but a pawn in Eadon's grand scheme, just another cog in the wheel. I know that I will never be ready to face him. He is ancient and I am young, and...I am afraid."

"As you should be... you bear a great burden, but you need not bear it alone."

"Why did Eadon make war in the first place?" asked Whill.

Araveal looked past the clouds to that faraway time so long ago. "He created the Draggard. In his time Eadon was a brilliant... there is no word in your tongue, to us it is a science word, call it life builder. He created things of beauty beyond words, flowers of such radiance and life, the sweetest fruit trees. He melded plant with plant and tree with tree. His work was a thing of renown and praise."

"But then he began to meld animal with animal. At first it was allowed, for he bred stronger and faster horses, larger bulls and beautiful felines. Then he unveiled his most abominable creation, he crossed dragon and elf, and created a draggard queen. It is said that the first of her litter were sired by him, and she gave him seven daughters. They in turn gave birth to the draggard as we know them now."

Whill was disgusted by the thought of the draggard being Eadon's children and grandchildren. He gained a new respect for the dark elf's insanity.

"My husband the king sent a regime of fifty soldiers to destroy the creatures and take Eadon into custody to answer for his crimes against nature."

Whill looked to the queen whom had quieted, she looked older that she had a moment ago.

"And he killed them all?" Whill guessed, the queen's nod prove him correct.

"Yes, and then he killed the next group and another after that. By then news of the warring had reached far and wide and a movement began within Drindellia that eventually proved fatal to our people. You see Eadon appealed with a silver tongue and pleading heart to those of us that had no magic. He told them that he was a victim as they were. That he was being attacked for being different from us as they were."

"Were they convinced?" asked Whill.

"You have met him, what do you think?"

Whill saw her point. She went on. "He promised them the one thing that they could not attain, he promised them power. He did something that no one had ever been able to do. He gave the non-magical, magic, as humans call it. They became his dark elves. We could not stop him then, and we may not be able to stop him now. We are less in number by far, but we have you."

Whill shook his head and looked into her dark pools of endless watching. "No. You also have the people of Agora, and you have the mighty Dwarves. I believe that if the prophecy is a lie, then I can at least be the one to bring you all together. Perhaps then we can defeat the dark elves, together.""Perhaps," she agreed.

Aurora was out of sorts in the strange elf city. She had not seen Azzeal since they arrived and Whill had been off doing whatever it was that kings did. She did not miss the attention of the white dragon-elf Avriel.

It was not until she finally gave in to the offer for something they called Lahakara that she felt comfortable there. What Lahakara turned out to be was what humans might call a bath house, but with many strong hands and flower scented oils. She was gently stripped of her battle marked and torn clothes and bathed in steaming water that smelled of forest and spring flowers. She was washed by the elf maidens from head to toe with soap and cloth, and then her hair was washed twice. The hot water did wonders for her aching body, it had been hell riding that dragon for days, and her arse had the bruises to show for it. She soaked for nearly an hour before being led out of the water and wrapped in soft towels.Through a stone archway and into the next room she was led. There soft music played from a flute player siting on the window sill. Beyond him through a large window was a view of the city and Thousand Falls beyond.

She was led to the center of the room where her towels were discarded and her maidens stepped aside for a tall red haired elf woman with sharp features. She wore a folded silk robe of purple with flowing wide sleeves. In her hand she held a smooth staff of black wood set with a large fiery opal at the top. The elf women smiled at Aurora as she looked up at her. She looked over her tall and muscled form with obvious admiration.

"Hello, I am Kreshna, if you would allow me I can mend your wounds and ease any pain you may have."

Aurora offered the elf her hand. The knuckles had been scraped bare by draggard faces and were crusted over with scabs. Kreshna indicated to a raised silk-covered bed upon which she could lay. She lay on her back and offered up her large hand. Kreshna's hands were half the size. The elf laid them over the wounds and closed eyes and smiled. A soft blue glow arose from the contact and Aurora's hand tingled. When the hands were lifted she beheld her skin renewed. In this way Kreshna healed her many wounds. Her job done, Kreshna bowed and took her leave and was replaced by twin male elves that put their strong hands to work rubbing out every ache and kink in her large muscles. Aurora napped at she was worked on. She was beginning to like the elves a great deal.

The queen took her leave after a time and Whill remained with the siblings. He gazed upon Avriel's body, beautiful still but missing the life force that had possessed it. The body was a shell, Whill realized then. The body mattered not; it was but a tool to house the spirit, and the body's animal needs and wants were just that.

Whill laid the back of his hand upon Avriel's cheek; it was warm. Tears came to his eyes and threatened to pour forth like the Thousand Falls. Avriel bent and gently nudged Whill's shoulder. With his free hand he touched her dragon cheek.

"I am sorry, Avriel; I do not know how to help. I have all the power I need, yet I am powerless."

Avriel mentally smiled upon him. *It is no fault of your own. I have a body, one given to me by the dark one. One day he will wish he had killed me; he will wish he had killed us both.*

Whill nodded in agreement and moved to stand before her brother. Zerafin's skin rippled and bubbled slowly. Here and there it browned and then blackened, but quickly the rot receded. The constant efforts of the healers were the only thing keeping him alive. Whill nodded to each of the dozen healers in turn and offered his thanks. One, an elf who looked no older than a child, stepped forward with a bow. "It is true, then? The One has come to us at long last?" "I am he," Whill said confidently.

"Then let us see the healing powers of the one who wields the blade of legend. Surely with the blade you can help your friend."

Whill looked into the elf child's eyes, wisdom and age far beyond his delicate features looked back. This elf was no child, Whill realized. More likely he was a great healer of untold years.

Whill set his jaw with determination and laid a hand upon Zerafin. He nearly jumped when Zerafin suddenly spoke. "Ah, Whill," he said with a cough. "You have made it here alive. I can rest easy now."

"We found the blade, don't you remember? With it I can—"

"No!" Zerafin cried with an effort that visibly drained him and the healers. "No, you cannot attempt to heal me. The bond that was created by the backfire spell I used is too dangerous. Eadon will feel your presence."

"There must be a way!" Whill protested.

"Go!" Zerafin stiffened with pain. "He knows...he feels you even...now...aaahhh!" He convulsed and began to shake. Whill reached for him but his hands were held fast by the elf boy's strong hands.

"He is being possessed..." The elf's eyes widened as Zerafin floated many feet above the bed, thrashing and frothing at the mouth, fighting the influence of Eadon through their connection, a connection that afflicted them both as one.

"Fight him, brother!" Avriel screamed in their minds.

"Please! I can help!" Whill shouted as healers began pouring into the room. Zerafin spun to stand upon the bed and his hands shot out to either side, sending the elves flying into the walls of vine. His eyes rolled back to show only bloodshot whites, and a voice that was not the elf's spoke.

"You can help him, boy, what are you waiting for?" said Eadon through Zerafin.

An elf flew to Zerafin's outstretched hand and was held by the throat many feet off the ground. Zerafin's face twisted into Eadon's maniacal grin. "How many more must die, boy, before you embrace your destiny?"

Knowing what was coming, Whill reached out to the air and cried, "No!" as Eadon used Zerafin to snap the elf's neck. The body of the healer then burst into flames and disintegrated to ash. Zerafin's face contorted in a scream of rage and he said in his own voice, "Kill me now! Quickly before he—" His voice was cut short by a scream of anguish as Eadon gained control once more. With an extended hand he lifted the weakened body of Avriel. In dragon form she roared as Eadon held her elven body by the throat.

Three healers attacked Zerafin with a host of multicolored spells. They were easily deflected and counterattacked by the possessed elf. Eadon blasted a hole through the chest of one and tore the head from another with the flick of a wrist, the elf's energy shield destroyed in a shower of sparks. The third elf was blasted through the wall of vine with such force that a large hole was torn in the living wall. Zerafin screamed in a deafening, booming voice, and the vines that created the house of healing withered with blackened death.

"Which will it be, hero? Your beloved Avriel, trapped forever in the body of a beast, or the warrior prince of Drindellia?"

"Let them go! It is me you want!" Whill screamed.

"Kill him or she dies!"

Whill frantically tried to think of something, anything that would help. Zerafin's white eyes and evil grin stared at him with sick satisfaction. Rage boiled within Whill and threatened to destroy him. The sword at his side hummed with power, he had but to reach for it.

"Decide, boy! Who shall die for you this day?" Eadon roared as flames rose up in a ring around the blackened house of healing. Whill unsheathed his blade, Adromida, with a cry of rage. Eadon's victorious grin spread across the face of Zerafin. Whill could not stand idly by while Avriel's elven body was destroyed. He had hidden and run from Eadon for too long. Now he held the greatest power given. The blade glowed white in his grip and the power it possessed poured into Whill, leaving him vibrating with energy. Before Whill could strike, Azzeal leapt through the flames and shot three glowing arrows at Zerafin in rapid succession. The arrows were deflected easily, and with his free hand Eadon shot writhing tendrils of black energy at the elf.

Whill summoned a shield around Azzeal, deflecting the energy attack. Azzeal extended a hand and yelled to Whill over the tumult, "Lend me the strength!"

Whill took the elf's hand and through their contact sent a rush of teeming energy. The surge caused Azzeal to stiffen straight and he gritted his teeth against it. With extended hand Azzeal hit the possessed Zerafin in the chest with a beam of purest white light. Whill poured power into the elf, and likewise Azzeal into Zerafin. Avriel's body was released and dropped to the ground. Zerafin's head snapped back and his body began to convulse. In his rage Eadon was trying to kill Zerafin through their spell connection. Azzeal redoubled his efforts, and a surge of power passed through Whill like none he had wielded before. Zerafin was lifted high, arms and legs extending straight out as he screamed, "Be gone from my vessel!" and fell to the floor.

In an instant it was over. Azzeal broke contact with Whill and ran to the side of his friend. Zerafin pushed him away weakly and crawled over to his sister's limp body. He looked up to the white dragon and smiled. "Your body lives."

Whill slumped to the floor of the destroyed house of healing and a smile crept across his face. "We beat him," he said to no one.

"He was not destroyed," said Azzeal. "I only freed Zerafin of his mental grip; with your help I destroyed the spell that bound the two."

"He may yet live," said Whill. "But there is hope. He has been beaten."

You are cured, brother!

Zerafin looked to his sister's dragon form while holding the head of her elven body in his lap. The fires that had circled the house of healing had died down, and healers and other elves rushed to the scene. Whill could not help but smile to himself. He had lent his power to Azzeal and they had successfully defeated Eadon, at least for a time. His mind spun with the implications of this new method's uses. He looked at Azzeal and caught the elf's eyes lingering upon the blade in Whill's hand. Azzeal met Whill's gaze but no guilt showed upon the elf's face. He nodded slightly and then set about helping Zerafin to his feet. Whill quickly joined to help, and together the three ferried Avriel's body away from the smoldering house of healing.

Whill,

If you are reading this I am no longer of this world. I hope that you have reached Elladrindellia safely. There you will be able to continue your training and learn things that I could have never taught you.

I pray that you have found the sword Adromida. With it I believe that you will fulfill the prophecy and bring an end to Eadon and his minions. I believe now, as I always have, that you will be victorious. You have been a wonderful student and dear friend, and I am thankful to have known you.

Remember all you have learned and apply what you know. I am confident that one day you shall be a great king like your father before you.

I am sorry that I could not remain at your side. But take heart that you are not alone in this. You will always find allies, as you have found in Roakore and the other companions. Tarren is strong in mind and body, and I am confident that with your guidance he will become a man of virtue as you have. Be true to yourself, my friend, and remember what you have learned. Do not worry about that which is out of your hands, and do not attempt to bear the entire weight of your destiny alone. Look to your friends.

If it is in your power to do so, please send word of my fate to my sister Teera. She worries about us both as always. If you are able to pay her a visit, she has possessions of mine that I have willed to you. She will be delighted to see you after so many years. Send her and the girls my love, and ensure her that my death means little given the grand life that I have lived.

One day you will rid Agora of the evil of the dark elves, and it shall know peace once again. This I believe with all my heart and soul. So go forth, my friend, knowing that I am with you always. You will never be alone, for we cannot all be alone together. Go forth and know that I love you as a son. You are a man beyond worth. I am honored to have shared the adventure of life with you.

Goodbye for now, until we dine with the gods...

Abram

Whill read the letter a second time with wet eyes and trembling hands, after the third time he rolled up the letter and put it away. He had been given it by Avriel's mother, whom Abram had entrusted it to. From his balcony within the vine-covered elven city of Cerushia, he sat and gazed absently upon the waterfalls that poured forth from the towering ridge to the west. Avriel was out there somewhere hunting, morning being her favorite time to seek out her meals. He sat alone in his meditative stance and reflected upon the past year. Not even a year ago he had been a carefree ranger of Agora, with Abram at his side and not a worry to be had. He had defeated a knight of Eldalon and won a fortune in gold, and he had seen his dream ship built by a master of the craft. He had fought pirates and freed slaves and torn a child from the clutches of death. Fame followed him and fortune smiled. Elves called him savior and dwarves named him friend. He was the son of a fallen king, hidden from the world for nearly two decades. He led men to victory and wielded great power. His legend was whispered throughout the kingdoms as his feats grew. He chuckled at the memory of the bar fight when the group had been together. Thinking back on the companions' time together, he longed for those days. Whill laughed at the irony of longing for a time in his life when he had been so confused and scared. He had been dealing with the truth of his lineage, and the prophecy. Looking back now he did not recognize his younger self. He had changed so much in such a short time. Eadon had seen to that. The torture was now a distant memory, one he refused to let his mind drift to. It was a constant struggle, keeping the demons from his mind. He fought uncontrollable fits of rage and quickly descending bouts of depression. His mind, if left to its devices, would have torn itself asunder. Therefore Whill had become the warden of his mind, and constantly had to keep at bay the plethora of maddening thoughts.

He thought again of Abram as he breathed deeply through an episode of particularly disturbing vulgarities and rage directed at him from a tormented inmate of his mind, one of the multitudes of self-hating phantoms. Love was the only thing that worked for him. Whill concentrated on pure love, imagined it washing over him and radiating from him. He pictured his spirit glowing forth like a sun, the energy around him connecting and pulsing in a megalithic tide of love. He smiled brightly and breathed deeply and focused upon the reality he had chosen. He had learned much from the elves, and already their techniques were helping him immensely. He was in possession of the greatest elven power likely ever created, Adromida, and he needed to be in complete control of his mind if he wished to wield it. Whill had set out to become a master of his self, and to learn as much of the magic he wielded as he could.

Abram had always believed in Whill, and knowing that the prophecy might be a lie left him feeling cold. If Kellallea had spoken the truth and Eadon was indeed Adimorda, the very elf who had predicted the rise of a dark lord, Whill did not know how he could ever beat the dark elf. Whill had been reasonably confident that he could defeat Eadon when he had believed the prophecy without doubt. Now he was not so sure. To think that he had been created by Eadon terrified him. He knew not how the dark elf could be defeated if indeed the blade Adromida was his, for it could not be used against him. Though the question remained as to why Eadon would make a blade of power that he himself could not wield, this question only gave credence to Kellallea's tale. If the legend of power taken and power given was true, then Eadon had to be given the power of Adromida, as he had already attained the greatest power taken.

Avriel came soaring down to land upon the balcony. *Good morning,* she crooned and set to grooming herself.

"Good morning," Whill replied with a smile.

He was amazed at her cheery mood since her return to her people. Even upon seeing her comatose body she did not react as Whill thought she might. It seemed that Eadon's words were true, and none but he could restore her soul to her body. The elves had been searching for an answer for more than six months, utilizing every text and their collective knowledge, some had even contacted the spirits, but to no avail. Eadon's magic was foreign to them, and it seemed that Avriel might never be helped. Even with the great power Whill possessed within the blade Adromida, he could not begin to understand what to do to help her. Whill had arrived in Drindellia in bad shape. He was malnourished and had lost a substantial amount of muscle mass. Though the elves could heal much with their magic, nothing could replace proper rest, food, and exercise. He had finally begun to get enough of each as of late. He felt safe here among the elves, as he had not in a long while. And though he had only been within Elladrindellia for two days, he was at home here. Autumn was upon the world, and the elven city was like something out of a dream. Native trees there were, their leaves covering the ground in a cascade of vibrant fall colors. Many of the different plants and bushes had been brought from the elven homeland, as had many varieties of trees. There were leafy ones as well as pines, and others such as the kornalla tree, which grew draping canopies of long leaves.

It did Whill's tormented heart good to behold such beauty after his nightmarish imprisonment for those six long months. He could hardly wait to explore Elladrindellia with Avriel. He did not leave his abode often, and he could not. Hundreds of elven followers had crowded the city for a glimpse of him. These were true believers, those who saw Whill as the savior of their people. He looked down at them from on high now and again, but mostly he remained in a high tower within a vine-and-stone building near the outskirts of the city. From one balcony he viewed the lush jungle, and from the other he saw the vast city. From all directions crowds of elves could be seen. When he peered out of his window they cheered; some flew by the windows and even landed upon the balcony to meet him (after asking permission). He had been visited by many of the elders, and the queen, Avriel's mother, came daily.

The barbarian Aurora Snowfell stayed in a room just below him. They had seen little of each other, however, due to Whill's seemingly endless meetings with a variety of elves. His least favorite ones were the grovelers; indeed, he favored skeptics and nonbelievers over these blubbering fools. They treated him as though he was a god, and he found it quite disturbing. Most other young men his age would have seized the power offered them, would have basked in the adoration of their followers, but Whill wanted none of it. The queen had told him this was what made him worthy; she also explained that had he been raised in such an environment as he now knew, he would have become a very different person. Perhaps it had been best to be raised as a normal Agoran.

He and Avriel had flown out and around Cerushia a handful of times. Gliding over the city of vine and stone, Whill marveled at the beauty of the elven creation. They melded wood and stone, vine and earth, to create an ever-changing living city of splendor. Large crystals hummed with stored power from the day's sun, and vines acted as conduits, drawing the power from the crystals and spreading it throughout the city. Similar crystals were used to collect the rays of the moon. The gathered energy was used mainly in fortifying the many wards and spells about the city. Not only did the elves build upward, but they also utilized the earth beneath them, building tunnels and caverns and passageways the likes of which would make a dwarf proud. If it ever came to it, the elven city of Cerushia could hold out against an enemy attack indefinitely. To break through its spell defenses would take a power unknown. Never, even within Drindellia, had the elves ever concentrated so much power. Cerushia hummed with life. Breathing in the very air lifted the spirits and cleared the mind. In comparison, Whill could only think of the smell of the forest in spring after a hard rain. He had been truly impressed with the elven city. He had expected to find wispy creatures glowing with inner light and living in huge tree houses; instead he'd found hard-working people who were quick to smile and quick to laugh.

Whill could not tell from looking at an elf whether or not it knew magic. He knew that a larger percentage of the population had no skill in the practice of Orna Catorna whatsoever, and were no more magical than the average human. Those who were not skilled in the arts were masters of other crafts—one did not have to be magical to create amazing things or accomplish extraordinary feats. Indeed, most things, be they sculptures or paintings or woodworks, were appreciated even more if created using no magic at all. The wisest of the nonmagic elves said it was because the gods had given them hands to do the mind's work, and that hands had a magic all their own, a special link to the mind and soul. It was after all from the hands of the casters that their spells poured.

The sun had grown in the sky, emerging from its morning cocoon of blazing fire, and now shone through the mist from the east. Whill looked out over the balcony. The elves below were dressed in a wide array of styles, but the basic theme was one of seasonal colors and even foliage and feather. Many others were not dressed at all, even those not in animal forms; lithe and beautiful they shone in the morning light. Whill blushed, though he had no audience. He doubted he would get used to that part of elven society.

Why do you blush? Avriel asked with a deep hum.

Whill jerked his head toward her as if he had been caught at something. *No reason,* he said quickly. *Come; let us be off, I begin training today.*

Avriel's smile could make a damsel faint. Now she smiled widely.

"What?" Whill asked aloud.

Avriel huffed smoke out of her nostrils and shook her head but said nothing more, and to Whill's relief she did not speak of his thoughts.

CHAPTER TWO

Black Rum and Pipe Smoke

Roakore thumbed through the book he had found within the elven library. He had yet to prove its authenticity, but he had a feeling. The elf Azzeal had ensured him that it had indeed been written by none other than the first Agoran dwarf king, Ky'Dren, but he was not about to take the elf's word for it.

He could not decipher a word of text, as it was written entirely in Elvish. Why would a dwarf write a book in Elvish? This was the burning question that filled Roakore's mind.

Upon his return to his mountain kingdom, he had immediately been bombarded with pressing issues. The human refugees he had sent to his mountain had arrived without incident and had been recovering from their journey. They had settled into one of the many vacant living quarters within the dwarf mountain and were doing well. They would hold out there until spring, when Roakore had vowed to help them rebuild their ruined town. Tarren had been particularly excited with the arrival of other humans, and had since been showing them around the mountain kingdom.

Roakore had been overcome with pride to learn that his son Helzendar, along with his teammates, including Tarren, had passed their trials. They were now no longer children by dwarven standards, which meant that Helzendar would be allowed to make the dangerous journey through enemy territory to Elladrindellia.

Tarren could hardly wait to set out to see Whill and the elven land, but before that journey could be made, Roakore was waiting to hear from the many search parties. He had sent them out to scour every inch of the inside of the Ro'Sar mountain kingdom. They were looking for a portal similar to the one that had magically taken Whill's company to the lost elven country of Drindellia. Roakore had always puzzled over how the draggard had suddenly poured into Ro'Sar those decades ago when the mountain was taken. It made sense that they could have come through one of the seven pairs of Gates of Arkron, magical elven portals created during a time lost to history. He would not leave until he was sure that the gate no longer remained within his mountain. It was possible that they had been removed once their purpose was through, but it was also possible that they remained, waiting to be used again. Roakore had vowed that would never happen again.

He pondered while he absently gazed upon the book. The only light within his personal quarters was a single burning candle. He had taken his late father's quarters, and it was here that he felt the closest to his father and king. His father had spent many days and nights here and was never to be disturbed. Roakore knew it was because he had had a large taste for spirits but preferred to drink alone.

Roakore raised a glass of wheat beer, a gift from the refugees, and offered cheers in the name of his father. He guzzled down the fine ale and chased it with a shot of black rum. There he sat through many more drinks, pondering the book on his desk until he finally passed out, mumbling of secrets and elven libraries.

Roakore awoke to a light tapping upon his shoulder and a soft voice calling his name. He smiled to himself as he dreamt but was shaken awake.

"Bah, what you want?" he grumbled and looked to see his royal brain, Nah'Zed, scowling back at him.

"Your highness—"

"I told ye a million times if I done told ye once, I be hatin' them fancy-pants titles! Call me Roakore, or King, or King Roakore."

"Right then, King, your search parties have all reported back."

Roakore jumped to his feet and looked around aimlessly for his boots, all in a huff. "Why didn't ye say so?"

Two hours later, Roakore had heard the reports of the many search parties. Nothing had been found. The report did nothing to quench his nagging feeling of trepidation. He had immediately ordered a second, more thorough search of the mountain. He wanted to be sure before he left his mountain kingdom once more.

Nah'Zed had not taken kindly to the idea of Roakore's leaving again, and did not waste any opportunity to tell him so. The truth was that Roakore did not think he was cut out for the tedious work of being king. He did not enjoy sitting idle within the mountain, dealing with the never-ending workload that came with his position. He longed for the road as his axe longed for battle. It was the reason he had often volunteered for lookout duty outside of the Ky'Dren Mountains when his people had lived there after the fall of his mountain. It had been on such a patrol that he'd first met Whill and Abram.

It was true that he was anxious to have his precious Book of Ky'Dren translated, and hear what secrets of his lineage it might hold. But the trip to Elladrindellia held other lures. He was curious to see the elven land, and he was worried about his elf friend Zerafin. The last he had heard, Zerafin was in a bad way, suffering from a rotting curse at the hands of Eadon, and Roakore was worried.

Roakore made his way to find a late breakfast, his many troubles following him down the dimly lit tunnels.

"It is gonna be amazing Helz!" Tarren promised Helzendar as he flipped through the page of a book he had been given by Lunara.

Helzendar eyed the colorful pictures of the elf land in the book with skepticism. "I don't know, looks weird to me. Why in Ky'Dren's beard did they cover all that pretty stone with them ugly vines?"

"Bah, they ain't ugly. Lunara says they actually strengthen the structures. And those, the crystals, they collect sunlight and power lanterns and things," he said, drunk with wonder.

Helzendar nodded. "Yeah, they got one o' them crystals up atop the peaks o' the Helgar Mountains. Powers the main city proper it does. A gift from the elves it was. They are a queer lot, them Helgar dwarves, usin' elf magics and such."

"Geesh! Those are harsh words against your own. Helgar was a king of Ky'Dren, you be knowin'," said Tarren.

"Yeah, I be knowin' me own history. I be son o' the king, ain't I?" said Helzendar. "What, you be likin' every human o' Eldalon?"

Tarren thought about it. "No, I guess not."

"Besides," said Helzendar, "I didn't say I don't like 'em."

"Yeah, well, the new door of Roakore that they put up last month was blessed with elf magic, you know. What's the big deal with using elf magic? Why do the dwarves dislike the elves so much?"

Helzendar was instantly flustered. "Why we be dislikin', eh? What's to like? They brought the dark elves here, didn't they? You know how many o' me clan died because o' the elves? Not to mention me grandfather and uncles. Roakore be the last o' his father's children 'cause o' them."

Tarren was sorry he asked, given Helzendar's reaction. "Yeah, I can see were there would be some bad blood. But we be needin' their help against the dark elves."

"Bah! You mean they be needin' our help to clean up their mess."

"Yeah, I suppose so," said Tarren. He hadn't thought of it that way before. He let the topic go and went back to his elven book. He couldn't wait to see Elladrin-dellia. More so he couldn't wait to see Whill once again. Thoughts of Whill led him to think of Abram. Tarren had been greatly saddened by the news of Abram's and Rhunis' deaths. They had both been men who'd seemed larger than life; he still couldn't believe they were dead.

His thoughts inevitably led him to frustration at his own age and weakness. He would give anything to be able to help in the coming battle. He could train with the dwarves all he wanted, but he would not be strong enough to be of help until he was grown. But one day he would be grown, and though the war would be over by then, there would still be evil in the world, and he had vowed to the spirits of his family that he would dedicate his life to fighting for those who could not. He would one day be a strong and powerful man with years of training behind him, and those of evil heart would quiver at the mention of his name.

Lunara finished healing the last of the injured human refugees. She had been hard at work for nearly two days mending the many wounds they had received when their town was attacked.

Holdagozz steadied her when she swooned from the exertion, and though she could have stood on her own she welcomed his support. He guided her to a chair within the makeshift infirmary and was quick to offer her a drink of mountain spring water, which she took thankfully. Though she used the energy within her staff to heal, her mind was thoroughly spent. She had spent countless hours in deep concentration mending bone and reconnecting muscle, and the work had taken its toll. Seeing this, Holdagozz offered to take her back to her room.

"I appreciate the offer, but I would remain here, I may be needed..." she said softly as she was hit with another dizzy spell.

"At least take a cot and get some sleep. We got a long road before us to your lands," insisted Holdagozz as he led her to a cot and covered her with blankets.

"You are coming with us, then?" she asked brightly.

"'Course I be, me place is by me king. And I would see you and Tarren to Elladrindellia safely."

She smiled at that and closed her eyes to much-needed sleep. Holdagozz watched her and looked out over the dozens of people she had healed. He was awed by her healing power, a power that had saved his very life. And though he was a strong dwarven warrior, made stronger still by her very hands, he was humbled by her ability to reverse sickness and injury and steal from death its helpless victims.

Not only did he marvel at her skill but also her beauty. He had never seen one who shone so with such radiating inner light. Her energy was that of a child, and she was filled with the wonder and awe of life usually beaten out of people by tragedy and age. Perhaps it was because she was young for an elf, young by all standards.

Looking upon her, Holdagozz was reminded of the beauty of life. He was reminded that miracles did exist, and where there was darkness, there too was blinding light. She had saved him from the clutches of death, had given him a second chance at life. He would be forever grateful, and always in her debt and at her service.

"Aye, Holdagozz, come share a drink. We have much to speak of."

He was jolted from his reverie by his king's hushed voice. Holdagozz felt his face flush from the knowing look he got from Roakore. He got up and followed the king to the common room that was part of the humans' quarters. Two large high-backed chairs had been set beside the large fireplace, and between them sat a small table and a bottle of black rum. They sat, and Holdagozz rubbed his hands together near the fire, waiting to hear Roakore's reprimand. None came.

Roakore poured two glasses of rum and together they cheered Ky'Dren and tossed the drinks back. Roakore poured himself and Holdagozz another and sat back to smoke his pipe and sip from his glass.

"I be gladdened that you'll be comin' with us, Holdagozz. It ain't the same out there without a good dwarf at yer side, I say."

Holdagozz took the compliment with a smile and lit his own pipe. "It's gonna be a dangerous road, it is…"

Roakore sniffed at the air and looked at his friend's pipe. "What's that ye be smoking, eh? That be no Shierdon leaf."

"Nah, it ain't," Holdagozz confirmed. "It be from the refugees you done saved from the shyte-eatin' draggard. Their main crop it is, an' it's got a smoothness to rival the best."

Roakore quickly tapped out the cherry from his pipe and offered it to Holdagozz with a lick of his lips. "Pack her full."

Holdagozz filled his king's pipe and handed it back. Roakore puffed up the fire slow and steady. His cheeks bulged and he blew out a swirling silver ring.

"Nah'Zed!"

"Yes, me king!" she said as loudly, clearly annoyed at being shouted at though she was sitting three feet away.

"See to it that a small barrel o' this weed finds its way to Silverwind's saddlebags. In return, give the humans a few pints o' me twenty-year-old Helgarian sweet rum."

Nah'Zed wrote swiftly and sent a dwarf off with the request. Holdagozz blew a ring of his own and wore it like a halo for a long moment. "Think they got any weed o' their own there, them elves?"

"Bah!" answered Roakore. "You'll never catch me smokin' no elf weed. Who knows what them folk do to it. Probably have magic farts for a week."

Helzendar coughed his last toke and choked with laughter. "Haha, rainbow farts!"

"Bwahaha!" laughed Roakore, and Nah'Zed joined in the mirth. Then Nah'Zed suddenly farted and gave an embarrassed "oh!" The squeak of a toot sent the two dwarves falling to the floor in convulsions.

"Magic farts, bwahaha!"

CHAPTER THREE
The Crystal Palace

Dirk was awoken by a shift in pressure in the room. The grip on his dagger tightened and his eyes opened slightly; otherwise he made no movement. He smelled the intruder and knew it to be Eadon. He relaxed his grip and sat up.

"I am done here. We return to Agora," Eadon said. He looked Dirk over with searching eyes. "Are you ready to meet your army…General?"

Dirk remembered his pact, reminded himself of his pledge of fealty. Such a pledge to Eadon could not be broken but on pain of death. Eadon had shown him how it worked by forcing a human prisoner to plead fealty, and then attempt to defy his will. He had convulsed and thrashed until finally, frothing at the mouth, he dropped dead. Dirk knew then that had he not told Eadon of Whill's location, he would have died. Dirk had asked Eadon why then did Aurora live—he had guessed correctly that she too had sworn fealty. Eadon informed him that it was due to the fact that she had tried to kill Abram, and he would have died had Whill not healed him. She had not yet moved against Eadon in any way, and therefore would live.

"We shall see how that feisty little icicle plays out," Eadon had said, to his own amusement.

He led Dirk through the halls of the tower of crystal. It jutted out in every direction and in every color, shining a thousand reflections in the midday sun. Within the mammoth crystal palace were rooms and halls, libraries and weaponries, servants and slaves, waterfalls and wine. Dirk felt like he was living in a waking dream, one as beautiful and mysterious as it was dark and disturbing. The crystal pulsed in unison with a low, almost soothing hum of power. The assassin had been given lavish quarters within the crystal palace. Krentz was even released to live there with him, though she still felt like a prisoner, they both did. But at least they were prisoners together, she had told him. Being with her brought him a peace he had not known without her. Whether they were ever freed from Eadon's clutches, he did not at the moment care. He was with her again. They fell asleep in each other's arms, shared stories of their adventures since parting those years before. They made love and they watched the sun rise and set through the multicolored walls of the crystal palace.

Dirk knew not how the thing might possibly work, and could not guess what great amounts of power it must have taken to do so, but the castle-sized crystal flew. He had been awed when he first saw the approaching crystal city, after he had been found and healed by Eadon. The thing had shot through the air at impossible speeds and come to hover over their heads. Eadon had grabbed him by the collar and flown them both up and into the crystal. Then the crystal shot off again in the direction it had come.

Inside, Dirk found a fortress teaming with dark elves and his breath was taken away. It was not the number of dark elves, which he guessed to be in the hundreds, but their appearance: they were Eadon's twins, identical in all regards except for the vacancy in their eyes, the lifelessness. The only others who lived within the crystal palace were select dark elves and women for Eadon's pleasures.

"They are me," Eadon had explained of the identical dark elves. "I call them my Afterthoughts. If I think it, they do it. They are alive but have no minds of their own. They have no power but through me. They see to it that my will is done."

Dirk followed the self-absorbed elf out onto one of the long shards that stretched out like a bridge. Below them was a sight that took Dirk's breath away like nothing ever had. An army of draggard, draquon, dwargon, and unnamable other beasts stretched for what seemed miles. They were in regimens of fifty, he guessed, and they must have numbered in the thousands.

"I have three such armies," Eadon said with great pride. "This one is yours." He looked deep within Dirk's eyes and drew so close it was intimate. He whispered in Dirk's ear, "Follow me and lead my army and you shall be a king and my daughter Krentz your queen. Fail me and you will see her die forever."

Dirk did not react to the threat. He simply stared forward, eyes locked on the impossible sight below them. "King and queen of what?" he dared ask. "This barren wasteland or a charred and dead Agora? One cannot be king of nothingness."

Eadon's head twitched. "Can't he?"

He let the unanswered question linger in the silent air of the crystal palace. After a time, as Eadon looked out over his magnificent creations, his pure killing machines, he said, "I will not lay waste to Agora. What happened here in Drindellia will not happen there. Here was a battle as you have never imagined." He seemed to warm at the memory. "Yes, the elves of the sun fought well, but in the end they killed themselves trying to kill us. Imagine an explosion of such magnitude it was as if the sun collided with the oceans. The sun elves scorched this land, not I." He turned once more to face Dirk. "If those on Agora surrender peacefully, I shall not have to unleash my army. But if they refuse, they must be convinced. I will be named king of all lands and the world will know peace."

"Until you find a new land to conquer?" asked Dirk.

"Precisely."

"Until the world is yours?"

Eadon grinned devilishly. "Until the world is mine."

Dirk resisted his body's urge to shudder at the thought. He looked down at his impossibly large army of monsters. His eyes drifted to what he knew to be one of the lost Gates of Arkron. Where in Agora its twin gate was located he did not know, but through it the army would pour. Through it the dark elf armies could travel from Drindellia to Agora in an instant, covering the land in darkness.

Dirk returned to the lavish room that he shared with Krentz and pondered the dark elf's words. He took off his enchanted leather cloak, his boots, and his clothes and joined his tattooed lover in the silk sheets of the large bed. Outside their wall the world was dark, but upon the ceiling of their shard danced a million multicolored suns, the stars greatly illuminated by the smooth clear crystal wall with its dancing colors. They lost themselves to each other and found a place far from the death and destruction of the world, a place where they could know peace and be left alone, a place that did not exist but in their hearts. They danced in the ocean of empty space and sang the song of the stars. Only together did they know such peace; only together did they know such love.

When they came down they held each other forever and thought of nothing, simply savored the glow, she with her pointed ears resting upon his chest, he with his arms and a leg around her. They remained as one while they slept, and when either stirred they danced yet again, long until morning.

CHAPTER FOUR
Training Begins

Whill flew with Avriel from the city, and shortly they landed upon an outcropping of stone and grass and dirt. The island was surrounded by a rushing river. Upon it was nestled a small cottage, a garden, and a well-kept yard. It was seemingly undisturbed by the violence of the river around it, which fed the Thousand Falls.

Avriel landed and Whill dismounted. He looked the place over and gave her a questioning glance. She spoke to him in his mind.

The Watcher is…different. He knows things, things that others only guess at. He is the most enlightened of our elders, regarded by all but himself as the reincarnation of Mallekell, the father of the second age of enlightenment. He is a monk, and insists that he is a simple farmer. He does not preach, nor hold what you call sermons, yet he will speak freely with any-one.

Whill swallowed hard and looked at the cottage with dread.

"What will he tell me?" Whill asked.

Only what you ask of him.

"Does he have no questions?"

None.

Her white scaled head turned to the river and she licked her sharp teeth. *I go to feed upon the river; his words shall be for you alone.*

Avriel leapt twenty feet into the air and extended her long dragon wings. They caught the wind as the sunlight caught her thousand scales, and the sight blinded Whill. He closed his eyes and called upon his mindsight. He sucked in a breath as he beheld Avriel in true form, her spirit as grand as a dragon and as bright as the god of light.

When she was beyond view, Whill reluctantly walked to the cottage. After a pause, he knocked on the door three times.

"Where I am from, knocking on a door thrice means the caller would like to dance naked under the moonlight" came the musical voice of an old elf.

Whill was taken aback by the statement. He was speechless. Suddenly the door opened inward and an ancient-looking elf, bent at the waist, cocked his head to look up at Whill from an odd angle.

"So you want to dance naked, eh, boy?" asked the Watcher.

"Uhh…," Whill stuttered.

"Hahaha!" The ancient elf laughed until he coughed, and coughed until he hacked. Finally he spat a hairball onto the doorstep. "Hmm." He hummed as he inspected it. "Silver trout does it every time." He pulled Whill's sleeve and pointed at the slimy hairball. "When in cat form, do yourself the favor of eating a silver trout." He turned abruptly and shuffled into the cottage. "Well, then, shut the door. Someone needs to try my newest batch of wine, and it may as well be you!"

Whill, still speechless, closed the door and followed the odd elf into his home. The cottage was strangely familiar, and then Whill realized that he stood in the center room of his aunt Teera's house, one he had lived in as a child. He marveled and went to the window to see beyond. There past the lawn the river raged, but not a sound found the room.

He turned to the Watcher. "How?"

"Why is the better question," the elf countered.

Whill shook his head. "Why?"

"Why did I bring what, where, and when is the question, and you ask how. Hmm. Indeed, you are curious."

Whill shook his head as if trying to clear it. He looked around and smiled as nostalgia washed through him in waves. His shoulders dropped and his muscles relaxed. And for the first time in a long while, he was at ease, he was at home. The fire crackled lazily, and above it a pot of venison stew sent delicious scents riding on the air.

Even the throw rug was the same, a pattern of moon and stars, symbols and glyphs.

"Thank you," said Whill.

The Watcher nodded and pointed to a chair opposite him. Whill sat as the elf poured two small glasses of wine.

"This wine is as old as you are, to the day," he said as he swirled his glass. He put his long hooked nose into it, nearly dipping it, and took a long, slow sniff.

Whill raised his own glass. "As old as I, to the day? Why?" He immediately regretted his words, thinking the word game would begin anew. To his relief, it did not.

"Why?" the elf asked the ceiling. "Hmm, why indeed? I suppose I thought it would be ironic somehow. It is silly, I suppose." He then lifted his glass in a toast. "Here is to your toe hairs: may they be curly and dry," he proclaimed, and took a drink of the twenty-year-old wine. His bushy eyebrows shot up so high, they could have been mistaken for leaping mice. His eyelashes fluttered and a shiver ran through his body as he swallowed. "It seems the wine is dead on. Try it, try it."

Whill skipped the swirl and smell, the looking and listening, and just drank. Flavor exploded in his mouth, sweet at first but then slowly balancing out to a harmoniously delicious medley of flowers and meadows. Again the flavor shifted, now to one of such intense bitterness that Whill nearly spat it out. He swallowed the wine and his palate was left numb.

"As old as you to the day, I daresay the hour."

"You know I was not...born, do you not? I was cut from my mother, I..."

"Yes, of course, but you are here all the same. Did you like the wine?" the Watcher asked.

Whill wondered for a moment and was about to say yes when a thought occurred to him. "Avriel told me that you asked no questions."

"How odd. I suppose I have never asked her a question." He took another drink.

Whill drank again. "It is bitter at the end."

"Many things of this world begin sweet and end up bitter, and others the opposite," said the elf.

Whill looked at him and then the wine. "I am like this wine," he realized.

"And the wine is like you. But like the wine, you can and will change. But enough of that. You did not come here to speak of wine, did you?"

Whill looked around the cottage again. Warmth filled him and joined in the wine lifting his spirits. "I have come here for training. I seek enlightenment."

"No, you do not. You wish for a way to stop feeling as you do. You wish for the nightmares to stop. You wish for your mind to stop torturing you. This I cannot help you with, for it is simply a choice."

Whill did not speak but listened, waiting for the help he sought. But the Watcher spoke no more. He simply waited and drank his wine.

"Where do I begin?" asked Whill.

"You have already begun. You are here."

"What next then?" Whill asked patiently.

"Next you must let go. When you can do that, you will be free."

"Let go of what?"

"Everything."

Whill breathed a sigh of frustration. "How? Don't you care about anything? How can your advice in this war be to let go?"

"The question is why," said the Watcher with a smirk.

"Why, then?"

"Because that is the only way. If the people of Keye let go, there would be peace. I seek peace, therefore I let go, and I know peace. This war you speak of, I know it not. I am not at war, and no one is at war with me."

"Eadon is at war with you," Whill countered.

The Watcher suddenly cocked his head and listened. Whill listened and waited also, but heard nothing. After a time the Watcher spoke.

"Avriel has caught a silver trout." He smiled and closed his eyes. "She is a good one for you; it is good that you have found one another."

"Yes, she is…she is dear to me. When I had thought her dead…"

"There!" the Watcher shouted so abruptly that Whill jumped in his seat. "That is the source of your problem."

"What is?"

"Your insistence on reliving old pains and worries. Do you like it?"

Whill shook his head, confused. "Do I like what?"

"Pain," said the Watcher.

Whill thought about it and shook his head. "Of course not."

The Watcher pointed to the pot. "If you would, the stew needs stirring and I am old."

Whill got to his feet and complied. His mouth watered as he smelled the small pot of stew.

The Watcher went on. "If you did not like pain you would not relive it. Of course you do. You believe that your pain defines you, as do most, but it does not. Nothing defines you because you need not be defined. Giving things names does not make them real. All that you need to know about yourself is that you are. That is the only truth. All else is simply making sounds to recognize a thing."

Whill thought about it for a moment. "I simply am."

The Watcher nodded and smiled. "You simply are."

"I am not Whill."

"You are not Whill, you are you, that which *is*. You believe that you can only exist as Whill, and therefore the captain believes he is the ship. But you are not your body, nor your brain. You are nothing and everything, the darkness and the light. Which one you choose to express is up to you."

Whill understood clearly, saw it all laid out before him, but quickly it was gone. He grasped at the glimpse as one would try and fall asleep to the same pleasant dream.

"I had it...but it left me."

This time the Watcher shook his head. "It cannot leave you, it *is* you. You still think that you are your mind."

Whill sat back heavily and slumped, resting his head in his hands. "I am insane," he sighed.

The Watcher laughed. "Of course you are, the mind is insane. See the spirit that you are, and you shall find sanity."

Whill lifted his head and the Watcher laid a strong hand upon it. Whill's body convulsed and went rigid as waves of energy neither pleasant nor painful coursed through his body. He soon found himself floating in a sea of dancing light. Explosions of energy boomed here and there, and lightning rode weaving currents from one explosion to another. A humming permeated from all directions as the dancing light flew like shooting stars. The Watcher floated next to Whill. Oddly, he still held his wine.

"Where are we?" Whill asked.

"We are in the cottage, but we are experiencing the inner workings of your brain."

"My brain!" Whill gasped.

"Yes. Quite busy, isn't it? I wish to show you something."

Back at the cottage, the Watcher pinched Whill hard on the tender underarm. A writhing ball of light shot up through the web of energy flow and lit a faraway part of the ocean of light.

"Ow!" Whill said aloud. Inwardly he was awed. "Do it again." He laughed; again the pain manifested itself as dancing light.

"Drink your wine," bade the Watcher and Whill complied, though he saw not the glass. Instead he watched as his sense of taste was manifested into a blazing light show.

The Watcher released him and they returned to the room. Whill blinked repeatedly and looked around, panting. "That was amazing!"

"Indeed. More amazing still is that, like the pain in your arm, your mental pain is nothing more than dancing light. If it dances enough along the same webs, trails are created. Then it can more easily travel again down the same path. This is why certain thoughts inevitably lead to the same conclusion, be they memories, beliefs, or thoughts. You must break the cycles within your mind if you wish to obtain the enlightenment you seek. For enlightenment is not a state of mind, it is the absence of mind."

Whill nodded in understanding. "I must give up my identity."

"You must embrace your identity. You simply are."

Whill understood. But he could not commit, could not let go. "Then I should forget that I alone may be able to stop Eadon? Is that what you are telling me? I just, what, grow a garden and daydream all day?"

The Watcher refilled both of their glasses and drank. "You do need food," he said matter-of-factly.

Whill was not amused. The Watcher chuckled. "You have been told by everyone that you are *the* Whill of Agora, the savior, the chosen one. Let me ask you. Do you feel like the legend you are supposed to be?"

"No!"

"Do you want the great power you possess?"

"No!"

The Watcher smiled. "Perhaps that is why you have it."

For the first time, the Watcher looked at the sword Adromida at Whill's hip, and his eyes went wide for a moment. His voice dropped and slowed. "The greatest power ever given…the greatest gift of all. And its twin, the greatest power taken, the greatest curse of all. They are the essence of existence, you know. Created to ensure that none could attain both, lest they become like a god."

Whill was startled. "You know of the legend?"

"I have heard it whispered in the rivers of time, yes."

"Kellallea said that Eadon's true goal is to attain both blades, and to ascend to the heavens."

"Indeed." The elf nodded.

"And you would do nothing to stop him?"

"It is not my place," said the Watcher.

"No." Whill nodded. "It seems that it is mine."

Whill drank down the last of his wine and stared at the mantel of his childhood. A pang of sadness threatened to rob him of breath as he thought of Teera and the girls. He had not seen the woman who raised him in too many years. How he longed for this all to be real, for his beloved aunt to come through the threshold, busy as a bee as always. She had taught Whill everything he knew about nonmagical healing. He imagined what it would be like to be there with her now, to show her how he had learned to heal.

He watched the fire lazily and daydreamed of roaming the countryside, curing disease and saving the dying. He could give people a second chance at life. Among the many powers he had discovered, healing was the most intriguing. He found no thrill in dealing out pain and death, though neither did he feel any remorse when killing the draggard, dark elves, or even the opposing gladiators. He thought of the rage that burned within him during battle, anger born of his torture. His mind was broken, he realized, and no amount of well-wishing was going to fix it.

"I see many things," said The Watcher suddenly with a flourish of the hands. "I see the past, solid, unchanging, always warning. I see the present, what is as it is in the moment. And I see the future, an eternal river of endless possibilities. I watch decisions alter the future, I see that which could have been, that which would have been, and that which can be. Eternal possibility lies before you, Whill. There are a thousand futures in which you fail, and as many in which you succeed."

"Well, then tell me what I did right in the futures where I succeeded," Whill blurted with frustration.

"If I began to meddle in the flow of time, a million new futures would play out before my mind. I would be likely to miss dinner to such a bother."

To that Whill sighed. The Watcher patted his leg with a strong hand. "There is no one way, no easy answer. Your life is for you to dictate, not I or the elders, nor a prophecy or a dark lord. You alone must choose your path. I only offer a way to not suffer while you travel upon your chosen path. I offer peace."

Whill smiled at the elf. "Thank you." He stood and fetched two bowls from where he knew them to be and two spoons as well. He scooped up helpings for himself and the Watcher. They drank and they supped, and the Watcher offered up what he thought to be the secret to happiness.

CHAPTER FIVE
A Dark Road

The dwarven search parties came back with the same report as before: they'd found no sign of any gate or portal or hidden tunnels that may have been used. It did something to silence Roakore's growing dread. Still, it was with foreboding that he packed the last of his things and prepared to leave his kingdom once again. Nah'Zed did nothing to quell her king's guilt; instead, she had quite the contrary effect. She reminded him that the world was at war, and his place was with his people. Roakore knew her to be right, and told her as much.

"But I be a creature o' action, Nah'Zed," he said. "I feel the call o' the road." He stood at Silverwind's side, packing the last of his provisions. In his hands he clutched the book of Ky'Dren. He remembered Azzeal's words and the elf's tale of a mountain within Drindellia, the dwarven kingdom lost to time. An idea had sparked in his mind when he heard the tale, a grand idea of such epic proportions that if he accomplished it, he would be given a seat among the gods. He dreamt of travelling to that most ancient of Dwarven Mountains and reclaiming it for the dwarves, if it existed. The possibility drove him to leave Ro'Sar, to abandon his throne for the beaten path, and to find the answers that would prove true revelations to the dwarven culture. He was going to retrace the path of Ky'Dren.

Little was known of Ky'Dren's early life. Dwarven history spoke only of the time after Ky'Dren appeared to the people and made his holy claims. Little if anything was ever said of where he came from. Roakore had ordered his clerics and historians to look into the matter, but without the great library within the Ky'Dren Mountains, little could be discovered of such matters. Therefore Roakore needed to have the precious book translated so that he might hear the tale from the dwarf himself, and he trusted none but Whill to do it.

Why Ky'Dren had never spoken of the lost dwarf home he did not know. Perhaps it was utterly destroyed and there was nothing to return to; perhaps the gods had told him to abandon the lost kingdom and start anew in Agora. But if the tale was true, and there was a lost mountain kingdom to return to, Roakore would be the one to attempt it. His mind raced with possibilities. He imagined the glory he would know. Not only would he be Roakore, king of Ro'Sar, who took back the fallen mountain, he would be Roakore, king of the ancient mountain of the dwarves. Wine and ale would overflow the mugs at the table of the kings, and the gods would cheer his health. He already had the high favor of the gods. In only a short year he had taken back his mountain, become king, and killed a dark elf, a draggard queen, and a black dragon. He could feel the power of the gods flow through him. He felt it in every strike, every blow. The power of the gods grew within him daily. He would ever be their weapon; his would be their right hand. He would lead his people to victory and salvation, or he would die trying.

Roakore stuffed the book in his belt and turned to the sulking Nah'Zed. "I be on a path that you would be approvin' of if I could tell you o' it. Trust your king, good dwarf, and know that I be takin' your counsel to heart. You have been a royal brain o' legend, and I be knowin' you will remind me son o' his duties in me absence."

She blushed and was gladdened by his words. His son Ror'Den topped the great stair and entered Silverwind's tower. He was a tall dwarf, taller than his father, and his eldest son by his first wife. Though Ror'Den was only twenty years old, his beard had grown to the floor and he had many scars to show for his part in the great reclamation. He was wise beyond his years and had a good mind for problem solving. His powers over stone had shown themselves early, and now he gave his father a good fight in the family tradition of stone wrestling.

It was a game similar to tug-of-war, but rather than a rope, the dwarves mentally pulled or pushed boulders against each other's minds.

"Me king." Ror'Den slammed his chest and bowed so low that even though his beard was folded over thrice and bound in leather, it still brushed the floor.

Roakore approached his son with open arms. "Ah, me boy. Just the dwarf I be wantin' to see. I am off to bring Tarren to the elf lands—me friend Whill awaits us there. You be in charge o' me mountain till I return, and king if I don't."

"Then let us hope that I ain't king any time soon," said Ror'Den sincerely. "I am honored by your choice, Father, but I would join you in your travels if you would allow it. I would see the world beyond the mountain walls."

"Bah, and I would have ye at me side, son, but for your value bein' here, watchin' over our mountain. That be a greater task than the road before me."

"Of course, me king."

Roakore slammed his fist to his chest and nodded. "Nah'Zed, let it be known that once again, Ror'Den be in charge in me absence."

Nah'Zed scribbled furiously on her scroll, then suddenly ran up to Roakore and embraced him tightly. He got a raised eyebrow and smirk from his son. He patted his devoted royal brain on the back and hugged her. After nearly a minute he had to pry himself from her clutches. "All right, then, I ain't on me deathbed. See to it things run smooth and I'll be back afore you can say dragon shyte."

"Yes, me king," Nah'Zed sniffled. She and Ror'Den left their king and descended the stairs. No sooner had they left than Tarren came sprinting up, panting, a wide smile spread across his face.

"This is gonna be great! Hey, do I get those neat goggles like you got?"

Roakore tossed him a similar pair. "Can't see nothing but wind tears without 'em."

Tarren caught the goggles and put them on. "Holy—!"

Roakore laughed. "Heh, I told ye in Kell-Torey that I would get a silver hawk o' me own."

"Wow," said Tarren as he stroked Silverwind's feathers. "Is it scary?"

"Bah! I don't know the meanin' o' that word." Roakore helped Tarren up into the newly reconfigured saddle and strapped him in. He took his place in front of the lad and took hold of the reins.

"Ready, boy?" Roakore asked, but did not wait for the answer. He kicked Silverwind's sides and snapped the reins. "Hyah!"

Silverwind ran to the ledge and leapt out into the air. Tarren laughed with joy and yelled gleefully, until they began to descend. A rush of wind hit them and his laughter was taken with his breath.

"Haha, boy, ain't it great?"

"Roakore, I…" Tarren gasped.

"Takes your breath away, don't it!"

"I think I'm gonna…"

"You ain't seen nothing yet! Bwahaha." Roakore pulled left and banked so hard Tarren thought he might fall off.

"Stop…I can't…" Tarren tried to warn the laughing dwarf but it was too late. His eyes and cheeks bulged and he threw up all over Roakore's back.

Roakore howled. "Turn your blasted head next time, boy! Ah, all over me new cloak."

Roakore landed at the base of the mountain where Lunara and Holdagozz were waiting with their horses. He leapt from Silverwind and threw his cloak to the ground in disgust. Tarren unbuckled himself, slid to the ground, and threw up again.

"How ye got anymore in ye, laddie?" Roakore asked. "That's gotta be your whole breakfast on me back!"

Lunara and Holdagozz had deduced what happened and chuckled. Lunara went to Tarren, put a hand on his shoulder, and rubbed his back.

"What did you do with the lad, loop-de-loops?" asked Holdagozz.

"Bah, ye be knowin' nothin' o' the art o' flyin'," Roakore grumbled. "Loop-de-loop, my arse. He got no stomach for it, I'm guessin'. Didn't but turn sharp and I was wearin' his food."

"I'll get used to it, Roakore, gimme another chance," Tarren pleaded.

"Maybe when the smell o' your puke wears off. Till then, you'll be washin' me clothes first thing when we make camp."

"Don't be so hard on the boy," Lunara interjected.

"Bah. The world be hard, you be knowin', hard as stone. Make somethin' weak, it'll stay weak. Bein' too soft an' easy with kids be the real abuse."

A regiment of fifty dwarves on horseback came galloping out of the gate behind them. They rode atop miniature brown and white Thendora Plains horses, thusly named because they were half the size of their kin, the great Thendoran warhorses. Even a miniature horse came up to a man's shoulders, and the smaller ones were perfectly built for carrying dwarves with their heavy weapons and armor. At Roakore's orders, no flags or banners were flown, nothing to indicate that the dwarf king rode among them.

Tarren mounted with Lunara and the group began the long journey through Uthen-Arden territory to Elladrindellia. It would take them the better part of two weeks to get to the elven borders, even though their horses were a long-distance breed. Traveling through Elladrindellia to Cerushia would be another ten-day.

CHAPTER SIX
The Cost of Fealty

Dirk attempted to mask his horror as he watched Eadon's army prepare to pour through the portal. He did not know where the portal led, but it didn't matter. Soon the already overwhelmed people of Agora would wake to a new nightmare. He knew then, looking out over the massive army of abominations, that Agora was truly doomed.

He had sided with the victor, it seemed. Krentz was safe, they were together once more, and as long as Dirk kept his promise of fealty to Eadon, they would remain that way. This fact should have brought more comfort to the assassin, but it brought none.

He stood next to Eadon before the dead land and its legions of monsters. He tried not to think too loudly, to clear his mind. But the images of burning towns, cities, women and children plagued his mind and pierced his armor of detachment. He saw the face of his sister, gone now nearly forty years. She had died at age two during a bad winter sickness that had swept the land. Dirk had vowed then that whatever god would take her as his own was an evil god, and he would strive always to eradicate the world of men of like heart. He was a killer true, but he was a killer of killers mostly. In his long career he had never taken a contract in which he had not known the target to be deserving of death. Dirk's services came with a high price, and thus he was hired to kill men of such worth. In his line of work his employers had been rich merchants, businessmen, bankers, and even kings. He was glad to help eradicate the scum of Agora. Being paid for it was a bonus.

"You must think me a prime target for your righteous justice," said Eadon without looking at him.

Dirk did not answer. He was not about to attempt lying to the dark elf lord. Eadon knew his mind; he could feel the constant presence at the edges of his consciousness, always watching. Dirk knew also that Eadon could see clearly his resolve to keep his vow, regardless of his conflicting morals. He did not attempt to hide his disdain for Eadon, for he could not regardless.

Eadon looked at him as he thought this, and he grinned. "You are a bold warrior indeed."

Dirk stole a glance at Eadon and gave a grin of his own. "I do not fear you."

"Indeed!" laughed Eadon. "The only thing you fear is losing your beloved dark elf tramp."

Dirk's upper lip twitched a snarl. "Such words for your own daughter?"

"Daughter of mine," Eadon said, as if to himself. "My children are legion; you look upon them as we speak. If ever I have failed, it is with her. She is weak minded, insolent, and a traitor."

Dirk quietly fumed, knowing full well that Eadon was toying with him, savoring the anger that he caused.

"But she has ever set the hearts of men and elves afire," Eadon added with a smirk.

Dirk ignored the barb, knowing his rage to ever be impotent against the powerful elf. He looked out past the horrid army to the ever-hazy sky of Drindellia. He loathed this place. It reminded him of nothing but death, of Agora's fate.

"Worry not of that. The sniveling humans of Agora will see that they stand no chance. The dwarves will hide in their stinking mountains, and the elves of the sun shall kneel to me, or they will die. Take heart, my assassin; you will be a king of men when this is through. Now, for your next—what did you call it? Contract?"

Dirk looked at the hated dark elf, his imagination running wild with hideous possibilities.

"You are to travel to Eldalon and kill Whill's remaining relatives; his grandfather, King Mathus; and every last man, woman, and child. Without their beloved leader, Eldalon will be driven to its knees."

Dirk returned to his chambers to say goodbye to Krentz. He stopped before the door, his hand a mere hair's breadth from knocking. He retracted his hand as if he had been burned. Shame washed over him and his throat constricted painfully.

For the first time in his life he was trapped; for the first time he was the victim of a more cunning and powerful foe. He had never before bent to the will of anyone; he would be controlled by no one. Whenever in his life he had been attacked by a bully, either physically or verbally, he would beat them down. He made such a scene as to show everyone in his circles that if you attempted violence or disrespect toward Dirk Blackthorn, you were a dead man. And now, because of his relentless pursuit of Krentz, he had sold his soul to evil in the name of love. For the first time in his life, he felt like an idiot.

If I do not do Eadon's bidding, or ever act against him, I will die. If I die, Krentz will lose what protection I can give her.

Dirk silently screamed and pulled at his black hair. His frustration swelled and his rage boiled at the impossibility he had been given. He could not even conspire against the dark elf. He had learned that the hard way when last he spoke to Krentz. They had been considering ways of escape and how they might break the oath. Dirk had been racked with a gut-burning pain that left him gasping on the floor. He could not resist, and for Krentz he gave in. Had the circumstances been different and Dirk did not have her to lose, he would have told Eadon to eat his own shyte and he would have died fighting.

He took a deep, calming breath, which came out in a nervous shudder. He opened the door and she was waiting. Before the door closed she had confronted him at the threshold. Tears streaked her eyes and he knew that she had somehow learned of his newest mission.

"You cannot do this," she said before he could speak. He avoided her eyes and shut the door behind him.

"I must—"

"You cannot! You should have never sworn fealty to him; you should never have found me. You will die because of me."

Dirk tried to charm her from her mindset with her favorite smile. He put a hand softly to her smooth, dark face. Her tattoos swirled slowly, churning like her emotions. She took his hand from her face and gripped is firmly with both hands at her breast.

"I will not die because of a dream you—"

"Then you shall be forced to do things that will change you forever," she said. "You may not die, but you will not be able to live with yourself if you become Eadon's monster!"

"What would you have me do?" he screamed, yanking his hand away. The crystal walls of the chamber rang faintly with his voice.

"You cannot kill the innocent; you are not an evil man. It will tear you apart..."

Dirk's face, Krentz saw, was one of resolve and determination. In his eyes she saw something she never had before. She saw the shadow of the man he might become if he continued down this dark path.

"I will do what I must to see you safe," he said.

"It is not up to you to keep me safe. I am not like your people. Your chivalrous sentiments are not for me."

"And neither are you like *your* people," he argued.

She ignored the statement, not letting him divert the conversation. "You cannot do this," she said, grabbing hold of his arm as he turned away from her.

"I must," he said firmly and pulled his arm from her grip.

"If you will do this, what will you not do? If you would kill an entire family, what will you not do?"

Her accusatory words cut through his enchanted cloak and leather armor to pierce his heart. He walked to the door and turned to her at the threshold. In her eyes was the smallest glimmer of hope that he might be swayed from his path. That hope was crushed when he spoke.

"I will do whatever it takes, Krentz. For you I would see the world burn."

He turned to leave but suddenly swooned and fell to one knee. He shook his head to clear it, thinking that it was his inner turmoil over Eadon's orders that had caused him to feel so...poisoned. He cursed under his breath and his head spun again, dropping him to both knees. He knew he did not have time. A panic fueled by the realization of what Krentz had done and what she might do sent a surge of adrenaline through his body and he shot to his feet. His eyes tried to focus on one of her images, but all he could make out was the needle ring on her left hand, which was held out toward his face. He staggered toward her like a drunkard and reached for her weakly. He took her by the shoulders as if to shake her, but ended up needing her to lower him to the floor. Tears welled in his eyes and he managed to utter, "Wh…what have you done?"

"Shhh." She whispered as a mother might. "Fret not, my dear Blackthorn. I love you. Remember that I will always love you."

Dirk struggled against the drug but quickly fell into oblivion.

Krentz walked briskly through the crystal corridor to her father's quarters.

"Father, Father!" she cried as she approached the door to his chamber and beat upon it. "Father, open the door! I would have words."

After a long moment the door finally opened, and Eadon scowled down upon his renegade daughter.

"You would have words, would you? What words would my spiteful daughter have?"

"I come to barter."

Dirk came to and found himself on unfamiliar ground. The brightness of the world stung his eyes. His vision was blurry and his head pounded. He tried to stand and found his legs unresponsive.

How did I get here? he wondered. He fought through the thick fog in his mind and the truth came rushing back to him. He had been poisoned by Krentz. They had been arguing about his mission and then he had fallen. She had said something to him as he passed into unconsciousness…she had said…goodbye.

His mind cleared and panic gripped his heart. What had she done?

"Krentz!" His voice was slurred, and the after-effects of the drug caused him to stagger as he stood. He looked around frantically and saw Eadon standing a stone's throw away, his form silhouetted in the churning light of what looked to be a portal. They were in a forest clearing, and Dirk knew from the foliage and trees nearby that he was no longer in Drindellia.

"What has she done?" he screamed and lurched toward the hated dark elf. His legs buckled but he found them quickly, the effects of the poison wearing off.

"Where is Krentz? What has happened?" he bellowed, his voice hoarse. Eadon grinned at him, thoroughly amused by the spectacle. Dozens of dwargons and draquon stood guard near to the portal, hissing and growling at Dirk as he stumbled toward their master. He ignored their warnings.

"What have you done, you son of a bitch?" he cried.

Eadon let out a long laugh. "As much as I looked forward to your services, assassin, Krentz made me an offer I could not refuse."

Dirk shook his head in denial and tears found his dark eyes.

"You are free, Dirk Blackthorn. I release you from your oath."

As the words were spoken, Dirk felt the difference within him immediately. His vision cleared, and as he slowly neared the portal, he could see Krentz standing behind her father, beyond the rippling threshold. Here form shimmered and wavered, but it was she.

"Krentz, no! What have you done?"

"Enough out of you!" Eadon roared. He raised a hand and Dirk was lifted from his feet and held in midair by the throat. His cries were choked as his hands clawed at the phantom noose that held him.

"You are free, but if ever we cross paths again, you will be mine even after your death."

He let Dirk drop to the dirt and turned to the portal. Dirk sprang to his feet and sprinted after him. As Eadon stepped through, it began to shimmer. Krentz lifted a hand in farewell and Dirk screamed. The portal closed as Dirk dove and he went through the empty space only to land on the other side in the grass.

Dirk got to his feet and screamed in rage. He then noticed the dozens of beasts that still guarded the portal. He was cornered. He planted his feet and drew his short sword and mind-control dagger. He threw the dagger at the closest dwargon, and when it stuck in the monster's thigh, Dirk yelled, "Kill them all!"

The dwargon roared in compliance, having no will to fight the power of the persuasive blade. The creature attacked the draggard to his right, grabbing its tail and with powerful arms swinging it to smash into the one next to it.

"The draggard are attacking your brother!" Dirk yelled to the other confused dwargon. The mammoth abominations were thick-skinned like a dragon and strong like a dwarf, but they shared the intellect of neither. Eadon didn't like his creatures thinking too much, which worked to Dirk's advantage. He went to work on the closest draggard. Using his enchanted cloak to ward off glancing spear and tail attacks, he rolled and twirled and danced around his attackers. He knew the beast's weak spots and he took every advantage. He hamstrung those he did not kill and threw darts into the eyes of others.

He caused such chaos that he was able to slip quickly out of the deadly ring of thrashing monsters. He retrieved his dagger from the dead dwargon and sprinted west toward a distant mountain range and away from the fighting guardians of the portal. He knew not where he was, but he knew that if Krentz had sworn fealty to her father, Eadon would give her Dirk's mission. That meant she would soon be in Kell-Torey. No matter which mountain range was before him, Eldalon would be west of it.

As Dirk ran, he retrieved a dart from his belt and jabbed it into his forearm. He felt the effects immediately as his heartbeat surged, his head cleared, and his lungs drew in twice as much breath. He doubled his pace as the drug coursed through his veins. He ran faster than a horse out of the woods and through a long field of golden wheat, but he knew he would soon need to find a horse if he was to make it to Kell-Torey in time to stop Krentz. He prayed that the far-off range was the Ky'Dren Mountains as he made haste to save his love from the beckoning of her mad father.

CHAPTER SEVEN
The First King of Elladrindellia

When Whill left the cottage, he was greeted by Avriel. Her dragon smile would have killed a deer from fright, but to Whill it was beautiful. She moved her head to the side to show Whill the large saddle upon her back. Thick leather straps wound before and behind her front legs to hold the large saddle in place.

"Where did that come from?" Whill asked as he stepped closer to inspect it.

Mother made it. You could fill a dwarven vault with the things she has made. Do you like it?

"I do indeed. No offense, but your scales are not the most comfortable to sit on."

She laughed, surely startling any nearby animals. *None taken. Come, try the new seat, I have much to show you.*

He didn't hesitate and stepped through the rung hanging from the saddle. The seat was well padded and soft, with flaps hanging from the sides to protect the legs. There were also a number of possible handholds upon the horn of the saddle. He took hold. Avriel leapt, beat her strong wings, and took to the sky.

Twilight was upon them as they climbed higher above the city. Far below Whill saw the constellation of lights aglow atop the many pyramids. The sun had just set, but its light had not. Rays of sunlight could still be seen gliding atop the encroaching twilight. Whill and Avriel soared gently on the warm autumn air; they flew between the heavens and the earth, between day and night. They existed for a moment between worlds, and Whill could have stayed there forever. Here his destiny could not find him, his pain was forgotten; his worries could not climb this high, and his cares could not follow.

What if we never return? he asked Avriel, absentmindedly gazing upon the last rays of light, like pillars to the heavens.

What do you mean? she asked, as if the thought had never occurred to her.

"I mean what if we were to leave Agora forever, find another place to live, a place far from this constant strife? I never wanted any of this. I was quite content with my life up until..." He paused and thought about when his life had started to spin out of control. *It was when I learned of my parents, within that vault,* he thought, and then felt guilty for it.

You would not leave Agora forever. For you would ever wonder of its fate, and when finally you were driven mad by wonder and guilt you would return to find a smoldering wasteland.

Whill knew her to be right. He could not abandon Agora if there was any hope that he might be able to help defeat Eadon. It seemed there was nowhere to go anyway; the elves had escaped only to be discovered a world away in Agora. The same nagging feeling of helplessness came back to him. He knew he stood no chance against Eadon. What could the elves possibly teach him in such a short time that would help him against a master of every school of elven magic? How could Whill possibly hope to defeat him?

Together he and Avriel flew over the Thousand Falls and beyond by moonlight. For nearly an hour they flew north over forests and streams, valleys and fields. Flying low to the ground they suddenly came to an end to the land. It dropped off to crashing waves and ocean spray. Whill howled as they broke through a foaming wave as it smashed against the rocks. Salt water fell from them like threads of silver in the moonlight.

Avriel rose above the waves and twisted in flight to face the land once more. She glided down gently toward the jagged rocks and through them into the mouth of a wide eastern-facing cave. Whill's breath was taken away as Avriel landed not far from the entrance. Crystals of all sizes and shapes protruded from the walls and ceiling. Even in the dull moonlight he could see the spectacular array of colors within the luminescent depths of the crystal. He dismounted and explored the nearby formations.

This and similar crystal mines are littered throughout the land, Avriel purred, and the crystal resonated with her dragon voice. *If only I had my voice, I could show you how the crystal sings.*

"Are these natural?" Whill asked as he glided his hand along the smooth surface of a crystal larger than he.

No, these are not. We helped them to grow long ago. They are used in many of our tools and weapons.

"It is beautiful," said Whill.

Avriel hummed in agreement and the crystal sang with her. *It is one of my favorite places to meditate.*

They remained within the cave throughout the night. They talked and rested, enjoying each other's company. When morning came, Whill was awakened with a gentle nudge from Avriel. She stared at the entrance of the cave in anticipation.

The sun rises, she purred, and there beyond the mouth of the cave the waters of the great ocean blazed to life as the sun rose into the morning sky. The first of the sun's rays shot across the ocean and onto the coast, and they shone on the crystals within the cave, illuminating them in a cascade of sparkling color. Whill could not help but laugh with joy as they seemed to bathe in color and light. Avriel's white dragon scales radiated with dancing, multicolored brilliance. She looked to Whill like a dragon goddess of lore.

Soon they began the flight back to Cerushia. The air was crisp and the day clear. As they passed over a clearing, Avriel's eye was drawn to a group of deer. She swooped down as silent as death and caught one in her jaws. Whill held on tight as she shook her head and broke its neck, and then choked back the deer whole. Then she took to the air once more.

"What is it like?" Whill yelled over the wind.

Eating deer?

Yes, he answered, this time in his mind. *Well, eating deer as a dragon.*

She hummed. *It is not the same as eating with fork and spoon.*

"Obviously," he chuckled.

The flavor is different. My dragon body craves...

Whill sensed her hesitation; it was not for lack of words. She was embarrassed by it.

Blood, she finally confessed. *The warmth of it, the bittersweet taste. I tried to eat like an elf might at first, but dragon teeth were not made for nibbling, and the use of silverware would be simply ridiculous.*

Whill burst into laughter at the thought of Avriel as a dragon, sipping soup with a huge spoon.

"What is so funny?"

He projected the image as hard as he could and soon Avriel had joined in his amusement. She laughed in Whill's mind in her elven voice, but she also laughed as a dragon. The dragon laughter, however, came out as a strange growl, which made it all the funnier to them. They laughed until Avriel's flying became erratic and she begged him to stop chuckling on her back like a chipmunk. That mental image only made things worse. They laughed until Whill's cheeks were sore and he was left panting as he leaned upon her smooth-scaled neck. She purred and glided along on a particularly warm current of air.

Midday arrived and the day had turned out to be pleasantly warm for that time of year, Will thought, then realized that he was used to the chiller climate of the north. Elladrindellia was at the very southeastern part of Agora, and therefore it would be warmer. He wondered if they had snow; he did not recall it in any of the books he had ever read on elves.

They reached Cerushia shortly thereafter, and Avriel flew to their abode on the edge of the city. There they were met by a messenger. They were summoned to the Summer Star, a pyramid named after its heavenly twin.

They took to the air once more and flew directly to the Summer Star. Once there they went inside, the door of vine and stone opened wide like a behemoth's mouth to accommodate Avriel. As they entered the pyramid, Whill saw that the capstone of crystal illuminated the space as if it were daylight. He saw too, the group of elves sitting in wait for him at a table in the center.

He knew the queen, who sat in the middle, and recognized a few of the elders who had sat with her before. They and other elves Whill did not know sat at the large round stone table. There were twenty-seven elves in all. His eye caught that of Azzeal and the elf offered him a friendly nod.

Whill strode to the table and looked around at the gathering of strange-looking elves, one of whom he could have sworn had an animal bone through his nose, and pointed ears split down the middle to form two points. There were male and female, some clothed in flowing robes of silk or gowns of vine. A few wore the armor of warriors, and the dirt upon their faces and their weary stares told Whill enough of their story.

A reflection of light from the queen's crystal crown caught Whill's eye. She stood and the others followed suit, and they followed her in a bow. Whill bowed back, his mind scrambling to remember something of elf custom that would pertain to his situation, but he came up empty. So he greeted the elves like he thought a king might—he was, after all, recognized by the elves as the king of Uthen-Arden, albeit the uncrowned king.

"Hello, good elves," he said at a loss for words more fitting his position.

They all looked at each other and shared whispered words. The queen's eyes watched the mouths of the others. "Thank you for coming so soon, Whill. Please do sit with us, as we have come to an impasse."

Whill took a seat and laced his fingers on the table. "Impasse?"

"Yes," said the queen as she too sat, followed by the others. "Some among us have suggested something which you must have a say in, for it concerns yourself."

Whill looked at Avriel beside him. She gave him a mental shrug. "What is it?" he asked.

"First you must meet the members of our gathering; it is small enough in number to warrant pleasantries."

The queen introduced each elf by name and title. The entire process took nearly a half hour. Aside from the members of the elder council and various representatives, Whill met masters of the various schools of elven magic, or Orna Catorna. He was not surprised to learn that Azzeal was a master druid, or Ralliad, as the elves called it. The other factions—that of Aklenar, seers of the future; Morenka, monks of peace; Arnarro, the healers; Krundar, the elementals; Gnenja, the warrior class; and Zionar, or psionists—were all represented as well. The was no Kennarra, or master of all schools of magic, as they had all stayed behind to fight for Drindellia, and none had yet attained that rank since.

Once all were introduced, the queen took her seat once again. "What we are here to discuss is the possibility that you could be given the knowledge of all schools, by each of the masters, and become a Kennarra."

"Kennarra?" Whill gasped. "A master of all schools of knowledge? How is that possible?"

The elf the queen had introduced as a master of Zionar spoke. His booming voice resonated throughout the temple in such a way that it seemed as though he spoke from all directions.

"It is possible, though it is shunned, for one to be given all the knowledge that another possesses. Only under certain…circumstances is it accepted."

"What circumstances?" asked Whill.

"Death," said the Zionar master. "One can pass on their knowledge at death to whomever they choose. Though mastery in an art is not granted until many trials, even then one must prove himself through the evidence of time and growth beyond the gift."

Whill shook his head as he began to understand. "No one is dying to give me their godsdamned power. I don't even want the power I have!"

"There are those of us who have wished to move on to the next life, to no longer hold death at bay," said a female elf, a master monk. "I would give my life to give you the gift of my knowledge. I would see you healed, mind and soul, for you carry so much pain and rage. You wear your scars like armor, and you revel in your pain."

Whill only sighed, tired of hearing of his rage and pain. They didn't understand.

"I am the one meant to find this blade," he said. "I am the one tasked with defeating your brother. I think I have a good understanding of power. The sword calls to me constantly, or I call for it, I do not know. But I know its power, I can feel it in my grasp, and I see no limits. I know that my imagination is the only limit, and it scares me, to know what I could do. I need your help, but I will not allow another to die so that I may gain more cursed power."

"Then you truly are an anomaly, Whill of Agora, to shun that which most hearts yearn for," said the queen.

Azzeal stood and bowed slightly to Whill. "There is one thing I believe we should all share knowledge of, a story that came to us from Kellallea herself." He looked at Whill, but Whill could not judge his feline eyes. "The ancient Kellallea told a tale of Adimorda that may be Eadon's greatest secret. Her story was thus. Eadon is Adimorda. In the ancient days of prosperity, long before the draggard wars of Drindellia had begun. Adimorda looked into the future with his great gifts of power and saw himself rise to power as the dark elf lord Eadon. He saw the very reality that he would set in motion to become so."

The elves stirred upon their seats. Exclamations and questions poured from the shocked gathering. "Please, this is but the beginning of the tale," Azzeal bade them with raised hand. "Kellallea spoke of an ancient spell, created in the days of the elven dawn, created by the gods themselves. This spell told of a way that one might attain the power of a god, and ascend to sit upon a heavenly throne. Two blades the spell named, the Sword of Power given, and the Sword of Power Taken. It was said that if one were to collect both of the blades, they would become a god. Eadon now has the greatest power taken, and he set into motion long ago a means to one day possess the greatest power given. He named the sword Adromida, the Blade of the Savior, only to convince others to do his bidding. The ancient one believes that the legend of Whill of Agora is but another fable created by Eadon."

Azzeal finished his tale and avoided Whill's eyes. The queen remained in her chair, motionless. The crowd was silent, none moving as they pondered what they had just heard. Finally an elder stood. "This tale, however unpleasant to comprehend and accept, carries with it the sound of truth." He looked at Whill. "The greatest puzzle we have recently faced is thus: Why did Eadon not kill you? Many would say that he sees in you a great apprentice, while others would state that Eadon needs you to transfer the great power of the blade to him. He asked you as much, correct?"

"Yes, sir." Whill nodded. "But whether the prophecy is true or a lie, Eadon would see me give him the power."

"Indeed," said the elf as he pondered. "But this spell of the gods, truth of it sparks in a far-off corner of my mind. I would need many days to explore my knowledge of this, though the truth of it may be lost to the destroyed libraries of our homeland." He looked to the others. "Have any of you heard of such a spell?"

Everyone looked around but none answered, until an elven woman stood. Whill could not guess her age, but if she were a human he would have said thirty. She wore a long gown of blue flower petals, which contrasted as the sky might against the snow, so white was her skin. Her eyes seemed to dance with deep blue flames, and when she spoke, she spoke as though in a trance.

"The seventh scroll of the ancient telling of Ardruin, verse nine-seventy-two, A Song of Swords: 'All eyes ever seek the heavens, all hearts their mystery. And so they will have a ladder to attain so high a dream, albeit one of two pieces, each got at great pain, each got by none named. The attainment of one shall be through great giving, the other through the taking of. That which is given cannot be taken, as that which is taken cannot be given. Let it be known that any who would seek such power, such a place among the gods, would do so with ill intent, as the son who desires the throne of his father." The elf sagged as she finished, and then became alert; her face was one of puzzlement.

"It is not true!" shouted a white-robed elf. He paused as the talking died down and he was noticed. "We have awaited the coming of Whill for thousands of years! Everything told in the prophecy has come to pass. Now, here he stands before us. Shall we let a rumor, spoken by one we do not see, cast shadow of doubt upon our faith? Shall we forsake our savior so easily, now, when he stands yet before us?"

Many elves stood in agreement. Others argued of logic and reason, blind faith and sound judgment.

"No!" yelled the elf over them all. "We shall not forsake Whill, for he is but our last hope."

Whill shifted uncomfortably and looked up to Avriel for support. Her dragon eyes relayed annoyance, and a hint of a snarl found her snout.

"Please! Please, I beg of you. Let me set foot past threshold before the argument begins, for I have yet to speak enough to offend." Zerafin's voice rose above all, and swallowed their words. Silence fell upon the gathering and everyone found their seat as the elven prince entered the pyramid. Zerafin was fully healed now, Whill could tell. He stood tall and proud, walking with strength and purpose. He made his way around the circle to his mother's side. With tearing eyes the queen put a hand to her healed son's cheek and kissed his forehead.

"Mother," he said with a smile. He looked up at the dragon eyes of his sister and smiled. "Sister."

Zerafin raised his hands to the gathering and eyed them all. His mouth opened as if to make words but then closed quickly as if the words eluded him. Finally he began slowly.

"My friends, my fellow elves." He looked to his mother once more. They shared a moment, and Whill was sure they had conversed. The queen nodded with a smile. Zerafin went on.

"My good elves of Elladrindellia, children of the sun, wielders of Orna Catorna, survivors of the exodus. With the blessing of my mother, and hopefully with your blessing as well, I have come to you to announce that I, Zerafin, son of King Verelas, do so from this day forth claim the throne of my father."

Whill was shocked, as were many in attendance. Through their constant if not always marked connection, Whill felt Avriel's surprise also, and then quickly he felt her swelling pride. Zerafin had for centuries refused the crown of his father, saying that Verelas would one day return to them. Whill watched Zerafin, and for but a second their eyes met. Whill understood then that Zerafin had only now accepted his father's fate, he had let go. Whill quickly shifted his mind from thoughts of Abram. His throat tightened and he chastised himself for being weak. He stood quickly to distract himself and began to clap. He looked around at the elves, wondering suddenly if elves clapped also, or did they have another way of showing cheers? Whether they were familiar with clapping or not, they stood one and all and clapped as well. Whill smiled to himself as whistles even pierced the drumming.

Zerafin raised his hand. "Thank you," he said and bowed.

Eventually the cheers died down and Zerafin was free to speak. "I have heard the tale of Kellallia, as you just have." He searched the faces of all in attendance, Whill's most of all. "As you also know, my family is of the order of Adromida, as are many of you." The elves who believed the prophecy religiously nodded their heads victoriously. Those more skeptical by nature stirred restlessly, feeling a verdict on the matter forthcoming from their new king.

"I will not rule out the possibility of the ancient one's tale. It has been confirmed to me from my sister and also the wise Azzeal that indeed it was she."

The tension in the room shifted and the believers' smug faces were taken by the skeptics.

"But as Whill said earlier, it matters not; either way, Eadon must force Whill to give him the blade voluntarily. The task of defeating Eadon remains. I feel in my heart that Whill shall be the one to finish this, prophecy or not."

Many elves nodded in agreement. Eadon remained the problem at hand. Whether or not the prophecy was a lie, the sword of Adimorda had been returned to the elves of the sun, and there was yet hope.

"We have yet a problem that must be spoken. While I was under the afflictions of Eadon's rotting curse, one which we shared as result of my counterspell, I shared a sort of connection with the dark one."

Avriel growled almost inaudibly, and many elves shifted uncomfortably at the thought.

"It was not a connection to mind but to body. My counter affliction spell bonded us together in sickness while the curse lasted. I was able to sense his, though he is many hundreds of miles off. Nevertheless, it was strong enough for me to notice strange shifts in the sensation beneath the pain. I have come to the conclusion that Eadon has discovered the secrets of teleportation."

The room was as silent as a tomb as everyone's mind eventually followed the train of thought. If Eadon could travel to any location at the command of his will, then he could also travel an army. It seemed the extent of his power was limited by only his imagination.

"We have hid from our destiny long enough, my friends. We hide no more. We have brought the destruction of our fallen brothers upon the innocent of Agora. Every day we have drawn breath upon this continent we have done so by the blood of children, human and dwarf alike. I am shamed by our shadow of defeat, always hunting, always breathing down our throats!"

Zerafin slammed the table and Whill jumped, so enthralled was he by Zerafin's flowing speech, and the promise of action that it echoed.

"I have seen my path. It is not one of running, or hiding. It is time for the elves of the sun to awaken, to rise as before against the darkness of tyranny and death, to strike out once and for all, with the armies of men and dwarves at our side. Together and only together"— Zerafin found Whill's stare and held it—"shall we be victorious!"

The gathering erupted in applause for the new king. To Whill's surprise, applause sounded as a dull roar outside and all around them, the words spoken by the king somehow reaching those outside and around the city.

"I call to arms every elf within Elladrindellia! We shall move as one, joining with the armies of dwarf and man, and we shall strike at the heart of Eadon's empire. With us shall go the blade of power given."

Whill cheered with the rest of them, and though he still bore the weight of responsibility in defeating the dark lord, he now had the beginnings of an army at his back. He smiled to think that he was beginning to bring the races of Agora together as one.

CHAPTER EIGHT
Chief

Night had long past fallen, and with it came a hard rain. Dirk paid it no mind as he approached the small town. He soon discovered it to be long deserted, given the destruction that remained. Most buildings had been burned to the ground, and all that remained of some were the skeletal remnants of their wooden frames.

At both ends of town pikes protruded from the ground, each with a human head atop it, man, woman, and child. Dirk turned from the sight in disgust. The hairs on the back of his neck shot up, and he realized he was being watched. The feeling came from behind him, between two burned-out but standing buildings. He made no move to give suspicion. He went about inspecting the town as usual. He called upon the jewels in his ears and listened through the rain. He heard nothing, and this did not bode well. If it were a beast or a draggard he would have heard its breathing.

Dirk listened while he walked toward the largest building; he listened for nearly ten minutes after he had slipped into the shadows between two buildings. Nothing stirred, but he felt the waiting. He felt the cold calculation and patience of a predator.

A dark elf, then, he thought, guessing that he had been tracked on the orders of Eadon. He needed to discover the location of his pursuer. From a pocket he withdrew a small speaking stone, a gift from Krentz. She had made most of his trinkets, and her creations were clever. Dirk whispered into the stone and threw it across town. It landed in a burned-out building and Dirk's voice boomed out of the stone. "Turn around now and you may keep your life."

A fireball ripped through the rain, leaving a trail of steam in its wake. Dirk knew then that indeed a dark elf pursued him, and it was weary. It was going for the quick kill, recklessly exposing its location in the process. It was a foolish mistake, and it did not make sense that Eadon would send a novice to dispose of Dirk. Instead he would send someone skilled in the arts. Eadon knew Dirk's abilities. He would send a master. The dark elf was toying with him; he was trying to convince him that his pursuer was weary, that he was a novice. Dirk was dealing with an excellent predator. He respected his tactics, though he would not fall for them.

There was a growl suddenly from the forest; Dirk knew it to be that of a wolf or wild dog. If nothing else, it seemed he was facing a proficient Ralliad that could change into a wolf. He assumed that the elf knew where he was, and it was possible that he was cornered, as the fireball had come from the other end of town, and the growl came from the opposite direction. Dirk was at a big disadvantage strategically. Again a growl came, and Dirk saw a pair of ice-blue eyes a few feet from the end of the alley in the thicket.

"Here, kitty, kitty, kitty," Dirk taunted and the eyes burned like blue flame. A huge brown timber wolf erupted from the brush and charged toward the alley. Dirk knew it was a trap; the wolf's master must be in wait at the other end of the alley. Instead of falling into the trick, Dirk charged the wolf, or seemed to.

As the wolf crashed through the underbrush, Dirk twirled his grappling hook once and sent it flying up and out. With his free hand he threw two poisoned darts at the animal. The hook caught hold of the roof ledge of the partially standing building to his right. He pulled the line taught and leapt into the air. He angled himself with the line and at the same time pulled himself upward while running along the wall. The wolf leapt for him and grazed his boot.

Dirk went up and over the ledge. Unhooking his grappling hook with a twist of the wrist, he crept quickly along the roof, contemplating what he had seen. The darts he had thrown had been dead on, yet they'd missed. They had not been deflected; rather the brown-

and-white wolf had become translucent and the darts had simply slipped through. It was as if the wolf was a ghost, or perhaps it was a dark elf after all. But no dark elf he had ever seen could make themselves as intangible as smoke. Perhaps Eadon could, but this was not Eadon's style. If he wanted Dirk dead, he would simply kill him.

He snuck a look over the edge of the roof. There was nothing to see but a fireball coming straight at him. With no time to duck and no protection to be found within the burned-out building, Dirk leapt over the fireball and extended his grappling hook with a flick of the wrist. The enchanted rope grew until it caught hold of the ledge on the adjoining building. Dirk swung out and wide intending to land on the adjacent roof. Another fireball ripped through the night and exploded where the grappling hook had caught. At that moment the ghost wolf slammed into Dirk and together they went tumbling.

They landed and Dirk rolled once and came up with a slash of his iron dagger. Dirk's suspicions of the wolf were proven right when the beast reared from the slash and growled. A bright red slash appeared upon its flank. The wolf's form wavered and turned translucent, then quickly back again, and the wound was gone.

Dirk dropped a smoke bomb that exploded with a deafening flash of blinding light. Behind him the wolf growled as he dove for the broken window of the crumbling stone structure. No fireball or wolf came at his back. The smoke bomb bad created a thick fog which covered the entire town in shrouds of gray. From a pocket he retrieved the glasses that a sun elf had created to his specifications under pain of death. He knew that the dark elf could not see him with his mind-sight, due to the spells upon his dragonhide cloak. But the dark elf had other ways of tracking. Dark elves could follow the aura of one's spiritual imprint, as clearly as a footprint in the sand. Dirk had of course remedied that problem with enchantments to his boots and attire. There were a multitude of tricks, however, and he assumed that the dark elf knew his location. The smoke had been more for the wolf, and it seemed to be working.

Dirk needed to even the odds and quick if he was to survive against the hunter and his pet. He had to take the wolf out of the equation. Quickly he took from a pouch a firestone and found the center of the room. He stood upon an old chair and scratched a symbol into the ceiling. Outside he could hear the low growl of the wolf as it stalked about, sniffing for a scent. He knew that the dark elf too was closing in. He finished the symbol and quickly made its twin upon the floor. It was a spell trap for snaring spirits, taught to him by Krentz. It would work, in theory; he did not know for sure, as he had never needed to use it before.

He finished the second symbol and put it between the wolf and himself. He heard a faint noise from the upstairs of the stone building and looked to the stairs back and to the right, but nothing stirred beyond the dark shadows of the passage. Dirk withdrew a dart, which, like the symbols, he had never used. This dart, like the six others of similar purpose, contained a silver tip and a poison of salted blessed water. He chucked the dart through the doorway as the spirit wolf stalked by; the dart hit the wolf in the neck. The wolf yelped and shook its head fiercely, it turned to spirit form and staggered back as the dart fell to the ground. Dirk readied another dart and his iron dagger as the wolf snarled and growled.

Behind him the wall exploded inward and he was forced to take a knee and shield himself with his enchanted cloak. A dark elf appeared through the destruction as if from out of the smoke and extended a hand toward Dirk. The assassin anticipated the attack and was ready as black tendrils of energy shot forth and were deflected by his enchanted cloak. Dirk twirled with the attack and came across quickly with his dagger. Behind him the wolf attacked, lunging at Dirk with hungry teeth and sharp claws gleaming. Dirk ignored the attack as his dagger was deflected by the dark elf's energy shield.

The dark elf came across with a sword slash, which Dirk rolled away from. At his back the wolf crossed the threshold and entered the area of space affected by the symbols. The spirit animal hit the force field as heavily as it might a large window. It realized its prison and thrashed about wildly, snapping and snarling at its invisible walls.

Dirk noticed the elf's slight surprise and predicted his next attack. As the dark elf brought up his hand to blast him with a spell, Dirk lunged forth with the speed of a viper. He knew that the only way to get through a strong energy shield was at its weakest point, which only occurred in the palm of the hand just before and just after a magical blast. The palm of the hand was the only place that the shield needed to be lifted, lest a practitioner release the spell within its own shield.

He plunged his mind-control dagger through the palm of the attacking dark elf as the spell began to emerge. The dark elf screamed in defiance, but before he could react, Dirk screamed, "Be still! You will not raise hand nor mind against me! You cannot, or you will die!"

The dark elf was silent but his face contorted with the pain of the struggle against the dagger's influence. "You were sent by Eadon, correct?" Dirk asked.

"Y...yes," the elf was forced to answer angrily.

"To kill me or take me captive."

The elf's face contorted as he fought the dagger. "To...kill."

Dirk nodded. "How do you control the wolf?"

The dark elf fought hard against the dagger. Dirk asked again, and intensified the dagger's force. "How do you control the wolf?"

The dark elf screamed against the wicked pain of the biting blade, fought against the mind intrusion, but the blade proved too powerful. His eyes rolled back and he shuddered with exertion.

"Tali…sman," he uttered and looked at his pocket.

"What is its name and what are its commands?"

"Chief, you hold the talisman, and summon, dismiss the same."

Dirk nodded thanks to the dark elf and in one swift motion hewed off his head so clean that it slid off the neck slowly. He retracted his dagger and searched the dark elf's effects. In a hidden pocket he found a small bone carving of a timber wolf, the talisman.

Dirk grabbed the dark elf's severed head and turned to the trapped wolf. It had stopped fighting the spell trap and simply stared at him as it sat on its hind legs. It looked at the head of its former master and cocked its own to the side; it let out a small whimper and disappeared to the spirit world. Dirk regarded the smooth bone talisman for a moment and then put it in his pocket. From the door of the building he threw a dart that hit the dark elf's body and exploded in flames. As Dirk left town, the building behind him went up in steadily intensifying flames. He set the head of the dark elf upon a pike that had been meant for the villagers. He took fifty paces and then threw a dart at the severed head. Dirk turned and continued on as behind him the dark elf head exploded on impact.

He kept to the road to make better time and ate what he could find off the trail. He knew how to be hungry, but he needed energy if he was going to make all haste to Kell-Torey. He knew himself to be just east of the Ky'Dren Pass. By morning he would reach the great pass, the only way into Eldalon by land. There within the gap in the mountains he would find the bustling trade city of the same name, and with any luck, he would find a faster way to Kell-Torey.

CHAPTER NINE
Inner Vision

Whill awoke within his silken bed the next morning feeling more refreshed than he had in a long time. Hope had begun to replace the nagging dread that had been his constant companion of late. The memory of a dream came back to him suddenly. He laughed and quieted himself quickly. He didn't know how he had slipped from it or it from his mind. It had been recent, just before he woke. It had been a dream of a memory. Whill closed his eyes as he reflected upon it. So clear was the memory that he felt a part of it.

Whill was but ten at the time. He and Abram had just left Sidnell, and the idea of being gone from Aunt Teera and the girls, warm baths and beds, had begun to gnaw at him. They followed the coast that rainy gray day, and young Whill was pulled from his homesickness by Abram.

"Are you hungry, lad?" he had asked.

Whill thought a moment. "No, sir, not yet."

"Good," Abram proclaimed and steered them off the road to cross a meadow of golden wheat, its beauty and vibrancy stolen by the dull day. "It is better to hunt when you are not hungry, lest you starve of misfortune."

He stopped Whill's horse and looked him in the eye. "Don't ever be caught unprepared; life is always waiting to kick your arse. Life kills all of us, don't forget. Every day lived means you were fighting, or someone else was fighting for you. Soon as you learn to fight, you learn to live." Abram dismounted and bid Whill do the same. "Now, lad, you have been learning things of great importance in my stead. Teera says you are a genius among geniuses, so now begins your lesson in living. For a brain to work a man must eat, and for a man to eat he must hunt. Reliance on others for food and drink makes one a slave to fortune, it causes dependence which hinders freedom. Understand, lad?"

Whill nodded. He did understand, as children understand all too well the limitations of dependency, the frustration at their size and weakness and inability to exercise their own will.

"Good, then. Today we hunt."

That had been the beginning of a decade of travel, adventure, danger, and learning.

Whill lay in his bed smiling at the memory, lost in the euphoria of nostalgia. They had hunted all day and into dusk when finally a big buck with an amazing rack of antlers crossed their path. Abram's arrow had flown true, and Whill had his first lesson in skinning and butchering deer.

Whill recognized the pain at the edge of his mind, encroaching on the sensitive thoughts. His pain wanted to bring him along in a sorrowful remembrance of his lost friend. Whill felt himself slipping, tears beginning to form, but quickly he smiled at the intrusion.

"This is not your place. I do not need you. Go away now," Whill said to his pain, and visualized his thought connections shifting down other paths.

"I am sorry" came a voice, and Whill jumped. "Avriel said that you were awake. I will go," said Aurora and turned to leave.

"No, no, I was not talking to you, I was…never mind," he said with a nervous laugh. "I was getting up anyway."

With a smile Aurora sat back on a thick vine chair, a mischievous smile creeping across her face as the vines of the seat shifted to the shape of her form. Whill swung his legs over the side of the bed and realized he wore no clothes beneath the silken sheets.

Aurora raised an eyebrow and her smile spread. "Thinking of staying in bed?" she purred.

"Uh, no! I mean—no," he stammered. He faked a yawn and stretched, attempting to recover. "But I am famished." He stood clutching the sheets and looked around for his clothes. He found the leg of the pants he had worn sticking out from beneath Aurora's bottom. She smirked at his wondering eyes.

"So am I…?" she teased and combed through her hair with long fingers. Her long, thick locks fell across her bosom and shoulder, brushing against her flesh. She wore still the furs she had worn within the arena, though they had not the dirt and blood of battle upon them.

Whill smiled weakly and went to his wardrobe. Many sets of clothes had been supplied to him. He chose loose-fitting pants and shuffled to get them on under the sheets. A breeze informed him that his sheet had fallen. A slight hum came from behind him and he felt his cheeks get hot. He tied off the pants and was pleased with their feel; they were light and airy and felt as if they were not there. He chose a similar shirt of white with light green patterns of snaking vines throughout. He found also that the sandals were very comfortable, like standing on moss.

Whill turned and raised his arms for Aurora, turning to show her the fit.

"You look like no less than a king," Aurora sang.

Whill scowled and rubbed his stomach. A hunger pang reminded him he had to eat. "Shall we find breakfast?"

Aurora gave a small laugh. "That will not be easy; it seems you have some admirers."

Whill walked to the balcony and the leaf curtains slid back slowly. Loud cheers emanated from below, startling him. A crowd of hundreds of elves had gathered and were cheering his name. As he walked out onto the balcony, many of the gathering crowd fell to their knees and bowed to the ground. It reminded him of the mob that had surrounded the house of healing in Sherna, after he had healed the infant.

Aurora came to stand by his side. "They worship you like a god-king."

Whill sighed. "I wish they wouldn't."

Aurora appeared perplexed. "What man would not appreciate such adoration?" She seemed to search his eyes for the reason.

"A man who does not feel he deserves it," he murmured, more to himself than to her. He looked out over the sea of smiling and cheering elves and his heart dropped. They saw him as their long-awaited savior, but Whill didn't feel like a savior. He felt like a fraud.

"But you are deserving of such adoration," Aurora said. "You have faced Eadon and lived to tell about it. Your deeds were known to me long before I met you. They are whispered in every village in every kingdom. You alone wield the greatest power given."

Whill was unmoved by her words. He turned from the balcony and mentally called to Avriel. Aurora put a hand to Whill's shoulder and he turned to face her.

"I have not known you long, Whill of Agora, but what I have seen has convinced me that you are a man of honor, strength, and courage."

Whill tried to turn from her, not wanting to hear more of his grandeur, but she held him firm. "Listen to me," she insisted. "You may not like the role you have to fill, few do, but—"

Whill tore away from her grip. "I can't do it, don't you see! I am not trying to be humble and I am far from righteous. This task is beyond me, the prophecy is a lie…"

"That may be, yes. The prophecy may be a lie. But you still possess the blade Adromida, and you are still the rightful king of Uthen-Arden. Do not waste your time complaining that you are wanted. There are far worse fates. Would you rather be wanted by none?"

"Yes!" Whill screamed and felt his rage boil to dangerous levels. He had to leave; he had to be far from her and his cursed followers. Without another word he unsheathed Adromida and flew from the balcony, nearly colliding with Avriel as she glided to meet him. He flew out over the city toward the Thousand Falls.

Whill! She called, but he did not respond. He needed to be alone.

Whill flew to the falls and landed between two of the rushing waterfalls as they spilled into the river below. He misjudged his landing and fell stumbling to the rocks and into the water beyond. He dragged himself up onto an outcropping of rock like a wet dog, cursing all the while.

"I think you need to work on your landing," a voice called. Startled, he looked in the direction of the sound and found the Watcher meditating on a lone rock jutting out of the raging water.

Whill sighed to himself. "I was looking for a place to be alone," he murmured, thinking the rushing water had drowned his words.

"If you were looking for a place to be alone, why did you land by me?" asked the Watcher.

Whill was speechless. He looked back toward the city and thought of Avriel. He now regretted ignoring her.

"I was about to get some lunch anyway," said the Watcher. "You shall have the privacy you sought." The Watcher turned as if to leave but stopped. "Unless you are hungry."

Whill's stomach growled at the mere thought of food.

"Well, then," said the Watcher. "At least there is a part of you that knows what it wants. Come." The old elf changed before Whill's eyes into a huge raven and flew off toward his small river island. Whill slowly elevated himself and floated clumsily to the island. The cottage of his youth was gone; he doubted it had been more than an illusion. In its place was a small pyramid made of what looked to be rocks from the surrounding river.

Inside, the pyramid had no walls, and Whill could find no binding element between the stones. It looked as though they had melded together.

"Do you like it?" asked the Watcher. "I made it in a dream." He chuckled as he added two large fish to the pan upon glowing coals. "You can imagine my surprise when I awoke and saw it had become real."

"You made it in a dream?" Whill asked, astonished. He ran his hand down the perfectly smooth, angled stone. "How is that possible?"

The Watcher regarded Whill. "How is it not possible?" he said with genuine curiosity. Shaking his head when no answer came, he went back to his cooking.

"It is amazing," Whill admitted and took a seat at the table.

"Yes, quite," the Watcher agreed. "I call it the house of dreams. I did not make the house to look as it did when you visited last, you did, or rather your subconscious."

"Why that house?" asked Whill.

"Why indeed?" said the Watcher. "Ask yourself that question. Those I have brought here, or who have come to visit, have conjured up many different abodes. Some from imagination, others memory, but always it is a place of great significance."

Whill nodded in understanding. "It shows you your dream home, then?"

"No," said the Watcher, his bushy eyebrows nearly coming together as he scowled over his cooking fish. He looked up at Whill and his expression changed to sympathy. "When you look on the house of dreams, your deepest desires are shown to you."

Whill cocked his head and pondered, looking at nothing. "My deepest desires are my old cottage?"

The Watcher only sighed and stood from the fire-place with the pan in hand. Upon two wide leaves he put the fish. He set marbled bread upon the small table, and poured two glasses of wine. Seeing no utensils, Whill dug into the fish, and before his mouthful was swallowed he was breaking bread. Wine washed down the fish with a fruity finish. The fish was excellent, and the sour bread added a fine balancing element to the meal. The Watcher knew how to pair food and drink. They ate for a time, and when the Watcher recognized Whill's distracting hunger was sated, he went on.

"It is not the cottage that you dream of, but what the cottage represents."

"What does it represent?"

"You tell me," replied the Watcher with a small laugh. "It is your subconscious."

Whill thought for a moment as he absently chewed his bread. Waving the piece from the loaf with his right hand, he surmised, "The cottage represents my child-hood, my aunt Teera, the girls…but not Abram. He was always gone when I was little."

"Until…?"

"Until…until I left with him." Whill's interest in the food was lost as he again thought of his old friend. "The cottage represents a time before my days upon the road began with Abram. A time of safety and security, a time of…" Whill stared off pensively.

"A time of innocence," the Watcher finished for him.

"I suppose," said Whill, and finished the last of his wine. "But what does it matter what my dreams are? All of that is behind us now."

"Indeed," the Watcher agreed. "Then why is it at the back of your mind? Why did you not conjure your family's castle, or one of the many other places that you have lived throughout your life?"

Whill pondered the question as he played with his food, not meeting the Watcher's gaze. "I do not seek my father's throne, or any throne. I want only peace and quiet, and a simple life. One in which I might come and go as I please, invisible to the world."

"Ah," said the Watcher. "You wish for a life that is not your own. You hold your happiness hostage until the world changes to accommodate your wishes, is that it?"

"No, I—"

"Why not simply leave this land, then? You have the great blade Adromida; surely you can live the life you have just described."

Whill met the Watcher's eyes and anger found his voice. "You know that I cannot do that."

"Why?" asked the elf.

"Because people depend on me."

The Watcher raised his brow. "Then you care more for the people than you do your own wants."

Whill thought for a long while, and finally answered. "Yes. I have a duty to help those whom I have the power to help."

The Watcher smiled and resumed finishing his meal, leaving Whill to ponder what had been said. Whill finished his food also and gratefully accepted another glass of wine.

"Who are you, Whill?" the Watcher asked.

"What do you mean?"

"Who are you?"

Whill's gaze moved here and there as he searched his mind. "I am the rightful king of Uthen-Arden, I am the supposed savior of the—"

"No, I did not ask who others think you are. Who do *you* think you are?"

"I do not know," Whill answered in a near whisper.

"Good, that is a start."

"How is that good?"

"Without labels and boundaries, there is room to grow," the Watcher answered. "What is important to you? What would you die for?"

"Justice," Whill answered without thinking.

"Justice for you?" the Watcher asked. "Or justice for all?"

Whill thought about it a moment. "Justice for all."

"Interesting." The Watcher appeared to ponder something. He nodded his head as he thought to himself. "That is quite a different answer than you gave me earlier. I thought you wanted a peaceful and simple life."

"Before…" Whill began, trying to find the words. "Before, I spoke…selfishly."

"Yes, you did," the Watcher agreed.

"Ugh!" moaned Whill as he set his head in his hands and weakly clawed his hair. "What is wrong with me?"

The Watcher laughed heartily and Whill raised his head to scowl at the mockery, but he found none in the Watcher's sympathetic face.

"What is wrong with you, my young friend, is that you were tortured for six months by a maniacal dictator. Don't be so hard on yourself. The brain storms I showed you when last we met are the reason for much of how you feel. You have the answers you seek, but your painbody refuses to let you see them."

Whill nodded, frustrated that he had learned so much from the elves, and yet lacked the strength to act upon his knowledge.

The Watcher became solemn and gazed upon Whill with vacant eyes and mournful words. "Eadon has shattered your mind and put it back together again. When I look upon you, I see two within one."

The fine hairs upon Whill's arms stood straight and a chill passed through his being that forced a shudder with the Watcher's every word. These were words of truth, a truth that Whill knew at his core, deep within the recesses of his scarred mind. There was a beast lurking within him, one that would devour him should the chains that bound it fail.

Whill realized that the Watcher had been speaking but had stopped; the old elf now looked at him patiently. "I am sorry, what did you say just now? I was—"

"You were thinking what I was trying to explain. You can feel the...Other inside, yes?"

Whill gulped and lowered his voice as if to hide his words from this...Other. "Yes, I feel him."

"Hmm." The Watcher clasped his hands across his belly and sat back. "This is good. Now you can begin to see the difference between your thoughts and actions, and this Other's."

"Yes." Whill smiled, a spark of hope beginning to form as he began to attribute his moods and emotions to not one, but two parts of himself. His mind exploded with rapid thought as he began to see clearly how the Other had been feeding off of him.

"It is like a parasite," Whill said.

"Indeed."

Again Whill lowered his voice a bit, though he knew how silly the idea was that the Other could not hear him, considering it was privy to his thoughts.

"But doesn't it know that I am onto it now? Won't it try to retaliate? Or hide?"

"No, it is quite sure of its supremacy over you. Remember, it is a part of your mind; it has been with you since your violent birth. If anything, it loves the attention we give it, no matter the context." The Watcher raised the bottle of wine. "Another?"

"Yes—," Whill began, but then came to a realization. "No," he said covering the glass with his hand. "I have had enough and…" He scowled at the floor and then swiftly locked onto the Watcher's gaze. "It…wants me to."

"Very good, my young friend!" the Watcher clapped, genuinely delighted. "When one becomes intoxicated with this particular drug, the veil separating them from their Other is weakened, too much of it, and they are possessed altogether."

Whill's eyes widened and he gave slow, exaggerated nods as revelation bloomed within his mind. Question then shadowed his mirth. "But you drink still when I have refused; do you not worry about your Other?"

"No," said the elf and took a slow sip of his wine. "My Other and I have an understanding. Over the centuries a healthy relationship forms if nurtured diligently. It is only one's survival instinct become conscious, after all, but all too often we are tricked by it to believe it is us, and we are it."

Silence filled the room as the Watcher sipped and Whill considered. It was a comfortable silence found between friends.

"What did Eadon hope to achieve in…splitting my mind?" Whill asked.

"He hopes that the Other will consume you. He has planted a seed that will be nurtured by you yourself until it outgrows its shell and devours you."

Whill tried to mask his sudden horror as images of his inner demon tearing free and his body falling like a discarded husk plagued his mind. He teetered upon the brink of terror as he imagined his Other wielding the blade Adromida.

"I am a fool." He looked suddenly to the elf, gratitude filling his heart. "If you hadn't helped me to see this, to recognize the Other…thank you, Watcher."

"You are welcome, Whill of Agora, and thank you."

Whill was baffled. "Thank you for what?"

The Watcher leaned forward and patted Whill's hand. "For needing me." He smiled.

As Whill walked to the door, the Watcher stopped him with a warning. "Be careful, Whill. The Other within you is very powerful. There will be a reckoning."

CHAPTER TEN
The Road to Elladrindellia

Roakore and his company made good time the first day. They took the less-traveled road that wound through the Uthen-Arden Kingdom from the Ro'Sar Mountains to the Elgar Mountains. The first of the towns they came upon was deserted as they had guessed it would be. Like so many others, it had been burned to the ground. Human and draggard bodies littered the landscape, rotting where they had fallen. It seemed as though no one had survived to bury them.

They made camp next to a small stream far from the road and the night went by quietly. Morning came and Tarren opted to skip breakfast, determined to fly with Roakore without puking.

"So you think you be ready to try again, eh, lad?" asked Roakore as the company readied their mounts to depart.

"I be thinkin' I can't be pukin' up what I don't eat."

"All right, then, mount up and keep your food to yer-self."

Lunara waved happily as Silverwind took to the sky. Roakore took it easy, ascending only high enough to graze the treetops.

"There be a trick to it, lad. You can't fight it; it ain't like being on the ground. You gotta just go with it, be one with the bird."

They flew ahead of the group and checked the road. All was quiet as they flew above the trees in the morning sunshine. The air was crisp with the smells of autumn as they glided along on a soft current.

"How you doin', lad?" Roakore asked.

"A lot better. I think I got the hang of it."

They traveled steadily east on the mountain road the rest of the day. Tarren dared a small lunch and managed to keep it down the rest of the flight. Night came and they made camp again far off the road under the bows of the everpine. A thick fog had gathered around the world, and heavy clouds hid the heavens in shadow.

The company of dwarves had brought with them enough food for fifty, and as much ale. The mood was light as they dined next to a blazing fire. Ale flowed freely and laughter spilled out into the night. Hold-agozz noticed Lunara's discomfort and moved to sit next to the elf.

"What is it, lady?" he asked as he offered her a pint. The dark dwarven ale had grown on her during her time in the mountain. She took it with a smile.

"The large fire and merrymaking, it is a bit of a ruckus, don't you think? We could attract unwanted attention."

"Bah," exclaimed Holdagozz. "Ain't none but trees to be hearin' us out here. What unwanted attention be there, anyway? That o' the draggard?" he scoffed. "Bring it on, says we!"

"What's that, Holdagozz?" asked one of the dwarves by the name of Philo.

"Lunara here be wonderin' if we be makin' too much noise and ruckus and such. Says we might attract unwanted attention, she does."

"Bah!" Philo roared and stood with mug in hand. "How's this for a ruckus?" he bellowed and guzzled his entire beer. Foam and drink poured down his red-tinted brown beard and he belched long and loud. From the fire he took hold of a branch burning at one end. "An' if that ain't enough to attract unwanted attention, maybe this'll be workin'." Philo turned and bent at the waist. He put the burning branch at the center of his backside and let rip a dwarven fart of epic proportions. A flash of flame blazed forth and his pants caught fire. The group roared with laughter and took turns lighting their flatulence.

Lunara rolled her eyes and tried hard not to laugh. Holdagozz stood up as if to join in.

"You wouldn't dare!" She giggled as he reached for a stick.

"Wouldn't I?" he laughed.

Just then Roakore landed and Silverwind's wings stirred the fire to leap high and bright. "Shut yer yappers, all o' ye!" he roared as he slid from his saddle, followed by his son Helzendar, who was nearly as tall. Dwarves grew to full height by age thirteen, but they grew thicker with every passing season. Roakore was twice his son's width. "I be hearin' ye for miles and then some. What, you think this is a party?" With the last word he grabbed the mug from a dwarf's hand, guzzled the contents, and smashed it over the dwarf's head. "Ye get a chest full o' fresh air and ye all go bat-shyte, eh? We be escortin' an elven ambassador o' Elladrindellia. Have some godsdamned respect, ye buncha dragon turds! Ruby group set a perimeter and quick as quick got ready. Move! Move!"

Five of the dwarves scattered to comply. He gathered the others round. "This be a stealth mission, and don't ye be forgettin' it. And ye be in the midst o' a lady elf o' the sun. Save the fart-lightin' for the taverns."

All were ordered to bed, as they would set out before the coming of the sun. Roakore slept in only short spurts, his ear always on the wind. He had seen something in the moon as he flew with his son after nightfall. Before the clouds captured the entire sky, he had seen a bloodred moon hovering there like the sapphire goddess herself, being swallowed by a wave of cloud.

The prophetic vision had not escaped his son; Holdagozz had pointed it out as Roakore too saw it.

"Sapphirian," he had breathed in disbelief.

If they had been on land they would have fallen to the nearest stone in reverie. As it was they could only bow forward in their saddles and pray.

"The gods be with us, Father," Holdagozz said tearfully.

"As they always be, son, as they always be. Such signs are always there for us to see. But ye gotta be lookin'. The gods be with us, all right, and they be warnin' us. There be bloodshed comin' on the morrow, best we make sure it ain't ours.

"Thank you, oh goddess o' the ancient stone," he offered to the moon as it was overtaken by star-killing clouds.

Later, as he lay by the hot coals of the fire, he smiled at the memory.

"Bloodshed on the morrow...bloodshed..." Roakore heard Helzendar mumble in his sleep, and he felt the fear that every parent feels. He reached in the darkness and patted his son's back reassuringly.

"Best we make sure it ain't ours," he answered.

Just then a song came to mind, and he sang it softly to the night. Many dwarves heard the song that night, and they sang it for years to come. The voice of the king, deep and strong but hushed as in lullaby, rose up into the night sky, and a tear came to Holdagozz's eyes.

There be bloodshed on the morrow, best we make sure it ain't ours.

There be bloodshed on the morrow, I seen it in the stars.

There be bloodshed on the morrow, the bloodred moon doth bode.

There be bloodshed on the morrow, death be somewhere down the road.

Long before the sun took back the heavens, the company was fed and on the road once more. At Roakore's orders they drove the horses hard into the afternoon. It was not until then that they stopped before a bridge. Roakore led Silverwind to a stream. The horses would have moved away were they not so thirsty.

Lunara stormed up to Roakore and shoved his shoulder. Though he did not move an inch, he understood her meaning.

"What do you mean by pushing the horses so hard? Are you mad?" Lunara demanded. "Even the sturdiest of dwarven breeds cannot be driven so long. Have you no knowledge of the equine?"

"I be knowin' 'bout dwarven horses, lady, and I be knowin' what they can take. Ask 'em yerself with yer elven tricks."

"One need not ask the obvious, good king, one must simply care to look," she replied.

"Bah." Roakore threw up his arms and turned to find food. She stopped him with a firm hand to his shoulder. He stopped and looked at her hand with a curious brow. "What be it?" he asked.

"What be it—that is indeed the question," she said quietly. "What be with you? I know that you would flee from nothing. You are not running away from something, you are running to something. Why the urgency, dwarf, what do you know?"

Roakore looked around at his unnoticing fellows. "Just somethin' me and me boy saw night last, somethin' in the heavens."

"An omen?" she asked, all seriousness and wide-eyed wonder. Roakore often forgot that she was young for an elf at only twenty-one. He took for granted her innocence in the face of her great power.

"Yes, me lady. I see blood on the road before us. Sapphirian has foretold of it."

"Then let us not ride into it headlong, but with a plan."

"I got me a plan," said Roakore.

"What is your plan, to go in axe first, screaming like a wild dwarf?"

Roakore looked at her dubiously. "Ugh…yeah."

Lunara pet Silverwind's beautiful shining feathers, startling the drinking bird and causing it to instinctively turn the color of the earth and stream for but a moment.

"Think for a moment of the effort that your goddess has gone to in order to bring you the omen," she said.

Roakore moved his eyes back and forth. "I'm listenin'."

"If she went to all that trouble, shouldn't we too show cunning, diligence, and due caution in the face of such a…dire omen?"

Roakore stared at her until she looked away. "Yer hired!" he said loudly, and walked away.

Lunara was momentarily dumbfounded but ran after him. "Hired?" she asked.

He turned and stopped so that she bumped into him, with her bosom to his face, given his height. He sputtered and apologized but she seemed not to have noticed.

"What do you mean hired?" she asked again.

"It means when one does a service for—"

"I know what it means in human and dwarf custom. What duty would you ask of me?"

"To be me adviser, of course, personal healer and such, and for it all the gold and jewels you could want and all the adventure you could stand."

Lunara squinted at his description. "Adviser, healer… you sound as though you are describing the elf word for friend."

Roakore scowled at that. "I guess I be, then, lady, I guess I be. Haha! Well, anyway, yer hired. Would ye lay out a plan for me and me boys? I want to see what you got." He leaned in close to her ear. "I doubted you would mind signing on with me crew, knowing that Holdagozz be at me side always."

He winked and walked away in search of his lunch, leaving Lunara to stare at his back, open-mouthed.

The dwarves dined and the horses ate, Silverwind went off hunting, and Lunara sang a song to the horses. Her staff glowed with the sweet melody that was her voice as it sang in Elvish of strength and healing and growth and rebuilding. All who heard the song were affected, horse, human, and dwarf alike. Her words surrounded them all, and all were held in attention and awe. Pulses of energy rippled from the staff and were felt as easily as seen. Like heat ripples above a blazing fire, her spell washed over everyone. And they all shuddered as the energy passed through them.

The belching dwarf Philo stepped forward as soon as the spell was through and raised a fist. "What's the meanin' o' this elven magic-makin' on us?"

Roakore stepped between Philo and Lunara, who was bent to a knee, recuperating from the exertion. "She be healin' the horses is all. She can't be blamed if ye felt a tingle."

"A tingle!" roared Philo. "It—"

"You be part o' me elite fightin' force, and we do things a little different here. Follow me to glory or be on yer own damned way."

"Sorry, me king—"

"Don't be sorry, just be sensible. Do ye not feel better than ye have in years? There ain't no fear to be had o' this one. She be pure as the driven mountain snows o' Ky'Dren's peaks, she be."

Lunara blushed at the compliment and the dwarves went to mounting their steeds. Roakore took to the sky with his son and they set out once again.

They flew ahead many miles and saw nothing to warrant the previous night's omen. The day had clouded over once again and a light rain fell, but aside from that, the world was quiet. There was no smoke on the horizon, no dark hordes of marching draggard. Still, Roakore sensed something coming, and he trusted his instincts enough to be weary.

Together with Silverwind and Helzendar he flew farther still, past yet another burned-out town, until finally they came to the fortress of Bhor'Alder. The old trading post had long ago been abandoned, having been used for trade between the Ro'Sar dwarves and Uthen-Arden. It was located perfectly between the Uthen-Arden capital city of Del'Oradon and the Ro'Sar Mountains. Since the invasion of the Ro'Sar Mountains, however, the trading place had gone into disrepair.

Roakore circled the stone structure looking for a sign of trouble. Nothing moved among the stone but long weeds blowing in the wind. The place was quiet, but Roakore's superstition was not quenched. He and his son landed outside of the stone structure and dismounted.

Helzendar was eager for some trouble, having heard the tales of his father's many exploits. For the dangerous trek, Roakore had allowed his son to take along the steel version of his wooden half-moon spear-staff. He held it at the ready as he scouted the deserted trading post with his father.

"Quiet as stone, lad. Listen close," Roakore bade him as he led the way into the quiet fortress.

Through the wide open archway they went into the main trading room. The vast hall had once been the epicenter of bustling activity, a place where dwarves and men traded their wares. It now stood quiet as a tomb, with only the soft moan of wind through its broken windows. There was only faint light here, but to the mountain-dwelling dwarves, it was enough to see clearly.

Roakore had come here many times a year in the early days before the invasion of Ro'Sar. Humans came from all corners of Uthen-Arden to trade food, pottery, ale, and supplies for the dwarves' masterfully created weapons and jewelry. He knew the fortress well, and using his knowledge of the layout of the stone structure, he led his son cautiously through the chambers and rooms.

They spent nearly a half hour searching for the cause of the previous night's bad omen but found nothing. Roakore and Helzendar came back to the entrance where they had started their search. There was only one place left to check: the wine cellar.

Roakore walked silently to the door of the cellar. He cursed under his breath as the large wooden door creaked on its rusty hinges. As soon as the door cracked open, a waft of stench assaulted the two dwarves.

"Bwah, what's that stink, Pa?" Helzendar asked, pinching his nose against the smell.

"That be the stink o' draggard eggs an' slime, or I be a bearded turd," Roakore answered. "Follow me close, lad, and not a sound."

Helzendar nodded his understanding and gripped his spear-staff tighter.

Roakore led him down the stairs cautiously. When the wine cellar came into view, the dwarves' eyes widened. It was no longer a wine cellar, but had been dug out for hundreds of feet on all sides. And though Helzendar was looking at hundreds of eggs, he could not help but puzzle over one question: Where had all the dirt gone?

Roakore froze at the bottom of the stair. Helzendar stopped a few steps short, glad that the stairs were stone and not creaking wooden ones. He and his father looked around the chamber of dirt, taking in the details.

Silently the lad and his father returned to the surface and did not speak or make a sound until they were far from the place.

"Holy flaming dragon shyte!" Helzendar exclaimed in a hushed whisper.

His father laughed. "Yer mam know ye be cussin' like a pirate?"

"O' course she do, I be learnin' from the best. She could swear a devil to blush, she could."

Roakore laughed all the more. But his face fast became serious. "There be nearly a thousand eggs down there. Ye know what that be meanin', lad?"

Helzendar did not have to ponder long. "A queen be nearby?" He scowled at the nearby tree shadows.

"No," said Roakore. "Them eggs be not fresh. What I think is there at least be some sort o' guard round."

Helzendar nodded his agreement and eyed the land with renewed vigor. Roakore whistled, and soon Silverwind was gliding toward them. As fast as she could carry them, they flew back to the others. Soon they came upon them and landed in a clearing next to the road. Roakore and Helzendar slid off of Silverwind and Holdagozz nodded at his king.

"What do you know? By the look o' your face, what? It be a dragon ahead?"

Roakore shook his head and grinned. "By the bloodred moon we did see the omen. We found ourselves a li'l den o' draggard."

Everyone perked up at that. Roakore pointed a thumb behind him. "There be bloodshed coming, boys. Best make sure it ain't ours."

He led them swiftly the few miles to the fortress; they stopped a few stones' throws away from the structure. The horses were tied off and the dwarves got into a huddle.

"What be the plan?" asked Philo eagerly. As weapons he carried twin war hammers, short and thick and made of steel. The heads of his hammers were as wide as dinner plates, and the handle half his arm length. They hung from straps above his elbows and swung lazily as he bobbed.

"Ye be rememberin' the ol' trading post o' Bhor'Alder? Well, the wine cellar be full o' draggard eggs, still stinkin'. Me boy and me be figuring that the queen has either moved on, or she be in wait. And there ain't no tellin' if any be guardin' the den. We're gonna go in fast and we're gonna go in hot."

He looked around at the group, picking out the quickest. "I be needin' two volunteers to go into the den an' flush 'em out."

When everyone raised their hands, Roakore pointed to the two he had already chosen. "You and you, get a small barrel o' lantern oil and be ready for me orders. The rest o' you prepare for battle. We be wakin' up the demons from their eggs."

Roakore took Lunara aside. "Would ye keep the boys at yer side? They ain't yet prepared for dangers such as this."

The young elf nodded. "Of course."

The dwarves split into two groups; one came in from the left, the other from the right. These were young, hearty dwarves who had survived the reclamation; they were Ro'Sar Mountain–born, and ready for blood.

The entrance to the trading post was surrounded as the dwarves took their places. Hatchets were drawn and the two runners nodded to their king that they were ready.

From one of the many bags attached to his saddle Roakore took two dragonsbreath bombs. He handed one to each of the runners. The two runners, Brendar and Du'Wren, looked at the bombs with wide eyes and eager grins.

"Now these here bombs pack more punch than ye be thinkin'," Roakore explained. "Ye be wanting a wide breadth when these go off. I be needin' you to pour a line o' oil all around and through the entire chamber. Brendar!"

"Yes, sir!"

"I be wantin' your bomb at the far end o' the den. And Du'Wren—"

"Sire!"

"I want ye to plant yer bomb near the entrance. We'll fry these demons right well. Now pull them plugs from them oil barrels an' give 'em hell."

"Yes, sir," the two dwarves said in unison.

Brendar and Du'Wren ran into the building, trailing oil, and disappeared. A few tense minutes passed and neither of them came out. When the unmistakable sounds of angry draggard began to come from the structure, Roakore nodded to Holdagozz to follow.

They entered the structure cautiously. Nothing was beyond the threshold but more sounds of stirring draggard. Holdagozz followed his king to the stairs and beyond. Once below, they saw Brendar fighting off a draggard. The dwarf was bleeding from many wounds and had abandoned his small oil barrel for his war hammer. In his wake lay two dead draggard. All around the den draggard had begun to stir. Many had hatched from their eggs, and many more were beginning to. Roakore ran to Brendar's aid and embedded his great axe in the draggard's head.

"Where be Du'Wren?" he asked Brendar.

Brendar pointed deep within the den. "I last seen him when we crossed back there."

Another draggard charged at the dwarves but was quickly put down by Holdagozz with a hatchet that sunk deep in the beast's forehead. Just then they heard the war cry of Du' Wren.

"Haha, ye beasties, come and get some!"

Roakore turned to Holdagozz. "Get Brendar to Lunara—"

"It ain't but a scratch," protested Brendar, though it was clear by the blood at his feet that the wounds were serious.

"Go on, now, the both of ye. When I come out with Du'Wren, light it up."

"Yes, me King," said Holdagozz as he led the injured dwarf out.

Roakore made his way through the draggard-egg-infested den. He could now see Du'Wren engaged in battle with two draggard. The dwarf wielded twin axes and in his strong hands they were deadly, but many of the beasts were quickly surrounding him.

Roakore barreled into the side of one of the draggard and sent it flying. Du'Wren smiled brightly at his king and attacked his foes with renewed vigor.

"C'mon, then, soldier, let's get clear o' this stinkin' den so we can light her up!" yelled Roakore as more draggard began to hatch.

He plowed a path through the growing draggard horde and reached the stairs with Du'Wren hot on his heels. They came sprinting out of the trading post with snarling draggard not far behind. Hatchets flew and the following beasts fell in a heap at the threshold.

"Light 'er up!" Roakore ordered, and the dwarves complied. Torches were lowered to the oil trail and flames quickly caught and started into the building.

Newborn draggard, covered in green slime, began pouring out of the old trading post. Hatchets flew into their ranks, two per dwarf, and the advance was quickly cut short. Screams of anguish rose up from the depths of the den and Roakore knew that the spilled oil had caught.

Suddenly Philo broke rank and charged three draggard as they came out of the building. Before he could reach them and before his king could give warning, there was a huge explosion from within the building. Philo was blown back many feet as flame and gore shot forth from the threshold.

A second blast ripped through the subterranean den and the ground shook with the retort. The dwarves cheered and pumped their fists in the air. Once the commotion had died down, the screams and cries of the burning draggard rose up with the smoke.

The beasts began to once again pour out of the building. Some were missing limbs, others were engulfed in flames, and all met the fierce battle cry of the dwarves. What draggard that survived the dragonsbreath explosion soon wished they hadn't, for it would have been a gentler death than what they faced at the hands of the dwarves.

The Ro'Sar dwarves had trained for twenty long years, always with the burning image of the hated draggard. They lived for nothing more than to kill the beasts, and they were very good at it. They had learned every weakness of the beasts, knew that they were soft behind the ear and under the tail, and as vulnerable as any in the eyes. The dwarves knew of and exploited every weakness, and even invented a few. One stout dwarf, the legendary belcher Philo himself, had learned quite accidentally that one could distract the draggard almost like a dumb animal if you spun and twirled your shiny weapons. Once proven, the idea had been adapted in everyday combat training.

The draggard were defeated in short order, and the spectacle amazed Tarren. He watched from behind Lunara and did not even try to get involved like Helzendar wanted to, though he could have, as Lunara was so engaged in the healing of the dwarves from afar. She flung swirling blue orbs of healing energy at the dwarves from both hands, one after another. She stood braced to the earth in a defensive stance, her eyes rolled back and head tilted likewise. She chanted all the while, and Tarren did not know for sure whether it was the wind or the supreme magic which caused her hair to dance like silver flame. Tarren watched as a bold dwarf misjudged a strike and got a draggard tail straight through his belly. Before Tarren could gasp at the horror, the tail retracted and Lunara shot a blue healing orb from her palm. The orb glowed around the wound, and it was no more. To Tarren's and indeed the dwarf's amazement, the wound healed as the skin came together and the dwarf fought on.

Tarren watched on wide-eyed as he saw firsthand the prowess of the dwarves. He realized just how much he needed to grow if he were to ever face something as nightmarish and powerful as the draggard. They were covered in small spikes, not pointed but jagged all the same. Upon their backs were larger spikes, the degree of which depended on the draggard build. They were not all of uniform size, Tarren quickly learned, but as varied in shape as humans. The smallest ones chilled Tarren the most; they tended to use all fours and were like little dog-sized monsters. The boy learned also the great prowess of the dwarves to be able to defeat such foes. It seemed that they housed the strength of two bulls. And while Tarren had seen the great loads the dwarves could lift, and indeed had felt their power in training, to actually see a dwarf rip off a draggard's arm and then smash its face in with it was something else.

Lunara ran to the dwarves once the fighting had stopped. "Get the injured to the tree line and away from the smoke of the dead! Put them over there." She pointed. "From left to right, dying to not."

The dwarves stopped in their victory song, even the badly injured, and just looked at her like she was a crazy elf. Holdagozz barked at them, "Do what the lady be sayin', ye bunch o' numbnuts, and right quick!"

"Quicker than quick got ready!" Roakore added.

The dwarves stopped in their victory song and found out the injured. They were sat next to the tree line, far from the smoldering trading post. A group went to collect heads to stake, and others set watch. Those who remained watched as Lunara went to work.

The young elf healer knelt next to the first dwarf on the dying side. He had a severed draggard tail jutting out from under his chin. Lunara set her hand upon the dwarf and took in a shocked breath. "His body yet lives, but his soul has passed."

She moved on to the next dwarf. As she removed the bandages, blood spurted from his neck and the dwarf went into convulsions. He bled from the mouth as well as the throat. Lunara put a hand to his neck and chanted softly. Blue tendrils of healing emanated from her hand as the other gripped her staff, and the crystal set upon its top glowed brightly. The bleeding soon stopped as Lunara extended her consciousness to the dwarf's life force. She coaxed bone, vein, and muscle back to form, and the skin to flawlessly meld. The astonished dwarf came to and stared at Lunara in awe. She moved on to the next in line.

So it went, and those who could be were healed. Only the two were dying after all, and four more with broken bones or severe gashes from draggard tooth or claw, tail or spike. Fifty heads they collected in all, and those were set upon spikes which were placed in a wide circle around the fortress. Roakore climbed to the top of the pile of headless draggard bodies and raised his great axe. "I be reclaimin' this here tradin' post for the Mountains Ro'Sar!"

The dwarves all cheered and chanted, "Ro'Sar!"

CHAPTER ELEVEN

Frostmore

The night ended in a morning shower. Dirk paid it no mind, his dragon-scale cloak easily protecting him from the elements. He toyed with the timber-wolf figurine as he rested from his trek. He had been traveling west toward the mountains all night, and now he had happened upon a town.

Had days been different, he could have walked into the bustling village virtually unnoticed and stolen a horse with ease, but these were dangerous times. War was upon the land, and the village was protected like a fortress. The forest had been cleared for nearly a mile to the north, and the lumber had been used to erect a high wall around the perimeter. Outside of the wall there were spikes jutting out in all directions. Watchtowers housing archers went around the wall, each a stone's throw from the other.

Dirk surveyed the village from on high and laughed to himself. *It would take but one dragon to turn your wooden town into a blazing inferno of death, idiots,* he thought.

He determined that the town was already overpopulated with refugees from the surrounding land. It would be beyond capacity with injured and sick, not to mention orphans and widows. Food would be scarce, and with winter closing in the stores would be tightly rationed, but no doubt the rich would continue to eat well. Horses would be highly valued; since the draggard found them particularly delectable, their numbers in Agora had plummeted.

The draggard were not the wild, frothing creatures that many believed. True, they were hideous in battle, but when not engaged in murder and carnage they were eerily civil. Dirk had watched them from afar on many occasions, trying to find something about them that he might use to his advantage. What he saw was a hive-like group of fairly intelligent animals. When he had asked Krentz about them, she had told him that every draggard was controlled by its queen mother or a dark elf handler. They gave orders, and they were carried out. The queen mothers shared a telepathic link with their offspring, and they could control their offspring from great distances.

Dirk considered how difficult it would be to steal a horse from the village, and weighed it against the likelihood of finding one elsewhere. He had no coin on him, and though some of his rings and earrings would have brought a pretty price, he could not sell them. They were enchanted and thus priceless.

Dirk was a master thief, burglar, assassin, and sneak, but taking a horse from this village was not something that could be done by stealth. It would take cunning. He studied the wolf figurine and thought of all he knew of such trinkets, which was little. He had heard of certain magic, considered a dark craft by most, that of capturing spirits and commanding them. He guessed that the wolf was a spirit that could shift in and out of the physical world with ease, as he had seen it do against his attacks. He also trusted that whoever controlled the figurine controlled the spirit.

He made up his mind and moved from the edge of the woods, away from the village. Under the boughs of a cedar tree, amid the autumn foliage and fire-colored leaves, he extended his hand and summoned the timber-wolf spirit.

"Come, Chief!"

The wind stirred the leaves in a small cyclone around him, and from the figurine came the faintest of light. The light speck traveled away from Dirk, and just before hitting the ground it exploded into the form of the brown wolf. Dirk had killed its master, and now he wagered everything that it could not kill him. The wolf growled at him and snarled, its haunches bristling and teeth bare.

Dirk held the trinket up and pointed at the wolf. "You are the spirit wolf Chief. I am Dirk. I have killed your master, and I now possess the figurine and therefore you. But I would not have you as a slave, but rather a companion. There is no reason that we should not both benefit from our situation."

The wolf only stared, growling.

"You are the spirit of a hunter, as am I. And I promise good hunting and great adventure. What say you, Chief?"

Chief stared for a time; he then became preoccupied with an itch on his rump. He gnawed for a moment, scratched his ear with a hind leg, then stood and shook vigorously. He then walked lazily to Dirk's side, stopped at his heel, and looked forward. Dirk let his hand rest gently upon the timber wolf's thick fur. Chief came up to his hip, and when in physical form, he projected a weight thrice that of a man. The wolf did not react to the touch and Dirk marveled at how real the spirit's projected body felt.

Dirk walked back toward the town and called to his newest weapon. "C'mon, Chief, we have ourselves a horse to steal."

Ten minutes later the town guard came alive and the warning horns blew as Dirk ran screaming from the tree line like he was on fire.

"Open the gates! Open the gates!" he bellowed.

Guards came to the wall and dozens of arrows were trained on him. He ran for his life and screamed again.

"Open the gate! Open the gate!"

Suddenly the three-hundred-pound timber wolf erupted from the brush at the tree line. Chief stopped and let out a howl that would consume nightmares for years. He then sprinted after Dirk, snapping his frothing jaws as he gained on him.

"Open the bloody gates! Shoot it! Shoot it!" Dirk screamed.

Guards scrambled and the gates opened, but not wide. The bowmen shot, but none hit the wolf, which was yet many hundred yards off. Dirk intentionally stumbled and the growing crowd at the wall cringed and gasped. They began rooting him on, and he smiled to himself.

He got to his feet and acted shocked that the wolf had gained so much. Bows rang out again and this time arrows rained down on the wolf. The arrows passed through Chief as he shifted quickly. Any who noticed it did not share it with others.

Dirk was thirty feet from the gate and the guards cheered him on with every step. He had begun to limp after he fell, adding to the drama and the entertainment and favor of the crowds. Ten feet away, cheers rang out and bows sang. He dove through the threshold and the gate slammed behind him. The men cheered as Chief, on cue, turned and ran back toward the woods, arrows following. The townspeople rushed to Dirk's side. He took his time getting up with help, and he held his bleeding arm, which he had cut.

"From where do you hail, good sir? You bring death at your heels," said a guard.

Another pushed through the crowd, a burly, red-mustached man. "Where in the hells ye get a timber wolf on your trail? They ain't of these parts, far from it!"

"Can't you see the man's hurt?" yelled a woman and offered to mend his wounds.

Outside the wall Chief howled eerily. Everyone froze and quieted instantly as the baying of the wolf lifted to the heavens and chilled bone. By then a crowd of hundreds had gathered, and whispers were spreading fast of the dark stranger and the wolf.

Dirk panted hard as if spent. He began to speak but faltered. Everyone hushed to hear him.

"Who I am and from where I hail is talk more suited to a good meal and wine. I have not the time for such pleasantries as of yet. Behold the wolf upon heels."

Just then Chief called to the night with his eerie cry and a snarl that echoed from all directions. To the chorus of the timber wolf's cry, Dirk spun a tale for the enthralled villagers.

"'Twas but the night last that we were attacked by this demon wolf. I know not from whence it came, for it fell upon my company like a ghost from a dream. Blood and cries of anguish were left in its murderous wake, and I, tasked as was my group to guard the gold of Lord Whittnar, was the only survivor. I ran west to this village, which I knew of from past travels, and lo, the wolf dined on my fellows while I have made it here alive."

Chief howled again and must have come closer to the village, as the sound of arrows could be heard at the wall. The crowd looked on, enthralled. Even the guards who had seemed suspicious were now convinced, it seemed.

"I mean to kill the wolf and have revenge in the name of my lord," Dirk said. "I will have vengeance. I will rid your village of this threat that I have brought on my heels. A share of my dead lord's gold to the man who lends me his best horse, so that I might vanquish this foe from on high!"

The crowd stirred and looked around for any who would offer up his steed. Many men volunteered, and soon the crowd was in an uproar of men wanting a piece of the prize.

Dirk raised his hands for the crowd to quiet. "No simple steed will face this wolf without faltering. This steed must be strong and brave; it must have known battle and be fast as the wind."

"Surely you speak of Frostmore!" a man's voice called out, and the crowd parted until Dirk saw the speaker and the horse he spoke of. The man walked to him and presented the tall, strong horse.

"Frostmore will see you swiftly to glory, but can you kill such a beast as this wolf? I would not see my best horse fall along with you."

Dirk spread his fingers in front of him and his many rings glimmered in the nearby light. "If we fall to the beast, all that I carry is yours—surely generous payment for such a steed."

The man nodded. "It is a deal; go with the grace of the gods, warrior."

Dirk nodded his thanks and shook the man's hand. He then mounted Frostmore and was led to the gates. He unsheathed his sword and raised it to the sky as the clouds parted to reveal the moon, and a howl rose up yet again.

"The wolf waits for you, stranger!" yelled a guard from the wall.

"Don't do it, brave sir!" shrieked a maiden.

"I must!" Dirk declared.

As the gates opened someone yelled from the crowd, "What is the name of such a fearless warrior?"

Dirk turned from the gate and eyed the crowd. "I am…" He smirked to himself. "I am Whill of Agora!"

The crowd gasped and Dirk charged out toward the wolf. The gates closed and men and women alike crowded to the top of the wall to see the battle. Dirk urged the horse into a fast charge, and Chief charged likewise. The villagers held their breath as three hundred yards away Dirk and the wolf continued their collision course. A woman fainted and men cheered as tension over the inevitable violence mounted.

Chief leapt high into the air with a snarl and Dirk struck with his blade. The sword sailed through Chief's form as the spirit wolf became translucent. The crowd cheered and Dirk sped on away from the wolf and the town. Chief landed and spun around to chase Dirk into the woods and beyond. The villagers looked after them for a long time, but the two were never seen again.

Shortly thereafter, but far away, Dirk laughed to himself and dismissed Chief to the spirit world, then pocketed the trinket once more. He spurred his new mount on westward toward the Ky'Dren Pass.

CHAPTER TWELVE
The Test of the Masters

Whill was surprised to find it afternoon when he left the Watcher's house of dreams. There Avriel was sitting in the sun waiting for him. She sat on all fours with her head to the sky, sunning herself in the bright rays that shone down from a cloudless sky. For fall it was very warm, like a northern summer it still seemed here in the elven lands. Avriel turned to Whill and smiled as he walked to her. He laid a hand upon the shimmering white scales of her shoulder.

"I am sorry that I ignored your call earlier, I needed to be alone."

It is of no concern; we all need time now and again. You have enough beings demanding of you, I do not wish to be another. I wish only to be at your side.

"You are a good friend, Avriel," Whill said and hugged the base of her neck. "Thank you."

Together they flew to Zerafin's quarters within one of the outer pyramids that made up the city's constellation. Located opposite the Thousand Falls, the pyramid lay near the edge of a jungle. One of the three sides of the pyramid was covered entirely with vine, all the way up to its crystal dome. High above the tangled trees grew their leaves wide and thick, their trunks green and slick. The canopy above left the jungle dark, but Whill could sense the many creatures within.

Before Whill reached the door of leaf, it parted and Zerafin strode out. He was in good form, his skin having fully recovered from the puss-filled rot that had infected him of late. He was as broad of shoulder as ever, and looked no worse for wear.

The elf king wore only a loose-fitting kind of robe the elves called a lokata. A sash tied at the waist kept its long sides from unfolding, and a high drooping collar arched from his neck to shoulder. The sleeves were short but deep and hung long at his sides as he approached Whill and Avriel with outstretched arms.

"My friend, it is good to see you well," said Whill as they shared a brotherly hug.

"And you, Whill." Zerafin turned from Whill, and as Avriel bent her large head to him, Zerafin stroked her snout and head. "Sister," he said, and a moment passed as they shared a private moment of thought speech. Then Zerafin looked at the two with a wide triumphant smile. "Well, then, here we all are in one piece. The quest was a successful one, though I deeply regret hearing of the loss of Abram and Rhunis. I wish I could have been there within the arena. I am sorry, Whill."

"It is no fault of yours, Zerafin…or should I call you king now?"

"No, no." Zerafin laughed. "I do not officially receive the crown until tonight at dusk. Even then you shall still know me as Zerafin Eldenfen."

"You are accepting the crown, brother; does it mean that you have…"

Zerafin looked at his sister stoically. "I have accepted that our people need a king, and Agora needs an elven king, for if we fail, I shall be the last. But by the gods I will be the first of many."

Whill was filled with admiration for Zerafin's bravery, for voluntarily taking up a mantle which Whill himself dreaded. Zerafin was a born leader, and had gained loyalty not due to his lineage or through intimidation, but through bravery and deed. Whill was glad to have Zerafin on his side. Soon he would be joined also by Roakore, and if Zerafin's proclamations reflected his intent, they would soon march to war.

There would be little time for training, Whill realized; it seemed he might have to accept the elves' selfless offer of knowledge in the arts. If he was to be of any help in the coming battle, much less the savior, he needed any help he could get.

We are being summoned, said Avriel to their minds. *We must return once more to the Summer Star.*

"What is it about?" Whill asked.

"It is my doing," said Zerafin. "Many of the masters have been gathered. They wish to know the extent of your abilities thus far. It is quite a mystery as to how you have done the things you have without a minute spent training."

"It is a mystery to me as well," Whill admitted.

"Then let us find out," said Zerafin.

Avriel carried Whill and her brother easily upon her back, and together they flew to the pyramid. Inside waited seven elves, each a master of the arts and the head of their school of knowledge. The queen was there as well, and, to Whill's surprise, the Watcher.

The inside of the pyramid was open space with a floor of sand. Directly across from the leafed curtains the masters sat upon the only seats within the open room, behind a long table set atop a landing. There were many items at the center of the room upon the sand, including a large bowl of water, a fire burning high from a large lamp, and a boulder half Whill's size.

Whill eyed the items curiously as he made his way with Zerafin to stand before the seated elves. Zerafin then took a seat at the long table with the others. The queen offered Whill a smile and began.

"Thank you for joining us, Whill. We have asked you here today to determine your abilities. As you know, elves train for decades, centuries even, to master the ways of Orna Catorna. For reasons unknown, you are able to do things that only students of the craft can do, though you yourself have not studied it. Would you object to a series of tests, much like those taken by initiates?"

"No, I do not mind, but I believe I may have figured out part of the mystery," said Whill. "I have found that in times of need, I can perform spells that have been used against me."

The elves traded looks but none spoke to this.

"We shall delve into those implications later," the queen said. "For now, let us begin. Behind you there is a large stone. Can you try to lift it for us?"

Whill looked at the stone, and with a lazy raising of his hand, he caused the stone to rise from the floor slowly. He let it float there and turned toward the elves. A few scribbled upon leaf parchment with feathered quill. Others nodded, and still a few remained motion-less.

"You may lower it now," said a tall elf with short, spiky black hair and a robe similar to Zerafin's. His dark skin told Whill that the elf spent most of his days in the sun, but then Whill remembered that many elves could change their appearance with but a thought. With elves, appearance meant far less than it might for dwarves or humans.

"I am called Arngil Enlar. I am a master in the art of Krundar."

"Greetings, Arngil," said Whill politely.

"Greetings. I am interested to see the extent of your abilities in my school of knowledge. Can you cause the flame to touch the stone?"

Whill looked at the fire. He remembered that he had sent it back at Eadon once before learning of Avriel's fate. He lifted a hand to the flame, and as his hand moved in the direction of the stone, so too did the flame until it engulfed the boulder.

"And the water, can you cause it to extinguish the fire?"

Before the elf had finished speaking Whill had turned and caused the water to rise up like a serpent and engulf the lantern, putting out the fire.

"And wind, I assume that you can control that as well?" asked Arngil.

Whill thought for a moment, unsure. "I do not know; I have never tried."

"Please do," said the elf.

Whill turned to the leafed curtains at the entrance of the pyramid. He extended his consciousness outward and beyond. Concentrating upon the unseen currents of air outside, he summoned them to him. Nothing happened at first, but then slowly a breeze entered the room. The curtains wavered gently as Whill's hold on the air currents became stronger. Suddenly they blew inward and a gale gusted through the room, scattering papers and sending Whill's hair dancing.

"Thank you, that will be enough!" said Arngil over the torrent.

Whill released the wind and faced the counsel of masters once again. Arngil said no more and took his seat. Whill could not tell from his face whether the elf was pleased or not.

Another elf stood. She was scantily clad in leaves much like Azzeal wore, and her green hair seemed to be intermingled with red and yellow moss. Whill assumed she was a Ralliad, or druid, like his friend.

"Greetings, Whill, it is a pleasure and indeed an honor to meet you. I am called Flouren En Fen, and I am Ralliad."

"Greetings, Flouren En Fen."

"Are you able to change form, be it animal or plant?"

"No," Whill admitted. "I have no skills in the school of Ralliad."

"Hmm." She hummed to herself. "Would you mind trying here for us today?"

"I will try," said Whill, unsure of what it was he should try, or even how to begin.

"We will start simply, then, with a test used for initiates." She pointed at a small pot that was set apart from the other items. Within the pot Whill could see a small seedling that had recently sprouted from the earth around it.

"Try to make the plant grow," she said with all seri-ousness.

Whill made his way to the pot slowly and squatted next to it. He put his hand over it but then self-consciously withdrew it. "I don't even know where to begin."

"That is understandable, as you have not studied the science needed to understand the process," said Flouren.

"Should I just will it to grow?" he asked.

"If you wish; this is not a lesson but a test," Flouren replied.

With a sigh Whill slowly extended his hand over the pot and closed his eyes. With his mind-sight he looked at the seedling and its small roots within the dirt. He wondered how he could possibly make it grow; plants needed water and light, after all. *Without sun and water it is impossible. But aren't those things just forms of energy? If I can give the seedling the energy it needs to grow in a form that it can use, perhaps it will work.*

Abandoning mind-sight he looked up to see every-one patiently watching and waiting. How long he had been studying the plant he did not know.

"Take your time," said Flouren patiently.

Whill nodded a thankful affirmation and resumed his pondering. With mind-sight once again he looked deeper into the small sprout. He saw the bright life force surrounding it, and the minute webbed tendrils of dancing light that swirled throughout. The seedling was tiny, but the closer Whill looked, the more intricate it became; it seemed there was no end to how far he could see into it. He quickly realized that this task was well beyond him. If he had time to learn its systems he would be able to do it, he was sure. But that was not the point of the tests, he remembered; he was being tested on raw ability.

Accepting that he could not figure out how it worked in such a short time, he stood from the pot and sighed. "This task is beyond my current knowledge," he told the group.

Flouren smiled at his words. "If I am not mistaken, you have not begun to try, you have only examined it. Did you know how to move stone from study? Or fire, for that matter?"

"No," Whill answered truthfully.

"Then please try to make the plant grow. Your abilities seem to be hampered not by lack of knowledge."

Whill wondered if he had just been insulted, however politely. He redoubled his focus and stared intently at the sprout. He willed the thing to grow, pictured the result he intended, and called upon Adromida. His palm face down, he directed his energy and will into the soil and sprout.

The dirt began to vibrate and shudder upon the floor. To Whill's amazement, the seedling grew. The growth was slow and stopped for a moment when he lost focus from his surprise, but it grew all the same.

He cleared his mind of expectation and emotion and willed the plant to grow once again. The pot shuddered and the dirt danced as water might on a hot skillet. The plant doubled and then tripled its size. A leaf and then two and three grew out from the main stem and Whill poured more energy into it. With his left hand he reached in the direction of the water he had used before, and from the bowl came a sphere of floating water the size of an apple. He directed the water to the plant, and when it hit the vibrating soil the plant shot up rapidly as if from a jester's sleeve. Up it grew until it was two feet tall and covered in orange leaves and flowers. Whill stopped, his work done.

He marveled at his creation with a delighted smile. He then understood how easy it would be to get caught up in the thrill of creation, and forget the morals of natural boundaries as Eadon had. He also understood that he should not have such powers, for he had not learned the ways; somehow he simply did it. He knew that many of the elves must be jealous of him, as many of the dark elves had been.

Abram's words came back to him then: "Power without wisdom is as a child with fire." Whill realized then that he was like a child playing with fire. He backed away from the flower he had created as if it had spoken to him.

"Well done," said Flouren, and many of the masters agreed. But the note of her voice had a begrudging quality, be it a faint one.

Whill looked from the flower to the seated masters, Zerafin and the queen. "I should not be able to do this," he said quietly, as if to himself. Louder still he repeated, "I should not be able to do this. I have not studied the art; I do not even know how I did it."

"We know, Whill," said the queen. "This is the very thing we are attempting to understand. Please, there will be time for reflection later. For now the tests must continue."

Whill nodded reluctant acceptance and closed his eyes to focus the mind. Another elf stood from his seat and with raised voice called out to someone unseen, "Bring in the volunteers!"

Through the entrance to the pyramid came a group of four elves. They each wore a lokata identical to the standing elf's, but where his was a dark blue, theirs were a much lighter shade. These too had swirling, darker blue tendrils embroidered along the sleeves and across the back. They were all women, and each looked at Whill as one would a worshipped relic of untold value. They smiled at him with a sincerity and joy usually only seen in children. They came to stand at his right and turned to face him.

"I am called Libratus," said the elf standing at the table. "I am master of the school of Arnarro."

"Greetings," said Whill with slight trepidation. He could see where this test was going and he didn't like it.

"Are you ready to begin?" asked Libratus.

"I do not want these women to be pained for my sake. I can show you that I can heal on myself."

"Please," said Libratus. "This is the will of the masters. These women have volunteered on their own accord; it is an honor to them. Precautions have been taken, no pain will be felt."

"You want to do this?" Whill asked the female elves.

"Yes!" said one.

"It is an honor, Whill...Whill of Agora," said another.

The rest nodded in eager agreement. Whill sighed with resignation. "Very well."

"Let us begin, then. Minrell, please step forward," said Libratus.

The elf to the left of the group stepped forward. A dagger appeared from under her sleeve, and with it she cut a long line along the palm of her other hand. She did not flinch as the blood began to spill; she only looked at Whill happily.

Whill quickly stretched out his right hand, and from it, writhing blue tendrils of healing energy snaked the short distance through the air and surrounded her injured palm. The elf shuddered slightly in apparent ecstasy of the contact with one so clearly revered. He ended the healing and looked as they all did at the elf's uninjured palm.

"Very good. And now, Drellen, if you would," said Libratus.

A red-haired elf with bright green eyes stepped forward and without warning plunged her own dagger into her exposed thigh and yanked it upward, splitting it from above the knee to hip and exposing white bone.

"In the name of the gods!" Whill swore and watched horrified as blood spurted from an artery. He quickly extended a hand, and the healing tendrils surrounded and penetrated her gaping wound. After a time the gash was healed, and though the elf swooned from loss of blood, she was all right.

"That is enough of this test! Do you understand? I will not abide more of this lunacy," Whill threatened.

Libratus bowed slightly, concern shadowing his brow. "We do not mean to offend. We only wish to know the extent of your abilities."

"Then I shall set fire to myself and be made anew. I will not see more blood spilled."

Libratus looked around as if estimating the other masters' consensus. "Very well. We have seen enough for now." He returned to his seat and the four female elves left the way they had come in. Whill saw disappointment in the eyes of those who had not gotten a turn, and he hid a small shudder at their fanatical mindset.

Next a gray-haired elf, ancient but strong-looking, stood. His lokata bore black and gray swirling patterns, and it hurt Whill's eyes to stare at them too long. The elf had silver-and-black-streaked hair to match, sticking straight up from his head in long pointed spikes. A ring adorned each finger and he wore many bracelets on each wrist. From his lone silver necklace a large oval onyx pendant hung heavily, and within the stone fiery tones danced wildly.

"I am called Ornarell, master of the school of Zionar," the elf said as he took long deliberate steps to the small stair and onto the sand. His eyes were almost unbearable to look at for too long, liquid smoke that seemed to churn the longer Whill stared, with a sudden piercing pinpoint of light that bore through Whill's very being.

Ornarell's eyes locked on his and Whill could not look away. He felt time slow and then detected a presence at the corners of his mind. Ornarell's eyes flashed and settled in a scowl, his pointed silver eyebrows arching like rooftops.

Suddenly Whill was not in the pyramid. There were no elves and no sand nor light. Whill was nowhere. A light pierced the darkness and stung Whill's senses— the light from Ornarell's swirling eyes, now alive with white inner fire.

"I have brought you here so that you might understand the power to be gained down the path of the Zionar," said the elf in a deep voice.

"Attempting to take over or delve into another's mind is a crime among your people. Do you mean me harm? If so, let's have at it. I have been a prisoner of the dark elves two seasons; you will not find my mind an easy fortress to conquer."

"If I wanted to conquer your mind, you would now be my puppet. That is not my goal. I have brought you here to help you understand what others of less… restraint might attempt." The elf's voice hummed and he seemed to glide closer, the smoky storm of his eyes flashing with silver lightning.

"Where is here?" Whill demanded. "If it is not my mind, then whose?"

"I have not invaded your mind; no crime has been committed here" came Ornarell's retort. He glided around Whill's corporeal form, his gaze never leaving Whill's as they turned in the darkness. "We are within the dream world. It can be made to be as elaborate as our own, but for these purposes, this will do."

Stubbornly Whill followed the elf's gaze, though the swirling silver fog made him disoriented and dizzy. He fought the sensation. He had not determined whether or not Ornarell had ill intent; he had not attacked, and Whill felt that he spoke the truth of the dream world—he had been here before many times, and had mistaken the familiar sensation for home, his own mind.

"And what is my test?" Whill asked. "To break free?"

"No, you could not break free if you tried," said Ornarell matter-of-factly.

"Then I am a prisoner here in this dream world of yours?" Whill asked, slight anger creeping into his words.

"Would you like to leave?" asked the elf, still moving around Whill with storm-torn eyes.

"Do I need your permission?" Whill retorted, pressing the issue.

"Of course not. Simply wake up," offered Ornarell.

Whill let his own stare bore into Ornarell's. "My will is that of the world, my thoughts become reality. Or have you not seen the previous tests? What then do you think I could do here in the dream world?"

"What can you do? That remains to be seen," said Ornarell coolly.

Whill closed his eyes and focused his will. He thought of the sun, and reached out to the ancient blade he knew still hung from his physical body. A rumbling arose in the eternal darkness of the conjured dream world, and with a deafening report, a sun was born far away. Giant waves spilled from the darkness and a mountain shimmered into existence. Next land and trees appeared and a blue sky above. Ornarell's eyes no longer dominated the reality of the dream world. The two stood upon a cliff at the edge of the land. To Whill's right the ocean crashed violently into the cliff, sending spray shooting high above their heads and turning to a drizzle that bathed them in seawater. Off in the distance but moving fast came a thunderhead. Thunder rolled across the land and the wind doubled as lightning battled within the rolling storm. Whill looked at Ornarell with a smirk. "Best take care. A storm is coming."

The elf smiled and then burst out laughing; his sudden hysterics were slightly unsettling, as were his maniacal eyes and lightning-charged hair. "The youngest of babes can conjure within a dream! But all too often their conjured worlds turn on them," he bellowed against the approaching storm. With his final word the monolithic thunderhead shimmered and changed into thousands of screeching dragons. They shifted from the storm's previous heading and bore down upon Whill. Ornarell was somehow now far away, observing from a distant cliff as the dragons dove to devour Whill. Finding his blade at his side, Whill unsheathed it and drove it into the ground. The earth heaved and rumbled and from the ocean came a serpent of such magnitude that it blocked out the sun and turned day into night. The shimmering green serpent opened its colossal mouth and devoured the dragons. It reared back and sunlight spilled onto the world for just a moment before it struck down from the clouds to devour Ornarell. The elf raised a hand as if to alter once again the corporeal form of the thunderhead-turned-serpent, and strike back at Whill.

Whill channeled massive amounts of energy and focused his entire being upon the diving green serpent. He could feel Ornarell's attempt to alter the dream creature, but Whill would not allow it. Soon Ornarell had frantically spent his conjured power and his will faltered. The snake crashed into the cliff and the world shuddered.

Whill opened his eyes and watched as a screaming Ornarell fell backward into the bench of the masters. He realized that virtually no time had passed here within the pyramid; they had been within the dream world, and there time had no hold, reason no bearing. Many jumped as the Zionar master slammed into the bench with a cry. Libratus moved to help the other master up, but his hand was shoved away. Ornarell got to his feet and took three quick strides to stand before Whill. So close did he come that their noses nearly touched. The Zionar master scowled his pointed-eyebrow scowl.

"I have seen enough. He has convinced me of his prowess in the art." Ornarell looked Whill over from head to toe. "Though I did not go very hard on him, he has passed my test...for now."

Strangely, Whill decided that he liked the mysterious if slightly dark Zionar master. He had learned from Avriel during one of their frequent, hour-long talks that Zionars mainly used their powers of the mind on animals, and aside from druids, they were the best animal trainers in existence. They could control entire herds of cattle or packs of wolves, even insects. Anything with a brain was fair game for Zionars, with the exception of the sentient races.

Zerafin gave Whill a questioning look, but Whill only shrugged as Ornarell returned to his place among the masters.

Next a young elf, bright-eyed and quick to smile, stood from the group. With her hands together under her long lokata, she bowed slightly to Whill, who responded likewise.

"I am Avolarra En' Kayen, master of Aklenar."

"Greetings, Master En' Kayen," said Whill and bowed once again.

"Greetings, Whill." She smiled. "Have you ever had dreams that came true?"

"Just the once, I think," Whill answered, trying to think. "It was during the spring, before...I dreamt of flying high over a battlefield atop a dragon. I saw the battles for Isladon and Ro'Sar before they happened. In the dream I watched the draggard hordes pour forth from the mountain, and in reality it came to pass."

"That is the only dream that has come to pass?" Avolarra asked.

"It is all I can recall."

She nodded as if to herself. "Do you ever know things are going to happen before they happen?"

"No...well, I don't know. Sometimes in battle, I can sense what my opponent is going to do."

"Interesting, do you ever have visions? Or hear voices?"

"No," said Whill, trying not to think about the Other.

"One last question for you, Whill. What will be my next question?" she asked.

Whill frowned. How could he know? Was he supposed to guess, or was he supposed to know? He tried to remember the feeling of the dream that had come true. He listened, seeing if the words from the future could be heard. He heard only his own busy mind.

"Nothing. You do not intend to ask another question."

Avolarra stared at Whill for a time and smiled. "That will be all."

Whill wondered if he had passed. What did his correct answer prove, anyway? Only Avolarra knew if she had intended another question.

Whill sighed deeply, ready to be done with these trials. He knew that the only schools left were those of the Morenka and Gnenja. He thought he had a good idea of what the warrior test might consist of, but what would a monk, or Morenka, want to know?

The Watcher stood and addressed Whill. "Greetings, Whill. You are familiar with my name as I am with yours. I have but one question for your consideration here today. If peace can be gotten through war, can war also be gotten through peace?"

Whill looked from the Watcher to the other elves in turn. He sensed a tension grow inside the room. He knew that this had been debated and preached by the Morenka for millennia. Zerafin himself had alluded to it once. The monk class chose a life of nonconflict while the others fought their eternal wars. Whill did not know what the Watcher wanted to hear, and he didn't know if there was a right answer. But he knew that his answer would lean toward one side or the other.

"No, war cannot be got through peace, but neither can peace be got through war," he answered. The Watcher smiled slightly. "War is born of conflict; it is the opposite of peace. Peace is born of harmony."

"Therefore," the Watcher said with a grin at his fellow masters, "peace can only be attained through the practice of peace, through harmony. Do you agree, King Whill of Uthen-Arden?"

"It isn't that simple," answered Whill.

A brief shadow of disappointment crossed the Watcher's old face but was replaced quickly by a smile. "Of course not," he said.

"If someone is trying to kill you, you kill them. That is the way of the world. You fight or you die," Whill argued.

"Thank you," said the Watcher. "This is all."

He turned to take his seat but Whill shouted, "Shall I just lay down the blade at Eadon's feet? Shall I live my life in laughter until Eadon and his minions turn Agora into the plagued death that has become Drindellia? You would advise that peace in this matter is the way to peace? We shall all be murdered whilst we meditate!"

The Watcher smiled sympathetically. "I would see this world and all in it healed. When all embrace peace, all shall know it. In error, those who want peace think they must fight for it, when in truth they must simply practice it. Until we learn the difference, we shall not know peace."

The Watcher returned to his seat and silence followed him. Whill heard the ring of truth in the Watcher's words; he felt it in his heart. He was saddened to think that he was simply feeding the fires of war, when there existed another possible path; he also regretted not being able to see that path.

An elf stood and threw back his cloak. Beneath it he wore leather armor interwoven with golden mail, and at his hip hung a sword much like Whill's. The elf looked to be in his twenties, but Whill knew better than to trust appearances. The elf had no hair to cover his pointed ears. His eyes were ice-blue orbs of focus. They bored into Whill as if his every flaw was on display.

"I am called Thryn 'De Bregeth. I am master of the warrior class."

"Greetings," said Whill.

Thryn nodded. "Are you prepared for your test in the art of the Gnenja?"

"I am."

"We would ask that you not wield the ancient blade. Nor any at all," said Thryn, regarding Whill with a steely demeanor.

"I will not wield it, but neither shall I be without it," Whill replied.

"Very well then," said Thryn. "Let the test begin!"

From the entrance came a dozen elves. They split and made a ring around Whill. To his dismay he saw that they were all armed. They wore armor similar to Thryn's, except that these warriors had black masks over their heads. So covered with the tight mail and leather armor were they that only their eyes could be seen. They faced Whill and withdrew their curved elven blades in unison.

One of the fighters surged forward, sword drawn back as if to strike. Quickly Whill moved as to unsheathe Adromida, causing the warrior to take pause. Whill took advantage of the hesitation and kicked sand in the warrior's face. Another fighter came at him from behind, his sword leading the charge. Whill kicked the sword out wide as the elf closed in. He got inside the elf's guard and landed a fist to the gut while simultaneously locking the elf in a standing arm-bar that left his sword arm turned up at the elbow. Whill landed a punch to the elf's face and received one himself. He spun the elf and himself around to face another attacker. Whill used the elf as a shield, keeping the others at bay while the elf struggled to break Whill's hold. With a snap Whill broke the elf's sword arm at the elbow and with a flat hand to the nose he sent him flying. The elf's sword dropped to the sand as two more warriors charged. Whill scooped up the blade with a kick of his foot and leapt over an attacking sword. He caught the blade and blocked a sword meant for his head. Steel sang on steel as the weapons moved in a blur. Whill parried every blow meant for him, first fighting two, then three elves at once. They came on hard and a fourth attacked his blind side, leaving Whill with nowhere to run. He leapt high and twisted as he came down to land upon the masters' table. He was forced to hop from the slashes at his feet and came down on one of the blades, pinning it. A kick to the face sent the elf reeling. Whill blocked and parried from on high, even scoring a grazing blow that left one of the warrior's shoulders bloody.

Whill leapt from the table, over an elf, and met the warriors head on. Deep within him something shifted. He felt the difference in him as the Other was awakened by the conflict. His senses became sharper, his reflexes faster, and he tore into the elven ranks with reckless abandon. Blades clanged in a chorus of speeding metal as Whill parried the attacks and kept the elves at bay. He received a hit to the leg that left a deep gash bleeding freely. His scream of rage echoed throughout the room, a scream Whill did not recognize as his own. He parried a blow so hard that the sword flew from the hands of its wielder. A kick to the knee bent the elf's leg back unnaturally and he hit the floor in agony. Another got too close and paid dearly as his sword was sent wide and high by Whill's parry. Whill slashed the elf's exposed armpit, leaving the warrior's arm dangling uselessly. Again an attacker came from behind, and Whill simultaneously blocked a blow at his back and retrieved yet another fallen blade. Whill took up the dual blades and sent them spinning in a blur of motion that sent the warriors back.

Time seemed to slow for him as his attackers rallied and came on again as one. Whill slashed wrists and hamstrings, laying low any fighter who got too close. Blades came at him from all angles, but Whill was always a step ahead. Every parry flowed into the next as Whill began to feel the elves' next move. A warrior came in hard from Whill's left, forcing him to block as another struck also from behind, forcing him to block again. A third stabbed forward, and without a free sword Whill was forced to kick the blade high and to the side. Whill twirled out of the trap and ran to the entrance of the pyramid. There he turned and engaged his closest pursuer. They exchanged three blows before Whill cut his hand clean off. Whill left the elf to his pain and came on hard, screaming all the while. His barrage sent the remaining elves backpedaling as their swords became twisted with Whill's parries.

"That will be all," said Thryn. But Whill paid him no mind. He heard only the movement of his opponents, the subtle change of their sword grip, the way their breath alerted him to a coming strike. He read their eyes perfectly and knew their minds before the strikes came. A boot to the chest sent another flying, and a twirling parry sent another blade through the air.

"Enough!" screamed Thryn so unnaturally loudly that the words shook Whill from his fighting trance.

Panting, he lowered his blades, as did the few standing elves. He looked around as if seeing the injured for the first time. Eyeing the two blades in his hands with a scowl, he dropped them to the sand and returned to face the masters.

"Those of you with injuries see yourselves and your brothers to the houses of healing," Thryn said. "You are dismissed." He nodded slightly at Whill. "That will be all. Thank you for the demonstration."

Zerafin stood. "The masters will take the time to reflect upon what they have witnessed here. Thank you, Whill. That will be all for today."

CHAPTER THIRTEEN
The Hunter and the Hunted

Aurora awoke to the soft song of lovebirds as they peered at her from the open window. Her sleep had been restless, haunted. In her dreams Whill's friend Abram, deformed and rotting from death, had croaked a cryptic song that played in her head still. She shook her head trying to clear it and forced herself to focus on something else, anything. But the song continued, steadily becoming louder. Even the birdsong somehow joined with it, then the faint breeze through the window. Aurora, barbarian of the frozen north, was chilled to the bone.

Always there is a coward at your back, coward at your back, coward!

"Stop it." Aurora pleaded as she began rocking herself.

Always there is a coward at your back, coward at your back, coward!

"Silence!" She yelled clamping her hands over her ears.

Coward at your back, coward at your back. The voice hissed inside her head.

"Stop."

But it would not stop. She saw not the room before her but only the vision within her mind. She closed her eyes only to see the face, his face, the one she had wronged so.

Coward.

She had betrayed Whill and befriended him. She had raised her hand against his dearest friend; she had tried to kill him.

Coward at your back.

"I had no choice!" She screamed. "It was for the good of my people."

Coward, coward, coward at your back...

"Stop!" Aurora bolted upright in bed, the lovebirds flew from the sill startled, but the voice had stopped. It had been a dream within a dream. Knees drawn to chin she held herself for a long time, and she cried. In her despair she called upon her goddess, she who sees all deeds and judges them not, she of cold and wind, ice and snow. To her goddess Skadia she prayed for strength, she of the harsh winter. Her mind settled, her emotions abated, and her thoughts became as placid as a frozen lake. Weakness, doubt, sorrow and despair, these were the ways of death. Only the strong survived the unforgiving motherland. In her long exile from Volnoss, she had softened in the warm sun, had forgotten what it meant to struggle against the unyielding tundra. She had grown weak.

The last few days in Cyrushia had been pleasant. She had allowed herself to indulge in the pleasantries of the flesh, pampered and catered to like a princess. But no more, she must realign herself with her mission, her destiny, her fate. She had left Volnoss in search of an answer, a way to secure her people's future in the changing landscape of the world. And she had found it. Eadon had promised her title and treasure, and more importantly the ancient Agoran homeland of her people. In return, she had given her fealty. Whill had promised her people freedom, and a place in the new Agora. She knew that Eadon's offer came with the shackles of slavery, but she had already spoken, and promises made to Eadon where written in blood.

She rose from her bed hungry from her slumber. The fruit and vegetables in abundance in her well stocked pantry would no longer do it. No matter how much of it she ate her hunger was never sated. *No,* she thought, *it is time I hunt.*

The idea of a fresh kill invigorated her and she was roused to her feet. The abandoned the elven light flowing gowns and dressed in her furs. She rummaged through her many gifts and came up with a suitable bow. The string drew back smoothly and a good tension was held by the smooth dark hardwood. It was a longbow, but it would suffice. Satisfied she took up her belt and sheathed her sword and made her way out into the city.

The day was mild and she wished it colder. She had never known a summer as hot as the season last. At first it had been pleasant, but soon the novelty of everwarmth wore off and she found herself longing to see her breath in the chill night.

Outside elves seemed to be everywhere. She looked around past the pyramids and crystal formations to the trees beyond. The vast shelf of cliffs that made up the Thousand Falls loomed to the east, and Aurora considered scaling it. She quickly changed her mind when she looked to the jungle to the west. The long hanging bows and thick canopy offered her foreign game, perhaps even danger. She walked towards the jungle politely nodding and smiling at the passing elves. She was very tired of feeling new. When she saw Kreshna she quickly ducked behind a fountain and took the closest bridge. Though the bridge took her in the wrong direction, it brought her away from the inquisitive elf. She was in no mood to talk right now; she was in the mood for meat.

Soon she was traveling swiftly down the vine walkways, some bringing her up and over the water, some down through moss lined tunnels. She came to the end of such a road and bounded into the jungle beyond. As soon as the thick foliage hid the city behind her she stopped and crouched low. She closed her eyes and breathed in her surroundings. Eyes open she took up the earth at her feet and smelled it. She sniffed the tree next to her, and the large red ferns that surrounded her. Her ears perked to the many sounds of the jungle. Random screeches and shrieks, singing birds and quick rustling of leaves played against a constant orchestra of whining heat bugs and a faint collective slither.

Aurora did not recognize the sounds of any of the animals, and she was elated by the challenge. She sprang to her feet and she ran. Hunger fueled her and the promise of the kill beckoned. Her muscular legs pumped harder and her feet were eager to comply. She sped through the jungle as though her barbaric frame weighed half its two hundred fifty stones. Over streams and under tangled vine she went, her senses tuned to every sensation, her body in harmony with the hunting grounds.

Soon she had found a game trail that began on the stony shores of a trickling creek. She sprinted down it deeper into the jungle. The tracks proved too small for her choice of game and she veered off the trail to run up the mossy bark of a fallen tree wide enough to allow two abreast. She charged up the log and where it had broken against another she leapt high into the air and with strong hands held fast a hanging vine. She fell for a few feet and was about to drop and roll when it caught. She kicked her legs and swung nearly to the ground and quickly up until she knew the vine was at its limit. Twenty feet up she released the vine to take another. She traveled this way until she found what she was looking for. She swung high and before her momentum turned at the top of the swing she grabbed hold of another vine and rode the two straight down to the jungle floor.

Aurora crouched and listened to the watering hole she had spotted. The soft trickle of the water emptying into a wide pond told her that it ran from the east, likely a branch of the waters that flowed over the Thousand Falls and into the ocean. Life teamed everywhere in the elven jungle. She had been bitten by a host of insects, none of which it seemed where poisonous. A snake which she thought must have been the king of his kind had almost been mistaken for a vine as she swung, but its fat middle had given it away. Likely the bulge had been its latest meal, and judging by its size it could have been a goat. Such a variety of birds there were that Aurora was overwhelmed by the beauty of their pluming headdresses and brilliant tails. Some had long curving beaks of yellow and purple, others were all black with strange shaped color patterns on their tail feathers only. These birds were nothing like the hawks and owls of Volnoss, whose color range consisted of black, brown and white. Given the world of snow and ice from whence she came, the elven jungle was a banquet of colors.

A variety of animal tracks both large and small dotted the muddy bank beyond the stones which mingled with the water. One in particular caught her eye, a split-hooved track that looked like that of a boar. She recognized also feline tracks nearly as large and knew that they belonged to an adult cat of some sort, perhaps a sabre. For the cat tracks to be dwarfed by that of the boar, it must have been large, and to survive as such a plump treat to the many predators of the jungle it had to be tough. Likely it had deadly tusks like curved blades with which it defended itself. She hoped to find out.

Aurora went to the water's edge downstream from the pond and found suitable soil to use, dark wet mud. She put down her bow and lathered black mud all over herself. She rolled in it until she was sure every inch of her body was covered. Taking up her bow once again she doubled back to the pond and found a suitable tree and climbed it until she found a good perch from which to watch.

She watched and she waited. The mud helped against the bugs. She became like the tree as she stood leaning amidst the thick drooping leaves and curtains of thin flowered vines which hung like tattered rags from the canopy above. The wind seemed never to find this deep haven, and her furs had become laden with her sweat.

The air had been chill in the city, but here it was nearly sweltering and thick with humidity. But the cool mud proved useful in this regard as well.

She waited high above the waters in anticipation of the coming prey. For a time incalculable due to the lack of sky she watched and waited and finally something approached. A rustling began behind her far below in the vegetation. Knowing that a chipmunk could sound like a wolf on the forest floor she could not tell its size. But when its feet fell upon solid earth she could guess at its length. She dared not move and scare it off, hoping that it was the giant bore. It continued on beneath her towards the water none the wiser and soon she could see it as it passed her tree.

Balancing upon two branches with only a shoulder to the tree to steady her she knocked an arrow slowly hoping that it did not creak. Her heart hammered in her chest as she beheld the beast below. It fearlessly moved to the water and drank noisily. It was indeed a boar and none like she had ever seen. She saw quickly how it could survive in such a place, its hide was covered in large plates of armor and tusks like daggers descended up its snout to its ears. Aurora pulled back her bow and let her breath out long and slow. She aimed for the crease in its plating behind the right shoulder and fired. The elven arrow flew true but deflected off of the plate armor with a twang. The horned hog didn't scatter; rather it turned with a snort and looked directly at Aurora with beady black eyes not befitting its horse sized head. It charged the tree she stood perched in and slammed into it with enough force to shake it. The horned hog reared and charged it again and again until Aurora found herself having to hang on. It backed up to the water's edge and snorted dripping snot from its large wet snout. It tore up big chunks of earth with its deadly tusks and sent it flying in all direction, clearly challenging Aurora. She stood tall upon the branches and answered the challenge with a war cry and leapt from the tree. As she fell she unsheathed her longsword and came down upon the hog with a powerful blow. But the horned hog proved surprisingly agile and darted toward the tree as if to charge it once again. Aurora landed and rolled once to absorb the impact and spun to her feet. The hog had already turned swiftly and was now charging her headlong, its tusks aiming to skewer her. She hacked at it as it charged past and landed a blow to the side of the head that left the hog stumbling in the underbrush. It reared on her violently and she came down once again with her heavy blade. She put all of her strength into the blow and this time broke two tusks and drew blood. Infuriated, the horned hog thrashed and tore at the earth. Aurora braced herself and the hog charged once again. It came straight at her, but she held her ground until it was almost upon her. As it barreled in Aurora spun out of the way and came around to plunge the blade between the thick plate armor near the hog's hindquarters. The blade sunk deep and Aurora held of tightly as the hog thrashed and bucked. Aurora pulled the blade free and the enraged boar turned on her with an open maw. She put all her might into a blow that broke teeth and cut through the beast's mouth splitting its head wide. The hog lurched and squealed but if came out only as wet gurgling. It fell to its side spent and Aurora was upon it in a flash. She positioned the blade between the armor plating of its shoulder and stabbed down and through the boar's heart. It tensed and died with a wheeze.

Aurora sat there panting electrified by the fight. Here stomach reminded her why she had ventured into the jungle and she went to work opening the breastplate. It was hard work but eventually she laid the chest of the boar open and cut out the large glistening heart. Aurora raised the heart to the heavens and said a prayer to her goddess and the animal's spirit. When she had finished she brought the heart to her lips and tore a chunk from it and ate. The heart of the horned boar was warm and melted in her mouth. She went into blood frenzy then, dancing and thrashing about. An energy that she had not known for a long time came rushing back to her, the strength of the beast.

Chanting her people's songs she set to work building a fire of deadwood. As the fire took on a life of its own she began gutting and quartering the boar. The guts she left for the scavengers, there would be no sign of the mess come morning. The plate armor took some time to remove from the hog's thick flesh; once it was stripped bare the job went quickly. With her heavy long-sword she chopped off the legs, rump included, and hung them to bleed from vines. She took off the head and hung it also, and cut the huge ribs from the spine. With her sword she chopped down small trees and made the frame of her smoking spit. It had to be wide and tall, and strong enough to hold the heavy slabs of meat; many strong hanging vines would help with that.

Once it was completed she carefully positioned the meat just over the raging fire. By now the wood that had been slow to catch was blazing, having had hours to grow. She knocked down the blazing logs and with her long poker spread the coals out evenly. The meat sizzled and the juices only added to the fire's fury. She let the meat char and set about gathering the large leaves nearby. When she added the leaves to the fire the smoke stopped altogether but then bellowed forth from beneath. The leaves were wet enough to last awhile, so Aurora set to making camp there a dozen paces from the watering hole.

With her sword she cleared a wide birth around her fire. An hour of cutting trees into spears left a barrage of pointed shafts jutting out in every direction. It was hard to tell where the sun was, but it was well past noon, she figured a few hours remained before sundown. If this jungle was anything like the dark forests of Volnoss,

Aurora knew that it would change into a different beast altogether. Creatures that now slumbered would surface to claim the night, and lesser creatures would cower in their dens. The smell of the smoking meat would bring them too, likely in legion. She had to show the predators of the night that she was not prey; tonight she was queen of this jungle.

She added a few more logs on the fire and a fresh topping of leaves and checked the nearest piece. It was coming along well, by morning it would be ready for transport. With the last remaining hours of light she set to work making a cone tent with trees and leaves. She set two more fires by carrying hot coals in a wide piece of bark to rest in the stacked wood. Soon her tent sat in the center of the three fires, within the ring of spear poles. There was little she could do about the network of vines and branches above her. If any predators dared drop down from up there she would have to deal with it with her blade. As a second thought she made twelve more spears and set them facing straight up throughout the camp. When the jungle began to noticeably darken, she was ready.

Aurora speared on of the front legs and laid it across the fire on her bracers. At the watering hole she filled her skin. With the coming of night came the feeling of a hundred eyes watching from the jungle beyond. The birds had stooped singing, and new and less beautiful calls filled the night. The jungle began to stir.

Aurora added more logs to the fire from the pile she had set near the tent; it was enough to keep the fires lit until morning. She thought of her homeland and her people, the Timber Wolf Tribe. For hundreds of years they had lived on Volnoss, exiled from the mainland after the Barbarian-Dwarf Wars. The barbarians had lived in Northern Eldalon and Shierdon, the capitol of their kingdom once being the Krozock Mountains, known now as Northern Ky'Dren. Relations with the young kingdoms of Eldalon and Shierdon had always been shaky; there had been many wars with the two. Lucky for the two kingdoms the barbarians were not interested in conquest, for every barbarian knew that they could have taken all of Agora. The barbarians were happy with their lot, and the tribes cared not for the land of their neighbors. But the humans were indeed conquerors, and ever they pressed. It was not until the Ky'Dren kingdom had grown fat and expanded over the pass to the north that the barbarians became truly threatened. Humans were weak, one barbarian could take down five, but the dwarves, they were a different foe altogether. Less than half as tall as a barbarian and nearly seven times as strong as the weak humans, the dwarves were like an endless pack of rabid dogs. When a dwarf got something in his head he would see it done, and with Holy Scripture driving their motives none could stand in their way, not even barbarians.

Attacked from all sides, the barbarians were nearly wiped out. Eldalon wanted what is now known as "The Horn", the northern most tip of Eldalon that looked like a dragon's horn when viewed on a map. The peninsula was a prime location for fishing, and a key strategic naval base. Shierdon wanted to expand its lands to the west including Lake Eardon, while the dwarves wanted the entire mountain. History had shown the barbarians to be savages, but like the tribal elders remind the children, "history is written by the victors."

The barbarians, mostly women and children, were loaded up on barges by the hundreds, ripped from their destroyed mountain homes, and sent to the frozen island of Volnoss. It had been the dead of winter. Half of the survivors made it through to spring, living off of buried roots and what fish could be caught in the frozen lakes with braided hair-line and bone hooks.

The barbarians of Northern Agora, the once proud and prosperous giants, had been reduced to a ragged community of refugees. It would be generations before they would become strong once again. Aurora reminded herself that now was the time. The barbarians of Volnoss had not been this powerful since the days of Talon Windwalker, and how they could use him and his wolf now. It was up to her she knew; she alone could restore her people to their former glory. But who would she use to accomplish her gains, Whill or Eadon? She had sworn friendship to one, and fealty to the latter. Though she no longer felt the power of Eadon within her, she suspected that her vow remained. She had hoped to have been free of it because she had fulfilled her promise; she had tried to kill Abram. But she now knew those to be nothing more than self-told lies, her way of wishing away the promise. She had thought of asking for the elves help in breaking the vow, Whill's even. But that would mean admitting her sins, and that would likely get her killed.

A rustling broke her out of her trance and she became alert and still. The fires crackled around her, and she was covered in a misty sheen due to the heat. She listened; it came again from behind her, and again from her side. Whatever they were they had her surrounded.

Aurora stood and unsheathed her sword sending liquid fire dancing up the face of the silver blade. She pulled it at a hard angle to cause it to ring loud and true in the night.

"I am warrior of the north, Aurora Snowfell of frozen Volnoss. Come forth and bleed with me!" She bellowed into the darkness beyond the dancing firelight that cast shadows thrice.

The rustling stopped dead and the howl of a large cat sliced through the thick air behind her, she did not flinch. All around her the cries rang out and she began to see sleek black feline forms in the shadows beyond the densely packed spears. Aurora growled back at them and grabbed a spear from the ground and threw it up into the air to catch it at the center of the shaft. She cocked back and led one of the moving shadows. As her muscles tensed for the throw a great growl stopped her dead. She scanned the canopy above her and soon found two fire lit eyes staring down on her from on high. If this pack had a leader, it seemed he was it. The great cat howled again unnaturally loud and Aurora could hear the other cats leaving. Aurora had not left the cats eyes, the feline orbs stared back unwavering. She blinked and the eyes were gone and a shadow was falling through the branches. A large black panther the size of her native timberwolf landed with a shower of sparks upon one of the fires. It did not react to the flames, but gracefully stalked off the wood and around the fire to stare at Aurora. She held fast her spear, ready at a moment's notice to impale the attacking beast, but it did not attack, nor did its demeanor hint to violence. It looked curious. There was intelligence behind those elliptical orbs.

"You are no cat," said Aurora as she circled the beast. "Show yourself as you were born."

The wolf leapt onto its hind legs and transformed into a tall elf that she knew instantly. "Azzeal," said Aurora, lowering her spear with a half cocked smile of disappointment. She had hoped for a fight.

"Aurora Snowfell, warrior of the north." The leaf-clad elf replied with a look to the hanging smoked boar. "Did you get...hungry?"

"Hungry for the hunt, I assume you understand," she said with a look to the panther tracks that led to his feet.

She took a seat upon the ground and poked at the fire as he regarded her. "Have you decided?" The elf asked.

Aurora froze as her eyes shot to his. He regarded her without expression, waiting. She knew that her answer would determine her fate.

He read my thoughts, he knows everything.

"Have I decided what?" She asked trying to mask her sudden shock.

"Do not play games with one so old child," he said as he took a seat opposite her.

Can I defeat him? She wondered. *Surely not, he is a magic user and more versed in combat than I.*

"When you move against my enemies, you will become the instrument of my wrath." Eadon had whispered to her as they sealed the vow with flesh.

"You have read my thought? Invaded my mind? I thought the elves of the sun shunned such practices," said Aurora.

Azzeal frowned and shook his head. "No, you were projecting in a language foreign to me. I know only that a great burden haunts your mind."

"These are dark times elf. Who has not a troubled mind?"

Azzeal nodded conceding the point. From the fire Aurora took the cooked boar that she had set aside to eat and offered it to Azzeal.

"Hungry?"

"I could eat." He replied and tore a piece off nodding his thanks.

They ate in silence for a time in which Aurora tried to mask her guilt and think only in her native tongue. She did not trust Azzeal, or any of them for that matter. It was hard to get comfortable around people whose personal power was impossible to tell by their appearance. Every second in silence seemed to stretch out impossibly long, becoming that much more awkward to Aurora.

"The great cats, they respect you, are you their leader?" she asked having to say something.

Azzeal groaned tearing meat from bone. "No, I run and hunt with them. They know I am elf. They wanted to kill and eat you; they were five in all, Shemba and her four cubs. They are nearly full grown and the two males will soon be banished from their mother's territory. Killing you was to be a right of passage."

"I did not need to be saved," Aurora replied.

"Perhaps I was saving the panthers," said Azzeal.

"You cost me five panther hides then it seems, what coin they would have gotten in Volnoss," Aurora added as she chewed the greasy shank.

"There is no way to know if you would have lived to sell such hides." Azzeal argued.

"Cut the dragon shyte elf. You seen me take on drag-gard bare handed," she proclaimed with a greasy clawed hand. "You interfered in my hunt."

"On my land," he said with a raised voice. "Consider the conquered hog a gift and speak of it no more."

Aurora was angry, nearly furious. She did well to keep her breathing slow and deep, and ignored her pounding heart. Little use it likely was. For all she knew the elf could see through to her insides. She felt as an open book to him, and her secret teased like a child echoing her wicked deeds.

Coward at your back

"What?" Azzeal asked as if she had said it aloud.

"Coward," Aurora heard herself say to her horror.

He cocked his head to the side searching her. Before he could utter question she said quickly. "My tribesmen have a saying, 'always there is a coward at your back.' It is a warning and reminder that the mightiest warrior a coward's dagger will take."

"You think that I conspire against you?" he asked.

"I..." she began softly, and then raised her chin, "I do not trust your people."

"That is understandable; it is best earned is it not? Have I not earned your trust?" Azzeal asked gazing deeply into her eyes, the light of the fire dancing upon his.

"We have drawn sword together, that counts for something," she replied.

"Indeed," he nodded heavily. "It is not I who you distrust then."

She averted his gaze pretending to hear something in the night. Acting satisfied that nothing was amiss she tossed the leg bone into the fire and drank deeply of her water skin. Wiping her greasy mouth she looked to Azzeal as if she had forgotten he was there sitting across from her, waiting.

"I had intended to preform a ritual of my people... it is private, sacred," she informed him as she offered her water skin which he nodded away.

"Then I shall keep you no further," he said to her utter relief. Her mind was chanting to her again and she had all she could do to not scream for it to shut up.

"Thank you for the meal," he said with a small bow. She nodded with a smile.

Azzeal looked up as if to leap into the night but then regarded her again quickly. "If you need help carrying your kill out in the morning I offer mine. I will be out until then."

Aurora held her composure against the perceived meaning behind the gesture. "Thank you, but I would dishonor my opponent if I did not myself carry it out of the wood."

"Very well," he nodded and turned again to look at the night. He leapt and spread his arms which became wings that lifted him through the lingering smoke to disappear into the night.

Aurora gave a sigh of relief as she watched him go. She opened her palm and found that she had drawn blood as she clenched her fist to distract from her thoughts. Relieved, she stripped out of her furs and laid them upon a large stone. She stood naked between the raging fires glistening in the cool night air and began the cleansing chant that would begin her long ritual.

From the branch of a tree not far from her camp Azzeal watched Aurora with feline eyes as she shuddered and stomped around caught in the throws of her native ritual. He had indeed heard her every thought and he had not needed invade her mind. She spoke within her mind so freely that one had only to listen to hear it. And though she spoke in her native barbarian tongue, he knew her words. He had been an ambassador to Volnoss three hundred years before. Aside from meeting the human "giants" as they were sometimes referred, Azzeal had wanted to see the fabled Icetooth bear that was said to be all white. Such a creature would add well to his shape shifting repertoire. He had studied the bears for two decades, and in that time he learned well the native languages.

As he watched her strong naked form dancing golden around the fires he pondered the situation. She had sworn fealty to Eadon, she could not be saved but by death.

CHAPTER FOURTEEN
The Elven Guide

"Bah! Eadon be the biggest bullshyter o' them all." Roakore proclaimed, silencing the dwarves who had been debating the dark elf's power.

"He ain't all powerful, he ain't no god. He be drawin' breath, and therefore he can be dyin'."

They had been on the road for a week and all had been quiet. They passed many villages as they crossed the Thendor Plains, some in ruins, others not. Those that remained were scrambling to prepare for winter. What soldiers the company encountered did nothing to hinder their passage across the lands. This was a road used for centuries by the dwarves going to and fro between the Ro'Sar Mountains and Helgar. Blocking the way of Roakore's company would mean certain death to the Uthen-Arden soldiers, and so they passed the dwarves every time without so much as a word. Roakore knew that they were being followed nonetheless, but it mattered not to the king. His boys were more than ready for a good fight.

They traveled on long through the day and into the night and made camp in a field along the road. Earlier in the day a few of the dwarves had killed a buck, and they did not waste any time skinning the deer and getting a strong fire going. The watch was set and Roakore barked orders to his men. Soon the sun was down and a dinner was underway.

Roakore joined Helzendar, Tarren, Lunara, Holdagozz, and the other dwarves by the fire. The always-animated Philo was in the midst of a tale of the reclamation of the Ro'Sar Mountains. They had all heard the story many times since the reclamation months ago, but none tired of it. Philo could not keep a seat while in the midst of his telling, and his animated face and constantly moving arms kept his audience enthralled.

"An' then Roakore blasted that hell-born dark elf clear out the mountainside. We charged out after the devil, an' to our delight we found an ocean o' draggard to use our blades on."

Tarren listened intently to the tale as he always did. He could almost see it in his mind's eye, and he yearned for such adventure and glory. *One day,* he thought, *one day I will rid the oceans of every last pirate scum there is, and such tales will be told of Tarren the great pirate-slayer.*

Helzendar waved a hand in front of Tarren's face. "What ye thinkin' on, eh?"

"Huh?" said Tarren as he was brought back from his daydream. "Ah, nothing," he replied dismissively.

"Nothin'? Judging by the big shyte-eatin' grin you was wearin', I figured it be somethin' more than nothin'."

Tarren only shrugged. "A girl, then?" Helzendar teased, shaking his head. "You humans get an eye for the girls early on, don't ye?" He chuckled.

"Naw, it ain't about no stinkin' girl," Tarren protested.

"All right, then, what, if not a girl?" Helzendar pressed.

"Jeesh, you never give up, do you?"

Helzendar gave Tarren a look of mock confusion. "Give up? What's that?"

They both chuckled. "If you have to know, I was daydreaming about...killin' pirates. When I grow up I intend on hunting down every last piece o' pirate scum on the seas." Tarren searched Helzendar's eyes for a hint of amusement at the idea. But Helzendar's face became serious as he pondered the idea.

"Hmm, Tarren the Pirate-Slayer, eh?"

Tarren grimaced and awaited ridicule, but none came.

"Ha! I can see that. Who better than you for the job, eh?"

Tarren lit up as he realized Helzendar was serious. "Yeah, I been thinkin' 'bout it a lot." His eyes widened as an idea occurred to him. "You could come with me, Helz!"

The dwarf scowled. "Me…on the open sea?" He shivered. "I don't want nothin' to do with the ocean. What with no land in sight, no rock, no stone—bah, ain't no place for a dwarf, it ain't."

Tarren sagged back down, crestfallen, and said no more of it. Philo had finished his tale to cheers for his king. Roakore might have told the dwarves to be quiet had he not been busy basking in his own glory.

The night went by quietly and the company was off once again before the sun. The next few days of travel took them on eastward and finally south to the borders of Elladrindellia. Roakore knew the moment he stepped onto elven land—one would be hard pressed not to notice the difference. The wind seemed to whisper as it blew gently through his hair. The trees became thicker, the grass greener, and while the rest of Agora's flowers wilted with the onset of winter, here they did not. It seemed to Roakore like stepping into perpetual summer. He saw the same thoughts in the faces of his weary dwarves. They had no trust for the elves and less love. The dwarves showed no animosity toward Lunara out of respect for Roakore, but he knew their hearts. There was still much deep-rooted anger toward the elves, be they sun or dark. Their kin had been responsible for the creation of the draggard, and the dwarves cursed the day those creatures had ever landed upon Agora's shores.

Roakore took to the skies upon Silverwind and then down upon the strange and vibrant land. It showed not a sign of draggard mischief. Here within Elladrin-dellia, one could forget that the draggard even existed. Roakore grumbled to himself. He did not like the fact that while dwarves and men died daily against the draggard and dark-elf hordes, the elven lands were untainted.

Roakore soon spotted an elf on horseback a few miles off, heading in the company's direction. The dwarf king steered the silver hawk around and headed back. The elf was likely an escort come to greet them. Upon landing among his dwarves, Roakore was quickly greeted by an excited Tarren.

"Helzendar said I could have the first ride over elven lands! Are ye headin' out soon again, Roakore?" He could hardly hide his jubilation at a chance to see Elladrindellia as few if any humans ever had, from the back of a silver hawk.

"Not now, lad," Roakore said with a passing pat to Tarren's head as he walked businesslike toward the company. "All right, lads, listen up! We got an elven ambassador headin' this way. I ain't givin' no more warnin' than this: don't be startin' no trouble while ye be here, ye got it? Else I will personally use your head to wipe a dragon's arse."

Lunara giggled at that and Roakore shot her a look but a wink quickly followed. Soon the rider reached them upon the road. He was dressed in what appeared to Roakore to be leaves, and rode a white-and-brown horse. A bow was strapped over one shoulder, and a banner of brilliant feathers blew in the breeze. The banner, made of many multicolored feathers, depicted rolling hills and a sun that set the sky aflame. The elf had hair of gold pulled back in a long tail; many a dwarf looked on at the golden hair with secret admiration.

The ambassador stopped his horse before the company and easily spotted Roakore beside the magnificent Silverwind. He greeted the dwarf king by slamming his fist to his chest and bowing in his saddle.

"On behalf of my people and Queen Araveal, I welcome you, good king Roakore of the Mountains Ro'Sar, to Elladrindellia. I am your guide, Nafiel."

Roakore nodded and addressed the elf. "Well met, Nafiel. We been at it since dawn, so now be as good a time as any to be eatin'. Would ye dine with us?"

"It would be my pleasure." Nafiel bowed and dismounted.

The dwarves were quick to set up Roakore's tent, which had not been used as of yet, and set to stoking a good fire. A mug was filled and a seat set for Nafiel before he had said hello to three dwarves. The elf laughed merrily as he watched the dwarves work together as one. Tarren was on him in a heartbeat with introductions of himself and Helzendar and questions that came faster than could be answered. Nafiel greeted the lad and gave a bow to Lunara. She greeted him in kind and introduced Holdagozz.

Shortly the food was set and the warm sun shone down upon the most unlikely of afternoon lunches. Now that the threat of the Thendor Plains was behind them, the dwarves allowed themselves more merrymaking and more ale. Roakore turned back a dwarf who entered his tent with another small barrel of beer.

"This ain't no party, it be but a lunch. Tell the company we move out quicker than quick got ready!" Roakore yelled after him.

Nafiel laughed as he always did. "They will be happy to reach Gallien. There a feast awaits your company, and drink from the southern vineyards of Estondar."

"Estondar, eh?" Roakore searched his memory. "I recall an Estondar white wine. A bit weak, but good elven wine all the same."

"I shall find your dwarves something strong enough, good king."

The company renewed their journey long into the afternoon with Nafiel as their guide. They had traveled nearly to the Thallien River and soon veered north to the elven village of Gallien. The small city of crystal-capped pyramids was nestled at the Thallien River's northern inlet. The delta and coast were speckled with elven fishing boats with their telltale fin-like sails.

Gallien's pyramids glowed and pulsed softly in the waning daylight. The pyramids, like those in Cerushia and every other elven city and village, were built to reflect the stars above. Here there were seven, and together they mirrored the constellation Gallien, which, like the village, was named after the ancient elf king.

Roakore landed and dismounted Silverwind as they reached the village. Elves had gathered in droves to see the dwarven company. They smiled and waved as the group slowly made their way to the heart of the village.

Tarren marveled, wide-eyed and open-mouthed, at the elven people and structures. Beside him Helzendar looked around with a curious expression.

"Amazin', ain't it?" Tarren asked. But Helzendar only shrugged.

Nafiel turned in his saddle and addressed the group with wide arms. "Welcome, good dwarves, to Gallian. Here you will find lodging suitable for such esteemed guests, and food and ale to replenish your tired bodies."

"Tired, eh? Who be tired?" Philo yelled. Nafiel only laughed and led them on to their lodging.

Gallien, like most elven villages, was made from living vines, stone, and trees. Vines wound together to create walkways and bridges where the water split the land. The woven vines grew together to create domed abodes and buildings. Many of the dwarves had never seen nor even heard of such strange architecture, and did nothing to hide their speculation about the structures' strength. Nafiel assured them to the contrary, giving examples of the structures' surviving oceanic storms and even tornadoes, but the dwarves seemed unimpressed.

Soon they reached the vine domes that would house the dwarves for the night. The horses were led to stable, and the dwarves wasted no time tapping their ale barrels. Lunara greeted many of her people with Tarren in tow. The boy introduced himself in Elvish before Lunara had a chance, gaining many smiles from the elves.

Elves had begun to crowd around the travelers, murmuring to each other as they eyed the dwarves with a mix of delight and apprehension. Likewise, the dwarves eyed the strange-looking elves, but with much less delight. Roakore noted this but shrugged it off. They would warm up to the elves soon enough. He hoped that Nafiel would make good on his promise of strong spirits.

Even as Roakore thought it, there came thin crystal glasses which were passed all around until everyone had one. Bottles also traded hands until all had filled their glasses. The dwarves looked at their too-small glasses and the yellow-white bubbly liquid therein.

"To friendships made anew and bonds forged between the races," said Nafiel. Roakore coaxed his men to cheers with a bellowed "Hoo-rah!" And drink rose skyward. The dwarves responded with a booming retort and slammed back their drinks one and all, while the elves sipped from theirs. Roakore soon learned why the elves only sipped from their glasses. The elven liquor was so tart that the dwarves all puckered their faces with slanting eyes as the afterburn of the strong spirits made them feel as if flames shot from their mouths and noses.

"Ahh!" came Tarren's scream, followed by Helzendar's hearty chuckle as the boy ran around in wide circles, holding his throat. Somehow it seemed the young lad had gotten a glass and quietly joined in on the cheers. Tarren blindly ran screaming and slammed into the dwarven supply cart that held a number of barrels of ale. He frantically pulled back on the spout of an already-tapped keg and lapped up the pouring beer as a dog would water. The dwarves erupted in belly-shaking laugher at the spectacle. Bottles began to float among the group again, and this time some dwarves didn't bother using the crystal glasses.

Lunara took the panting boy by the shoulder with a scowl. "Come, we will find you some water. I will not be healing you of your stupidity."

"Ugh-huh," Tarren could only moan sickly.

The dwarves tapped their barrels, and frothing mugs were passed to the elves. Cheers were made and the mood became light. The dwarves took up their instruments and began to sing songs of old. The elven spirits had put them in a right jolly mood and together their deep booming voices and melodic chants gained the attention of all nearby elves. Dwarven drums brought to mind mining picks and falling hammers and the deep heart of dwarven mountains. Hatchets clanged in rhythm and pots were struck; even barrels of ale were used as the music grew steadily louder. Philo began a melody upon his miitar, bending the strings and plucking out a busy progression. Wind pipes moaned and fiddles danced as the elves too joined in and blended perfectly with the melody. Beautiful elven voices rose up to join the dwarves' booming ones, and dancing began all around the company as more and more elves poured in to get a glimpse of the king of Ro'Sar and his hearty dwarves. Elven flutes and whistles, fiddles and horns joined in the merrymaking, and together the dwarves and elves sang to the heavens.

As the first song ended, Roakore stood high atop the supply cart and with outstretched hands began the old dwarven song, "The Beauty o' the Gods." His dwarves came in and the elves joined too, and soon a version of the song never heard in all the lands rose up and rang out for miles.

The rivers they be pretty, and the lasses they be too.
The mountains set me heart to singin',
and me love, so do you.
There be one thing that stands above, high atop the rest
And no, it ain't a cold-filled pint, nor fair bouncing breast.
It be a thing o' eternal beauty, it be fire in me soul.
I'll search it to the mountain's heart, till me hands
be dead and cold.
It be the shining in me eyes, it be the heart at me core.
Gold and silver and gem and jewel, and it be so much more.

The beauty o' the gods, lo
The beauty o' the gods.
The demons tried to hide it away
The beauty o' the gods.
The beauty o' the gods, lo!
The beauty o' the gods.
I'll search it out till dyin' day.
The beauty o' the gods.

The crowd joined in after a few choruses and the song went the length of three. Holdagozz bowed to Lunara, who laughed as she too sang for the entire world to hear. She bowed slightly as she beamed at her friend. The night had become intoxicating—the instruments and harmony, so many voices singing as one. Holdagozz bellowed laughter as he spun Lunara round and round, twirling through the streets of dancing elves. The dwarven dance had quickly been taken up by the clever elves, and now hundreds laughed and sang and danced. Smoke from dwarven and elven pipes floated higher with the song. Ale flowed freely from dwarven barrels, and the elven spirits made many rounds.

CHAPTER FIFTEEN
Bandits on the Road

Long into the night Dirk rode. He did not rest until an hour before dawn. As soon as the sun broke the horizon, he began again on a steady pace. Before him the Ky'Dren Mountains grew with each of the horse's steps.

During the night he had come to a crossroads and taken the pass road. The road to the Ky'Dren Pass was much wider than the last, and it was kept up much better as well. This was a major trade route, and it was kept in good shape for the wagons. Though trade had slowed, and there were many more road bandits about these days, heavy traffic could still be found.

He soon came to the remains of a burned-out fire and the telltale signs of a camp. Dirk studied the ground for a few minutes and determined the party to have been few. A cart, two horses, and no more than five men, he estimated from the tracks upon the soft earth. By the depth of the cart tracks he knew that they carried a heavy load. He doubted that they were farmers, as the Ky'Dren Pass was the better part of a day away, and no one would be hauling food that far with a starving countryside in every direction. Likely they were a group of bandits, robbing the countryside to amass enough money to live out the winter to come. Either way, Dirk needed to catch up to them. He needed to eat, and though he could hunt, or better yet have Chief catch him live game, he had no time for all that.

He urged Frostmore on faster as noon approached and his stomach growled. Within the hour he came upon the wagon and horses. He saw them many miles off from on high, at the crest of a ridge that opened into a wide valley of forest and stream. He suspected that well-armed lookouts traveled behind and before the wagon. He had not seen but he had heard through his enchanted earrings the faint but distinct sound of horse's hooves. The sound grew fainter as it traveled away from him: he had been seen. Likely the trailing lookout was off to report Dirk's approach to his comrades.

Dirk withdrew the wolf-shaped bone trinket and called to the spirit wolf once again. "Come, Chief." Within seconds a smoky mist emanated from the trinket and took the form of the huge timber-wolf ghost. Chief looked Dirk over for a moment, then sat lazily on his haunches and began to groom himself.

"Listen up, fella!" said Dirk. "There is a wagon ahead, three men upon it, I suspect, and two lookouts both before and beyond. I have been spotted by one of the lookouts; he now rides to warn his friends."

Chief continued to groom himself and ignore the assassin. He yawned and looked as bored as a wolf could look.

Dirk went on. "I need you to hunt down the horseman and keep an eye on him."

Chief's ears perked up at this, the mention of hunting. He opened his maw in a panting smile and wagged his bushy tail slowly back and forth. The spirit wolf's ears perked and began to scan the surrounding forest independent of one another. Dirk now had his full attention.

"If the lookout or any of his friends attempt to harm me, kill them. If not, leave them be and stay out of sight. If I require your aid, I will make this call." Dirk whistled a quick chime. "That is to be your call from this day forth. Understand?"

Chief barked his acknowledgement and Dirk chuckled at his intelligence. "You will make for a good companion."

Again Chief barked.

"Go on then, boy! Good hunting."

With that, Chief darted into the underbrush and soon disappeared. Dirk urged Frostmore on once again toward the wagon and a likely ambush.

He had determined that there were no more than five men in the group, three upon the wagon and two on horseback. Still, he could not know how many might be atop the cargo. He decided that if he came upon the wagon and saw fewer than three people on or near it, he could expect an ambush. The two horsemen, he knew, were on lookout duty, so if the wagon contained only two men, a third was most likely hiding, no doubt with an arrow nocked and ready.

Dirk came upon the wagon as it slowed before crossing a short bridge. The rider and driver jumped down from it and began to unhook the horses to drink from the slow river. Dirk could see as he approached from a few hundred yards that the big-wheeled wagon was not made for human transport. Its wooden sides came up no more than a few feet, and a leather tarp covered whatever cargo was beneath.

Dirk approached the wagon slowly. With the help of his enchanted earrings, he could hear as the lookout slowly stalked him, now on foot. And beyond that sound were the quiet steps of Chief, stalking the lookout.

He raised a hand in greeting as he came closer to the two who acted as if they were not aware of his presence. Dirk played along.

"Hello there! Hello!" he yelled.

The two men flinched as if they had been startled by him. "Hello!" the burly driver called back. His tall and lanky rider rested his hands atop the canvas nonchalantly, no doubt inches from a hidden crossbow or blade.

"You mind if my horse shares the river with your fine steeds?" Dirk asked as he dismounted. The driver rubbed his beard and nodded permission while eyeing Dirk's horse. Dirk knew that he was puzzling over Dirk's lack of baggage. The rider inched his hand closer to the tarp flap and eyed Dirk. Chief quickly moved from the tree line behind Dirk and back again, giving him the would-be ambusher's location.

Dirk stroked Frostmore as the horse drank, and addressed the men with a pleasant smile. "I am in need of food and coin if you have it, and I will swiftly be on my way. Tell the men in the woods to lower their bows and come out peacefully and I will spare your lives."

The rider's hand froze and he looked at Dirk, dumbfounded. The driver, however, eyed Dirk with renewed interest. He looked him over once more, seemingly noticing his attire for the first time.

"What are you about, stranger? Ain't no men in the trees. Alls there is is all ye see of our company. We want no trouble."

"What am I about?" said Dirk as he continued to stroke Frostmore. "I am about to spill blood, unless your rider quits reaching for his weapon under that tarp, and your men come from the woods."

"There ain't no men in the woods, I said once, and I ain't gonna—"

Dirk cut him off with a loud whistle. A snarl and a scream tore through the woods to their right, first one man's scream and then another. In an instant the rider had thrown back the canvas and had a crossbow at his shoulder.

There was a twang and a bolt came rushing at Dirk. He turned and pulled both sides of his cloak out wide, causing the bolt to skid harmlessly across and to the river. The rider cursed and reloaded with trembling hands as another scream ripped through the quiet day. A bloodcurdling howl followed, and Dirk threw two darts in rapid succession, one at the rider's neck, the other the driver's. The two men fell with a thud.

Chief came bounding out of the woods and leapt atop the unconscious men. "You're a bit late for those two," Dirk told him. Chief cocked his head and regarded Dirk curiously. "Never mind. There is one more of them, in the woods or on the road ahead. See that he doesn't surprise me."

Chief crossed the bridge, sniffing as he went, already on the trail. Dirk checked the pockets of the snoring men. He took what coin they had and pocketed it. It would be sufficient for his needs.

Under the bench seats of the wagon Dirk found bread, but it was stale and hard. He went to the back and uncovered the tarp. Below he found half a dozen wooden shovels still caked with dirt. He turned back the tarp further and found lanterns and iron crowbars. The men's personal effects were mingled with ten large chests. Dirk took hold of a crowbar and smashed the lock upon one of the chests. It took many blows but it finally broke; it was a cheap lock, made by human hands, most likely. Within the chest he found many watches, bracelets, rings, and jewels.

Grave robbers, thought Dirk. The men must have been on a long quest to have amassed such a pile of jewels. He could not imagine how many burned towns they must have sacked, or how many graves they'd robbed. A fortune was laid out before him, and Dirk wondered why so few men were there to guard the wealth. Likely the party had consisted of many more, but they had slowly been thinning out the group, making each slice of the pie larger.

It was now clear that the thieves had not been traveling to the Ky'Dren Pass. They would have been seen for what they were with a wagon full of family heirlooms, gems, and jewels. Dirk surmised that they were either still on the hunt or headed back to their base of operations, wherever that may be.

Dirk found their food stores among the cargo, and loaded Frostmore with two packs of them. Footsteps approached from the woods behind him, and he could tell that the person limped. The slow, singing sound of a sword being unsheathed came through his enchanted earrings. He turned toward the sound and saw the man hiding beyond the underbrush. Neither moved as Dirk held his gaze and the man's eyes passed over his two fallen companions.

"You will not get away with this, thief!" yelled the man.

Dirk threw back his head with a laugh. "Ironic, that is, being called a thief by a thief." He moved to the wagon and folded back the canvas. "How many died for this bounty?"

Angrily the man countered, "I ain't tellin' you nothin', you—"

"You have been injured by my wolf. You drag your leg and trail blood. The beast likely snapped your bow; you have a few blades but no strength. I could kill you within the minute. So please, I tire of these games. Come out from the woods and have a word, or you will die." Dirk looked to the opposite side of the road and yelled to the other hiding man, "You too there, in the brush behind the tall oak. Come out or die—you have one minute!"

Dirk turned from the cowards and took an apple from the wagon. With a satisfying crunch he began to eat while he hummed a tune and waited. Soon the two men came hobbling out of the woods, swords sheathed. One of the men had found a stick to help himself along. Both had a bloodied leg and torn pants. One wore only one shoe. They hobbled over to the wagon and grudgingly waited for Dirk's instruction. The assassin looked them over but did not speak, merely ate his apple to the core. The sun finally broke through the clouds and shined warm light upon the road ahead.

"Ah! But it looks as though it will be a pleasant day after all," he told the men nonchalantly and fed the apple core to Frostmore. From the wagon he found what meager medical supplies they had and threw them to the men. "See you tend to your wounds."

The men tore the cloth into strips as they eyed Dirk suspiciously. "What are you playin' at, stranger? You need someone to drive the team and wagon, is that it? Well, I'll tell you what! Viggo Varrox ain't gonna be too pleased you meddled in his business—"

Dirk sprang from the side of the wagon with inhuman speed and had a dagger to the man's throat before the sentence ended. Surprised yelps escaped the men.

"Your next word will be your last," Dirk whispered into his ear. He looked at the other injured man, who was backing away slowly.

"You there, fetch a barrel from the wagon."

The man complied without a word and set the barrel down at Dirk's feet. "Put your right hand on the barrel both of you, one on top of the other," Dirk ordered, and released the loudmouth.

The men looked at each other and at the barrel. Grudgingly they obeyed. In a blur of movement Dirk stabbed his dagger, Krone, through both of their hands. The men cried out in pain but soon became placid as the dagger's effect took their minds. They looked at Dirk with empty stares.

"You and your friends will turn this wagon around and head straight to the barricaded town one day's march east and south. You will give the contents of this wagon over to them and tell them that it is a gift from Whill of Agora. You will then offer yourselves to their service and live out the rest of your days glad that you did not die here today. Do you understand?"

Both men nodded agreement. "I understand," they said in unison.

Dirk retracted the blade and the men clutched their wounded hands. "Tend to your wounds and prepare to leave."

Just then Chief came back across the bridge, dragging a screaming man by the ankle. The spirit wolf stopped at Dirk's feet and he gave him a pat on the head. "Good boy." He grabbed the shaken man and put his hand atop the barrel. "Chief, if he moves, I want you to rip his throat out."

The man shuddered as the wolf crept to within an inch of his face and growled. Dirk whistled a tune and gathered the unconscious driver and rider. He put their hands over the whimpering man's and stabbed through them all with the dagger. The two men screamed awake suddenly but soon became calm as Krone compelled them to obey Dirk. He recited the same instructions to the three men that he had to the others.

Dirk left them tending to their wounds soon after. They would follow his instructions, for they were weak minded and easily controlled. Dirk had rarely met even an elf who could resist the dagger, much less any human.

He ate as he rode and made good time the remainder of the day. By nightfall the mountains towered before him and he knew the Ky'Dren Pass to be only hours away. He rode on through the night and thought of nothing but Krentz.

The sky had gradually cleared and now there was not a cloud to be seen in the darkened heavens. He had not dismissed Chief all day, curious about his stamina within the physical plane. All day the wolf had darted ahead down the road to disappear around a bend or hill, but always he came back. Sometimes he would take to the woods for such long durations that Dirk thought he had returned to his own plane of existence, but always he returned. He was curious to learn more of the spirit wolf. *Chief.* The name played in the back of his mind, sparking the faintest light of recognition. But it seemed that the information was long ago learned or only overheard. He could not pinpoint where or when he had heard it.

Dirk shifted uncomfortably in his saddle, weary from travel but not able to spare a moment of rest if he was to stop Krentz. He still could not believe that she had sworn fealty to her father, a fact that disturbed him more than a little. He feared that he would be too late to stop her from reaching Whill's kin, from killing them all. If he allowed that to happen, he did not know if she would ever forgive herself for such a heinous act. He had to save her, and then...

Dirk wondered what his next move would be. If he did reach her in time, he would likely have to fight her. She would be compelled to carry out Eadon's orders; there would be no resisting. To resist meant death. But Dirk could not let it reach that point. He could not make her decide, for she would choose death. Instead he would have to trap her, and then...

The only help Dirk could imagine for breaking Eadon's spell of fealty was Whill, but Whill thought him a traitor, and rightly so. Dirk did not regret what he had done; for the sake of Krentz he would do it again. But he hoped that saving his kin from certain death would be enough to regain Whill's trust. The dwarf Roakore, however, was a different story. The dwarf king would try to kill him on the spot.

One thing at a time, he told himself as the road before him turned once again.

CHAPTER SIXTEEN
The Dragonlance of Ashai

Aurora didn't sleep that night. She sat cross-legged between the fires for most of it, entranced by the sounds around here. The jungle had a savage lull to it, a primal element that helped one forget the trappings of the mind. Here one needed be alert at all times, ever in tune with their surroundings. The random death cries of those creatures that failed to do so echoed often throughout the night as a reminder to all.

At some point light found its way once again into the dark depths of the jungle. Aurora had spent part of the night braiding vine and building a sled to carry the meat. She took each heavy piece down in turn and wrapped it in large leaves and secured them with vine. The spears were pulled and added to the smoldering fire, and the logs were scattered. Aurora didn't concern herself with a possible wildfire, the vegetation here was damp. She headed towards Cerushia feeling rejuvenated. During the ritual dance the barbarian goddess had spoken to her. Aurora was now resolute; she would leave shortly and journey to her homeland. Once there she would challenge the chief, and once victorious, she would lead her people against the dark elves and share in the spoils of an Agoran victory. The ancient barbarian lands would be restored, and again her people would know pride.

It was slow going through the jungle dragging nearly a thousand pounds of boar meat. By the time she reached the city it was past midday, and she was soaked with perspiration. She had washed off the mud during the night, but her ritual dance required that she cover herself in the blood of her kill. She came dragging the smoked boar into the city and gained many stares from the elves. Over an arched bridge of stone and straight through the market square she dragged her wares. She drew stares from the elves every step of the way. Finally she reached her dwelling and released her burden with a relieved sigh. She knew that she must have looked every bit the part of the savage barbarian.

The vines door opened and Kreshna greeted her with a wide smile, until she saw the dried blood. She regarded the leaf-wrapped smoked meat curiously. "You spent the night in the jungle?"

"Yes, I was in the mood for the hunt," said Aurora as she unsheathed her sword and began chopping the tusks from the boar head. Kreshna jumped as the blade hit and sent a tusk flying off.

"These will make an excellent necklace don't you think?" said Aurora.

"The horned hog was nearly wiped out for its tusks and plating," Kreshna replied looking concerned. "We brought them here to live in the jungle so that they might thrive."

"Yes, the plating would make a fine shield. I feel honored to have been allowed to hunt the treasured beast," said Aurora as she continued to work at separating the many tusks.

"We-."

"The elf Azzeal took part in the meal, if he allowed it I assumed it was alright." Aurora told her standing to her full height, the act left her towering over Kreshma.

"Have you seen him?" she asked and went to collecting the severed tusks.

"I...no I haven't." Kreshna replied as she looked apprehensively at the tusks being piled in her hands like firewood.

"No matter", said Aurora adding the last of the tusks. "See that these and the smoked meat, and all of the many gifts make it to the harbor."

Kreshna gave her a quizzical look. "You mean to leave?"

"Indeed. It is long overdue," said Aurora. "There is a storm coming. I have little time and much to do. I have tarried long enough. The people of Volnoss need a leader, and I intend to be it."

"You will need a crew; someone who knows these waters, someone to help you introduce the elves to your people."

"My people know of you, if we share anything with the dwarves it is our...their opinion of you all. They do not adjust to change well."

"I can do it. You have warmed to me, to us, in such little time."

Aurora looked her over in thought."May as well be you then." She said and turned to enter her dwelling. A large crowd had gathered near to them. They did not stop but traffic had slowed considerably as the elves gawked at the spectacle.

"Thank you Lady of the North," Kreshna said with a bow.

"See to it we are ready to leave this night."

Aurora bathed and took the better part of an hour braiding her hair. She let the blood remain on her furs; her people would find it appealing. It was for the same reason she had allowed her wounds to be healed, but had insisted that the scar tissue remain. She would need all the help she could get if she was to depose chief Icethorn

Aurora worried for her people. She had not been home in many seasons, and when she had left the land was plagued by draggard and whispers of war. The seven barbarian tribes of Volnoss cared not for the plight of the dwarves and man, and the elves were hated strangers. They planned to dig in and take what was left of the mainland. But Aurora knew that it would not work. If Volnoss did not side with Whill they were doomed, she had to show them somehow. Or would Eadon be the Victor of this battle, would she be leading her people to their doom? She had not heard from Eadon at all, nor could she feel his power humming within her as she once had. Was she free? In the end it didn't truly matter. All that mattered was that she kill Chief Icethorn, and to do that she would need help. She was confident that she could take the man, but she had no delusions about being able to defeat he *and* his dragon, the very one that had dropped her father to his death those many winters ago. To defeat them both she would need help, and she intended to get it.

She left her room as elves came on Kreshna's order to have Aurora's things taken to the waiting ship. Soon she was standing before Whill's door. She knocked and waited nervously. It had been hard to quiet her mind in the presence of Azzeal, and it was no easier around Whill. The door opened and Whill was quick to offer her a smile and greeting.

"Aurora, please come in."

She ducked under the threshold and entered.

"It is good to see you. Things have been so busy these days, I regret that we have not had more time to visit," he said as he moved to the table and offered her a seat.

"Think nothing of it," she replied taking a seat that was to her as a child's.

"Tea, water?" Whill offered.

"Nothing, thank you. I have come to tell you that I will be returning shortly to Volnozz."

"You intend to challenge your chief?"

"He is no chief of mine, but yes, I intend to kill him. I am confident that I can defeat him alone, his dragon is a different matter."

"His dragon?" Whill asked.

"Yes, the very one that killed my father. I have no beast with which to challenge his, no one has. It is with his dragon that he has taken control of all tribes and named himself Chief of the Seven. If I can defeat him and become Chief of the Seven, then you will have the support of Volnoss. I promise you that."

"And you need my help?"

"Yes, surely with your great sword you can create a beast that could challenge the dragon."

Whill shook his head and looked to the blade. "I wield it yes, but I have neither the knowledge nor skill to create such a beast."

Aurora was disappointed and did not hide it. She looked on hopefully as Whill seemed to ponder the problem.

"Perhaps a ralliad could be of use, Azzeal may agree to it."

"No!" Aurora blurted but quickly composed herself. "I would not have any risk their lives for my cause. No, I could not ask it of Azzeal, or any other. I should not have asked such a thing."

She got up to leave towering over Whill. "I must go."

"Wait," said Whill standing too. "I will contact Avriel. Perhaps the elves possess an enchanted weapon for such a purpose."

"I would be honored," said Aurora as she sat back down.

She watched as Whill became distracted. He remained that way for some time and she assumed he was talking to Avriel. Finally he looked to her with a satisfied smile. "Avriel has told me of a weapon that will aid you in your fight, the Dragonlance of Ashai. She will see to it that the lance finds your boat."

Aurora's smile grew wide and she sprang from her chair and wrapped Whill in a hug. His laugh was smothered by her large bosom as he patted her big back. "You are a true friend and ally Whill of Agora."

She held him at arms length beaming. "I shall not fail you in rousing an army that will make the draggard quiver."

CHAPTER SEVENTEEN
The Other

Whill waited patiently for Zerafin to arrive. Avriel seemed not bothered by her brother's lateness a bit as she sat at the entrance to their new home. Whill had requested new lodging, as he could not move a foot from his old abode without being confronted by a worshipper. He had chosen one of the many towers jutting from stone outcropping along the Thousand Falls. The upper level was wide and open, its balcony easily large enough for Avriel. The lower levels were more suited to human standards and Whill was grateful for the elves' consideration. The inside of his quarters looked like any of the dozens of inns he and Abram had ever stayed in. All the accommodations were present. He had a small stove on which to cook, a pantry stocked with seasonal vegetables and fruits, even a bath fed by the waterfall, its water warmed by a sun crystal.

The only way to the tower was by air, but one could leave by simply diving to the deep waters below. From the balcony the entirety of the Cerushia could be seen. The falls fed dozens of small rivers, all of which eventually connected with another larger river and those into one which led to the sea.

Whill went out onto Avriel's balcony and joined her as she lay gazing out over her city. Her deep hum vibrated in Whill's chest as he placed a hand upon her head.

"Were you sleeping?" Whill asked.

Avriel projected the feeling of a smile onto Whill. *No,* she hummed in his mind, half sighing. *I was caught up in dragon memories. There is so much to know, so much to see. In this form I can recall entire lives of the dragons of its line. I can sit for hours, lost in the exploits of the dragon's kin. I feel their triumphs, I know their pains. Humans have been a nuisance for centuries, and the dwarves—they hate dwarves with a passion.*

Whill stared in admiration at the city glowing in the night. But Avriel saw it not; her mind saw the rolling hills of ages past, battles with dwarves, men, and even elves. She could look even to a time in Agora when the dragons ruled the land. And back farther still, to a time of long migration from a faraway land. Whill shared her vision through their mental connection.

The dragon-lore historians have been delighted in my tales and insist on longer and longer hours of recital. I am convinced that they hope I am never gone back to my elven body.

"Do you want to go back? Will you miss your dragon form?" Whill asked.

I wonder who she was, this dragon, Avriel said solemnly as she spread a clawed foot before her and cocked her head, considering it. *I do not feel her soul here. Without me it is empty. I fear that the body will die without me.*

"Your body will die without you," Whill reminded her.

I know this, she said with a hint of anger. *I am the reason for it. I gave that life in your name, Whill, and I will give this one.*

"Stop talking like that," said Whill, half annoyed with this worship of him, and half at the fact that she had tried to kill herself.

But it is true.

"I know, and I would give my life for you, but I do not need to be sav—"

No, you cannot, Avriel blurted. *You cannot die for me. I am nothing of importance compared to—*

"Please," he pleaded.

Just then she cocked her head and listened. *Zerafin is here. I shall return.*

Whill backed up from her as she stood and took a step and leapt from the balcony. Whill ran to it and watched her fall to the gathering mist below, and after a heart-hammering moment, she suddenly broke through the mist, parting the fog with her gliding wings.

It was only a few minutes before she returned with Zerafin on her back. "The masters have come to a decision, then?" Whill asked as Zerafin dismounted.

"Didn't you tell me that this one would learn patience?" Zerafin asked his sister. She hummed a dragon laugh.

Whill stood before Zerafin, trying to convey patient waiting, but his tapping foot gave away the ruse.

"This is the masters' decision," said Zerafin as he withdrew from the bags book after book and stacked them in Whill's arms. There were seven books in all, with thick silver bindings.

"These are the seven scrolls of the art of Orna Catorna. They contain the theories, spells, and science behind each school," Zerafin explained.

"I am to study them all?"

"Yes. The masters wish for you to read them all and then appear before them again."

"How long do they expect that to take?" Whill thumbed through the huge Elvish volumes. Strange diagrams and formulas in a mathematics more advanced than any Whill had ever seen filled the pages. He was reminded of all of the rare books and scrolls Abram had insisted on him learning from as far back as he could remember. It had seemed Abram was always trying to prepare him.

"You have seven days to complete them, one day for each volume," said Zerafin.

"Of course." Whill laughed. "One day for each giant tome of ancient elven magic. I had hoped to get in a little light reading while I visited Cerushia."

"It is good to see you in high spirits, as you should be. As should we all. Together we will bring about a new age of men and elves, one of peace and prosperity." Zerafin gave Whill a pat on the shoulder.

Avriel did not hide her pleasure in seeing her brother warm up to Whill in such a way. Zerafin stroked her snout and walked to the balcony ledge. "You had better get to work on those early, Whill. I would start with something light, perhaps the book of Zionics." He grinned and leapt from the balcony to the waters below.

Whill looked at Avriel with a sigh. "It looks like I have some work to do."

Long into the night he skimmed through the many tomes. He was amazed by what he saw, descriptions of such magic as he had never thought possible. Spells and potions and transmutation and healing, mind reading and wielding the elements—it all fascinated him. Whill's appetite for knowledge and his love for learning and lore kept him up all night, until the sun rose once again beyond the balcony.

Whill hardly noticed the morning and then day pass by as he delved into the first volume he had chosen, Arnarro, the Way of the Healer. In it were diagrams of the insides of bodies, from elf to man to horse and cow. The workings of the nervous, skeletal, and muscular systems were outlined in great detail. Also there were wards and spells, theories and assumptions, lists of herbs and roots and ointments and ales. When Whill finished the first tome past midnight that night, he felt refreshed. He had read stories of legendary healers who, at their strongest, were known to have healed hundreds of soldiers simultaneously. Some had even dared to bring back others from the dead, but that always ended badly.

Whill dove into the next tome, the Way of the Ralliad. He soon was distracted by an idea he had come across in the last tome, in a chapter dealing with brain trauma. He recalled the Watcher's warning of meddling with his own mind, but he ignored it. He turned his consciousness inward; he turned his mind-sight on itself. He studied the inner workings of his mind, watched the rivers of thought and the constantly firing connections. From the sword he pulled a steady flow of energy and focused it upon parts of the mind he had discovered to be the centers of learning and memory. He sent great tides of energy into his mind, deep within the web of lightning sparks.

There was a great surge pulled from the blade, and Whill realized he had not intended it. Again a surge and a ripple ran through the entire web of dancing light that was his mind. Whill watched as a surge centered upon one area, and from it came a shadow of writhing black lightning. Another surge and it was gone. He pulled back from his mind and willed the blade silent.

He opened his eyes and his hackles rose as his senses screamed. Before him, seated in Whill's exact posture on the moonlit balcony, was the Other. He looked as Whill knew he must have looked during his torture. His doppelganger stared at him through bleeding eyes. His hair hung in filthy clumps of dirt and blood. His cheeks were sunken, his teeth like dried bone. Torn, scorched, and filthy, his clothes hung from him like rags. Gashes, bites, bruises, and burns covered his exposed skin, and a long cut from the left corner of his mouth left him with half a grin.

It was not the appearance of the Other that scared Whill the most, it was when he spoke, for from his mouth came Whill's own voice. It was pained and spiteful; it was venom to the ears.

"Hello, Whill," the Other hissed.

A shiver ran down Whill's back that did not go unnoticed by the apparition.

"You are not real," Whill said with strength and purpose. He closed his eyes and after a time opened them to find the Other still there. He too blinked and looked around expectantly.

When nothing happened, he raised a hand. "Let me try." He coughed. "You are not real!" he yelled and pointed at Whill with a bony finger and broken nail. The Other squeezed his eyes shut and waited. Mocking Whill, he looked around and finally quit the facade. "Well, then, I guess we are both real," he said, bored.

Whill stared, wide-eyed. "I am insane."

"Yes, my friend, you are, and you're also a selfish bastard, and a coward," spat the Other.

Whill was confused. "How am I selfish?" He looked around. "And why am I arguing with an illusion?"

"You left me there!" the Other screamed, and visions of his cell flashed through Whill's mind.

"I didn't—"

"You left me there! Alone, cold, beaten, bloody, starved, and dying, you left me. You turned away when the dark elves came. You closed your ears to my screams, and you closed your eyes to the horror."

Whill found himself sobbing as images of his torture, images of the Other shackled to the stone, flashed through his mind. "Stop…" he breathed, barely able to speak.

The Other's voice shifted to a strangled whisper. "And I was left to feel everything."

"No!" Whill mewled as pain shot through him and wracked his body, leaving him shaking.

"I was left to see everything. I was left to hear my very bones snap, the rip of muscle and flesh, the festering of maggots and gnawing of rats."

"Stop it!" Whill screamed and sent a blast of energy from his hand that went through the Other and exploded against the far wall.

"Of course you would attack me. You hate me. You hate yourself," the Other spat.

"Stop," Whill cried weakly as anguish washed through him, leaving him lying on his side like a child, curled in utter misery, hiding from the world.

"Without me, you would have never survived," the Other sang through broken teeth. "And you shan't be rid of me now."

The pain suddenly subsided and eventually Whill was able to sit up with effort. The Other stared absently at the floor as Whill knew he had for those long maddening breaks between sessions.

"The Watcher warned me of you. You are the Other. You are Eadon's doing."

"I am your doing!" the Other countered, annoyed. "You were too weak, as you are now. Get rid of me and you will cease to be."

Whill believed the truth in his words. He was too weak. The few memories the Other had shown him had left him babbling in tears. The Other was his tortured self, and he held the memories of it all. Whill suddenly felt bad for him.

"While you were...away," the Other began, "while I endured the torture for us, I also learned. I delved into our torturers' minds; Eadon's included, and learned a great many things, things you cannot know without me." He looked at the many tomes scattered on the floor between them. "Even with your precious books."

"You are the reason for my unexplained powers?" Whill said breathlessly.

"Our powers since then, yes. Our ability to perform Orna Catorna before the torture was the result of our father's spirit working through his blade. What we have done since has been a result of what I gleaned from the dark elves. The battle in the arena, fleeing from Eadon, the test of masters—all me," the Other boasted.

"It is not true," said Whill, thinking back. "Before I held my father's blade I healed Tarren, and the infant in Sherna. That I did alone."

"Perhaps," said the Other.

Whill stared at his tortured apparition for a long while. His heart sank as he realized once again that he was having a conversation with himself. "What is it you want?" he asked.

"I want what you want. I want to kill Eadon and destroy his dark armies. I want to see a million draggard heads staining pikes. I want the dark elves to pay for everything they have done!" he yelled, having worked himself into frenzy. Then his expression calmed and he added, "But I need your help, as you need mine."

Whill sat up at the confession, the Other's first real sign of weakness. "My help with what?"

"I want what you want: I want to exist. Help me to gain the blade of power taken, and we can become like gods."

"The blade—Eadon's blade? I do not want what he wants, I don't want to be like a god, I don't—"

"It is the only way! Don't you see that now? The prophecy is a lie! We are not the chosen one! We are meant to give to Eadon the blade Adromida. It has been his plan for eons!"

Whill thought about it for a moment, not agreeing with the Other, but at the same time seeing no other plausible way. "What would you do with Nodae, the sword of power taken?" he asked.

The Other lifted his chin. "I would manifest a body, and then I would leave you at peace and take your pain and your nightmares with me. You could reclaim our father's throne, and claim our birthright."

"And you?" Whill asked. "What will you do?"

The Other grinned knowingly. "I do not want to be you. I already am you. I could destroy you if I wanted."

"But you would be destroying yourself. You are my ego. Your entire existence depends on my safety."

The Other nodded, conceding the point. "Indeed, you need not fear me. I am your only hope." He grinned. "And I have a gift for you, to help you understand what we can achieve together."

"Go on."

"I learned many things when Eadon was meddling with our mind; I was able to learn many secrets. I can help you to restore Avriel to her elven body."

The words slammed Whill in the heart like a stone and hope lit his heart. He believed the Other.

Who were you talking to? came Avriel's mental voice as she landed suddenly upon the balcony. The pages of the many tomes riffled under the wind of her wings.

Startled, Whill looked from her to the Other, but he was gone.

"No one," Whill stammered, and stood on aching legs. He now felt the hours spent so long sitting.

Avriel regarded Whill as she folded her wings. "You said that you could restore me to my elven body. Who were you talking to?"

Whill's eyes widened in terror.

CHAPTER EIGHTEEN

Heldensvargen

The next morning Dirk awoke to a tongue bath from Chief. The wolf lay next to him as he was rousing, and when Dirk got up, the wolf remained.

"Hmm, getting tired then, are we?" he asked with a gentle nudge to the lounging spirit wolf. "Ah, I bet you have a hell of a fight left in you." He took out the timber-wolf figurine and gestured to Chief. "You did well. We will make an excellent team. Now go and rest, back to wherever a spirit wolf calls home."

Chief panted happily and dissipated to mist that swirled up and into the trinket. Dirk put it away with a pat to his pocket and began his day's journey.

Well before the chill began to leave the air in the afternoon light, towns and villages began to become more prominent. This was old country, places that had been around for a thousand years and more, the human roots of the Ky'Dren Mountains.

Here in the shadow of the great mountain range, and all along the mountain's spine, was one of the greatest seats of wealth in all of Agora. The Ky'Dren Mountains touched all of the human kingdoms save Isladon, and trade with the dwarves flourished. Over the centuries more and more human villages and towns, even kingdoms, had grown around and along the mountain. As the dwarf population grew and the Ky'Dren kingdom was carved out within the range, so too did humans, who supplied nearly all dwarven food. The dwarves had carved halls and tunnels from the northern Icewind Seas to the Nordon Sea in the south, nearly one thousand miles long. They did nothing but toil away in their mines and tunnels; always did the fires of Ky'Dren burn.

"Always a hammer falls in Ky'Dren" was a well-known Dwarven saying. The dwarves and humans thrived for centuries due to their symbiotic relationship. Humans grew food and raised livestock, and dwarves created masterful weapons and metalwork. Gems, jewels, and diamonds flowed from the mountains on rivers of gold and silver as payment for the food. The only other export of the Ky'Dren dwarves, and in its own right widely sought, was beer. Dark dwarven ale was the favorite of the humans.

Dirk rode through the largest village he had yet encountered. It felt more like a city as he went. He knew his geography enough to know it to be Heldensvargen. He had never been here before, but he had met a few men from the region. They were easy to tell by their ridiculous accent and tendency to always sound like they were asking a question. The Heldensvargen accent spread far north and south of the Ky'Dren Pass, but curiously, their Eldalonian counterparts, who also traded with the dwarves, had no such accent.

Dirk nodded to the women on the streets, which here in the center of Heldensvargen were cobblestone. Fine houses flanked both sides of the wide street, with the ditch at the center of the street and lined with mint and flowers. Stonework that could only be dwarven adorned the short wall set before the wooden homes. Great pillars, known to the dwarves and humans alike as the arms of Ky'Dren, supported most archways and the corners of homes and buildings. Aside from being known for its goats and its spirits, this was a land renowned for glassblowing, and it was home to a center for masters in the art. There were more than a few jokes about the wives of glassblowers, but if one were smart he would not utter such trifling words among the sharp-chinned people.

Dirk paused before a pub called the Bearded Ram. He was contemplating stopping for a quick blond ale when a drunkard was pushed out of the swinging front doors by a much larger man.

"I tell ye, I tell ye the truth, I saw it with mine own eyes as right as I see your ugly face now, Ortenfelth!

You listen not to the words of a drunk, but godsdamnit, drunks have eyes too, ye know!"

"All right, Koshker, all right! Enough of that. Even if you're telling the truth and you did see a big winged beast overhead, so what? Strange things been creeping around the world for a time now." Ortenfelth led the drunkard along the few steps to the road and turned him around.

The drunken Koshker whirled back on him and nearly fell, and then, stumbling, came to rest against Frostmore's shoulder. "We must prepare! It is a sign, I say."

The innkeeper waved the drunk away and turned back to his pub. "These be dangerous days, fortune-teller. We don't need you makin' 'em any darker with your babblings." He turned at the door, tapped his nose thrice, and pointed a warning at Koshker.

The drunk kicked at the ground and screamed vulgarities. "Don't listen, then! Deny your heritage, deny my gift! But you will not be able to deny death when it comes for your nonbelieving arses."

He stumbled and lurched and again caught himself with Frostmore. Dirk patiently looked down at the man, coughed, and gave him a friendly smile. "What is it you saw, good sir? I would like to hear your tale."

"Tale!" said Koshker. "It ain't no—." He stopped, seeming to see Dirk for the first time. He peered closer and his eyes went wide. He whispered, "The man in black upon a steed of noble blood," so quietly that if not for his enchanted earrings Dirk would not have heard. The man stumbled backward and fell but quickly sprang up again. He fumbled backward like a blind man and went in circles as might a caged beast.

"I would hear your tale!" Dirk yelled after him as the man began to run for his life. Dirk kicked Frostmore into quick pursuit. The drunken man scrambled between two buildings and Dirk followed, the alley barely admitting his horse. Dirk leapt from his saddle and threw his grappling hook as Koshker attempted to climb a high gate. The hook caught hold of his pants, and with a yank from Dirk, Koshker fell flat on his back from on high. Dirk was upon him in an instant. "I would hear your tale—Koshker, is it?"

The drunkard babbled and clawed at the ground as he tried to squirm away on his belly. "The man in black with the shadow of a wolf...poison in his touch and death in his stare."

Dirk grabbed him and spun him around roughly. A hard slap across the face sobered Kroshker quickly. "Enough of your riddles! How do you know me, what did you see?"

Kroshker mewled and refused to meet Dirk's gaze. "This mornin'. I seen it overhead, flying northwest, the winged beast from my dreams...and death rides atop." The man was almost chanting.

"Who is the rider? Is it Krentz?" Dirk asked.

"She is the rider before the storm, the harbinger of death, the daughter of the destroyer..." Kroshker's voice rose with every word, such terrible titles and twisted riddles that Dirk backed away, disgusted.

A great shadow passed overhead and all at once a rumbling began, with a low hum that quickly grew. Screams and shouts of warning echoed throughout the village and the town bell tolled with an eerie reverberation.

"They come at your heels, they come for us all, abominations of the dark one..." Kroshker stood as if pulled up by strings, and a creepy smile spread too far across his face, cracking his lips. "She is the harbinger of death! Death! Death...!" Kroshker chanted as his face contorted with every word.

The rumbling had grown to the power of a small earthquake as Dirk ran and leapt atop Frostmore. The crazy fortune-teller followed, never stopping in his dark proclamations. The bell tolled and the screams swelled as Dirk quickly backed Frostmore from the alley. The rumbling swelled and shook the very earth as the screams became a deafening orchestra of terror. Dirk turned with a jerk to see what nightmare came crashing through the village. A horde of draggard and dwargon stretching far off to the horizon descended upon him, the sky was blackened by beating wings... Dirk was swallowed by the marching destruction and all was black...

With a shuddering breath Dirk tried to scream but could not. He looked around the alley, bewildered, not knowing where he was. His head snapped to Frostmore and when he saw the horse blocking the alley where he had left him, he sighed with relief. It had not been real.

"...she is the princess of darkness, the destroyer of hope. For you she will murder the world." The drunkard's voice came back to him with its eerily musical chant. But his face had returned to normal and his mouth no longer grinned so wickedly it threatened to split his head in two.

"Enough of your poisonous tongue, trickster! Another word and I cut it out," Dirk threatened, brandishing his dagger.

"My tongue, my tongue you would take?" the man raged, spittle flying. "My tongue makes not the words true, murderer, remember that...remember that." Kroshker gave him a maniacal grin.

Dirk punched Kroshker in the mouth, snapping his head back. The drunkard stumbled backward and fell, clawing the wall as he went.

"Beat me, kill me...kill me now and be done with it," Kroshker babbled through blood and tears. Dirk could see that he had split the corner of the man's mouth badly with the punch. A shiver ran down his spine as he was reminded of the man's splitting mouth and cheeks in his temporary illusion. Kroshker now groveled on his belly and tugged at Dirk's pant leg.

"Kill me now and spare me the sight of the village aflame, the blood and darkness and death that is surely to come. Do it! Do it now!"

Dirk kicked the man's clutching hand away and backed out of the alley. He left Kroshker crying and babbling. Dirk decided to go and get that beer after all.

The pub was serving lunch at this time of day, but Dirk was in no mood for food. The well-polished bar was a square at the center of the large room. It looked able to seat more than fifty, with tall stools which at the moment were mostly empty. To the left burned a large fireplace, and many large, fur-lined chairs were set there, a perfect place for a weary traveler to warm his bones. But Dirk was not a weary traveler, he was a thirsty one.

"A pint of the house ale," he asked of the bartender wiping out fresh glasses from the kitchen.

"Coming up, sir," answered the man, though he was much older than Dirk.

As the drink was being fetched from one of the many barrels that lined the inner square of the bar, Dirk scoped out the pub. At the bar sat three other men, each sitting alone at his own section of the wrap-around bar. They stared off into the distance or the inside of their mugs, unnoticing of their surroundings, much less Dirk.

The ale was set before him with a frothing head that slid down the side of the mug to add to its appeal. Dirk offered a thankful nod and put back the beer with a long guzzle.

"Another, if you would," he said as he wiped froth from his mouth.

The bartender gave him a strange look and eyed his clothes, particularly his cloak. He refilled Dirk's glass swiftly and set it before him. "It takes a good bit of work and time to brew good beer. It is nice to see it enjoyed," said the bartender.

Dirk was tempted to tell the man he didn't need to be taught how to drink beer, but he thought better of it. He did not need to be drawing attention to himself. "The road makes one thirsty is all, good sir. I truly enjoyed your ale; I have had many lonely miles of cold and miserable road as of late. Your ale was my reward for the toil and patience. This one"—he raised his glass—"this one I shall savor."

"Glad you like 'em. 'Twas a good batch we had this time round. Keeps getting better with the makin'," the bartender boasted as he returned to wiping glasses.

Dirk nodded agreement and drank. He had not known how sore he was until now. Every ache and pain he had acquired from riding so hard now screamed its reminder. He had medicated darts and even healing trinkets, but if he used them for every menial pain he felt, they would soon be spent. Dirk saved such things for times of true need.

He finished his beer and set payment and a fine tip on the bar. As he left, the bartender called behind him. "Thank you, sir, and mention our house brew to any who might ask of such things. The Bearded Goat is the name."

"Will do," Dirk said over his shoulder and walked out into the midday sun.

He gathered up Frostmore's reins and walked through town for a bit to work out his stiff legs. Though he would rather not tarry, such things were necessary if he was going to make the long ride able to stand, much less fight. His growing anxiety would devour him before he got to Kell-Torey if he let it. He needed to remain calm and focused. Stressful situations were his business; he would not let himself come apart over this one. To clear his mind, he focused on what he knew.

Eadon wished Whill's Eldalonian kin dead. He had first tasked Dirk himself with the killing of every man, woman, and child related to Whill. Dirk had heard the tales and knew the stories, but more often than not, stories were just that. They often grew as large as the many tellers' imaginations, becoming grander with each telling. But for Eadon to order the royalty of Eldalon killed, Dirk knew the stories had to be true. Whill was the rightful king of Uthen-Arden, being Queen Celestra's son.

Krentz had sworn fealty as payment for Dirk's freedom. It was she whom Eadon would task with the deed now. Kreshka had mentioned a great winged beast flying overhead. Had that been Krentz upon a dragon, or gods knew what twisted creation of her father's? Dirk was not quick to take the man's word, being the crazy drunkard he had seemed. But Dirk was unsettled by his proclamations. The man had known things. And though Dirk was slow to admit it to himself, he feared that the man's every word was true.

"She is the harbinger of death." The words echoed in his mind until Dirk cursed to himself to shut up, which gained him a strange look from many passersby. He patted Frostmore and gave the horse a few strokes. He forgot his sore legs and aching body and mounted the horse. With a few clicks of encouragement from Dirk, Frostmore led them through the town and closer to the Ky'Dren Pass.

One more town separated him from the pass towers and the pass itself. The town was of no consequence, but the towers posed a far greater problem. The ancient towers had once been used to house thousands of soldiers during the times of war between Eldalon and Uthen-Arden. Though the warring had been brief, back centuries before when borders were being disputed around the mountains, the conflict had ended with a massive dwarven force pouring into the pass. The dwarven king then claimed the pass to be dwarf land, between the mountains and stretching to their very base on each side. They then destroyed all military outposts within said territory, Eldalonian and Uthen-Arden alike. The two human kings had not been pleased with the claim, but they had not disputed it. To fight the dwarves on the issue would have been disastrous.

The pass towers on the Uthen-Arden side of the mountains had survived the sacking by the dwarves. They now stood as relics of a time lost to history, though they remained manned with soldiers.

Always had the pass been open, but now, with a war raging throughout the lands, the pass was closed to any of Uthen-Arden. The Ky'Dren dwarves had sided with Eldalon and Eadon's opposition. And as such, they were at war with Uthen-Arden.

Times were rough for the once-thriving towns along the eastern spine of Ky'Dren, as the dwarves had cut off trade to the kingdom completely. Though the stop of trade hurt the dwarves as well, it only strengthened Eldalon's economy. With Uthen-Arden cut off from the dwarf trade, Eldalon was the sole supplier to the dwarves, with the exception of the dwarven sea trade to other countries, though it compared not to the heavy land trade.

Dirk did not feel like explaining himself to any soldiers, and intended a far berth around the five towers set in a semicircle a mile apart at the base of the mountains, guarding the miles wide opening to the pass. Getting by the dwarves would be another thing altogether. Any man attempting to sneak through it was mad. It was virtually impossible, given that at the pass' most narrow was built a two-hundred-foot-tall metal gate, guarded by hearty dwarves tougher than the stone they called home.

Dirk's anxiety grew as he traveled down the pass road. Already the towers were coming into view as the land flattened into a valley leading to the roots of the mountain range. If Krentz had passed overhead and was on her way to Kell-Torey, there was no way he would be in time to stop her. He didn't have time to sneak through the pass; he needed to get through as quickly as possible. He needed to tell the truth. He had knowledge of a plot to kill the royal family of Eldalon, a king who to Dirk's knowledge was a good and just man.

Dirk kicked Frostmore's flanks and mud flew in their wake as they darted off toward Tower's Watch. Fog had begun to roll down the mountain with the waning of the afternoon, and overhead the gray clouds choked out the blue sky. Dirk stopped only to let Frostmore drink from a trough within the village before he was off again, followed by the scowl of the establishment owner. He barely took in the village around him; his eyes and mind alike were set to the distant Ky'Dren Pass.

In a blur of yelping and scrambling villagers, a few of whom were grazed by the big stallion, Dirk flew through town. Frostmore doubled his speed once out of civilization. He raced with a determination to match his new master, as if reveling in a rider of equal endurance and strength.

As the road led down into the sparsely treed valley, Dirk withdrew the timber-wolf figurine and called to his hunter.

"Come, Chief! Adventure waits."

Ghost mist swirled out of the figurine and Chief came to form against a blurred backdrop of racing earth. The wolf solidified on the run and gave a howl at finding himself in the midst of such a swift hunt. He looked across to Dirk and awaited the details.

"We charge toward the Ky'Dren Pass. There are those who would stop us from reaching it. If any try, take them out!"

Chief growled loudly in response and looked ahead hungrily as together, wolf, man, and horse charged on after the slowly dying sun. They veered off the road, which in this area did not change the terrain much. Frostmore never slowed and Chief charged ahead with supernatural speed into the fog to guide the horse. They tore through it recklessly, trusting in the timber-wolf spirit. The towers in the fog looked like mammoth obelisks, each with a glowing beacon atop. Dirk grimaced as they came through a thick patch of fog into beaming daylight. Though it was dreary out and clouds had won the heavenly battle, Dirk could be seen clearly now to any who might be looking. Quickly Chief led them to the closest patch of fog in the ocean of mist rolling from the mountainside.

No shouts or horns rang out in their wake; they had gone unseen thus far. The towers shifted as they went and were soon behind them. Dirk set his sights on the nearing Ky'Dren Pass and followed Chief through the slowly thinning cover. Rather than curse his luck that the fog was leaving, he was glad to have had it. With it they had flown unhindered where they would have otherwise been spotted.

Ahead was the true test, a fogless two-mile stretch of randomly guarded posts. They would surely be seen, but they could not be stopped. Dirk knew that Krentz would be slowed considerably having to fly over it. He doubted she would be dumb enough to fly through the pass.

A horn blast and distant calls of alarm rang out, and demands of name, title, and rank and commands to halt followed in Frostmore's charge. Dirk rode low to his saddle and brought his cloak around for protection. Chief suddenly dug in and came to a stop. Just as gracefully he shot off behind Dirk. It was but a moment before the startled whine of a horse and the cry of a terrified man rang out behind them. Chaos was left in Dirk's wake as Chief intercepted his pursuers.

Ahead the mountain split and on each side the walls seemed to open to welcome him in. A flag caught his eye and he watched as three riders, each wielding a lance and in full armor, moved into his path and began a charge that set the four on an unavoidable collision course.

"Chief!" Dirk called against the wind. The three lance-wielding knights spread out a horse's length and barreled in. From inside his boot Dirk took two darts, and with a quick apology to Frostmore, he stabbed them into the horse's neck. Frostmore jerked and protested briefly before the drug kicked in. Then he gave a startled cry of wild delight and charged toward the knights with renewed vigor that far surpassed his fastest speed yet.

Dirk gripped the reins so hard that his hands became numb with strain. His legs pumped to keep in rhythm and he quickly realized he would need strength to match Frostmore's. Carefully he reached back and retrieved a third dart from above his boot. He stabbed himself in the leg and put the dart back. The mechanism that held the darts swallowed the spent one and replaced it with a new one with a soft click of gears.

The distilled adrenaline from the blood of a terrified man coursed through Dirk's veins and caused the reins to seem loose. "Chief!" he screamed as the knights charged toward them. Dirk steered straight for the knight at the center as the other two knights took places behind him. He would have to face them all in turn.

Dirk gracefully jumped up to stand upon his saddle, and with a scream of "Chief!," he leapt forward as the lance of the charging knight bore down upon Frostmore. Dirk caught Frostmore's neck with his outstretched arms as his body twisted and a swift kick came down upon the shaft of the knight's lance. Dirk ran up the lance as its tip sank deep into the ground. The horses grazed each other as they passed around the dug-in lance. The assassin took two quick skipping steps up the lance and slammed a boot into the knight's helmet, knocking it flying off.

Dirk landed upon Frostmore's rear and clutched the saddle's back, while not ten feet away the next knight barreled in. Dirk unsheathed his sword, dropped back into his saddle, and gave a war cry. In the corner of his eye he saw a wisp of fog shoot past and slam into the charging horse and rider. Chief hit them with a force not lent from his weight. Horse and rider were thrown wide, and the timber wolf abandoned physical form and flew as writhing smoke. The third rider closed in and screamed in terror as Chief came to form on his back.

Dirk laughed as he urged Frostmore onward past the fallen knights. Another horn blew and the zing of arrows took to the sky. The barrage came sloping down upon them and Dirk threw up his cloak. Two arrows rattled off of his enchantment and another sunk into the saddle.

Dirk steered Frostmore toward the small watchtower from which the arrows had come. From his hip he took a thick dart. Carefully he twisted it at the middle and caused it to click twice. He threw the dart and it stuck to one of the supporting struts of the elevated tower. A second later there was a blast of smoke and fire and the groan of splintered wood. Dirk steered directly between the failing struts and threw another dart at the underside of the tower, which tilted and tipped with a protesting screech of wood. Dirk rode on as men scrambled out of the collapsed tower and another explosion destroyed what was left of it.

Dirk saw ahead that the chase had caught the attention of the dwarves. They waved, hooted and hollered, and cheered Dirk on as he charged toward the dwarven post. Arrows fell in his wake as Frostmore sped away twice as fast as his pursuers. Once he had passed the border, the dwarves closed up ranks behind him. The pursuing Uthen-Arden soldiers reined their horses to a stop before the border.

"This man has clearly broken our laws, and likely killed our soldiers. We demand that you hand him over for justice, in the name of King Addakon!" proclaimed an Uthen-Arden soldier.

Dirk had stopped a hundred feet beyond the dwarven border; he and his horse stood panting steam from their mouths into the cool evening air. The effects of the dart had still to wear off, and Dirk yet felt invincible. He knew the dwarves' aversion to elf magic or any sorcery, real or imagined. Therefore, while the dwarves were busy facing off with the swelling number of humans, he quietly dismissed Chief to his plane.

"Your King Addakon is dead. The dark elf Eadon has taken his place and assumed lordship over your lands. You blindly follow one who would see you all burn!" he told the soldiers, trying to gain the favor of the dwarves further.

The soldier sneered and trotted his horse down the line. "Lies!" he said over his shoulder, more to his men than Dirk.

"Are they?" said Dirk from across the dwarven barrier. "Why then do your men search each other's faces?"

The soldier—a general, given the braided golden sash over the right shoulder of his armor—looked at his men. He turned his horse, and with a sneer he dared a step closer to the border. The border was marked by a line of smooth stone half the size of a one-wagon road. It stretched on for miles in a straight line, connecting the two ranges that made up the Ky'Dren Mountains. The general's horse took another step, this time upon the stone border.

"Come a bit closer an' everyone here will agree that ye be trespassin' and so be deservin' what yer about to be getting'," said a gray-haired, wild-eyed dwarf, and dozens grumbled agreement. Human and dwarf soldiers alike tensed and waited for the general's next move.

The general stopped his horse in mid-step and his sneer disappeared. "You would threaten a general of the Uthen-Arden army? Where do you think this will lead, dwarf?" the general asked, but he did not advance.

"It be leadin' to an arse-whoopin', boy, and the name be Dar'Kwar!" yelled the old dwarf. "I got more dents on me forehead than ye got about yer whole shiny armor. This ain't a fight ye be wantin', laddie."

The general looked speechless for a moment but quickly recovered. "Our fight is not with you...this day. Let the man in black face me here upon the stones of the pass border. Dwarves such as you enjoy a good fight, do you not?"

He dismounted from his horse and let it be taken by a soldier. He stood upon the stone border, his heels resting upon the Uthen-Arden side. With a slow, purposeful pull, he withdrew his short sword and accepted a handed shield, as the metallic song of his blade rang out through the still air. The sun had begun to set behind the mountain range, illuminating the dark clouds with the colors of twilight. Overhead the sky looked to be from a dream.

The general was a big man, yet he was comfortable in his familiar armor. Dar'Kwar's proclamation of "boy" had not truly been befitting for one of his size. He looked to be in his early forties and his hard eyes and weathered skin told a tale of their own. Dirk did not doubt that he had seen battle in his day, but neither did he have the time to prove himself. Unfortunately, the dwarves had perked up at the mention of a fight between the two. They looked at Dirk and the gray-haired dwarf, who appeared to be their commander. Dar'Kwar crossed his arms. "It be yer move, lad."

Dirk gave Frostmore a calming stroke and dismounted. The horse looked ready for another mad dash. Dirk unsheathed his mind-control dagger and the dwarven hook sword from beneath his cloak. The dwarven blade got the reaction he had been counting on from the dwarves: they clapped and hooted for Dirk.

Not to be outdone, the general turned and raised his arms to the sky, gaining a cheer from his men. It was the wrong thing to do around Dirk. The assassin sped across the stretch of hard-packed earth and across the stone border. He planted a foot on the general's back before any of his men could utter warning.

"Ooohh," muttered many of the dwarves and men alike as the general was sent flying and staggering forward to fall on his face many feet from the border stones.

The general shot to his feet, and a cheer issued from his men. Dirk was impressed with his speed. The formidable veteran general gave Dirk's boots a knowing glance and smirked at him as he looked him over with newfound interest. He slowly stalked his way back to the stone border and threw down his sword and shield. Reaching across his body, he began to unstrap his armor. Loudly he addressed them all.

"This outlaw has the advantage of enchanted armor, weapons, and trinkets. He is a spawn of the enemy's draggard whores, no doubt!" Armor fell from him as he spoke. "You all saw how he flew across the ground like a coward at my back, his feet fueled by elven devilry!" He threw aside his breastplate and bracers. "Let him face me as a man! Let him face General Straun with but his bare hands."

The last of his armor hit the ground and he stood there naked before them all. Dirk rolled his eyes and held back a colorful vulgarity. The dwarves were sold, it seemed, for at the mention of elven devilry, their attitudes had shifted quickly. They had, after all, seen Dirk's impossible speed firsthand. General Strawn had been smart in forcing a bare brawl, smart enough to realize he could not defeat Dirk armed.

Dirk had three options: surrender, kill the general and likely be killed by the humans and dwarves alike, or fight naked. He unlatched his cloak and threw it to the old dwarf.

By now a crowd of a hundred dwarves and Uthen-Arden soldiers had come to witness the fight. The wind picked up and a light rain began to fall, leaving the border stones and the general's muscular form glistening in the waning twilight.

Dirk added the last of his gear to the pile and stepped barefoot onto the slick stones. Ten feet away, General Strawn did the same.

The general had numerous scars across his body; it appeared that he had been in his share of battles indeed. He was a head taller than Dirk and nearly twice his size, with thick, knotted muscles covering his lean body. His thick black body hair only added to his beastly appearance in the quickly growing downpour.

Dirk did not have the tree-trunk arms like General Straun, but neither was he weak. The two men circled each other as lightning suddenly ripped through the heavens, and thunder boomed, shaking the ground. Oil-soaked torches were lit by both men and dwarves. The twilight sky was at that most transcendent point, when the vales between night and day collided for a time. Shadows were born slowly across the land; this was a time when phantoms of the twilight swam in and out of one's vision. It was said that in the twilight the spirit world was opened, and ghosts could be seen in the corner of the eye. Dirk's father had taught him that this strange time was the best for executing an ambush. Men's eyes played tricks on them when shadow and light collided, and if you could move like a phantom, you could move unseen.

The men paced faster now as the torrent of cool rain shone as a million burning drops on their skin. Fists cut through the rain as both men took a shot at the other. Dirk had only feigned the punch after seeing the general's eyes decide to strike. Rather than punch, Dirk sent Straun's strike down and wide with a blocking arm.

He was inside the big man's reach in a flash and landed a swift elbow to the chin that sent the general staggering back. Dirk leapt with a quick spin and brought a heavy kick down meant for Straun's neck. But the big man was faster than he looked. Straun deflected the kick and countered with a sweeping kick of his own. Dirk went with the momentum of the trip. He leapt from the one planted leg, and it looked as though he would smash his head against the stone. In a great show of strength, Dirk caught himself with his hands, and arching his body he leapt with his arms back onto his feet.

Straun attacked with a barrage of fists, forcing Dirk back and blocking frantically. Dirk's heel found the edge of the stone border on the dwarven side and he began an assault of his own. Both hands came from his chest as he double-blocked a jab and hook. As Straun's hands went wide, Dirk brought his in to box the general's ears. The blow landed and Straun jerked and screamed in agony.

Stumbling back, Straun found his left hand bloody from his ear. His nostrils flared as his murderous eyes found the assassin. Like a charging bull blind with rage, the big man charged and Dirk did the same. A big right hand came barreling in toward Dirk's head as he twisted around and under the blow. Coming up behind Straun, he kicked him in the rear as he passed. Straun had anticipated the strike and arched his body forward with it, lessening its impact. He recovered quickly and stalked Dirk in a circle, waiting for the assassin to attack. Soon the general seemed to realize that Dirk was not attacking, only reacting. With a growl he came in swinging. Dirk blocked the blows and countered with a body blow that the solid man absorbed easily. Straun landed his first punch, and though it was a glancing blow that rolled off Dirk's chin, it sent the watching soldiers into a frenzy of cheers.

Dirk reached up and, pretending to nurse a sore jaw, took hold of a fake tooth and twisted it. He bit the fake tooth, crushed it, and swirled the liquid in his mouth. Straun came in hard again with a barrage of fists. Dirk turned them aside without backing off, and when Straun came in too hard, Dirk made him regret it with a quick jab that left the big man's nose bloody. In a rage Straun barreled in, and ignoring Dirk's rib-crushing flurry of punches caught hold of the assassin's arm and tried to take him to the ground with a sweep of his legs. Dirk shifted his weight and with a twist brought them both crashing to the stone.

Dirk wrestled himself on top of the general and rained hammer fists down on his nose, sending blood spraying. Straun punched up from below, unable to connect with anything but a glancing blow. Straun threw Dirk from him in a rage but the assassin was on him in a flash, choking him from behind. Straun immediately lurched backward in an attempt to crush Dirk beneath him and shake him loose. Dirk bit the big man on the neck as hard as he could and forced the liquid from his mouth into the wound. Straun screamed and raked at Dirk's eyes but the assassin quickly shoved away from the howling man.

"You!" Straun spat, accusation bathing his voice as he held his neck. "What have you done, you sneaky coward?" He stumbled and nearly fell across the border onto dwarf land.

"It seems I have won," Dirk answered nonchalantly, wiping dirt and blood from his arm. Lightning crashed upon the mountainside and the big Uthen-Arden general charged the assassin with murder in his eyes. Dirk met the man blow for blow and noticed as the poison went to work.

"The harder you fight, the sooner you will die," Dirk warned and slammed a quick jab into Straun's chin. Straun roared and with surprising speed hit Dirk with a powerful uppercut that sent the assassin flying back. Dirk wavered but recovered quickly, cursing himself for letting his guard down. If the fist had been a blade…but it seemed that Straun had used the last of his strength in the blow, and now he panted upon his knees. Dirk walked to the poisoned and beaten man. "Admit defeat in this match and I shall provide you with the antidote."

Straun looked up at Dirk weakly, impotent fury burning in his eyes. "I know who you are, with your tricks and trinkets and a dagger up your arse," Straun spat, and fell into a coughing fit that left the rain to wash away blood. "You are the assassin Dirk...Black..." Straun grabbed his stomach and wavered on the brink of consciousness. "You...killed my...ahh!" He screamed as the poison ran its course. "My brother...Wren..." Again he fell into coughing.

The Arden soldiers urged their general to get up, to keep fighting. The dwarves became restless at the inaction. "Be ye beat or be ye fightin', Uthen man?" a dwarf yelled.

Straun grabbed Dirk's calf and squeezed as convulsions wracked his body. "Wrendel Kwarren. You know the name. Wrend..." He shuddered and fell to the stone.

Dirk knelt down to the dying man's ear and whispered, "Your brother was killed because he owed a very powerful man a fortune—a fortune he lost after his child slavery ring was destroyed. Your brother was as low as they come, and he got what he had coming to him."

Straun twitched and thrashed with rage as Dirk strode across the stone border toward the mountain pass. Immediately two soldiers moved to retrieve their general. They dragged him across the stone and a medic began working on him in vain. The only thing that would help Straun was the antidote. Dirk himself was immune to the poison and many others due to his methodical taking of them in small amounts.

Dirk retrieved a dart from his gear and skidded it across the border. "That is the only thing that will help your dear general," he said to the soldiers. He returned to his gear and began to dress. The gray-haired dwarf eyed him with a frown.

"What was that ye did to make him falter?" asked Dar'Kwar.

Dirk pulled on his pants and looked at the dwarf incredulously. "I punched him in the face. Ain't you ever seen a fight?"

"Ye know what I be meanin' you did."

Dirk only shrugged and put on his shirt, coat, and cloak. "All I know is that I won the fight, and now with your blessing I will continue on my journey, for I bring important information to Eldalon that may determine the fate of the royal family themselves."

Dirk moved to mount Frostmore but a strong dwarven hand stopped him. "I heard the man call ye Dirk Black-thorn." He searched Dirk's eyes. The assassin wondered if word from Roakore about Dirk had yet spread this far, if at all. He did not know if the king had returned. Dirk looked at the dwarf's hand, but the gray-beard was not to be intimidated. "I am Dirk Blackthorn. I am friend to Whill of Agora, Rhunis the dragon slayer, and your king Roakore."

"Roakore, ye be sayin'? It ain't wise to be utterin' lies with the name o' me king tied to 'em," Dar'Kwar warned.

"He is a wide-shouldered dwarf, about this tall. Wild brownish red hair, big axe, kind of moody."

Dar'Kwar scowled, obviously not finding the dark man funny. Dirk pulled his arm loose and mounted Frostmore. "What will it be, good dwarf, shall I be given passage or nay? If not, I must go now with all haste around the mountains to the sea, possibly to the cost of your king's allies, and Whill's line."

At the mention of Whill's family line, the dwarf perked up and his scowl disappeared. He knew as well as any other Ro'Sar dwarf the high esteem in which Roakore held Whill, and the friendship they had forged. It had been for Whill that the king had left his mountain.

"I will see you through the pass meself," Dar'Kwar said.

The dwarves waited behind for the Uthen-Arden soldiers to withdraw as Dirk headed for the pass.

"Assassin!" Straun bellowed from the border. His soldiers had given him the antidote and he stood in the rain shaking his fist. Dirk and the dwarf turned to regard the furious man.

"I will not soon forget you, Dirk Blackthorn!" Straun bellowed.

"Thank you! I usually only get that reassurance from the ladies!" Dirk retorted, and turned once again for the pass.

CHAPTER NINETEEN
Dwarves at Sea

The dwarves awoke with the sunshine and groaned one and all. The ale had flowed freely the night before, as had the elven spirits. And even though Roakore himself felt as though a dragon were kicking him in the temples, he roused the others. He kicked dwarves in the shins and hollered orders.

"If you be feelin' like shyte, it be 'cause ye can't be controllin' yerselves and that be your own doin'! Get your lazy arses up, we got a boat to catch!"

After a breakfast of fish and bread, the company stood before a great fin-sailed elven warship. It had been sent to await the dwarf king's arrival. Roakore admired the ship with awe. He noticed Tarren at his side looking quite ill and patted the lad's shoulder. "Mark me words, boy, I be gettin' me one o' these."

Tarren had seen that wide-eyed look before, when Roakore had promised him that he would one day own a silver hawk. But the boy too stared at the great ship in wonder. With such a vessel he could chase down any pirate of the sea. He could rid the world of them all. Tarren imagined himself and Helzendar, maybe even elves, sailing the seas of Agora and beyond, hunting down the murderous scum.

"C'mon, Silverwind!" Roakore yelled to the sky. Two fingers disappeared under his dark beard and he whistled. "There be room enough for ye on the ship!" But the silver hawk did not appear.

The dwarves made their way onto the ship, many of them grumbling low and eying the vessel beneath them suspiciously. The deck was not planked but seemed to be made of a single piece of wood, black and polished to a high sheen. The rail was three entwined vines as thick as oak branches. The three masts seemed to grow out of the deck, and from them long sails billowed in the wind.

Roakore was the last dwarf on board and he whistled to Silverwind one last time. Still the bird did not appear. "Bah!" He turned, grumbling about stupid birds, and boarded the ship.

"Have you sailed before?" Nafiel asked as they began to turn out of the harbor.

Roakore looked for rowers or any explanation as to how they were moving. "Aye, I sailed plenty, but never on an elven ship."

"Ah." Nafiel smiled. "Then you should enjoy this."

The warship left the harbor slowly and was soon sailing northeast across the Gulf of Arden. Tarren and Helzendar joined Roakore and Nafiel at the front of the ship. There was little wind and the elven ship moved along at a slow pace as the group looked out over the waters.

Roakore looked at Nafiel with an arched brow. "Be this all she got?" he asked, unimpressed.

Nafiel grinned at that and hollered to the captain, "The good dwarf king Roakore wishes to see her best speed."

The captain nodded and bellowed a command in Elvish. From below deck came four elves who quickly made their way to the stern and stood shoulder to shoulder. Roakore looked on curiously, as did the rest of his men.

"I suggest you find a grip upon the rail," Nafiel warned as he himself wrapped an arm around it. Roakore scoffed at that and waited for the four elves to do something.

The elves began chanting in unison and raised their arms to the heavens. What wind had been at their backs died and Roakore laughed and shook his head. His men joined in and released the rail, now feeling silly for having held onto it. But then the wind picked up, slowly at first, then growing until the sails were full and the ship was speeding through the still waters. Still the dwarves did not see the need for the security of the rail. Nevertheless, Roakore nodded to Nafiel, pleased.

Roakore was about to say that the speed of the ship left much to legend when a huge gale took his breath away and the ship lurched forward as if something had slammed into it. The elves chanted all the louder and the gale doubled in strength. Roakore was thrown, slamming into a cannon with a ping. He got to his feet laughing, and using the rail he fought the momentum of the ship and returned to Nafiel. Tarren was still laughing, and Nafiel tried without success to hide his smile.

"Now this be sailin'!" Roakore roared over the gale as the ship sliced through the waters at breakneck speed.

"Your bird seems to have changed her mind," Nafiel yelled over the conjured wind.

Roakore spun his head back and forth and spotted Silverwind behind the ship. She gave a squawk and pumped her wings to catch up.

"Fly, girl, fly!" Roakore laughed, but his words were drowned by the wind. "Nafiel, let's slow her down a bit an' let me bird catch up, eh?"

The elf turned and motioned for less speed. Everyone lurched forward as the wind wielders let up on their spell work. Silverwind caught up quickly and circled the ship. The dwarves cheered and coaxed her to come aboard but she would have none of it. She squawked angrily and disappeared, changing the color of her feathers to match the sky above. There was a delighted murmur from the elves aboard and laughter from the dwarves.

"I think yer bird be pissed!" Philo laughed and took a long drink from a frothing mug.

Roakore scowled at him and slapped the mug from Philo's lips. "No drinkin'! Ye be on dut—"

Roakore suddenly flew over the rail and sailed through the sky, out over the dark waters of the Gulf of Arden. "What ye doin', ye damned crazy bird!" he bellowed and beat upon invisible talons.

Silverwind changed back to her natural color and the dwarves and elves alike laughed to see such a spectacle. Roakore hung kicking and screaming from Silverwind's claws. The bird circled the ship and dropped unceremoniously Roakore into the water.

"Dwarf overboard!" yelled Philo.

"Bah, he'll be all right. He ain't wore no armor since we entered Elladrindellia, he ain't about to be sinkin'," said Holdagozz as Nafiel scrambled to keep Roakore in sight as the ship passed by.

"But can he swim?" asked Tarren, concerned.

"Yer damned right, me king be a swimmer. Look!" Helzendar pointed and everyone looked. The ship had slowed to a stop and the dwarves cheered their king on as he swam to them.

Nafiel went to the stern and almost fell overboard as Tarren bumped into him.

"Sorry." He smiled sheepishly.

Nafiel only smiled and pushed back the right sleeve of his lokata. He extended his hand toward Roakore and the swimming dwarf was thrust up onto the suddenly bulging water. The water rose beneath Roakore and snaked up and over the ship. Roakore landed with a splash at the bow of the ship to the many cheers of the dwarves.

He got to his feet, soaking wet and swearing. Silver-wind flew overhead and gave a cry. The wind wielders began their chanting anew and the ship set off once again for Cerushia.

Tarren stood at the bow long after the dwarves had been shown to their quarters below. A barrel of ale had gone with them and already the boat shook to the rhythm of stomping feet. He could not wait to see Whill again. The last he had seen of him had been seven months ago in Kell-Torey. Nafiel had informed him that the ship would make it to Cerushia by early morn-ing. For Tarren, it would be a long and sleepless night.

CHAPTER TWENTY
The Greatest Enemy is Thy Self

Whill would not tell Avriel about the Other. He could not, not yet. He still had to work out what in the hells was going on for himself. He convinced her to let it go after too long, telling her he only wanted to fly and to rest his mind. She looked at the open tomes and projected her smile.

"Come then, we shall explore the rivers," she bade him, and lowered her shoulder.

Thankful for her understanding, he climbed up and strapped in. When she was sure he was secure, she took two leaping steps and dove over the balcony and fell with the waters of the falls. To Whill's shock, she did not extend her wings at all and dove straight into the cool frothing waters. They dove deep, and when finally Avriel emerged, she swam up swiftly and shot out of the water and into the sky. Water fell from her glowing white scales like rain as she soared toward the moon.

For nearly an hour they flew in silence. Avriel gave Whill the space she knew he needed, and he was grateful for that. He wondered if he was crazy, and laughing at that he wondered how crazy he was. Could the Other truly be more than a delusion? Could he have his own sense of self outside of Whill? The Other believed it, and the implications of this did not escape Whill. But the thought remained: what if the Other was somehow created or implanted inside Whill's mind? The Other might not even know it—or worse yet, he did know it and was meant to betray Whill. If Whill gave in to the Other, and together they somehow took from Eadon the sword of power taken, would the Other then destroy Whill's mind and betray him? This and many questions filled his mind as they flew out over the jungle.

Sensing Whill's tired weight, Avriel flew them back to their abode. Whill climbed down, exhausted, and found his bed easily. He was soon asleep, within the realm of the Other.

The nightmares found him quickly, and memories of his torture troubled his sleep. In one his legs were hacked off by a swinging pendulum, only to be healed as the blade swung away and then returned swiftly. But the worst dreams were the memories of what he had done. Men and women alike were put before him, and the dark elves' promise of an end to the pain should he himself take up the tools of torture. Whill had not been able to resist long.

He awoke in a cold sweat with a strangled cry to the soothing voice of Avriel.

It is all right, Whill, I am here.

"Avriel!" he panted and looked around wildly.

You were dreaming. It is over now, the Other is gone.

"What did you say?"

You spoke a name in your sleep—the Other.

Whill shivered. "What did I say?"

You said…you said that he did terrible things. "He killed them," you said over and over.

Whill put his hands to his hair in manic frustration. "What is happening to me?" he pleaded, realizing that the Other was exercising control over him. These were the Other's thoughts and feelings, not Whill's. He cleared his mind and fought for control, and eventually he found it. Long, deep breaths brought him back to himself and calmed him. Avriel looked on with worry etching her scaled brow.

"I need to eat." Whill forced a smile and squinted at the bright morning light. "How long have I slept?"

The entire day and night. I was worried you would not wake.

"I am all right now," he assured her and went to the vast pantry. After a large meal of vegetables, fish, and tea, he felt more himself. He had needed the rest, as fitful as it was. He still had the books to study and now only four days left to do it in. He returned to his place among the tomes and began anew the book of the Ralliad. Avriel curled up near the balcony ledge and slept lightly while he studied.

Against the advice of the Watcher, Whill had tampered with his own mind. He had somehow inadvertently freed the Other from his mental prison. But he had also been successful in expanding his own memory and capacity for learning. The tome before him came alive in his mind. He flipped through pages quickly, gleaning all of the information with but a glance. It was not even dark when he finished the book of the Ralliad. Excitedly he tore into the next in line, *The Way of the Warrior.*

Whill absorbed every word, saw clearly in his mind's eye every technique and form, and soon had devoured that tome as well. It went the same for the remainder of the books. Page after page flew before his eyes as he scanned them. He called upon his sword when he felt the ache of such long sitting, or when his focus wavered. By the end of the next day he had finished all seven tomes, and his head swam with the great amounts of information he had gained. He was exhilarated to learn that he could call upon any chapter or page from the tomes at will, seeing the words anew with but a thought. He could not wait to practice his newfound knowledge.

Avriel had left early in the afternoon, but Whill had been too absorbed in his trance-like study to say good-bye. Now she returned and Whill ran to her.

"I have finished them all!" he proclaimed joyfully.

How can that be?

"It is not important right now," Whill answered, dodging the question for the time being. He was not sure if what he had done to his mind would be frowned upon. "I think I can help you return to elven form. But you must know something before you consider it."

Over the next hour Whill explained to Avriel what had happened. He told her about the Other, and the offer he had made. Avriel listened intently, interrupting with only a few questions here and there. Whill was afraid she would think him crazy, and rightly so. But he had to tell someone, and he was glad he had. Avriel did not stand in judgment; rather she looked upon Whill with concern.

This…Other, she began. *He says that he is the reason for your abilities since your torture? And he claims to know the spells necessary for my transformation?*

"Yes, that is his claim," Whill concurred. "Do you think that this is a trick of Eadon's?"

Avriel thought long on that. *It is hard to say. He tortured you those long months for a reason, it would seem, beyond his hoping to instill a murderous hatred for him. Likely his plans are twofold. It is possible that Eadon intentionally split your mind in two in hope that the Other would eventually take control.*

Whill nodded his agreement. Avriel went on. *If what the Other says is true, and together you can defeat Eadon, take from him the blade of power taken, I cannot see the Other's acquisition of the blade ending well.*

"Nor I," Whill admitted. "I should speak of this with the Watcher."

Can you control the Other?

Whill remembered how easily the Other had left him a babbling mess, with only a few mental projections of his tortured memories. "I do not know," he answered. "If I cannot...I possess Adromida, and therefore so does he."

And this Other, you say he is the embodiment of your ego?

"Yes—no—it is possible that he is the embodiment of my tortured self, the...pain body."

Avriel looked out beyond the balcony in silence. Whill sensed a shift in her mind, a sorrow. He guessed she was contemplating the transformation, what it would mean to her dragon form. Whill walked to her side and laid a gentle hand upon her muscled shoulder. Her scales were smooth as glass beneath his hand. He noticed her tears and gazed out over the city with her.

What will become of this body when I am gone? Avriel asked the night.

"I do not know," said Whill. He sighed quietly, wishing he had all the answers, wishing for once he could help her.

We shall see. We do not even know if you can do it. I must think about this. Avriel stood. *The dragon-lore masters seek my presence as always. Do you wish to come with me?*

Whill looked at the tomes he had devoured. He mentally flipped through pages in his mind at random and knew that he had retained it all. He shrugged and stepped up into the saddle. "I would love to hear your tales."

CHAPTER TWENTY-ONE

Through the Ky'Dren Pass

Dirk followed Dar'Kwar through the many miles of the Ky'Dren Pass. He was pleased that the dwarf had heeded his words and pushed his dwarven horse at a good pace throughout the night. Soon the sun rose behind them and Dirk saw far off in the distance the mouth to the pass and Eldalon beyond.

The night had been a dark and cloudy one, the thunderstorm having played out, leaving the world wet, dark, and silent. Wind barely stirred here between the high mountain cliffs, where at their highest the walls of the pass reached a thousand feet. Dirk knew that below him ran hundreds of tunnels connecting the two mountains. Legend even had it that beneath Agora ran thousands of miles of tunnels connecting all three dwarven kingdoms. Many, however, doubted that claim, arguing as they always did that the dwarves were known to make the long aboveground journey to see their kin, and if they had underground tunnels to travel, why use the roads? But every time a sinkhole was heard of somewhere in Agora, people thought it was proof of dwarf tunnels.

Dirk imagined having to live or travel through those tight spots and enclosed spaces on a daily basis. The idea caused him to shudder. He was a man who always had an escape plan. Before Dirk even entered a building, he liked to have two escape routes, if not three. Being trapped under those low ceilings with only forward or backward to go would be maddening for him.

Now that the sun had come up, Dirk could see clearly what had only been hinted at by the occasional far-off lantern along the pass wall. He had drawn his hood over his face and, in looking through it, had seen the pass walls occasionally, but he was not going to strain the magic within it with hours-long use. It was much too great a tool to be misused. With his hood he could hide his face from any, while being himself able to see clearly through it, night or day.

Now with the sun's light he saw the awe-inspiring monument which was the Ky'Dren Pass. At some spots along the thirty-mile pass, the walls looked like castles. Towers grew out of the walls along the pass, and arching bridges connecting railway systems there were both high and low. Pillars were carved below great buildings both large and small, and monolithic monuments towered over travelers, statues of gods, heroes, and kings alike adorning both walls for miles.

One statue in particular caused Dirk to insist on stopping and taking pause. The statue of Ky'Dren loomed five hundred feet above the pass, said to have been made for him by his son, who, like his father and his descendants, could move stone with but a thought. The statue depicted Ky'Dren, the first dwarven king, standing tall and strong with one foot on each side of the pass, connecting the northern and southern mountains. He stood with an axe in one hand and his pick in the other. Atop his head sat his crown and his armor was covered in silver.

Dirk was awestruck by the statue and thought on it for hours. To be held in such esteem as to be commemorated so laboriously and venerated for thousands of years after you were gone was an incredible feat. But Dirk knew also that nothing lasted forever, and as the stars saw one day to the next, so too would they see Ky'Dren's statue fall and be forgotten. The stars turned, as did the wheels of time, and only the gods bore witness to all things, and only the dead remembered.

Dirk needed sleep, as did Frostmore, but he had no time for such pleasantries. He knew that the horse could not take much more of this. Already Frostmore was thrashing randomly and chomping impatiently at his bridle. Dirk needed a fresh horse, loath as he was to depart with Frostmore. The horse had proven to be a good one.

An hour more they rode and finally came to the dwarven outpost on the Eldalonian side of the pass.

"'Ere then," said Dar'Kwar. "Here we will find food and drink. You and your horse be lookin' like rest wouldn't hurt ye, neither."

Dirk dismounted with a grimace and took a moment to steady his legs. He had been riding for days and felt every bump in the road. He knuckled his back and stretched before following the dwarf to the nearby outpost.

The dwarven outpost was more like a town than anything else. Here trade between the dwarves and the people of Eldalon thrived still. It was early morning and already the markets were crowded with dwarves and humans alike. Here were human tailors, farmers, medicine men, and other peddlers. Long caravans filled with vegetables and livestock meandered up the many mountain trails, and likewise, dwarven wagons came down, likely filled with kingly treasures.

There were also Eldalonian soldiers within the pass marketplace. They, however, were more interested in armor and arms than jewels and the like. Dirk followed Dar'Kwar to a group of his kin and accepted a steaming pot of porridge gratefully. As he ate, he eyed the Eldalonian soldiers, looking for the highest-ranking man among them. He found what he sought as a tent flap opened and out strode an armored soldier adorned with the telltale golden sash of a general. Dirk handed off his bowl with a thank you to the dwarves and headed toward the man. Dar'Kwar followed.

The man stood facing the morning sun with closed eyes. "Excuse me," Dirk said to the man's back, and he turned and regarded Dirk curiously.

"What is it?" He turned his face to take in the day's warmth once again.

"I have information that may mean life and death to the royal family. I seek your audience," said Dirk in a low voice as to not attract attention.

The general looked Dirk over with renewed interest and then at Dar'Kwar behind him. "Please," he said, gesturing toward his large tent. "We shall speak inside."

Dirk entered the tent, followed by Dar'Kwar. The general closed the flaps behind them. "Please, sit." He indicated to the chairs opposite his long desk. "Care for a drink?" he asked as he poured himself a dark amber whiskey.

"Please," said Dirk.

"Mind dwarven whiskey, or is it too early?" the general asked them both.

"Bah, be it ever too early for dwarven whiskey?" asked Dar'Kwar with all seriousness.

"Whiskey is fine," answered Dirk.

The general set the drinks on the desk and squared on the two. "I like to know who I am drinking with." He took a moment looking at the dwarf. "Dar'Kwar, I believe, from near Uthen-Arden side?"

"Aye, Dar'Kwar I be."

"You, however, I do not know," he said to Dirk. "If I had to guess, I would say sword for hire."

Dirk only nodded. "Blackthorn, Dirk. Well met…?"

"General Harris Steely," replied the general, offering his hand as he eyed Dirk.

Dirk shook it and General Steely took his seat. "Dirk Blackthorn. Where have I heard that name before?"

"I do not know, General," Dirk replied. "I have not ventured often or for long within Eldalon. Any word of me would have likely come from Uthen-Arden. Just as likely those words are false, given the tongues of those speaking them."

"Hmm." The general still eyed Dirk with a hint of speculation. "Not a friend of Uthen-Arden, I take it."

"Not as of late," replied Dirk and took a swig of the whiskey.

Dar'Kwar laughed and drank also. "Not as of late, indeed. This one came charging through the Uthen-Arden ranks in a race for the border night last. Was challenged to a bare-arsed duel by one General Straun, he was. And won the fight, I should add."

"General Straun. I know of him. He made it through the ranks under King Addakon—he's just the kind of scum Addakon likes. Did you kill him?"

"He will live," Dirk replied coolly.

General Steely nodded and shot back his drink. "I assume you were racing for the border to warn Eldalon of this danger you speak of. What do you know?"

"I have knowledge of a conspiracy to kill the entire Eldalonian royal family line. With your cooperation, I hope to make all haste to Kell-Torey to warn the king."

General Steely mulled over Dirk's words. "Who is behind this conspiracy?"

"The dark elf lord Eadon wishes it so. He wants to wipe out Whill's entire line," Dirk answered.

"This Whill you speak of, he is the one said to be the rightful king of Uthen-Arden?" the general asked, intrigued.

"They are one and the same, sir, yes."

"And what is your stake in this, Dirk Blackthorn? By the looks of you I would say that you are a blade for hire. Surely you are not a soldier. Why should I believe you? Suppose you are trying to get close to the king for the very reason you warn of?"

"I wish to see Eadon's every plot and aspiration fail. I wish to see him dead. If I can be a thorn in his side, then I will do everything within my abilities to do so."

"Why?" the general asked.

Dirk ground his teeth as he thought of Krentz. "I have my reasons."

The general stood from his desk and poured refills for them all. He drank from his glass as his eyes wandered in thought. Finally he returned to his seat and clasped his hands together upon his desk and met Dirk's waiting eyes.

"I consider myself a good judge of character," the general began, and Dirk fought to not roll his eyes. "And you, sir, I do not trust. There is much you have not told me."

Dirk had the urge to stab the man in the neck. He didn't have time for this. He was about to get up when the general's demeanor changed.

"But there may be truth to your words. A claim such as this cannot be taken lightly. Is there anything more you wish to tell me?"

"Only that every minute we tarry may be detrimental to your good king's health."

"Well," said Dar'Kwar. "Me work be done here. I thank ye for the whiskey, General. Now I return to me post." He slammed a fist to his chest with a slight bow to the general, nodded at Dirk, and made for the door.

"I do not have to remind you that what you have heard is not to be repeated, do I, Dar'Kwar?" said the general to the dwarf's back.

"No, Steely, you ain't for remindin' me o' shyte," Dar'Kwar retorted and left the tent.

"Now do you wish to tell me more?" General Steely asked.

Dirk did not answer but finished his whiskey instead. The general's eyes never left his until Dirk's glass was empty.

"Another?" the general asked.

"No," answered Dirk flatly.

The general nodded, still taking a measure of the man. "Where did you say you came across this information?"

"I didn't," Dirk replied, annoyed.

"What are you hiding?"

Dirk didn't like where this line of questioning was going. Beneath the desk Dirk's hand came to rest upon his mind-control dagger, Krone. He had hoped to gain the support of the Eldalonian army, but it seemed that the curious general would not give it. He decided to try another angle before resorting to more drastic measures.

"I am an ally to the one known as Whill of Agora. He has sent me on this quest," Dirk said as if finally coming clean. "As you may know, Whill has made powerful enemies. At his request I have been hunting the would-be assassin from Uthen-Arden and recently lost their trail outside of the Ky'Dren Pass, Uthen-Arden side. As you may also know, Whill is the son of your late princess and queen of Uthen-Arden. Your king is his grandfather. It is for this reason the dark elf Eadon wants the Eldalonian line wiped out."

"Why then does this Eadon keep Whill's uncle, King Addakon of Uthen-Arden, alive if the rumors of the alliance are true?" the general inquired.

"Addakon is dead by Whill's own hand more than six months now. Eadon has since been impersonating the king."

The general began to laugh but found no mirth in Dirk's face.

"You know this to be true, or you should. Has not the king of Eldalon informed his generals of such things?" Dirk pressed.

The general scowled at the slight. "You say you lost 'their' trail. Why not him or her?"

"Because if I had been close enough to know if they were a he or a she, they would be dead."

The general clenched his jaw and squared his chin. "And you mean to tell me they slipped through the pass unnoticed?"

"No, they did not go through the pass, they went over it. Any reports of that?"

The general met Dirk's eyes and looked upon him as he had not before. "Guard!"

A soldier tore into the tent with his sword half drawn. "Sir!" he yelled upon entering, searching for trouble.

"Search out the commander of the Third, Blood-rain. Bring him here immediately," barked General Steely.

He sat back down and stroked his short beard. In his eyes and on his face Dirk saw that the man was now concerned. From a drawer he pulled a pipe and leaf bag.

"Do you smoke?" the general asked.

"Opium on rare occasion, but not the leaf. It leaves my lungs heavy," replied Dirk.

When the general realized Dirk was not making a joke, he laughed. Dirk struck two of his rings together, and from one a small flame danced to life from the spark. He reached across the desk, offering to light the pipe. The general nearly went cross-eyed gazing at the magical flame as he bent and puffed the pipe to life.

"That is a fine elven trinket you have," the general admitted through a cloud of smoke, with a hint of jealousy at such a prize.

Dirk nodded and blew out the fire from his ring. "It comes in handy."

Heavy footsteps approached outside, and soon the tent flaps opened wide and in strode a tall soldier. He looked to be about thirty, and Dirk could tell by the way he carried himself that he was comfortable in his armor. He was a lifetime soldier.

"Sir!" he said smartly and saluted the general.

"Commander Bloodrain, please repeat to me your report of the northern wall from last night," said General Steely with a glance at Dirk.

"One hour before sunrise from the northern tower watch, I received a report of a winged creature flying overhead."

"What direction was it flying?" the general asked.

"Northwest, sir."

"Was it bird, dragon, draquon…?"

"The lookout thinks it was a small dragon."

"How did a small dragon fly across the Ky'Dren Mountains without being seen by the dwarven lookouts? They are stationed every mile."

"Sir, the lookout said that he only saw the beast when it flew through the hovering smoke of the outpost campfires. Otherwise it was invisible."

"Was the man drunk?" General Steely asked.

"No, sir, he is not the kind of man to drink while on duty," said the commander with a darting glance at the whiskey glasses.

"Wait outside, please," ordered the general.

When they were alone, Steely leaned once again toward Dirk, his pipe to lips. Dirk struck the rings once again and relit the pipe. The general smiled through teeth that clutched the pipe, admiring anew the fire ring.

"There are two possibilities now, it seems," the general surmised as he leaned back and blew smoke forth. "One, you saw the very same creature and have worked its existence into your story." He eyed Dirk suddenly and sat up. "Or two, what you say is true. In any case, this winged creature must be investigated. The commander says it was flying northwest, which fits your story. Twenty miles northwest of here is the home of the duke of Bristle, cousin to the king and possibly your assassin's first target."

"Then that is my destination," said Dirk as he got up from his chair. "I could use a fresh horse, mine has been pushed to its limits, I am afraid."

The general nodded. "I will provide you with a horse. Come. If this creature was seen last night, we may already be too late."

CHAPTER TWENTY-TWO

Secrets

The boat that Aurora had been gifted was a near replica of a barbarian fishing boat. The elves had accounted for her size when designing it; the stairs and archway to go below deck admitted her easily. Six long oars came out the sides, and these too had been crafted with barbarians in mind. The sails however were elven fin sails.

All of her many gifts had been loaded, along with the smoked boar. She was pleased to find the boat had already been stocked with provisions. There were barrels of water below deck, along with wine and ale, bread, smoked fish, cheese, and a variety of vegetables and fruit. It seemed as though there were enough provisions to last months of travel. She did not need months; it would take the elven ship little more than a week to traverse the waters to Volnoss, having to make a wide berth of the dark elf occupied Island of Fendora.

As the lines were thrown onto the dock and the boat began to pull away, a large flame-colored jungle bird flew over the ship. It circled twice and swooped down. Aurora was not surprised when the bird transformed as it landed, and soon Azzeal was grinning up at her.

"If you do not mind the company I would see you to Volnoss. The waters are dangerous these days, especially when traveling near to Fendora Island."

Aurora tried to hide her disappointment and suspicions. He knew something, she was sure of it. But why then would he let her live if he knew of her betrayal? She guarded herself from her thoughts and feelings and let a welcoming smile find her face.

"It would be an honor to have you, Azzeal. But does not your duty to your king command that you remain at his side through this? I feel my plight is but a trifling thing to one such as you."

"Quite on the contrary lady of the north. In these dark times allies are far from trifling things."

"Very well then, welcome, and thank you."

"My pleasure," he said with a bow."

The boat left harbor without the use of the oars. The small elven crew consisted of water weavers who steered the ship north through their magic. Aurora had not slept in the jungle, and she felt the affects of the long day in her tired muscles. She left Azzeal, Kreshna, and the others and went below deck. In her cabin she found the dragonlance among her things.

The weapon was smaller than she would have guessed it to be, no longer then her sword. She took it up and inspected it curiously. What material it was made of she could not tell. The shaft was rough and black like coal, with no pointed end. An assortment of gems the size of coins was the only thing to adorn the strange shaft. Aurora rubbed a thumb over one and suddenly the lance multiplied in length not once but twice with a reverberation of singing metal. The pointed end slammed through the wooden wall of her cabin and into the room beyond. Aurora was pleased. She thumbed the jewel once again and the lance retracted.

She undressed and got into a bed that had been made with her great height in mind. As her boat was steadily guided north Aurora tried to sleep. She tried to prepare herself mentally for the coming battle, but the thought of Azzeal left room for nothing else. The elf's presence loomed over her, suffocating her mind, confusing her thoughts. Why was he here? What did he know?

She lay there for hours unable to sleep. When she could take it no more she bolted out of bed and stormed out of her cabin tearing the sheets from the bed and wrapping them around her as she went. When she reached the stairs to the deck Azzeal was already coming down them. He reached the bottom and raised an eyebrow to Aurora. "Lady."

"Shove your lady up your arse Azzeal. What do you know?"

"I am not the one that need be answering for any-thing," said Azzeal. He looked up the stairs wearily and gestured to her quarters. "Perhaps we should discuss this somewhere more private."

"Private!" she fumed. "How can there be any privacy when you elves can read minds."

"Hear stray thoughts." he corrected her.

"One in the same!" she countered and turned annoyed to her quarters. Azzeal followed.

When the door was closed Aurora sat upon her bed and watched with trembling hands as Azzeal waved his hands at the walls and murmured to himself in Elvish. If the elf had learned her secrets she knew that she would die. She was not afraid of death. She was afraid of dying as a liar, with no honor. She had lost that when she attempted to kill Abram.

"You may yet regain your honor. It comes down to decisions," said Azzeal.

Aurora looked to him startled. "I spoke to myself in my native tongue, yet you understand."

"I do."

"Then you know all." She resigned herself to her fate. Azzeal chuckled.

"You need not fear my judgement, I mean you no harm."

She was surprised by this and did little to hide it. She wondered if he knew the whole of it, perhaps he misun-derstood, perhaps...

"I know that you swore fealty to Eadon, I know that you attempted Abram's life."

A tear itched its way down Aurora's face and was soon followed by many more. She broke down in sobs and fell to her knees; she felt her sheets pile around her legs but cared not. She was powerless to do anything but clutch at Azzeals leafed robes and cry. She cried like she had not since childhood, since the day her father plummeted to his death those years ago. She had disgraced her father's memory, he who had himself been the victim of a coward. She deserved nothing more than death.

Azzeal bent to his knees and took her head in his hands. She reluctantly met his gaze through teary blurred vision. "You are right to feel disgrace upon yourself, but do not tarry there long. Soon it will tear you apart."

"I deserve death," she lamented sobbing.

"You are dead. When you have sworn fealty to Eadon, that was the moment of your death. Now you are free to choose. You can still do the right thing. The only reason I have not killed you myself is because I made a promise once to one of your people, and I have seen your heart."

"How can I be saved?" she asked hanging on his every word."

"It will not be easy, as the right path often proves. But it is possible."

Aurora shuddered a few steadying breaths and tried to get ahold of herself. She felt cleansed of the pent up guilt, but the purging had sapped her strength. Azzeal helped her to lie in bed and covered her with her sheet and a thick quilt.

"What promise did you make?" she asked.

Azzeal smiled and sat in the chair next to the bed. "Talon Windwalker." he said and laughed at the face she made. "I assume you know your history then. It was more than two hundred years ago. He once saved my life. When I offered mine in return he told me instead to help one of his kin if ever I was to find one in need. And I have."

"Thank you." Aurora smiled.

Azzeal stroked her hair away from her face with a smile. "Rest now Aurora. Let dreams trouble you not. Be at peace."

CHAPTER
TWENTY-THREE

Visitors from Ro'Sar

The next day Whill awoke to Avriel's soft voice in his mind. *Word has come that Roakore and his dwarves have arrived.*

He shot out of bed and dressed quickly. Together he and Avriel flew from the Thousand Falls and headed to the northern coast of Elladrindellia less than ten miles away. Soon they spotted Roakore's company traveling the road to Cerushia from the coast.

They were spotted quickly and alarmed calls of "Dragon!" rose up from the dwarves as Whill and Avriel flew overhead. Avriel landed a few hundred yards ahead of them. Roakore's booming voice could be heard yelling at his dwarves.

"Hold, ye dolts, the dragon be an elf friend!"

Arguments broke out as Roakore tried to explain. Whill dismounted and headed toward the company.

"Best you stay here for the moment, Avriel. The dwarves will take some convincing, I imagine."

Indeed. I doubt many of them will accept the explanation, or care. To them a dragon is a dragon. It will be easier if I leave.

Before Whill could argue, Avriel leapt from the ground and took flight. Whill watched after her, worried. She was quiet as of late. He knew it had to do with her possible transformation and the fate of her dragon body.

Turning from her, Whill saw Tarren running toward him down the cobblestone road that led to the coast.

"Whill!" Tarren yelled joyfully.

Whill smiled brightly and jogged to the boy.

"Whill!" Tarren called again, waving his hands. He reached Whill and slammed into him with a hug.

"Tarren, well met!" Whill laughed as Tarren wiped tears with his sleeve and beamed up at him.

"Well met indeed!" Tarren laughed. "I thought I would never see you again!"

"As did I. But alas, we meet again." He held Tarren at arm's length and looked him over. "You've grown."

"Yeah?" Tarren beamed. "I been trainin' with the dwarves. Look at this!" He flexed a bicep. Whill squeezed his arm and gave the boy an impressed look.

"They put some muscle on you, eh?"

"You're right, they have, they are a tough lot!" said Tarren. He pulled Whill with him eagerly. "C'mon, you gotta meet my friend Helzendar, he's Roakore's kid."

Tarren led Whill to the dwarves and Roakore gave Whill a bear hug, lifting him off the ground. "It is about time you arrived!" Whill teased when Roakore finally put him down. "How was your journey?"

"Bah!" Roakore spat. "It was a right bloody one. Ran into a draggard hive we did, and set fifty heads to pike! They had made their stinking nest in an old trading outpost."

"Was anyone injured?" Whill asked, looking past Roakore with concern for the dwarves.

"Those who got hurt were lucky enough to have Lunara around. Those who were killed…well, they be in the halls o' the gods now, and their mugs be full."

"Lunara?" Whill asked.

"Ah, yes, where be me manners?" He turned to his dwarves. "These be some o' me finest fighters. Warriors all, they be."

"Well met," said Whill in Dwarvish and slammed his fist to his chest, a great gesture of respect from one of such a name as he. "It is good to see the dwarves of Ro'Sar returned to their home and in good spirits. I am honored to meet you all."

As one the Ro'Sar dwarves slammed fist to chest and bowed.

"Aye." Roakore turned Whill to the right with a hand to his shoulder. "This be me boy Helzendar, one o' me strongest and bravest."

"Hello, Helzendar," said Whill and offered the dwarf boy a hand. Helzendar squeezed Whill's hand in a crushing grip that could have been a full grown man's.

Lunara and Holdagozz came forward to stand beside Roakore. "Ah! And this be General Holdagozz, one o' the toughest dwarves you be meetin'. And this elven beauty be Lunara, as good a healer as yer likely to be findin', and she be not much older than yerself."

Whill gave Holdagozz the same dwarven sign of respect as the others. He could not help but notice the broad-shouldered dwarf's thick knotted muscles, like tree roots winding around his exposed arms. It looked as though the dwarf had not an ounce of fat on his body.

"Lunara. That is a beautiful name," said Whill as he took her hand and gave a small bow.

Lunara smiled with a blush and took a quick inhale. "Thank you. It is good to finally meet you, Whill of Agora," she said. She took back her hand as if she had been given a great gift and clutched it to her chest.

Roakore coughed and Whill realized that he and Lunara had just been staring at each other, smiling stupidly, and all eyes were on him. "Well, then, well met!" he said cheerily to them all. "Come, I welcome you all to Cerushia!" He wrapped one arm around Tarren and the other around Roakore, and they headed to the elven city. Behind them the dwarves broke out in one more traveling song that took them into the city.

O'er rivers wide and prairies plain
Far from shining jewel and silver vein
The road has led we nigh astray
Our feet they march all through the day.
O frothing mug and grandest feast
Be just reward for we at least
O'er rivers wide and prairies plain
Far from shining jewel and silver vein.

Roakore's company sang them all the way into the heart of Cerushia. There at the city square, a great clearing filled with the tallest flowers and multicolored leaves awaited a gathering of thousands, and Zerafin. The dumbfounded company was led by Nafiel to the grand gathering. From the elevated city square most of the city could be seen, and the sun reflecting off of the massive ridge that was the Thousand Falls was astonishing. The dwarves were awed one and all. They followed a stone walkway that led to a large circle of stone. Upon the stone stood Zerafin; his mother, Queen Araveal; many of the elders; and the seven masters. A dwarven-lore master there was also, furiously scribbling as he bore witness to the meeting.

"King Roakore of the Mountains Ro'Sar!" Zerafin announced. "My friend," he said more personally as Roakore greeted him with a bear hug that sent the elves into joyful laughter.

Zerafin raised Roakore's arm to the crowd and proclaimed, "From this day forth I proclaim an allegiance with the Ro'Sar dwarves, to be recognized by all of my kin. Together we liberated the human kingdom of Isladon, together we took part in the reclamation of the mountains Ro'Sar!" Zerafin took Whill's hand also and raised it to the heavens. "And together we shall liberate all of Agora!"

The crowd cheered for Whill, for Roakore, and for their Drindellian prince who would soon be king. Whill was happier than he had been in a long time. Again he felt that old brotherhood he had once known. Abram and Rhunis were there too, in Whill's heart and mind. He saw the smiling face of his oldest friend. *Ah, Abram, you old dog, I wish you were here,* he said to himself as a conflicted tear found his cheek.

CHAPTER
TWENTY-FOUR
Blood and a
Black Rose

General Steely provided Dirk with a fresh horse and chose four of his best men to accompany them to Bristle. Dirk laughed to himself, thinking forty men would not help them against Krentz, let alone four. Krentz had sworn fealty to her father, Eadon, and Dirk could only imagine the power he had bestowed upon her.

They rode into Bristle shortly after noon. Nothing out of the ordinary seemed to be going on in the village, nothing to indicate that an assassin upon a winged creature had been here. General Steely led the group to the small castle set atop a wide hill, the home of the duke of Bristle.

Before the large wood-and-iron door they dismounted and the general knocked. No one came to answer. After a long pause the general knocked again. Dirk knew it was useless, the place was too quiet. No guards walked the ramparts, and no sound came from within. Dirk knew they stood before a tomb.

He threw his grappling hook over the wall and pulled it until it caught. "Hey!" yelled the general as Dirk began expertly scaling the wall. He slipped over the top, quietly landing in a crouch. Listening, motionless, he wound the elven rope and returned the hook to its place along his belt. Below he could still hear the banging of General Steely, and his calls to anyone inside.

Dirk wasted no time in entering the castle. From the roof he came down a short set of stairs that led to a long hall. Doors lined both sides of the hallway and Dirk went to the first on his left. He pushed the door open slowly and saw no movement within. A large four-poster bed sat at the opposite wall near the wide windows. Two lumps in the bed caught his attention.

Dirk walked to the bed and hesitated before throwing back the sheets. He feared what he knew he would find: the bodies of Krentz's victims. Seeing the bodies would make Krentz's crimes real, her fall complete. Dirk knew her as a dark elf who shunned her people's evil ways; she had always been quick to laugh and good at heart. Though she could be a fierce warrior if forced to fight, she could also be gentle, kind, and caring. Once Dirk saw the bodies of her victims, all of that would change.

He took a deep breath and threw back the blankets. An animalistic mewling left his throat as Dirk laid eyes on the two dead bodies. He barely registered the crash and groaning splinter of wood as the general and his men began slamming something large into the front door below.

Dirk stared at the seemingly sleeping faces of a mother and her daughter. The girl, no more than six years old, clung to her mother as they slept. Likely she had been scared by the storm and had crawled into bed with her mother in the dark of night. Their peaceful faces showed no sign of terror; they had been killed in their sleep. The lack of blood and the small puncture wounds in their bedclothes, just below the breastbone, told Dirk they had died instantly with a thin dagger through the heart. With trembling hand he reached for the single long-stemmed black rose that had been placed in the child's small hand.

Dirk jumped as the door was smashed open below, the boom of impact reverberating through the entire building. Boots hurried throughout the castle as doors were slammed open and rooms were searched.

"In here! By the gods, they are all dead!" yelled a man down the hall.

Other such proclamations echoed throughout the castle and fell upon Dirk's ears like lashes of a whip. A chill ran through his body as he took up the rose and stood, unable to tear his eyes from the dead.

"The duke is dead, and all of the servants," the general said from behind him. Then Steely saw the mother and child. "By the gods, his wife and even…little Annabelle. What kind of monster would do this? What kind of demon would take the life of a mother and child?"

The general's words tore through Dirk as he looked down upon Krentz's victims. Rage welled within him with Steely's every curse. He wanted to strangle the man just to shut him up. This wasn't her; it was not the Krentz he knew. It made him sick to think he had been prepared to do the very same thing. If she had not sworn fealty to her father, Dirk would have held the killing blade. Had it been easier for her because she was a dark elf? Was it truly in her blood? When the moment came, would Dirk have been able to do it? Krentz had been able to, and quite efficiently. His urge to save her swelled as his anxiety grew.

"Where is the next royal in line?" Dirk suddenly yelled, grabbing General Steely by the edges of his breastplate and shaking him. Steely scowled at the intrusion but his face lost all anger when he saw Dirk's haunted eyes.

"Where?" Dirk demanded.

The general seemed to remember his high station and shoved Dirk away hard. "You are not running off alone ahead of me and my men. This is a matter for the Eldalonian army. You are in possession of knowledge that must be contained and dealt with by the king's men."

General Steely took three deliberate steps toward Dirk and looked him dead in the eye. "Until this entire affair is over, you are my prisone—"

From nowhere Dirk produced Krone and jabbed it into the general's hand. "Silence!" he commanded in a hushed whisper as blood dripped and the general froze.

"Sir." A voice approached from down the hall.

"Tell them to leave us," Dirk hissed.

"Leave us!" General Steely was forced to blurt out, though Dirk could tell the general was trying to fight the effects of the torturous dagger. Its real strength was in its euphoric effects should the victim stop resisting; good behavior was rewarded instantly, while bad behavior was punished painfully. To the approaching soldier, the general simply sounded gruff.

"Now tell me where the next in King Mathus' line can be found," Dirk ordered.

With a grimace and shaking with effort, General Steely hissed, "Southwest a day's march, McKellian's Cross, Lord Grendial…"

"And what would the closest target be beyond that one?"

Steely ground his teeth and after a silent scream that left his eyes bloodshot, he broke. "North to the Twin Lakes, Castle Carlsborough…Kessleton is the name." He cringed.

General Steely glared at Dirk with murder in his eyes. To force such vital information out of such a devoted soldier was akin to death. Dirk knew that he had made an enemy for life. But the general would have to get in line.

"You will not yell out when I take back the blade. You will wait here until you have counted one thousand heartbeats, and you will never speak of me again. You have no memory of me. Say it."

"I have no memory of you," droned the general.

"No memory of who?" asked Dirk.

"No memory of you."

"Who am I?" Dirk finished.

"I don't know." The teetering general drooled.

Dirk retracted the dagger and walked out of the room, back to the stair and onto the roof. From there he took in a quick lay of the land. He looked southwest beyond the horizon to where he knew the closer village McKellian's Cross lay, likely Krentz's next stop. Then his eyes traveled north to where he knew Twin Lakes to be. Krentz would take the targets at Castle Carlsborough after McKellian's Cross.

Dirk ran along the wall and leapt. Catching his grappling hook on a gargoyle, he swung down smoothly, guiding his descent with his left hand. He landed and dislodged the hook with a whispered word. The rope followed him, winding itself back up into the mechanism as he walked. By the time he had reached his horse, the rope was again on his belt.

He sped away from the soldiers and their questioning yells at his back. From a strap he took a dart and jabbed it into the horse's neck. The next dart was for him. The adrenaline hit them both and they flew off northwest. Dirk intended to get there before Krentz did. He rode on into the night and his mind was haunted with images of what Krentz was now doing to the family at McKellian's Cross.

The general would still be on the trail of the assassin, but they would follow the trail south to her next kill. And Dirk would be waiting for her in the north. He had to put an end to her spree, no matter the cost.

CHAPTER
TWENTY-FIVE

Treason

Music took to the skies as harp and fiddle, flute and reed rang out, marking the beginning of the festivities. Whill had been too preoccupied with his studies and that twisted figment of his imagination to know that a grand celebration had been planned. He soon learned that Zerafin's crowning would be that night.

The queen motioned to a nearby elf and he quickly came forward. "See to it that the dwarves are shown to their special quarters and their every need is met."

The elf bowed. "Yes, my queen."

As the dwarves were being guided away by the queen's help, a blast of lightning erupted from somewhere in the crowd. All in the blink of an eye screams and crackling thunder tore through the jolly gathering. The lightning snaked its way toward Whill as a blade came at him from behind. Two more assassins blasted fire and black spells at him.

Time slowed to a crawl for Whill, and in the ocean of elven faces he saw the grinning apparition of his tortured self. "What would you do without me?" the Other asked.

Time surged forward and sound crashed into Whill. He unsheathed Adromida and the thunder was devoured by the vibrating hum of the blade's sheer power. Whill raised his free hand and the lightning hit an invisible globe of energy and shot back at its wielder. The blade at his back was blocked and driven into the ground by Roakore's massive axe. The fire was absorbed by a black globe that swirled in Ralliad master Flouren En Fen's outstretched hand. Whill raised his arm and the four assassins were lifted into the air to slam together and then violently smashed to the center of the stone circle. Elves quickly parted from the four assassins as they slammed to the ground. There was an ear-piercing roar and fire rained down from above. Avriel landed and impaled one of the dark elves with a razor-sharp talon. She trapped another with her other clawed foot and with a snap of powerful jaws bit his head off. The crowd reeled in shock and the dwarves gave battle cries. Hatchets flew through the air only to freeze mid-spin by Roakore's command of the metal blades.

"Stop!" commanded Queen Araveal and Roakore in unison, and the dwarves froze in their charge.

"She is my daughter!"

"She be princess Avriel!"

At mention of her name and title, the white dragon Avriel seemed to realize what she was doing. She flung the lifeless body of the dark-elf assassin and pawed her bloodied lips as if to hide them. Not able to stand the gawking of the crowd, she sprang shamefully into the air and took flight toward the Thousand Falls.

One of the two assassins still breathing unsheathed his blade and charged Whill in a blur of motion, but Whill was faster. He blocked the attacking blow with Adromida, and on contact the assassin's blade disintegrated to ash. The assassin slammed into Whill's energy shield and his head snapped to the side as Philo barreled into him with a crushing tackle. Underneath, Philo the elf cackled and proclaimed in Elvish, "Lord Eadon take you all!"

Zerafin, sensing what was coming, reached forward and mentally pulled the dwarf from the dark elf. The Krundar master Arngil stepped forward and with a clapping boom caused stone from the circle to heave like ocean waves and wrap around the elf. There was a great muffled explosion as the assassin blew himself up. The stone from the circle shot out in every direction, and so too did the hands of a dozen elves and Roakore. The flying stones stopped in midair, reversed direction, and slammed back on themselves. With so much force applied by Krundar earth movers, the stones could only collapse in on themselves, entombing the remains of the assassin forever in a smooth, round boulder.

All eyes went to the last assassin and everyone froze. The dark elf stood among two dead elves of the sun who had been trying to protect his hostage. Tarren looked at Whill wide-eyed as the dagger pressed to his throat drew a trickle of blood. Whill flashed back to the same scenario upon the pirate ship. Tarren would have died then. It seemed to Whill for an eerie moment that death had returned to claim Tarren, as it had first meant to those many months ago.

"Tarren!" Lunara shrieked and with a clawing hand shot a spell of green multicolored light, but it was absorbed by the staff of the Watcher who seemed to suddenly appear.

"That way ends badly," he warned Lunara, who was held back by Holdagozz.

Ten feet away from Tarren, Whill held Adromida with both hands. No blood came from the bare hand that squeezed the blade. His gaze bore down into the dark elf and the elf began to shudder. Tarren was released and the dagger was dropped. The boy slammed his short staff into the dark elf's face. The assassin squeezed his head painfully as he dropped to his knees.

"Tarren, come away from him!" Lunara yelled as his mother might, and the boy staggered backward.

In agony the dark elf glared at Whill. Blood ran from his nose and ears and he shook violently. Through clenched teeth he growled, "Sun elves do not... invade...another's...mind...aagh!" He screamed as Whill stepped closer and scowled.

"I am not a sun elf," Whill answered.

The dark elf ceased in writhing convulsions as Whill bore down on him with his mental assault. The Other was in control now, and he tore through the dark elf's mind. Whill sent more power surging through himself and the dark elf screamed in anguish.

"Enough!" commanded the queen. "Release him!"

Whill looked at the queen, and for a moment the insane eyes of the Other regarded her. Then Whill blinked and released the dark elf.

"We must learn what he knows. He must be questioned," said the queen.

"I know all that he would tell," Whill informed her. He sheathed his blade and regarded the whimpering assassin. "He is of no value alive or dead."

The queen regarded Whill with apprehension and turned to her guards. "Take the prisoner away; he will be dealt with later." She then addressed her help. "See that this mess is taken care of. The festivities will not be interrupted!"

Whill went to Tarren and put a hand to his shoulder. "Are you all right?"

Tarren did not look too shaken from the incident. Rather, he looked furious. "I am fine...thanks, Whill."

"Come," Zerafin bade Whill and Roakore. "We must speak in private."

Whill looked at Tarren with worry.

"I will watch over him," said Lunara.

Whill smiled at her gratefully and followed Roakore and Zerafin to the carriage.

They were brought to Zerafin's pyramid in short order. Inside, the place looked more like the interior of a castle than anything. Zerafin led them into a large library at the heart of the structure. He gestured for them to take a seat at a round table at the center of the room. "Cider, wine, ale?" he asked from a small cabinet as he poured himself a glass of wine.

"Ale," said Roakore.

"The same," Whill concurred.

Zerafin brought the drinks and joined his friends. He handed them each glasses and lifted his own.

"To Abram and Rhunis!" he said.

"To Abram and Rhunis," Whill and Roakore repeated and clanged glasses.

Zerafin drank deeply and put his glass down. His demeanor changed in an instant. "This tale of Kellallea the Ancient One, do you believe it?" he asked Whill.

Whill took a deep breath and sighed. "I do not know what to think anymore. I have thought it over for a long time now and am no closer to revelation."

Zerafin nodded but Roakore scoffed. "Bah! That old elf was crazy! Whill be the one to defeat Eadon, don't ye be doubtin'."

Zerafin nodded with Roakore's every word. "That may be true, and it may not. Either way, the elves of Elladrindellia and the humans of Agora need hope. They need something, someone to believe in, and that someone is you, Whill."

Whill began to argue but Zerafin cut him off. "Think about your people, your father's people!" He slammed the table. "By the gods, man, your name alone stirs hope in the hearts of men. You have not seen the world these six months. Agora has been tortured by the dark elves right along with you, my friend. Your father's people need you, they want you. For nineteen long years they suffered under Addakon's rule, and now they suffer under Eadon's. You—"

Whill slammed the table and it jumped, causing the drinks to teeter. "Do not speak to me about my father's throne and my responsibilities to my people! It has taken you five hundred years to claim the throne of *your* father. I am twenty years old! I cannot be held responsible for the fate of an entire continent, I will not!"

He found himself looming over the table, his knuckles white as he leaned on them. The sword at his belt hummed and vibrated.

Zerafin looked at the sword and Whill. Roakore silently looked from one to the other as he slowly sipped his beer. Whill closed his eyes to calm himself and sat back down. Quietly he spoke. "I do believe Kellallea's tale. Eadon wants me to try to kill him. He wants me to give him the greatest power given, and he wants to become a god."

Silence followed his words and for a time no one spoke. Zerafin set his laced fingers upon the table.

"I ask much from you—*we* ask much from you. I cannot imagine the burden you carry, but I would help you bear it."

"Aye, as will I," Roakore declared. 'You be what gave me the strength to be facin' me haunted mountain again. I said to meself, if this lad be findin' the strength to face his rotten fate, then so too I be. You ain't alone, laddie. We be much alike, we three, one an' all redeemin' our fallen fathers and lost lands. We three be kings, and we three be havin' to lead. Ain't none of us likes our lot—we would rather it were someone else had our problems—but there ain't no one else. Our people be lookin' to us, and I for one ain't for lettin' 'em down!" He guzzled back his beer, walked to the cabinet, and poured another from a small barrel. Returning to his seat he took a long pull and slammed down the mug. Froth leapt from the mug and wet his beard.

"So who gives a good godsdamn about the prophecy bein' true or false? Whether you be the son o' a king or living happily in Fendale playin' trouser sticks with a fair lass, you still be livin' through this war." Roakore scowled at Whill.

"Well, I would rather be...playing trouser sticks!" Whill yelled and his face twisted in laughter. Roakore gave a bellowing laugh and the three burst into fits of laughter. None could form the words "trouser sticks," and with each attempt it only got worse. Whill laughed until his sides hurt and his cheeks were sore. After a time they settled down and, parched, they raised their glasses.

"Don't say it!" Whill warned Roakore.

The dwarf grinned, threatening to send them back into hysteria. "To bein' in a sinkin' boat with good friends," he said.

"Hear, hear!" They clanged glassed and drank.

They talked for more than an hour about everything and nothing at all. Roakore sat back with his pipe, and the familiar Eldalonian tobacco smoke reminded Whill of Abram. He could just imagine him sitting there across from him, leaning back after a good meal, of which he had savored every bite, pipe hanging from between his teeth, causing him to grin as he held it. To Abram, life had been a thing to be enjoyed. He always found the good in a situation, and he wasted not a moment. He rolled with bad fortune and never expected more than he earned. Whill knew that he shamed Abram's memory with his behavior. Abram had not raised him a warrior so that he could feel sorry for himself, and he had not raised him to be selfish.

Whill was reminded of a time when he was just twelve years old, and Abram had brought him to a mission in Brindon, west of Lake Eardon in Shierdon. Abram had made Whill volunteer with him for three days, tending to the sick and dying. He had forbidden food for the duration, for both Whill and himself.

"Here the skills of healing that Teera has taught you will be tested, but so too will your compassion. We will not eat for three days, and we will test our selfishness," Abram had told him.

Whill never forgot those three days. He helped to bandage festering sores, tended to children sick with the barking cough; he made comfortable the dying, and spent endless hours sponging fevered foreheads. After the first day, the hardest part was feeding the sick. He became frustrated with the infirm who left the precious food dribbling down their chins. Abram too helped and he watched Whill closely.

By the second day, Whill was sick with hunger. He began to feel like those he helped to treat. His stomach felt sunken, and he was occasionally wracked by hunger pangs that left him panicking for food. But he kept it to himself as those around him did. If the four-year-old girl coughing herself to death could starve with dignity, then so could he.

By the third day, Whill had become accustomed to the burning emptiness in his belly. He moved slowly, weakened as he was. He drifted along the dozens of beds, tending to people's needs on a schedule he had become accustomed to. He learned what people needed by watching their eyes, and he was well liked by all. The tending Mothers of the Flame said that he had the bedside manner of a saint, and he began to take great pride in his work.

Whill saw so much senseless pain and suffering that he became outraged at any god who would allow it. The Mothers of the Flame had tried to comfort him with their dogma and their explanations for such things. They spoke of the great plan of the father of the gods, but to Whill, any god whose plans included the suffering of innocent children was neither a loving god nor one to be praised. The Mothers blamed the devils for sickness and death, and praised the father when someone turned around and got well. Little credit was given to the efforts of the healers for miracles of health. Whill had learned from Abram that the lack of simple cleanliness caused most illness, not devils or demons, and though the use of boiled water during treatment and surgery had been shared by the elves hundreds of years before, most healers did not practice it. Agorans were slow to change.

Whill made it through the third day and spent the fourth eating frequent small meals and resting under Abram's supervision. The Mothers and healers feared he had contracted something, but after a day of replenishment and rest, Whill insisted on getting back to work. They remained there at the mission in Brindon for six months, and Whill made many friends and helped many people. He also lost a lot of friends, young and old alike.

Now, sitting with Zerafin and Roakore, Whill looked at the ancient blade of power at his hip. With it he could heal legions. He smiled at Roakore's pipe smoke and was thankful for his old friend. Whill knew what he had to do.

"I can help, therefore I must," he said aloud, stopping Zerafin and Roakore's conversation. He looked at them with the renewed vigor of resolution. "I accept now that my life is forfeit. I will give myself for this cause. The people's pain will be mine; together we shall fight against death."

"Together," Roakore agreed.

"Together," Zerafin said with a smile.

CHAPTER
TWENTY-SIX

Carlsborough

Dirk pushed his horse hard that night. He had injected it numerous times with adrenaline and knew that it could not take much more. He had stopped administering the shots to himself. He needed real rest. He had other useful trinkets and the like that could restore strength, ease pain, and enhance endurance, but there was no replacement for real sleep and dreams, at least none Dirk had yet found.

He soon came to a small farmhouse that looked to have been long abandoned. One half of the building had been burned out, and the fields had not been tended to in a season. Draggard attacks were not as frequent here in Eldalon; this place had been an exception, it seemed.

He dismounted and retrieved the timber-wolf figurine. "Chief!" he said loudly. Swirling smoke poured forth and Chief was soon standing before him, awaiting orders. "Check the house and then the barn. If nothing is found, take to the woods and keep the perimeter clear of any intruders."

Chief barked once and sprang off toward the farmhouse. After a few minutes the ghost wolf had decided the house was clear and began his inspection of the barn. Dirk tied off the horse and ventured into the house himself. He found what he had hoped he might find within: a bed. Kicking off his boots with a groan, Dirk produced a headband with a single green crystal at its center. He had not had a good night's sleep since leaving Eadon's crystal palace, and if he wished to have any chance of stopping Krentz, he would need all the rest he could get. Dirk put on the headband so that the dream crystal was at the center of his forehead. He lay back on the old down bed and instantly fell into a dream-filled sleep. He would sleep for an hour and then take to the road once more.

Chief stalked the perimeter of the farmhouse, following the scent of a deer. He followed it to the woods but stopped when it traveled too far from the territory he had been tasked to watch.

Returning to the farmhouse, Chief sensed the nervous horse's fear. He resisted the urge to attack it, though he could sense that the animal was exhausted and would soon die. His instincts told him to strike, but his loyalty to the holder of the figurine stayed his animalistic urge. He looked at the window of the farmhouse in which he knew his new master slept. His master. He had known many over the centuries—humans, elves, and even a dwarf for a time. Many of his previous masters had fallen to a new one. He was intrigued by this new master, a cunning hunter and able fighter. Chief was eager to see what trouble they might get into together.

Dirk awoke an hour later, feeling alert and mentally refreshed. The soreness was out of his body and he felt strong. He left the farmhouse and swore to himself when he saw the dead horse. Chief trotted over and sat on his rear and held his head high, sniffing. Dirk gave him a look of accusation. The wolf sneezed and pawed at his nose. Shaking his head, he trotted to the dirt road and waited.

"More likely 'twas I who killed the horse. Damn!" Dirk said to Chief and joined him on the road. Dirk gave a big, reaching stretch and took a full deep breath.

"All right, then, boy, it is less than ten miles to Carls-borough. Let's see if we can beat the sun. C'mon, Chief!" he yelled and took off in a run. Chief barked and chased the black one.

Dirk ran down the darkened road with Chief at his side. All the while, Krentz would not fly from his mind.

His thoughts drifted to the years they had spent together. They had known true freedom then, and though they'd had droves of draggard and dark elves on their heels, they felt alive. They trained daily, and Krentz forced Dirk to master all weapons. She lent him her magic, and Dirk became a master of his weapons quickly. He remembered the endless hours spent throwing darts at flies, which at the time he'd found ridiculous. He never hit the damned things, but still she pushed. When finally he succeeded and tacked a fly to the wall with a dart, he leapt in celebration, or meant to. Instead he found himself paralyzed, with Krentz holding a clawed hand toward his head, a look of concentration twisting her beautiful face. Her tattoos swirled and shifted and Dirk felt his mind tingle and buzz.

Soon she released him and he gasped. "What in the hells was that?" he asked angrily.

"I captured your brain activity when you successfully hit the fly with the dart, and then I embedded that pattern onto the mental connections for that action," she panted.

Dirk shook his head, exasperated. "Come again?"

"Just try and hit another fly." She waved him off lazily. "My curious lover, try again."

Dirk sighed and rubbed his head. He spotted another fly and took a dart from one of the many ridiculous dart-filled straps she insisted he wear during practice.

"No!" she yelled. "Do not take the dart out until you mean to shoot."

Dirk huffed and grumbled, "You know, you still owe me an apology for the invasion of will."

She opened her eyes and regarded him with a smirk. "See if you want one in a minute. Go on, try on the next fly."

"Who gives a good godsdamn about the fly?" Dirk yelled, and in his anger he reached for a dart and flung it in a violent outburst. There was a thump and a buzzing died instantaneously. Dirk stared open-mouthed at the newly tacked fly. He laughed, cocked his head to regard the insect, and laughed all the harder.

"Holy dragon shyte," he mumbled and eagerly searched for another fly. Thud went his dart through another fly and into the wall. Thud, thud: a dart from each hand hit a fly on the wall. Dirk laughed and spent all of the darts from his straps. When he noticed he was out, he reached for one of his sheathed daggers and threw it at a fly with joyous anticipation of yet another perfect throw. Clang! The dagger bounced off the wall.

"You have yet to do that, therefore I cannot embed it in your—"

"Yeah, yeah, yeah." Dirk spun his hand in circles. "You be ready, then. The perfect throw is coming up," he said as he threw and missed and another dagger clanged to the floor.

It was many days before he hit a fly with a dagger, but after that he never missed. Krentz had told him that the method she used was one shunned by the sun elves, and Dirk had thought them idiots.

As the first rays of the sun began to shine above the pine trees, Dirk saw a village come into view. He slowed to a walk to catch his breath and inspected the village from afar. Few people were about at this early hour, and Dirk quickly spotted the stables of the small village.

Sometimes the best place to hide was in plain view, so Dirk stayed with the road and headed straight for the stables. He quietly instructed Chief to go around the village and wait by the road without being seen. The spirit wolf faded until he was nearly invisible and quickly disappeared into the trees.

Dirk slipped between the stables and an inn and came around back. Behind the buildings there were only foggy wheat fields, pastures, and piles of manure. A row of maples separated the fields from the property behind the buildings that made up Main Street. A few buildings down, a woman came into view and splashed the contents of a bucket into the thicket. Dirk slipped into the stable through the open back door. His hood was pulled down over his eyes, and through it he could see the heat aura of only six horses and one human. The stableboy was shoveling hay from the attic down into a wooden bin. Dirk chucked a dart up at the silhouette of the boy, and a soft thud told him that it had hit home. The boy would likely wake to a good lecture about falling asleep during chores.

Quickly he inspected the horses. A tall white-and-brown-speckled mare caught his eye. He did not bother with a saddle and led the horse out of its stall.

Stroking the horse's neck, he spoke to it as he would a friend. "Will you run well for me, beauty?"

He petted the horse for a minute and from his hand fed it oats from a bucket nearby. "The apples are fat this time of year, Beauty. How about we get some?"

He leapt atop Beauty's back, and grabbing a handful of his mane, he gave the stallion a soft kick. Beauty reared, shot out of the back of the stables, and with a leap cleared the small wooden fence. Dirk steered Beauty on toward the road on the other side of town. He knew that he was hours ahead of Krentz, and he had only a few dozen miles to go.

Well before noon he arrived in Carlsborough, one of the many large towns dotted all over the Twin Lakes. Centuries past, this had been barbarian territory. And though the tribes had since been wiped out or run out, many of their monolithic structures still stood. Many of the thousands of giant stones had been scavenged to be used for nearby castles and buildings, but many more remained, too big to be moved. Strange patterns had been laid out by the barbarians, and weathered statues of foreign-looking humans with long heads could be found easily. While the barbarians could have used the stone to build impenetrable fortresses, instead they'd built monuments to their gods.

Dirk stopped at the nearest inn and tied off his horse. The place was empty but for a man preparing the bar for the day's business.

"We don't open before noon 'less you the king of Eldalon," the man said as he stopped in his polishing of glasses and gave Dirk a once-over. "And you ain't him." He went back to his work.

Dirk walked to the bar and put a small sack of gold coins on it with a clang. "No, but I spend like a king," he said and took a seat.

The man limped over to Dirk and appraised him with renewed interest. "I hope a man who carries that many blades is a friend to the lordship, or he ain't welcome here no matter how much gold he be carrying."

Dirk toyed with the idea of stabbing the man in the heart. There was something about the bold man's way of speech that irritated Dirk. He had a few old scars on his face, causing small patches in his red beard. Dirk guessed his limp was a result of battle also. Judging by the man's righteous proclamations about the lordship, he was either a retired soldier or guard. There were enough of those around these days. More men than not ended up in the kingdom's armies, and fewer came home every year. The draggard wars had raged on for two decades, and every village had its share of lost soldiers.

"I am here with intention to thwart an assassination attempt on your lord, but first I must eat. Fighting dark elves calls for a big breakfast," said Dirk dryly.

The man laughed, but quickly his smile was smothered by uncertainty as Dirk opened one side of his jacket. The barkeep saw the dozens of darts, daggers, and gleaming throwing stars and gulped.

"You're serious, ain't you?" the man asked, wide-eyed.

"No," said Dirk. "I am Whill of Agora. And I am hungry."

The barkeep looked perplexed. He ran a hand through hair that wasn't there and brought it around to rest on his open-mouthed chin.

"Whill of Agora. You don't say." He turned from Dirk and placed the glass he had been polishing with the others. He put a hand to a wide center beam as he bent to retrieve his dropped towel. "Now that is a tale worth a beer at least."

There were four quick thuds as four darts hit the wooden beam between his spread fingers and thumb. They hit in such rapid succession that it sounded as though a woodpecker were drumming away.

"Please, good sir, I have no time for games. Two orders of your best breakfast dish for two gold coins and a story to tell."

✕

Dirk had just begun his second plate when people started pouring into the inn. Dirk smiled to himself as he dug into his biscuits and gravy. His second glass of goat's milk washed down a slice of pork.

As he had anticipated, the barkeep's story had spread like wildfire. Not an hour had passed since he rode into town, and he bet that everyone knew he was there. He needed to gain the audience of Lord Carlsborough, but he also needed to eat. By this route he expected to have his audience by the time he had finished his breakfast.

And so it was not a moment before he washed down his last drink of milk that a guard arrived and came to stand behind him. Dirk regarded the soldier over his shoulder; the man raised his chin with an air of importance. The crowd that had been eyeing Dirk with anticipation fell silent. The guard's purposeful cough became the only sound.

"Sir, Lord Carlsborough would have word."

Dirk stood and wiped his mouth. "Excellent in all regards, good sir," he said to the barkeep, and left three gold coins on the bar.

"Lead me to your lord," he instructed the guard.

The guard led Dirk on horseback up the winding hill upon which sat Castle Carlsborough. Dirk veered to the side of the road and off for a moment.

"The castle is this way," said the lord's guard.

"Yes, it is quite hard to miss. But I promised Beauty here some apples," said Dirk as he plucked an apple from one of the many trees which lined the road to the castle. The land of Carlsborough was lush with growth of flower and fruit, the lake effect keeping the air moist and perfect for farming.

Once Beauty had eaten his fill of the treats, they continued on. In short order Dirk stood before Lord Carlsborough. The old man looked to have had a rough morning. He sat upon the dais of the great room upon at a tall chair surrounded by guards—twenty of them, Dirk quickly counted. It seemed that the lord was scared.

Dirk disregarded pleasantries and strode forward purposefully. He did not miss the faint flexing of many of the guard's sword arms.

"You have heard of your kin, then? Surely you do not guard yourself so heavily against word of Whill of Agora?"

Lord Carlsborough took a measure of Dirk. Behind his bushy eyebrows and long nose, suspicious eyes regarded the assassin.

"You are he?" he asked in a strong voice.

"No," said Dirk, shaking his head. "But I am a friend of the man, and I knew his name would gain me audience."

The lord cocked back his head and let out a pensive breath. "Who are you, then?"

"Dirk Blackthorn." He could have used one of his many other names, but he wanted Eadon and Whill alike to know what he had done.

"Why have you sought my audience?"

"I am here to make sure that you and your entire family is not murdered."

The lord smirked at the comment. "You alone?"

"Yes," answered Dirk seriously.

Lord Carlsborough laughed and a few guards joined in.

"With all due respect, Lord Carlsborough, these guards will be of no help to you. The one who hunts you will tear through them as if they were children. I assume you have heard what happened to your kin to the south. Their fate shall be your own lest you heed my words."

Lord Carlsborough shifted uncomfortably in his chair, considering what Dirk had said. "Yes, the horrible news reached me this morning. What are we up against?"

"A dark elf, and possibly a dragon or some other nightmarish flying creature."

"And you have the skills necessary to fight off a dark elf and a dragon?" the lord asked, the humor having left him.

"I do," said Dirk.

Lord Carlsborough mulled over his options for a time. "And why should I believe your tale? You have no credentials to back up your claim. It is possible that you yourself are a spy, or better yet, an assassin."

"If I had been sent here to kill you, sir, you would be dead."

"How dare you threaten the lord in his own keep?" yelled the captain of the guard and stepped forward, hand on hilt.

Dirk did not let his gaze waver from Lord Carlsborough. The lord raised a hand, gesturing for his captain to hold. "A few weeks ago this Whill of Agora fought within the Del'Oradon arena. There are tales of a barbarian woman and a man in black who fought alongside him and escaped with him. Are you that man?"

"I am he," said Dirk with a nod.

The captain leaned in and whispered to his lord. Dirk called upon his enchanted earrings and the hushed voices of the two became clear.

"Sir, I do not trust this man. We have all heard the tales of the man in black who fights with Whill of Agora, but the odds that this man is he, sir...Furthermore, who alerted this man to the murders of your nephew and his family? How does he know it was a dark elf? I would advise strong caution with this one."

Dirk had heard enough. There was just no time for all of this. From his pocket he withdrew two darts and threw them in rapid succession. They exploded in a cloud of thick white smoke among the twenty guards and their lord.

The captain's warning echoed throughout the keep as Dirk brought up his hood. From behind it he could see through the smoke perfectly. He sprinted forward as the captain screamed panicked commands.

"Protect the lord! To me! To me!"

Dirk silently sprinted to the right through the smoke. The guards all looked like drunkards, blinded and coughing as they were. They were easy targets for his darts. He threw five consecutive darts on the fly and five guards fell to the floor. Alert to his fellow soldiers' fall, the closest guard unsheathed his sword and came forward swinging. Dirk came under the ghost swing and hit the guard with a devastating uppercut that left him crumbling to the ground. Moving quickly behind the guards, Dirk came around and kicked the captain in the back, sending him sprawling on the floor through the smoke. The lord yelped when Dirk put his dagger to his throat and pulled him back against the wall.

"Krellentia!" Dirk bellowed and the smoke from the dart-bombs began to fade. When it cleared enough, the captain of the guard saw that his lord was in mortal danger.

"Hold!" he ordered his men.

"Like I said, Lord Carlsborough, if I had been sent here to kill you, you would be dead," said Dirk, loud enough for all to hear. He withdrew his dagger and released the man.

Lord Carlsborough instantly felt his throat and moved away from Dirk. The lord scowled at him as he checked for blood but found none. He looked to the soldiers and back to Dirk.

"They are sleeping, I assure you. Now, shall we plan our defense, or are you not convinced?"

The lord waved away what fog remained before him and shouted to the ceiling, "Will someone open a gods-damned window? Captain!"

"Sir!"

"See that these men are tended to. I will speak privately with Blackthorn."

"Sir?" the Captain began to argue.

"Then you will protect my family from a dark elf?" Lord Carlsborough yelled. The guard lowered his eyes impotently. "All right, then!" said the lord. "See to it that this castle is locked down for the time being. And put the village on alert."

The captain of the guard bowed, and with a quick "yes, sir," he marched to fulfill his duty. But Lord Carlsborough grabbed him by the top of his breastplate and pulled him near.

"We have known that the fight would come to us sooner or later. I am counting on you, Barldan. You are my best man." He released the captain with a slap to the chest. Barldan forgot his passion and nodded to Dirk.

"Yes, my lord."

Dirk followed Lord Carlsborough to a door at the rear of the keep. The lord took a torch from the wall into the room with him. Once inside he bade Dirk close the door and lit three more torches along the wall.

The firelight, along with a faint glow that came from three slits in the stone no larger than murder holes, lit the room. The lord motioned to a chair opposite a large oak desk with deer antlers melded seamlessly into the wood. Many volumes lined the walls, and stacks of papers strewed the dark-finished desk. Dirk realized that this was Lord Carlsborough's personal study.

"It is whiskey for me. What is your spirit?"

"I hear good things about Twin Lakes white wine. Have you any?"

"Of course!" said Lord Carlsborough, smacking his head. "Good call, sir. I have a bottle, vintage fifty-one forty-five, given to me by my brother." He rummaged in the bottom of his wine cabinet. "Aha." He blew dust from the bottle and wiped its label. "Twenty-five-year-old wine on the day I die," he mused and seemed to lose himself to nostalgia. He shook himself out of the trance and smiled in grandfatherly way at Dirk. After retrieving a wine opener, he sat.

"Ever had wine aged so?" he asked Dirk as the cork popped free.

Dirk was reminded of the centuries-old wine he had shared with Eadon. "Never," he answered as the gold goblet before him was filled. Lord Carlsborough lifted a matching goblet and made a toast. "To Dirk Blackthorn, the only man to hold a knife to my throat and live."

Dirk nodded and touched goblets. He took a long, slow smell of the crisp white and drank. He sampled the wine slowly, letting it sit in his mouth for a time before swallowing it shallowly. The remaining wine danced on his tongue, and as he opened his mouth and took the air, the sweetness of spring exploded in it. A quick tartness followed and finished with a fruity tail.

"I have drunk elven wine that could not stand up to this masterpiece."

"Indeed." The lord nodded and followed the wine with a large shot of whiskey. He lit a pipe with faintly quaking hands and puffed the smoke, only to drink again from his goblet. Dirk watched him as he poured another shot for himself.

"Lord Carlsborough," said Dirk.

"Hmm?" The lord jumped as if he had forgotten Dirk was there. The assassin had seen it before—men who thought they would not see the morning drinking themselves stupid.

"This is the first time you have faced certain death?"

The lord focused on Dirk and scowled as he put down his glass. "Of course not! I did my time for my country. I fret not for myself; I am an old man who has had a life of hard work and good fortune. It is for my family that I worry. This town is home to my two sons and their six children and wives." He looked at Dirk with sudden brave determination. "What do we do?"

CHAPTER TWENTY-SEVEN

Zorriaz the White

Whill left Zerafin's abode and used the sword to fly to his home in the Thousand Falls. He found Avriel there on the balcony, curled up and looking smaller than usual. Whill touched her consciousness and found it sad.

"I can do it," said Whill as he walked to stand by her. She raised her big head and regarded him through dragon tears. "Do you trust me?"

Avriel slowly nodded. *I trust you…*

"I…the Other read Eadon's mind during the torture. I learned this spell also," said Whill.

Avriel shook her head. "But you do not remember it, the Other does. And if you are mistaken…I do not want to die like this."

"I can do it. I must. You are slipping away, Avriel, the dragon is taking hold. All day you recite your dragon memories to the lore masters. You hesitate for fear of your dragon form; what of your elven body?"

Avriel sighed and the balcony vibrated. "It seems that if you cannot do it, then no one can."

"Then we fly. We do it now."

Whill rode Avriel to the house of healing in which her body was preserved by the ever-diligent healers. A line of elves stretched from the door and over a small bridge across a slow river, and still the line went around a corner from pathway to the cobblestone street. These elves were giving gifts of energy to their beloved princess Avriel.

She circled the house of healing and landed upon the well-manicured lawn of clover. Her clawed feet sunk slightly into the earth and water pooled around her claws. Zerafin was there, as were the queen and a handful of elves. Avriel's still form lay upon a silken white bed. Mesh curtains made up the walls of the house of healing, and they danced slowly with a light breeze. The sun was on its way down beyond the Thousand Falls, and the elven buildings and pyramids of the city had begun their soft nightly glow.

"Both of Avriel's bodies must be brought close together," said Whill to the nearby elves. They looked to the queen for guidance.

"How do you know the spell required to move her soul from one body to the next?" asked Queen Araveal, taking a step between Whill and Avriel's elven form.

"I do not understand how I know it, but I do," answered Whill. "Avriel has decided... I must be alone for a moment, pardon me."

Whill left the house of healing and followed a winding garden path to a small stream. He knelt on the bank and sat on his legs. With a deep breath he closed his eyes and spoke to the Other.

"I would have words with you now," he said in his mind, and looked into the slow-moving water of the stream. The reflection of his tortured self stared back at him, and grinned.

"You said you could heal Avriel. Is that true?"

Slowly the Other nodded and smiled wider, cracking his chapped lips.

"And in return for your help, you seek the sword of power taken?"

Whill's reflection moved on its own, leaning closer to the surface.

"You know this all to be true. Do you wish to see Avriel restored? That is the only question. If so, give me control to do my work."

"No!" yelled Whill immediately. "Give me the knowledge that I must know to help her myself."

"I cannot," said the Other, annoyed. "You cannot take knowledge from me unless you embrace every memory that I am. Are you prepared to remember those six bloody months?"

Whill shook his head, as did the reflection of the Other.

"No, you cannot bear the memories," the Other agreed. "You are too weak."

Whill shuddered as he stared into the Other's blood-shot eyes. He heard the chains and the whips, felt the constant ache of the cuffs.

"Do what you must," Whill said and closed his eyes.

He felt nothing happen within. He opened his eyes and looked at his hands and realized he hadn't willed his arms to move. He rose and turned back toward the house of healing, yet he did not command his legs. Whill tried to speak but found that he could not. All he could do was watch and listen.

"Stop fighting it or my hand may slip," the Other warned out loud. Whill calmed himself and focused instead on his connection with the blade. He could not stop fighting the invasion of his body, and he did not like where he was being kept. He saw through his eyes, but the view was down a long, strange tunnel. The sounds of the world became mangled, twisted and mixed with strange whispers and screams in the dark. He felt monsters at his back, always beyond the corner of the eye. Whill realized that this was the part of his mind in which he kept the Other.

The voices became louder and the screams closer. Whill panicked, knowing that he could not get out, could not take control. If he fought for dominance, Avriel would not be helped. He tried to calm his mind and focus but he could not. The voices were now like booming explosions in his ears, the echoing unbearable. Whill mentally screamed and the Watcher cursed as he walked into the room.

"Be calm!" the Other Whill yelled, and many elves jumped.

Inside the twisted depths of his mind, Whill flew from the voices and the screams, the whispers and the sneers. He willed himself to not be in control, but out.

There was a flash and Whill was standing across from the Other, who still controlled his body. A sparkling silver tether of twisting light connected Whill's astral form with his physical. The Other Whill looked at him and grinned.

Between them lay Avriel's elven body and her dragon form. Avriel's voice came into his mind, and to Whill she sounded scared. "You...there are two of you."

Whill looked from Avriel to the onlooking elves. He realized then that they could see his astral projection through their mind-sight. They looked at him curiously; the queen regarded him with concern. When

she spoke, she did not address Whill's body but his projected self.

"Can you control...yourself?"

Whill's projection nodded.

"Look!" An elven healer pointed. Whill looked too
and watched as his body slowly began to change. Cuts
appeared upon his bare arms and face; bruises and festering wounds sprouted from his skin. Blood trickled
from his eyes, nose, and ears as the Other was manifested through him. His wrists split above his palm, and
from the wounds, thick, barbed chains erupted. One
wrapped itself around Avriel's elven ankle, the other
around her dragon leg. The barbs sank deep into each.

The other unsheathed Adromida and held it above
his head with both hands. Whill panicked, thinking
that the Other meant to kill both Avriels. A gale struck
the house of healing, sending the thin curtains flapping noisily as a whirlwind surrounded them all. Whill
watched as the Other chanted in a language he had
never heard before. His voice boomed, shaking Whill's
corporeal form.

The Other pulled massive amounts of energy from
Adromida and a surge coursed through his body and
down the bloody chains. Both of Avriel's bodies stiffened and heaved. Elves hurried to be out of the reach
of the dragon's thrashing claws and deadly tail. Again
a surge of power rippled through the blade to the two
bodies.

As Whill watched, an elf gasped, and though her eyes were closed, Whill knew that with her mind-sight she saw what Whill saw. There at the center of Avriel's dragon chest shone a bright white orb. The Other used the steady current of energy from the blade to capture Avriel's soul with energy and slowly guide it out. The dragon roared and thrashed and the Watcher sent another surge of energy from Whill and into the dragon body. The encapsulated soul of Avriel rose from the dragon body and was guided across and into the chest of the elven body. There was a blinding surge of power and a humming from the blade Adromida. Avriel's body convulsed and arched like a bow upon the white sheets and slowly floated above the bed. Then the chains suddenly receded and Avriel's body fell back to the bed below.

Whill watched as his body wavered and fell to the ground. Suddenly he was pulled forward as if an invisible wave had crashed into him. He returned to his body, gasping for breath. His wounds were gone, and there was no sign of the Other.

"Avriel!" Zerafin called to his sister as he lightly tapped her cheek.

Whill got to his feet and pushed through the crowding elves. "Is she alive? Did it work?" Whill begged as he pushed forward and watched as Zerafin and Araveal tended to her.

"She is not breathing!" Zerafin said helplessly as he intensified his attempts to revive her. He surrounded her with blue tendrils of healing but her condition would not change.

She will die came a voice in his mind.

"We had a deal!" Whill shouted and received many strange looks.

You never agreed. I would have your word, said the Other.

"You have my word! You shall have the blade Nodae. Now help her!" Whill pleaded.

Very well, said the Other.

Whill's hand reached out toward Avriel, and from her a mass of black energy swirled into his palm. Avriel's body arched and she gasped for air. She blinked, confused, and breathed the precious air into her lungs.

"The dragon!" she screamed and fought those who held her down. "The dragon, do not let it die!"

"The body of the dragon lives, fret not, sister," said Zerafin as he stroked her sweat-covered brow.

"Whill." She smiled as he came close. She reached out and he took her hand. It was warm to the touch. Whill looked into Avriel's elven eyes for the first time since she had tried to end herself so long ago.

"You did it," she said as tears welled in her eyes. "Thank you, thank you."

Queen Araveal took Whill by the arm and gently urged him aside so that they might speak privately. She smiled at him, but Whill saw slight apprehension in her eyes.

"You have given me back my daughter. I am forever in your debt." She squeezed his hands softly.

"She is all right, that is all that matters," answered Whill, hoping that she would not ask what he knew was on her mind.

"May I ask—," she began, but he cut her off quickly.

"You may, but I cannot answer what I do not yet understand."

Araveal watched him closely and Whill could hardly bear her scrutiny. "I must know for the sake of my people, was that...other, was it the dark one?"

"No," he answered truthfully.

After a time she smiled, but he could not be sure she believed him.

"That language you spoke, do you know of it?" she asked.

Whill shook his head. "I have, it seems, though I do not know the words."

Queen Araveal did not hide her concern. "Is there anything I can do to help?"

"Allow me to see Avriel," he answered with a grin.

The queen laughed. "Of course. Thank you once again."

Whill bowed to the queen and the bow was returned. Avriel had sat up but was still being checked by the many healers. Her elven body had been kept from wasting away by their constant vigilance. Still, blue tendrils surrounded her as the healers extended their consciousness out through the energy ribbons. After a time they were satisfied that she was well.

"Yes, yes, I feel fine, spend your energies on…" She meant to say the dragon's name, Whill knew, and he watched as her eyes wondered and she looked to be remembering something. "Her mother had intended the name Zorriaz," said Avriel as she reached from her bed to touch the body that had contained her. The body of Zorriaz the White, daughter of Kyrayn, daughter of Knorr, daughter of a thousand dragons before her.

"Zorriaz is her name. Zorriaz," she said to no one as she leaned closer and stroked what had once been her snout. The body of the dragon breathed slowly and steadily, and the heart kept a constant rhythm. But there was no spirit within, no soul for the vessel to serve, and so it slept. Without the effort of the healers, it would remain motionless until it died of starvation.

"I am sorry, Zorriaz," Avriel said. "I am sorry that you were forced out of your body to save someone who tried to die. I would see the return of your dragon soul. I would see you live and fly high as a dragon can fly." Her elven tears fell upon dragon claw.

The inner glow that illuminated the house of healing wavered and pulsed randomly. The wind once again stirred the thin silken curtains, and many elves looked around apprehensively. Whill had just performed a spell no one had ever seen, and there was palpable tension in the air.

Zerafin looked around. "The house of healing remains rich with psychic and spiritual residue. The energy of the magic performed hangs in the air like humid summer dew. Look with your mind-sight, Whill."

He did, and he saw what Zerafin had meant. Magical residue swirled in clouds of sparkling light all around the house of healing. But Whill did not understand the concern he had heard in Zerafin's voice. Surely such spells let off residue.

They do, said Avriel's voice in Whill's head. *But the wielder of such spells is supposed to take back the leftover magic. You, it seems, did not.*

Is that bad? Whill asked.

It can have some…interesting results.

Why didn't someone, I don't know, absorb my leftover magic?

Avriel looked from the surrounding magical discharge to Whill. *Because that power is from the blade Adromida, and none would dare take it ungiven, for the legends say it means death to any elf who would attempt to wield it.*

Apparently Zerafin was privy to Avriel's side of the conversation, for he turned to Whill with a pensive look. "You should absorb the leftover energy. Your spell is still alive in this place."

Avriel looked around with renewed wonder. "The very spell that helped me back to my body…"

"No, sister. These things are not to be meddled with," warned Zerafin, and Whill began to understand. Avriel meant to summon the lost dragon soul, Zorriaz, or somehow already was.

"You may return now," Avriel said to the high, ascending folds of fabric that were the ceiling.

"Avriel! This is not something to be toyed with!" Zerafin yelled.

The wind had picked up, and the air, thick with buzzing energy, became suffocating. Whill reached out with his mind and found resistance, but then Avriel let down her shield for him. When he made contact with her mind, he heard a constant chanting in a dozen Avriel voices. Whill realized she was chanting a spell, a big spell.

Avriel glared at her brother as he took their mother by the shoulders and backed up with her as if protect her. The queen shoved off from her son's guidance and stepped forward purposefully.

"The laws of the elves of the sun forbid this form of Orna Catorna. Stop at once."

Avriel smiled to her mother and spoke a word. "Zorriaz."

With his mind-sight Whill watched as the swirling magical residue converged upon itself. Electric humming and snapping emanated from the quickly forming dense orb of power. The energy swirled into a speck no larger than a coin and suddenly shot forth blinding light. Everyone who had been watching with their mind-sight reeled back as if their eyes had been scorched. Whill held his head in pain and forced himself to look once more. All sound ceased, not a thing stirred within the house of healing, and all watched as a shimmering dragon soul drifted into the body of the dragon.

There was an explosion of sound and action as the dragon soul returned home. The white dragon Zorriaz lurched to life, spewing flame that engulfed two stunned healers.

CHAPTER
TWENTY-EIGHT
The Assassin

Late into the afternoon the townspeople scrambled to prepare for the expected attack. Water was pumped from the wells constantly as every bucket that could be found was filled and either stored away at strategic locations or used to wet the many thatch roofs. Lord Carlsborough had ordered every harpoon to the castle walls, though Dirk thought they would be of little use against the enchantments Krentz had surely laid upon her mount.

He guessed that Krentz would use the same stealth she had shown in Bristle. If so, there was little to worry from the dragon mount unless she called to it for help. If she was alerted to the village's anticipation of her attack, she would use the dragon to cause chaos. Therefore, Dirk's plan was for the town's preparedness to be as inconspicuous as possible. If he could lure Krentz into the keep after her targets, his plan might work.

Dirk reminded himself that he was here for Krentz, after all; he couldn't give a damn about the village. If she had not sacrificed herself for him, he would be the one to fear tonight.

The day passed and the village was prepared as well as possible. The women and children were brought to the subterranean chambers of the keep; there they would not suffer the wrath of the dragon at least. These chambers had been built for this very thing, and had been needed at times throughout the centuries. As much as Dirk loathed the idea of being trapped in the catacombs of the castle, he knew he might very well have to make a final stand there.

As twilight began to mark the end of the day, Dirk walked the parapet of Castle Carlsborough. He gazed down on the castle, memorizing its layout. He needed every advantage he could get.

The castle sat high atop the largest hill, overlooking the distant lakes. The rolling hills on which the village was settled shared the same magnificent view. From this high perch Dirk still could not see the other side of the lakes before the horizon; they were two of the largest in all of Agora.

Dirk took note of the high outer wall of the castle, and the still-higher inner wall. Many of the massive barbarian stones had been used in the making of these walls, and though this was not a large castle, its walls were made of huge solid slabs. It could withstand the bombardment of heavy siege weapons easily. A dragon could hurl itself against this ancient keep, which looked as though it grew out of the hill.

Though there was no moat, there was a steep incline to reach the level castle landing. Boulders had been tethered against the side of the walls by many chains, boulders that could flatten a shed. When set loose, the stones could flatten enemy soldiers storming the castle from all sides. In a ring around the castle hill, under the well-kept grass, were thousands of pointed metal spears. Levers in the castle set in motion a chain reaction of gears and pulleys, causing the spikes to rotate on their hidden platform and stick out straight. The trap was tested monthly and kept well oiled. But all of these things would not stop a shadow, could not keep away one coming from the sky. The dragon harpoons would be enough to deter a normal dragon, assuming he was not out for revenge. But Krentz's mount would be a gift from her father. Likely it would be one of his own creation, and powerful.

Dirk made his rounds and attached an explosive dart to the tip of every harpoon spear. He had given the spearmen code names consisting of colors. On his command, the different harpoons would be shot off. The captain of the guard had personally ordered his men to obey Dirk's command, though Dirk knew it begrudged him to do so. If the men obeyed his orders and did not misfire in a fit of dragon fear, they might at least be able to turn away the dragon. Dirk was not concerned; he cared only for facing the rider.

The sun set slowly and time ticked in Dirk's mind like the lamenting church bells of Bellowsblood, the village of his youth, where fall seemed the only season and pumpkins the only crop. The village had been the birthplace of Stefayn Bellowsblood, one of the most celebrated lore masters of Eldalon. His monster and ghost lore had become the staple of Agoran superstition centuries past. The village had become a testament to the man, and survived mainly by selling Bellowsblood mojo dolls, Bellowsblood boards of conjuring, and other namesake items. Many believed the items worked, and they were often used in medicine.

The night arrived and they waited. The men below in the village, the many teams of spearmen ready to spring from under heavy tarps, the bowmen behind the murder holes, and the swordsmen waiting in the courtyard below and beyond the doors of the keep—they all knew fear. Dirk wondered what kind of pandemonium he would witness this night. From his pouch he took the wolf figurine. He had warned the soldiers that a timber wolf fought with him, but he doubted they had believed him.

"Chief," he whispered. "Come."

The swirling mist set the ramparts aglow as Chief came to form in a few heartbeats. Instantly Chief became curious of their environment. He sniffed at the edge of the castle wall and panted with exhilaration.

"The time has come, boy. As we speak, she rides on wings of death. Harbinger of death…"

Chief cocked his head to the side as Dirk trailed off and his eyes drifted to the stars. A hushed bark snapped him from his dark imaginations and he saw the world once more.

Through his hood the nighttime veil was lifted, and the world was shown to him. Little was unseen. His body tensed as he spotted a bright heat signature far off to the south. From his perch he gave a small howl. Chief stared at him, seemingly unimpressed, and gave a strong, keening howl himself. It was the warning signal: the assassin had arrived. Krentz was coming for the blood of Whill's line.

Dirk watched as the creature flew steadily toward the town. As it neared, it became apparent that it was indeed a dragon. He looked from under his hood and saw nothing—it was invisible. Dirk knew then that the beast was indeed one of Eadon's silverhawk dragons, and its rider was Krentz.

The dragon-hawk glided over the town without as much as a sound. Over the hill it went, and once over the castle, a figure leapt from the beast. It twirled, falling some thirty feet and landing without a whisper.

Dirk watched on high as the crouched figure listened in the shadows, its armored head scanning the perimeter. Dirk had ordered three guards to stay at their stations for the duration of the night. He knew that these men would die, but it had to look as though everything were normal lest Krentz think her element of surprise gone, at which time she would turn to the brutal destructive force of the dragon.

A blade whizzed through the air, and with a thud one of the guards gurgled to the floor. Three quick, well-placed leaps took the dark-elf assassin up to the castle wall. The nearest guard found a sword through his chest and fell with a puzzled look on his face. The third jumped over the wall.

Dirk reached into his pocket for a spell-dissipating throwing star and looked away for but a second. When he looked back toward the assassin, he found her three feet away. A blade came down as Dirk's dagger shot out and up. A clawed hand shot out at Dirk and there was a flash of silver light. Dirk quickly turned into his warded cloak's thick folds and rolled away, deflecting the spell. He came around suddenly with a lunging strike with his short sword. Metal clanged and sparks flew as the blades crashed into each other's enchantments.

The lithe form of the dark-elf assassin moved as a ghost. Dirk could barely make out a full-faced helmet behind the shadows that seemed to cling to it. Dirk threw a dart as he spun and came in with a dagger slash but had to move away quickly as the dark elf unleashed a powerful blast that shook the stone. Nearby a dragon screeched, and Dirk heard a spearman give warning.

"Dragon!" he screamed, and fire split the night off near the eastern wall.

Dirk was blasted off the wall to land in the courtyard. He came up out of the roll and climbed stairs to the upper wall three at a time. "Red team and yellow, purple then blue—fire!" Dirk screamed, and to his surprise the spearmen followed his command to the letter.

Red team, which consisted of two harpoon teams, shot from two locations toward the belching flame. Boom! A blast shook the castle as the first of the darts exploded against the dragon's protective enchantments. Boom! Another lit the sky. Two quick, buzzing shrieks rang out as yellow team shot their harpoons. One dart missed but the other exploded in a shower of shimmering blue dust. The dragon lurched and slammed into the castle as Dirk ran toward the beast. Behind him the dark elf charged, flinging deadly daggers at the spearmen. A thud marked the death of one soldier of blue team. Dirk leapt high up and off a short wall. Spinning in the air, he threw two explosive darts at Krentz and threw his grappling hook as he leapt out over the courtyard. The hook caught and wedged in a crack in the stone, and Dirk glided to the opposite end of the courtyard.

There was a shriek as the awkwardly flying, convulsing dragon wavered as if injured by the blasts. The guards began to cheer, but soon the cheers ended as fire poured up and above the side of the wall in waves. The dragon beat its massive wings and once again gained a high position over the courtyard. Purple team and blue team fired in unison, and Dirk closed his eyes as the flash bomb went off, followed by the darts of silence. The dragon was blinded and suddenly hovered in a soundless vacuum. The dragon lurched, disoriented, as Chief leapt from the wall with a growl and, landing on its snout, began to claw and bite savagely. As the dragon and spirit wolf battled out of sight, the dark elf leapt down to face Dirk, who stood in the shadows by the keep door.

"Krentz, there is a way to overcome this, you must not do this!" Dirk cried.

The graceful dark elf slid her sword into a sheath as smooth and black as her tight armor. No cloak trailed behind, no coat hung from her shoulders. The armor appeared seamless; smooth and dark, it contoured the body perfectly, every muscle and curve carved into it.

"Beyond this door lies your quarry, women, children…I know what you did in Bristle, I saw the mother, the daughter, the black rose. Please—"

Dirk was forced to duck behind the stone archway before the keep door as three throwing stars cut into the stone. Dirk threw a blinding dart at the assassin's feet and came in with a barrage of sword and dagger strikes that pushed his opponent to defend or die. Serpents of blue flame shot out at Dirk but were absorbed by his cloak. He felt the hum of power as his many enchantments were strengthened by the energy. Sparks flew from his blades as the dark elf met him blow for blow.

The dark elf stepped back, and from her left hand shot crackling lightning. Dirk pulled his cloak around him but it did not spare him the brunt of the blast, which sent him hurling through the air to slam into the wall once more.

Dirk rebounded quickly and came in low. From a leg strap he flung a dart at a pillar to the left of the dark elf. The dart hit and there was a click as the back of the dart exploded and ten smooth, round steel pellets shot toward the dark elf while Dirk came in with a low sword swipe. The missiles deflected in a shower of sparks against her energy shield as the dark elf met Dirk's blade and with blinding speed caught him with a kick to the ribs that took him off his feet. He slammed into a pillar with crushing force and slid to the floor. The dark elf turned from him, conjured a green fireball in her palm, and hurled it at the keep door. Surprised screams of pain came from the burning wreckage as smoke billowed out of the keep door.

Out charged the captain of the guard and a dozen soldiers. The men screamed and charged the dark elf bravely. The assassin flung her hand out wide and every last man was slammed back against the wall. Dirk glanced at the dark elf's feet and cursed her closer, into his trap.

"Hey!" he screamed as he got up and threw a dart bomb at her face, followed by a flash dart and seven consecutive throwing stars. The assassin redirected the missiles to blast into many of the guards, who had begun to get up and shake off their daze. A harpoon came slicing through the air only to explode midflight in a quick blaze that left only ashes falling slowly through the air. The dark elf reared on the harpoon team and blasted them from the wall with a ball of lightning.

"Krentz!" Dirk screamed. "Stop this madness now!"

She turned and regarded him with a cocked head. She raised her left hand and there was a black rose held in it. Her right hand moved to her neck and peeled back the faceless mask. Krentz shook her head and her hair spilled out and down her back. Tears pooled in her eyes.

"Oh, Dirk, my love," Krentz cried and stepped closer. Another step brought her a foot from the trap. Her face came into view clearer in the moonlight, and Dirk watched in horror as her cries turned to laughter and her face contorted in a snarl.

"No, she will not stop; we will not stop until every human of Whill's line is dead." She laughed. The captain of the guard howled and charged, his blade meant to impale her suddenly. With a clash she sent his sword flying and sliced through his armor, leaving an X of blood across his chest and glowing edges on the armor. The guard fell and stared dead-eyed at Dirk.

"Krentz," Dirk began.

"No, my dear boy," laughed the dark elf. "I am not Krentz."

The face of Krentz contorted and the tattoos swirled. The hair turned blue from the roots to the tips, and Dirk looked into the eyes of a dark elf he recognized. She was one of the twins he had seen in Eadon's floating palace of crystal. She was a twin!

Dirk whirled to the right as a sword slashed across his cloak and back, cutting the cloak in half and slashing a long gash across Dirk's shoulder. Both dark elves came at him then, but the Krentz-impersonating twin stepped on his special trap. There was a click as she stepped on the loosened stone he had put his bomb under, and for a brief moment Dirk was satisfied to see her surprised. He threw a cyclone dart at her feet as the trap exploded in a raging ball of fire. The dark-elf twin was caught up in the cyclone of burning dragonsbreath and, screaming, was lifted up into the night by the explosion. Dirk braced himself as the whirlwind pulled in everything in the courtyard not tied down.

He had only a few darts that could cause such havoc and he rarely used them, but facing both of these dark-elf assassins at the same time was cause for such extreme force. The dark elf's sister came at him in a rage of slashes and powerful blows. Their blades sent showers of sparks into the cyclone above as the dark elf pressed Dirk toward the whirlwind.

Boom! The dragon slammed into the wall of the castle and roared in a rage. Fire leapt up into the whirlwind as the dragon clawed its way up onto the castle wall. It spotted one of its riders and belched flame down on Dirk. He dove to the left and rolled himself into his cloak as the flames engulfed the courtyard.

When the fire subsided, the dark-elf assassin was there, chopping down at him from on high. A cross-blade block stopped the attack but the dark elf slammed down on him, trying to pin him. Dirk rolled onto his back, heaving with his legs. The dark elf twirled through the air to land on her feet as Dirk got to his. The dragon roared again and cocked its head as if to breathe fire once more. Chief flew from nowhere and landed claws first on the dragon's face. The beast reared and slipped as the cyclone pulled on it as well. The dragon-hawk crashed into the courtyard as it pawed at its snout, trying to dislodge the spirit wolf, but Chief would not be budged. The ghost wolf became translucent as the great clawed paw came at him to squash him. When the hand receded, the wolf turned to physical form and slashed at the snout and eyes. Blood and feathers had begun to fall from the furious dragon-hawk's face.

The burning body of the other dark elf landed upon the stairs to the wall and rolled to the bottom. Dirk followed his attacker's eyes and saw fear there. He grinned.

"Chief, kill the burning elf!" he ordered and threw Krone at the dragon. Chief had clawed and bitten enough to weaken the dragon's magical defenses, and Dirk's enchanted dagger plunged through it. It twirled through the air and into the dragon's mouth, wedging itself in the soft skin between the dragon's teeth.

Chief landed upon the burning dark elf just as her healing light began to glow. The spirit wolf bit her neck and shook violently, trying to break it. Sparks popped and flew from the dark elf's energy shield as the spirit wolf raked with vicious claws that carried with them the mysterious power of the other side.

The other assassin snarled and met Dirk once more in battle. She flung a ball of fire at him but it was absorbed by his enchanted left glove. The gems within the glove began to glow with the absorbed power. Dirk took advantage of her surprise and shot the glove out forward, sending the pent-up energy in a shockwave that crushed the center of a giant pillar. The pillar was one of four that held the giant slab of the upper floor, and it shuddered and cracked when its supporting pillar crumbled. Dirk had chosen that very pillar because it was above the thrashing dark elf and Chief.

Dirk's opponent screamed as the slab buckled and cracked and fell with crushing force upon her sister and Chief. Seeing the tide of the battle turning, the guards rallied their courage and poured out of the destroyed keep door. Men scrambled to man the harpoons, not daring to imagine what had happened to the last spearmen. By the dozens they poured, and their quarry was the dark elf. Dirk pressed his attack in a blur of spinning sword and dagger. The dark elf looked from Dirk to the charging men, then to the dragon that sat upon the wall like a statue, paralyzed to move against him, and finally to her sister, crushed beneath the weight of the stone, her energy shield flickering and sparking against the great weight. With a cry she shot a glowing orb of energy at the center of the attacking men. It exploded with a bang, sending many men flying through the air, and still they charged.

Whirling away from Dirk, she darted to her sister's side. Dirk looked up at the dragon and screamed, "Kill her!" The mind control dagger Krone forced it to obey.

The elf skidded to a stop before her crushed sister and with raised arms began to mentally lift the stone slab. The dragon roared and leapt from the wall onto the slanted broken slab. The pinned elf's energy shield died in a show of webbing lightning. Beneath the stone slab the dark elf fell to one knee with the effort of keeping it off her sister. She trembled and quaked, and from her mind curled tendrils of healing energy. The guards came with a dozen swords that exploded against her shield. The men pounded with sword and axe, weakening her shield. Dirk threw the last of his dragonsbreath darts at the trapped, dying elf. The bomb exploded on impact with the elf's energy shield and the explosion cracked the slab further, causing it to break off at the high end and come crashing down upon the courtyard.

The dragon-hawk slammed a huge front paw down on the remaining twin. With a grunt she ducked under her protective shield as it absorbed the blow. With a scream of rage she blasted the dragon with a massive surge of lightning that left her trembling, her energy spent. The guards slashed and stabbed as Dirk came at her from the right, whipping daggers in rapid succession. The dark elf began to tremble and shake. She screamed so loud that it was instantly deafening. The daggers were deflected by the shield but it was wavering. The dragon rebounded from the wall and slammed the dark elf into the far wall. She shot out of the destroyed wall and charged at Dirk with murder in her eyes and her sword leading. Dirk braced himself, but the blow never came. The dragon lunged forward and struck like a snake, catching the dark elf in its jaws with a snap. The teeth clamped down and she screamed as her energy shield was taxed to exhaustion. The dragon shook its head violently and slammed the elf down, shattering the stones beneath her broken form. Dirk came down with his sword, stabbing her in the chest as a dagger found her throat and drew blood.

"Where is Krentz?" he demanded. Blue healing energy swirled around the sword in her chest. She coughed red and grinned with bloody teeth.

"Gods take you, worm," she snarled as a weapon clattered upon the stone. Dirk realized it was the mind-control dagger he had wedged between the dragon's teeth. The dragon was no longer under his control. Dirk pulled his blade from the dark elf's chest, and blood gushed for a moment but stopped as she used what power she had left to heal the mortal wound.

Dirk stepped back from the dragon that now glared at him with ice-blue eyes of cold fury. The guards followed Dirk's lead. The dark elf laughed and no longer gurgled from her wounds.

"Now you will die,—" she said, and was bitten in half by the dragon. Her torso and legs stood for a moment and then slowly fell to the knees and stone. The dragon shook its head and sent the upper body over the castle wall.

Everyone looked at the dragon in a defensive crouch, but the dragon looked at Dirk. No one moved. Dirk slowly sheathed his sword, and then his dagger. The dragon watched his every move.

Dirk squared up on the dragon from ten feet away and put out his empty hands. "I have no quarrel with you, dragon. It seems that our enemies were one and the same. We have no quarrel with you."

The dragon-hawk reared and ruffled its large silver feathers, causing it to appear double its size. Feathers crowned the dragon's head around two large, straight back horns. From behind a beaked snout, the dragon's intelligent eyes looked to the dead dark elves and to Dirk. Finally the dragon lowered its gaze and turned to climb the broken wall and be away.

"Silver dragon-hawk!" Dirk yelled.

The creature turned from the wall slowly and regarded the assassin.

"Where will you go? You have no home. You are defying your maker and you know not the world."

The dragon-hawk's feathers changed to match the stone and night sky above. Only the eyes were left to see clearly. The dragon-hawk listened.

"I too have been the dark elves' captive, I too would seek revenge! I can show you the world; I can lead you to more of our enemies. I know of an island of dragons—I can lead you home, whatever you wish. Let me be your rider and I promise you friendship and loyalty."

The guards watched on wordlessly, thinking Dirk insane. The dragon-hawk regarded the stars for a time and then knelt upon the stone wall, offering a boost to the first saddle rung. Dirk slowly climbed the broken wall to stand next to the dragon. There was a terrifying moment of anticipation as he put his boot up onto the dragon's leg. Dirk climbed up to sit in the forward seat of the twin saddle. He took the reins and nodded down at the astonished guards as the dragon-hawk leapt and soared out into the night.

CHAPTER
TWENTY-NINE
King Zerafin

Zerafin redirected the dragonsbreath of Zorriaz high as Whill raised a hand and squeezed the air, and the dragon's mouth clamped shut. Fire instead raged out of its nose as it reared and its tail sent four elves flying.

"Zorriaz, stop!" Avriel yelled and the dragon obeyed. The flames subsided and she walked toward Avriel. With the aid of the other healers, the two engulfed elves were tended to, healing blue energy surrounding their burnt bodies.

Zorriaz bent her neck to meet Avriel's gaze. The dragon smelled her hair and stared at her through large eyes. Avriel lifted a quivering hand as tears ran down her face.

"Hello, Zorriaz. Be still, you are safe here," Avriel crooned.

"Are you mad?" Queen Araveal screamed at her daughter.

"Zorriaz wanted to return. I simply helped her."

"You are out of control, Avriel!"

"I am centuries old. I do not need mothering."

The queen stepped forward into her daughter's space and Avriel could not hold her gaze. "I speak to you not as your mother but as Queen of Drindellia! There are laws of conduct for a reason. Do you think you are the first to wish to reverse death? It is forbidden."

Avriel bravely stepped forward to meet her mother's glare. "You allowed such a thing in my transformation, Queen Araveal."

"And my punishment will be the relinquishing of my crown," said the queen with a raised chin.

Avriel jerked back as if slapped. "Mother, no," she whispered.

"It must be so. I have willingly broken the rule of resurrection and I shall be punished accordingly. If I as queen do not uphold my people's laws, then I am not fit to rule. Such is the way of the elves of the sun. You, my dear daughter, shall also answer for what you have done. I do not know how you did it, but you did."

"I did it!" Whill suddenly blurted. Everyone in attendance turned to look at him. "I summoned the dragon soul, for it lingered still, unable to return to its vessel but also unable to move on. She is right, it wanted to return, but Eadon's spell made it unable. I simply opened the door, if you will."

The queen looked from Whill to Avriel, then left and right to the elven healers. "Is that what happened here?" she asked.

Heads slowly nodded agreement.

"Very well. I have been mistaken," she said to the group, and looked into her daughter's eyes. "It appears as though Avriel is innocent," she said, and lingered long in her gaze.

A man who would lie for you truly loves you, said the queen in her mind, and Avriel smiled.

Beware. It also means that he would lie to you for you.

Avriel's smile disappeared as her mother turned and left, with a quick glance at Whill.

Whill watched from the balcony as Avriel combed her long hair. It had grown down to the small of her back these six months, and Whill liked the look. In her bright white gown of golden lace, she looked every part the princess of Elladrindellia.

He moved from the balcony to stand behind her. Through the mirror he smiled.

"What?" She blushed.

"And thine eyes had not seen, nor had thine ears heard, until they beheld thee," he said to her reflection.

"A reciter of elven poetry?" She smiled brightly. "I had not thought you the type."

"I have read some, but rarely does life mimic such verse," he said with a grin.

Her room in the palace near the heart of the city faced the city's gathering hill, the very hill upon which Whill had been attacked, and Avriel had killed her kin. A light breeze blew through the open balcony door, and upon it rode elven music.

Whill was struck by the memory of another elven poem. He looked in the mirror as he began to recite it, and then recoiled with alarm.

"I had thought her dead for so long," said the Other. He reached a broken-nailed and bloody hand toward the surface of the mirror, and Whill jumped to grab Avriel. He pulled her from the mirror as the hand reached. Whill pulled her up and held her to him. Looking back at the mirror, he saw the Other was gone. Only his terrified reflection stared back at him.

"Whill, what is it?"

Whill scowled at his reflection and leaned closer, inspecting the mirror and the room within it. There in the reflection, leaning cross-armed against the balcony door, was the Other.

"Powerful things, mirrors," said the Other. "I am surprised one such as her would risk one." He cocked his head at Whill. "Have you ever thought her to be vain?"

"Whill, is it the Other?" Avriel asked quietly.

He looked at her wide-eyed and nodded slowly. "Can you not hear him?"

She shook her head and put her hand upon his shoulder. "What does he say?"

The Other laughed. "Tell her I love her."

Whill picked up the carved chair that Avriel had sat on, and with a growl he smashed the mirror. Avriel backed from him and the flying glass.

"It will not be that easy, my cowardly friend," laughed the Other from the balcony.

"You leave her alone, you sick, twisted son of a—"

"Do not take our mother's name in vain!" the Other screamed in a sudden rage that made Whill blink. "You ungrateful worm! I give us back Avriel, I bear the brunt of our torture, and this is what I get." He walked toward Whill slowly, threateningly. "You forget, I am you. Remember that when you look at her. Remember that when you touch her," he said, and was gone.

Whill blinked and looked around the room, to the broken mirror and into Avriel's eyes. "I...," he began, but could not find the words. The way Avriel looked at him took his breath away. Sensing this, she quickly smiled and dared walk to him. He turned from her and her hands clung to empty air. He left her there and hurried out into the night.

Whill walked through the congregation of elves, and though he tried to hide himself, a commotion began to commence around him. In short time he was so surrounded by gleaming elves that he could not press through the crowd easily. Whill thought to call upon Avriel so that he could fly far from there, but then he remembered she was an elf again. He began to panic. His breath came in short, frantic gasps and his chest tightened.

"Let me pass!" he bellowed, and all talking ceased in a heartbeat. The dismayed elves parted before him as wood to an axe. Whill sighed, embarrassed, and offered apologies as he quickly walked through the crowd.

"Bah!" came a voice. "Ain't no king alive who's got to be askin' crowds to be movin' for him, nor any need to apologize for expectin' common sense!" Roakore roared as he split the crowds before him with his sheer presence. He scowled at the crowd as he met Whill.

"I be guessin' common sense ain't so common round these parts," he said to the elves. "Eh, laddie?" He slapped Whill on the back hard enough to make him stumble. Roakore put him in a one-armed headlock, pulling him down to the side as they parted the crowd.

"C'mon, then. We got ourselves a right large beer tent set up already. The kegs be tapped and the spirits be flowin'."

Soon they came to the dwarven tent. Some fifty dwarves cheered when their king and Whill walked in. Whill found a mug in his hand instantly and was cheering with raised glass before a word had been spoken. So many mugs clanged against his that when he went to drink, he found no ale left. Roakore hurried him along to a center table with fine, high-backed oak chairs. The king himself poured Whill a golden mug and together they had a proper cheer.

"To the three kings and the three races!" a dwarf cheered, and all the dwarves guzzled.

"To pissin' on a dragon's tail!" another put in. Laughter and drinking filled the tent.

"To Whill o' Agora!" yelled another, and again they drank.

Whill wondered how long they could keep this up. He yelled over the crowd, standing taller than all. "To the good dwarves o' Ro'Sar!" he cheered, and they drank to themselves.

"To hoggin' on damsels!" Philo yelled, and ended his cheer with a loud raucous burp. There was silence for a moment as dwarves looked at each other curiously.

"Hear, hear!" said Roakore, and they all drank.

Thankfully, the dwarven cheers subsided for a time and Whill was introduced to yet more of Roakore's warriors. Philo slammed his fist to his chest and snorted to clear his throat. "Well met, Whill. I hear you got yourself a blade o' power." His eyes went to the sheathed blade. Whill reflexively turned it from the dwarf. Their eyes met and Philo took on a serious tone. "It ain't the size o' the sword o' power, laddie, it be how you use it," he said, straight-faced. Suddenly the dwarf burst into frantic laughter that was taken up by all.

Roakore pushed Philo to the side. "Go on, ye maniac." And Philo stumbled off in a fit of laughter.

Whill watched, amused. As always, Roakore had lifted his spirits. Just being around the hearty, life-filled dwarves made him feel better. For a time he forgot about the Other, and everything else.

The party raged on into the evening and soon night-time was upon them. By the time Whill and Roakore exited the dwarven beer tent, the gathering hill was unrecognizable. Lights of every color floated around the hill, and elves dressed in elegant gowns danced all around them. Music filled the air as minstrels played. Elven children were among the large crowd of elves. Many had come to see the crowning of their new king. Fire pits raged and the smell of food filled the air. Fireworks the likes of which Whill had rarely seen exploded randomly throughout the city. A large, open-sided, leafed tent had been erected, or grown, Whill could not tell. Hundreds of stone tables and chairs had been pulled from the earth for any who wanted to eat comfortably.

Tarren found Whill and bounced up and down, waving at him. Whill gestured him over with a smile.

"Holy shyteballs, Whill! You see that tent go up? Wildest thing I ever seen, and the light show—oh, man, you should have seen 'em lettin' them off!"

Whill laughed and ruffled the boy's hair. "The elves seem to know how to throw a party."   "Lunara says you and Roakore need to be over there before Zerafin is crowned." Tarren pointed west to a podium that had been erected at the edge of the hill overlooking the Thousand Falls.

"When is his crowning?"

Tarren shrugged "Beats me, but the queen and a few others are already over there."

"Have you seen Avriel?"

"No, but I can't wait. I haven't seen her in a long time. I heard what you did, helping her back to her real body. How did you do that?"

"I don't know," said Whill absently as he scanned the crowd for her. As he turned in his searching, he was startled to find Lunara suddenly in front of him, smiling brightly.

"May I have this dance?" she asked with a small bow as the music turned soft with strings and flutes.

"Uh, I...," Whill stammered, and Tarren chuckled. "It would be my pleasure," Whill finally said and offered her his arm. Together they made their way to where the dancers had gathered. Whill looked around quickly, trying to determine what dance the elves were moving to. Lunara laughed and took his hands in hers.

"It is simple, follow my lead," she said as she put his hand upon the small of her back and held his other straight out to the side. Twirling, they found their place in the crowd, and Whill was quick to catch on to the simple elven dance. The music picked up and Whill tried to keep time with Lunara as the dancers twirled round and round. The pair received many looks both curious and jealous from the elves.

"How are you enjoying your visit?" she asked as they settled into an easy rhythm.

"Ah, it has been interesting so far, to say the least. But I like it here. One can almost forget the worries of the world."

"Tarren seems to be enjoying himself." She nodded to the boy. Whill saw Tarren dancing with an elven girl his age.

"Indeed he does," laughed Whill as Tarren smiled wide-eyed at him. "Thank you for taking care of him these last few months. If there is anything I can ever do for you, do not hesitate to ask."

"I imagine I could think of something," said Lunara coyly, and Whill felt his cheeks get hot.

"May I be cuttin' in?" a slightly drunken voice piped up. They looked to see Holdagozz standing behind them.

"Of course, good dwarf," said Whill. He kissed Lunara's hand and smiled. "Thanks again," he offered, and she smiled back.

Holdagozz took hold of her, and lifting her high spun round and round. Together they disappeared in laughter into the ocean of dancers. Whill had thought he and Lunara had gotten a lot of looks, but it was nothing compared to she and Holdagozz.

Trumpets cut through the music and the dancing stopped as everyone looked to the raised podium where the queen now stood. Whill cursed to himself and found his way through the crowd to stand next to Roakore near the podium.

A busy-looking elf interrupted their greeting and hustled them into place. "No, no, King Roakore, you are to stand here, and you—"

"I be standin' where ever the hells I be standin', busybody."

The elf huffed and looked as though she might cry. "I apologize, good dwarf, but the queen has her plans and I do not wish to see them thwarted."

"Of course, I be sorry for me bad manners. Point me in the direction."

The elf sighed gratefully and led Whill and Roakore to the podium.

Together they stood with a host of elves about the podium. Whill recognized a few, but most he did not. Cheers rose up as Zerafin and Avriel walked toward the podium to strong drums and rushing overtures. Together they climbed the podium and waved at the crowd, which erupted in cheers.

Avriel took the spot next to Whill with but a smile as the queen stepped forward to speak. The music fell to the background and the queen addressed her people.

"This night we celebrate the crowning of our new king, and with his crowning, the end of an age. For five hundred long years we have lived here, refugees of Drindellia, our homeland. But the dark elves have found us, and once again our peace is threatened; once again war has come to our lands. For five hundred years we have remained hidden, and we have restored our once-great power. I am here today to say that we hide no longer. Once and for all this battle will be ended, and I implore you all to do what you can to see the dark elves defeated."

Queen Araveal took up the crown of the lost king of Drindellia and Zerafin took a knee.

"Zerafin, my son, I offer you the crown of your father, and with it the mantle of king. Do you accept the crown, and all of the responsibilities and duties that come with it?"

"I do," said Zerafin with a raised chin.

"Very well," said the queen with watery eyes as she lowered the crown to sit upon his head. "Rise, Zerafin, first king of Elladrindellia!"

Zerafin stood and walked forward to stand before his people. The elves cheered their new king. Many teary-eyed minutes passed as applause rose up above the city of Cerushia. When finally the cheers died down, Zerafin addressed the elves.

"Long has my mother served our people. She has seen us safely from our lost homeland to the new land. She has procured us a new home, Elladrindellia, and by her guidance we have thrived these last five centuries in peace. I am thankful to have had her as a queen through such trying times."

Applause for Queen Araveal rose up and she took a long bow. Zerafin waited for the applause to die down. "Now war is upon us once again. Our fallen brother means to spread the same darkness as he did in Drindellia. He seeks to rule all of Agora. And I, like my father before me, shall die trying to stop him if need be. I, along with the brave men of Agora and the hearty dwarves of Ro'Sar, Helgar, and Ky'Dren, choose to fight!"

Cheers rose up with the king's every word, and Whill was reminded once again that he was not alone in this. They had all suffered under Eadon, and they all had no choice but to fight or die.

"I ask you now, elves of the sun, are you with me?"

The crowd erupted in cheers and proclamations of loyalty. Whill found himself one of the beaming crowd as he too cheered. Before them Zerafin stood in armor of gold. His cape blew steadily to the left as a breeze picked up and seemed to grow with the mood. To Whill,

Zerafin looked like a god, and if any should wield such a blade as Adromida, Whill thought, it was he.

Looking out over the crowd of thousands of elves, Whill felt the spark of hope. He imagined the thousands of unseen elves throughout Elladrindellia, the legions of dwarves within the three mountain kingdoms, and the armies of his fellow men. He imagined them as one army, and a surge of electrifying hope coursed through him. He had to unite the races.

Whill knew then that it was not his duty to kill Eadon, it was merely his duty to try. If he could successfully bring the wrath of humans, dwarves, and elves down upon Eadon, he could give them a fighting chance.

Zerafin turned and motioned to Whill and Roakore. They joined him upon the high perch. He took one of their hands in each of his and raised them to the sky.

"Together we shall know victory! Together we shall make our claim!"

CHAPTER THIRTY
The Dragonlance of Ashai

Guided by Azzeal, Aurora's boat was steered wide of Fendora Island. The days at sea went by slowly as her anticipation grew to unbearable levels. Aurora did not like the vast never ending ocean. There was nowhere to go and little to do. She spent the time on deck practicing with the mighty dragonlance or sparring with the elves. Her nights were spent with Azzeal in her quarters. She and the elf often discussed the implications of her vow to Eadon.

"The fact that you can no longer feel his power within you means little." said Azzeal, to her dismay. She hoped beyond reason that she was somehow free of the curse of her promise, but Azzeal assured her that she was not.

"But you can still defeat the chief and lead your people."

Aurora was confused by it all, spells, curses, magic. She did not like it. Better that you saw your enemy for what they were; better to fight with but a blade. She considered magic a coward's weapon.

"As we speak I conspire against Eadon's will, yet I am not pained as I was in Del' Oradon. Doesn't that speak to the possibility that the curse is lifted?"

"Not necessarily." Azeal cautioned. "Spells of this sort tend to depend greatly upon the resolution of the swearer of the pledge. The less your promise is held in your heart, the less affected you may be."

Aurora thought she understood. The promise had never been close to her heart. She was passionate about securing her people's fate, and she had been faced with the alternative of death. The future of the barbarians was all she was worried about. She would surely die in the coming days or weeks, she had accepted that now. But she was determined to die honorably, and for her people.

Azzeal told her the legend of the Dragonlance of Ashai. It had been created by its namesake many centuries before. The story of the dragonlance was one of loss and sorrow, despair and regret. Ashai was an elf that had been a master krundar and gnenja.

"We elves had been expanding throughout Elladrin-dellia for a century. Ashai and his large family had migrated to the southern most tip of our new country. There they began what is now known as the city of

Elwrenden. But there at the rocky coast, nestled among the many large caves beneath the cliff, slept a dragon. The industrious elves eventually woke the beast that had slumbered for centuries there within the deep recesses of the coastal cliff."

"The day the dragon awoke, the ground heaved and a deep growl echoed forth from the earth. Ashai was there at the seashore below the cliff, and he alone saw the dragon arise from its slumber. It is said that a one-hundred foot cliff was torn asunder as the silver dragon emerged from it as if it were an egg. The waters boiled and raged, animals fled from the coast in droves, and for miles around the cry of Kryshra pierced the air." said Azzeal with a hand through the air. Aurora listened enthralled by the tale.

"Ashai was badly injured by the blast that marked the dragon's rebirth. Burnt and bloody he watched help-lessly as the great silver dragon spread his impossibly large wings and took to the skies in the direction of his village. It wasn't until the next morning that he was spotted by elves returned from fishing. Among them was one skilled in healing, and he was made well again. Together they ventured wide the destroyed and smok-ing cliff and made all haste toward Elwrenden. They found the village in ruin."

"Anguished, Ashai frantically searched the smolder-ing waste that had been his home. Inside he found the charred remains of his family. They like so many others had died seeking shelter from the rampaging dragon. Time passed and the village was rebuilt, and eventually the story of Kryshra the Silver passed into history. But Ashai never forgot, he never let go. The elf poured himself into his studies for decades, single-mindedly focused on one thing, revenge. He became a master gnenja, ralliad, and pzionar. Ashai's father-in-law and master metalsmith Krel D'orren made for him a dragonlance with which to avenge his daughter. Into the cold enchanted iron was poured strength and great magic."

Azzeal stroked the rough surface of the coal-black dragonlance with a far-away stare.

"Seventy-five years passed and Ashai became strong, but no word came of the great silver dragon. Ashai gathered all the wealth he had amassed since the cursed day and offered his fortune for any information about the dragon. The years passed and the reward that had so excited the human fisherman and merchants slipped into legend. Then one day word came to Ashai of a sighting out to sea. Ashai set sail immediately and after weeks at sea he caught the trail of Kryshra."

"Did he find the dragon?" Aurora could not help but blurt out.

Azzeal smiled at her shaking his head. "Yes, upon an island nearly five-hundred miles to the west of Agora. He found the dragon, and he faced it there upon the rocky beach. He killed the beast, and was never seen again. The dragon was found with this lance through its heart, and no sign of Ashai."

Aurora looked to the dragonlance with renewed awe. "What happened to him?" asked Aurora.

Azzeal shrugged, "likely he was disintegrated by dragon fire.

Aurora thought of the story of the dragonlance often the remainder of the voyage. The lance had been crafted with vengeance in mind. With it, she would have hers. After nearly a week at sea they came upon Volnoss from the west.

Immediately Aurora knew that trouble awaited them. A storm had gathered above the island, and far off on the horizon dancing lightning hinted at a great disturbance. Aurora looked from the spectacle to Azzeal's knowing eyes.

"What is it?" Aurora asked.

"It is a rift, a portal not unlike the once we traversed once." said Azzeal.

"Where does it lead?"

"You know where."

"Drindellia," Aurora whispered as she looked once again. She could feel Azzeal staring at her still; she imagined his mind searching hers.

"The dark elves come for your people, they come to destroy your homeland." said Azzeal and turned her to look at him with a strong hand. "You can rally your kin against this invasion, it is your destiny."

"You knew about the portal, you have come to see that I do not side with Eadon." said Aurora and Azzeal nodded.

"This is the way to your redemption. Help us destroy the portal and your honor will be restored."

CHAPTER THIRTY-ONE
A Favor to Ask

With the arrival of Roakore and Tarren, and the transformation of Avriel, Whill no longer sought solitude. He moved from his Thousand Falls cavern and took up with the dwarves. The rugged dwarves did not put up with crowds around their doors and were not shy about shooing gawkers. Whill was able to go to and fro much easier with the thick-muscled dwarves clearing the way.

Lunara too stayed with the dwarves. She and Tarren had grown quite close, and Whill had the feeling that they would remain that way if either of them had a say in the matter. Whill watched her watching Tarren, and in her face he saw motherly love. He understood then why Abram had left him with Teera for the better part of ten years. It was for this reason that he sought to be alone with Lunara.

Her room within the dwarven quarter was to the left of the main chamber and down yet two more tunnels. The elves had melded stone and crystal to create a large dwarf-like mountain abode. From the outside it was a large pyramid, but inside were stone tunnels, chambers, and halls. It had been fabricated after the Ro'Sar Mountains.

Whill knocked on her thick wooden door and she answered as if she had known he was there.

"Hello, I was…may I come in?" he asked.

Lunara nodded with a smile and opened the door farther, gesturing him in. After he passed, he noticed her slight hesitation at the door as she seemed to ponder whether or not to close it. She closed the door and turned to greet Whill.

"What brings you to my room?" she asked with the faintest of devilish grins. Her eyes were drawn to his sword, as were everyone's. Whill remembered Roakore saying that she was his age, and he thought he could tell. There was a light in her eyes that he had not seen in many of the elves, the look of curious adolescent excitement that many humans shed by their fourteenth year. Whill felt a kinship to her because of it.

"I have come to ask a favor, one of the utmost importance," he said, wringing his damp hands.

"Well, then." She beamed. "This calls for tea! Please have a seat." She led him to the small low table upon which sat a white teapot with swirling golden inlay. They each took a seat on soft cushions and Whill watched silently as she prepared the tea.

From a similar covered dish she scooped crushed tea leaves with an ornate silver spoon. Into the pot she dropped three spoonfuls of tea and returned the spoon and dish lid with delicate, practiced movements. She smiled at Whill from across the table.

"I have made great progress this last year in what would you call...water weaving? Watch." She set a red crystal upon the table and whispered to it. The crystal hummed and suddenly sprouted a high flame. "Deklen en!" she proclaimed dramatically and laughed at Whill's surprised smile. The flame shrank to half its size and burned steadily.

Lunara blew her silver hair out of her face and extended her right hand palm down toward a water basin. She turned her hand up, and out of the basin rose a slowly churning serpent of water. The water grew out a foot and broke apart from the basin. She guided the water serpent toward the table, and once there gave Whill a quick pensive grin and began waving her hand slowly back and forth. The water serpent began to move in a circle over the flame. Fire licked water as the small water serpent formed a circle, seemingly swallowing its own tail. It continued to churn and circle the flame like a wheel of water until it began to bubble and boil. With barely contained excitement for her work, Lunara directed the water into the teapot without so much as a splash. With a wide smile she covered the teapot and lifted it by the handle. With her other hand she took a small strainer that matched the set and poured Whill a cup of tea over the sifter. She tipped the teapot back until only a drop hung from the spout. She carefully moved to pour for herself, making sure the drop found her cup. Once her cup was half full, she stopped and laid the teapot on its tray. She looked up at Whill with anticipation and turned her cup around so that the handle did a full cycle. Then she looked at Whill's cup. Thinking she meant him to mimic her and hoping he was not ruining some tea ceremony ritual, he turned his cup as she had hers. Lunara gave a smile and a small laugh and raised her cup with Whill and drank. She closed her eyes as if savoring the flavor. Whill thought he saw her lips make words as she returned her cup to its saucer. Whill did the same.

Lunara opened her eyes and blinked as if she had been daydreaming. "What favor would you seek? Ask it of me and it shall be," she said with a smile and eyes that never left his.

Whill leaned forward onto his arms. "My path is one of war and death, my quest likely suicide. I would see to it that Tarren is looked after, that he is loved in my stead. I would ask that you watch over him."

Lunara's eyes glistened and her nostrils flared as her breath came to her quickly. Her hand found his across the table and she squeezed. "You would ask this of me, to be as mother to your child?"

"His guardian, yes," Whill clarified gently.

Lunara straightened. "And should you return, as you doubt—when he has become used to me as his nurturer, you would take him then?"

Whill squeezed her hand back and could not help but smile at her hopeful gaze. "You would remain as you were, until he is a man of his own mind to choose."

Sobbing laughter escaped Lunara as she answered, "Yes! Yes of course. It would be my honor."

Whill sat back, happy that he had one less thing to worry about. "The lad loves you already, and there are things you can teach him that I cannot," he said, and suddenly heard the same words from Abram. He turned toward the sound and found himself in his childhood cottage. Abram and Teera were talking by the fire.

"He loves you already, and you can teach him things I cannot," Teera said, looking nervously in Whill's direction. He followed her gaze and saw that there in a swath of elven cloth was an infant. "This child...I must know."

Abram turned away from her as if it were an old question.

"It is best—"

"The fallen king of Uthen-Arden. My brother disappears for ten years to become a knight of another kingdom. Letters come few the first year and rarely after that. I read your tales of adventure and folly, how you were rising through the ranks of the Uthen-Arden army. Assigned to the king's very own guard, you said.

And then you return to me on the heels of news of the assassination of King Aramonis."

Teera jerked Abram around to face her. "Brother," she pleaded. "What trouble have you gotten yourself into?" She glanced at the infant Whill. "What trouble have you brought upon us?"

The memory froze and the Other walked out of the shadows behind Abram.

"He leaves after this conversation, not to return for a year."

Whill looked around bewildered and then angry. "What game is this?" he demanded.

"Game?" The Other looked around, his blood- and grime-soaked hair whipping. "There is no game here. I simply wanted to share with you my fondest early memories. We cannot forget from where we came." The memory around him swirled into smoke and became utterly dark.

Whill groped blindly and his hands found nothing but thick liquid and warm flesh. Muffled noises surrounded him, along with a steady, thunderous heartbeat. There was a jolt to his surroundings and he felt the jar of a fall. The heartbeat slowed and skipped, beat four more laborious times, and was still.

Muffled voices screamed outside of the womb and there was an explosion that shook all things. Silence followed. Whill floated there terrified, longing for the soothing heartbeat that had been his world. There came a long slice in the darkness and light poured into Whill, jolting his senses. Hands came for him and pulled him from his mother and he was lifted into the cold biting air. Pain hit him for the first time and he heard himself let out a gut-wrenching cry.

"That was the moment of my birth," said the Other, "and I have been with you ever since."

Whill was thrust back to Lunara's room and the biting cold followed him.

"Whill?" came a concerned, muffled voice. "Whill!" Lunara came into focus across from him. He sat up straight quickly and looked around, confused.

"I…sorry, I have…what happened?" he asked.

"Nothing, you just trailed off for a moment. What was it? It looked as if you remembered something important."

"How long?" he dared ask.

Lunara shrugged with a frown. "Just a few moments. Are you all right?"

Whill nodded and sipped his tea, hoping she did not think him insane.

Whill? Avriel's voice entered his head.

Lunara perked up as if Avriel spoke to her as well.

"Of course, Princess, please enter," said Lunara brightly.

The heavy wooden door opened and Avriel strode into the room. She stopped abruptly and Whill followed her eyes to the teapot and cups. She looked from the set to Lunara with an arched brow. Across from Whill, Lunara straightened and lifted her chin. Whill looked from one to the other, knowing he was missing something. Nothing was said of it, however, as Avriel smiled and walked forward.

"King Zerafin requests your presence," she said to Whill.

He nodded, finished his tea, and rose with a smile at Lunara. "Thank you once again. I am forever in your debt."

"It is my honor," she responded with a sweet smile.

Whill and Avriel walked down the hall and through the main room without a word. Whill could sense something bothering her. "Did your brother say what this is about?" he asked, not knowing what else to say.

Avriel shook her head. "The tea ceremony—did she say what it represented?"

"No." Now he was curious. "I assumed it was just tea."

Avriel gave a short, forced laugh. "It was a ceremony of offering."

"Offering what?" asked Whill hesitantly.

Avriel stopped and faced him. "An offering of self. Lunara has given herself to you."

"What! She didn't...we didn't!" he stammered.

"I know. To you it was just tea. But to her it was...she will give herself to no other."

"But it was just tea!" he blurted.

"To you, but to her it was sacred."

"But doesn't she know...I mean you and I..."

"I have not made my feelings known to anyone. I have been a dragon as of late, if you recall."

"Of course," said Whill. "I didn't know if elves had a different way of...knowing or making these things known."

They left the dwarven abode and strolled through Cerushia toward Zerafin's home. At some point Whill took Avriel's hand and together they talked and laughed through the brilliant afternoon.

CHAPTER THIRTY-TWO
The Looking Glass of Araveal

Whill and Avriel strode into the pyramid at the edge of the city and found gathered there Roakore, Holdagozz, and Zerafin. The main hall was set up like a war room. At the center was a circular table with a low bottom and edges that rose up, the kind of table found at any bar in any tavern in Agora. Roakore even had a mug in hand as Whill and Avriel approached.

"Welcome. Please have a seat," Zerafin bade them.

The closer Whill got to the strange table, the more his curiosity grew. He came to the edge and looked within the lowered center. What he saw caused his breath to skip and his eyes to widen. "This is amazing," he uttered in admiration.

The table dipped to the center and flattened out again into a giant map of Agora. But it was more than a map; it was as if they looked down upon Agora from the stars. Whill stared in awe at the lifelike map. It had moving clouds and rain, rippling oceans, and even ships out to sea, tiny dots upon the vast blue ocean.

"Is this actually real?" Whill asked, astonished.

"Ain't it the damnedest thing you ever seen, lad?" said Roakore dreamily.

"It is real," said Zerafin, joining them at the table. "In a sense, it is the accumulated memory image of hundreds of elven druids who looked down upon the world from the clouds. This, the Looking Glass of Araveal, is my mother's doing. She fabricated it and set into motion its creation. It has been and will be a critical tool in the war. Let me show you. Choose a town in a kingdom."

Whill looked around Agora and spotted his hometown. "Sidnell," he said.

Zerafin turned his high-backed chair and put his hands upon two crystals that jutted from his place at the table. There was no physical sign that Zerafin had done anything; if he had made a command, it had been in his mind. Suddenly Whill felt as though he were falling as the map turned and shifted and the view zoomed swiftly down upon the land and to the upper right corner of Agora. Whill gasped as Sidnell was displayed to him in living clarity. It was the actual view from elven memory.

"They flew over every last stone's throw of Agora?" said Whill, amazed.

"Yes, but there are places the memories do not show," Zerafin explained.

Once again the map backed up and dropped them in the middle of Uthen-Arden's Thendor Plains, a few hundred miles north of Del'Oradon. There upon the ocean of grass was a strange rippling disturbance. The image contorted too much to be made clear.

"What is it?" Whill asked.

"A portal," said Zerafin with a pensive frown. "Thrice we have sent scouts to discover the source. The first two groups did not return. The third reported back this morning. It is indeed a portal, or rather some sort of rift. The one survivor of the group said that from it marched an army of draggard."

"How many?" Avriel asked.

"We cannot guess. The Looking Glass of Araveal's images are replenished on a weekly cycle, and this disturbance appeared two weeks ago. There is no way to tell how long the draggard have been moving."

"Where do you think the portals lead?" Holdagozz asked. Whill knew the answer before it was spoken.

"Drindellia," Zerafin answered. "And there are more."

At Zerafin's mental command the map panned out and once again the entire continent and its surrounding islands could be seen. "They are here," he said as bulges swelled in the map, Whill realized its surface was water. There were six bumps in the map in all. There was one over the Thendor Plains, and also one in Eldalon,

Isladon, Shierdon, the ancient Uthen-Arden naval outpost Fendora Island, and Volnoss, the northern island of ice, the very place Aurora was headed.

"These may all be portals to Eadon's hordes in Drindellia?" Whill said softly as he brought to memory the location of each.

"Yes," said Zerafin solemnly.

"Then it's settled! We need to be destroying 'em!" said Roakore, slamming the table.

"Of course they must be destroyed," said Zerafin, annoyed. "But we must use cunning and patience—"

"Bah, I had about enough o' patience! Patience had me sittin' on me arse for twenty years afore reclaimin' me mountain. Patience be the way o' the weary, an' dwarves ain't weary," Roakore spat.

"He is right!" Avriel yelled over them all. Zerafin nodded in agreement, but looking at his sister, he realized that she spoke to him.

"Roakore is right, we must strike these locations and we must strike quickly. The gods only know how long these portals have stood open," she said to her brother.

"That is what he would expect." Whill shook his head and leaned forward to study the map. "They could be traps."

"Eadon would not have known that we have the looking glass," argued Zerafin.

"Wouldn't he?" said Whill. "If Eadon has assassins here inside Elladrindellia, why not spies?"

"You are right," Zerafin conceded. "Spies there may be, and he may know about the looking glass."

"Bah!" Roakore bellowed and threw up his arms. "We need to be warnin' Eldalon and Isladon. Trap or no trap, it bears lookin' into."

Whill pointed at the Fendora Island disturbance. "From here to Fendora is what, a few hundred miles?"

"Yes," answered Zerafin hesitantly.

Whill stared at the island for a time and finally nodded. "I must go there."

Zerafin and Avriel began to object immediately and Whill had to shout over them. "It is the only way to know the truth!"

"And if it is a trap?" asked Avriel.

"You cannot yet face Eadon," added Zerafin.

"I can never face Eadon!" Whill cried, and the room became as silent as a tomb. Avriel lowered her gaze and Zerafin only stared blankly. Roakore looked as though a reassuring word lay upon the tip of his tongue.

"I know what you all would say, but it is not true. I cannot defeat Eadon—I was never meant to, and the prophecy is a lie. But what is true is that I wield the blade Adromida. I possess a great weapon in this war. And though I may not defeat Eadon, I can still defeat his armies."

Avriel shook her head in denial. "The prophecy is not a lie, I do not care what Kellallea claims. Perhaps *she* was a lie."

"True or not, we cannot rely upon a prophecy alone," Whill argued. "If your beloved prophecy is true, it will matter not if I go to Fendora Island, for I will come to no harm."

Avriel sighed in frustration but said no more. Zerafin looked to Roakore, who scowled at the map.

"What be your plan, laddie?" he asked, and all eyes went to Whill.

Whill gazed down upon Fendora as a god might. "A full frontal assault. I am done running from Eadon and his minions."

"We will make it a coordinated effort, then," said Zerafin.

"No. I must do this alone."

"When would you leave?" Avriel asked, not hiding her displeasure.

"I will see the Council of Masters, as I have been summoned, and then I will investigate this portal," Whill said with finality.

"I'm goin' with ye, laddie," Roakore interjected.

"I said I—"

"I be the godsdamned king o' Ro'Sar! I be goin' where I please!" yelled Roakore. "One o' these damned portals was in me mountain, an' this fancy-lookin' glass don't show what portals might yet be in our mountains."

"Very well," said Whill, surrendering to the stubborn king. He looked at Zerafin. It was apparent that the meeting had not gone as planned.

"And once through the portal? Likely there is an army waiting," said Zerafin, eyeing Whill and Roakore.

"If there be an army waiting, then we'll kill 'em all," Roakore promised.

CHAPTER
THIRTY-THREE
The Book O' Ky'Dren

Dirk urged the dragon-hawk on steadily east toward Kell-Torey. He knew that to try and pick up on her trail again was a waste of time. Dirk had no way of knowing how many assassins Eadon had sent after Whill's family, but he did know that the elf lord would send his daughter after the biggest target.

Dirk flew on into the morning, thinking of nothing but Krentz. Had she been the one to kill the mother and daughter after all? Had she killed others of the bloodline already? Had he been mistaken about Krentz being given this mission? Either way, he had to get to Kell-Torey. Whether or not Krentz was the weapon, he had to stop the assassination of the king and his family, if only to be a nuisance to Eadon.

Traveling from the Twin Lakes to Kell-Torey by horse-back would have taken him weeks, but he guessed that the dragon-hawk could do it in days. He hoped that his guess about Krentz was correct, and he would have a chance to intercept her in Kell-Torey.

He used his time to refine his plan to stop her and take her captive. She had sworn fealty to her father and would not be able to disobey his will intentionally. Dirk would have to play his cards right if they were both to live through the confrontation. He was not sure if he could defeat her given the gifts that Eadon had likely bestowed upon her. His only advantage was his knowledge of her abilities and fighting style. Krentz was a powerful Zionar and warrior. Her ability to invade the minds of her victims had led to the creation of most of Dirk's many weapons and trinkets. His hood had been enchanted to protect Dirk against such invasions, among other things, but he did not know how it would hold up to its creator.

He pondered the possibilities and played out the fight in his mind as he fingered the timber-wolf figurine in his pocket. He had not dismissed Chief during the last battle; the spirit wolf had simply disappeared when the heavy column had fallen on him and the dark elf. Dirk did not know if the spirit wolf would return when summoned, and he was anxious to find out. But he had no time to find out; he would have to wait until the dragon-hawk stopped to rest.

They flew on into the afternoon under the cover of the dragon-hawk's camouflaged feathers. Dirk had not gotten more than an hour of sleep in days and his eyes were heavy. Trusting that the dragon would not eat him if it hadn't already, he tightened the saddle strap and quickly fell into a much-needed sleep.

Whill was awakened by a banging at his door. He arose and threw on an elven lokata.

"Who is it?" he asked, shuffling to the door.

"Answer the damned door and ye be findin' out!"

Whill opened the door to his friend and the dwarf king rushed inside and went straight to the small circular table of thick wood.

"Go on, then, close the door before someone finds me," Roakore barked.

Whill complied with a smile. "Are you hiding from someone?"

"Someone? Bah! I be hidin' from everyone," Roakore answered as he laid a tome upon the table with a thud. "Can't get away from curious elves ever since we got here. There be lore masters, historians, Ralliad masters, jewel crafters, nobles, elders, an' every godsdamned elf in the city wantin' to see me."

"I know what you mean," said Whill, joining his friend. "I had to move to a cave in the thousand falls to get away."

"I be believin' it." Roakore stared absently at his book.

"Can I get you anything?" Whill asked.

"Ye got anythin' to wet the whistle?" said Roakore, tonguing his mouth. "An' ye best be openin' a window if you got one."

"No windows," said Will, getting up to fetch a drink. "The elves even built dwarven wind tubes into this mock dwarf mountain."

Roakore eyed the room and walls with a scowl. "This ain't nothin' like a dwarf mountain."

Whill turned from the stacked gifts he had received as he inspected a bottle. "It is as good a copy as I have ever seen."

Roakore only grumbled and lit his pipe.

"Elven cider?" Whill asked.

"Cider? Lad, give me somethin' that'll be turnin' me curlies straight."

Whill frowned at his friend and returned to the table with the cider, a bottle of dessyberry wine, and a brick of cheese. The elves had given him a pile of gifts, and he was thinking about getting a separate room for it all.

"What is on your mind, Roakore?" he asked as he poured him a glass of dessyberry wine. "You cannot be this flustered over curious elves."

Roakore nodded thanks for the wine and gulped down the whole thing. He offered the glass and Whill pulled back the bottle stubbornly.

"What is going on? Are you nervous about traveling through the portal?" Whill asked.

Roakore moved his mouth as if to speak but could only stutter.

"You can still back out," Whill teased.

"Back out!" Roakore finally stammered. "Nervous? I ain't been nervous since the time it burned to pee. No, it ain't that, it be this damned book. It be the reason I be here."

Whill focused then upon the tome of Ky'Dren and reached to touch it. Roakore flinched but let Whill take it up.

"The one you found within the elven library. Of course, you wanted me to translate it then. Roakore, I had forgotten."

"You can read it, then, and tell no one what ye learn?"

"Of course. What are you afr—what do you think you will find?"

"I ain't for knowin', but I ain't for likin' the implications laid by that Azzeal. Says Ky'Dren was from Drindellia, an' yer right for thinkin' I be afraid o' that book, if I was ever afraid o' anything." Roakore's eyes never left the book; they seemed to look through it. His eyes widened and one twitched now and again.

Whill filled Roakore's glass and cut a chunk of cheese off the block. The dwarf just stared. "Don't read it, then," said Whill.

Roakore's incredulous eyes snapped to him. "I got to be knowin'. This be the word o' Ky'Dren."

Whill laid the book on the table and straightened to the task. "Look at this writing." He whistled. "It is beautiful…and long. Roakore, this will take all day to read."

"Then we be readin' all day," replied Roakore, snatching up the bottle and pouring himself the wine.

"Wait!" said Whill, suddenly excited. "I changed parts of my…I can speed-read this book."

"Well, that don't be helpin' me to speed-hear it."

"No, but I may be able to share the experience."

"How about we just read it normal-like," said Roakore, puffing on the pipe between his teeth.

"No, I can do this. Move closer. Here." Whill indicated to the left of himself and got comfortable. Roakore shuffled his chair over noisily and with a frustrated sigh. Whill laid the book out and put a finger under the first page, then placed his left hand upon Roakore's forehead. The dwarf followed the hand apprehensively until he was cross-eyed looking up at it.

"Don't be fryin' me damned brain!"

"You have my word." Whill took three calming breaths. He began to read slowly in his mind and mentally projected it onto Roakore. The dwarf gasped and laughed. "Faster!" he begged.

Whill picked up the pace until he was scanning a page in a few seconds, the entire tale coming into view in his mind. A sweeping landscape of mountains deep and valleys long played out. Gold and silver and diamonds and jewels, thriving dwarven cities and a kingdom of peace stretched out before their imagination as a tale of glory and sorrow was spun. During those times, the dwarves named the elves friend, and from them they learned many things, including stone melding.

Ky'Dren spoke of his line, for he named himself the twenty-seventh in the line of Du'Wrenden, and eldest son to the king. The dwarves had prospered for centuries and lived well from trade with the elves. The mountain kingdom of Du'Wrenden thrived until the arrival of the dragons. The elves called it the great migration; the dwarves called it a war waged by the gods. Du'Wrenden was overwhelmed overnight by thousands of dragons, and while the dwarves were as legendary fighters as any, the dragons were too many. The elves at first helped in the battle, but quickly their dead piled and their resolve waned. They drew back on the sixth day and offered to help the dwarves to retreat. The dwarves would have none of it. The dwarf king refused and the dwarves closed themselves up in their mountain. For more than a year they held out inside their mountain, and for more than a year the dragons waited. The beasts continued to arrive throughout the year, and soon their numbers doubled and then tripled. They marked their territory one hundred miles around the mountain in all directions, and killed any trespassers by the droves. The dwarven lore masters eventually agreed with the elves: this mountain, it seemed, was an ancient dragon breeding ground. The dragons were there to breed and lay their eggs, and they would allow no threat to their young. The elves took their losses and retreated from the shadow of the mountain, forced to bring their trade with them.

Supplies were immediately rationed, but as the year wore on, the supplies dwindled and the dwarves slowly starved. Tunnels had been ordered dug, and some hunting came from the surrounding forests. But always the dragons sniffed them out. Dragon fire engulfed the tunnels and dragon claws dug them out all the way back to the mountain. No matter how many miles the dwarves dug, the dragons always found them. It was believed that the dragons could hear or feel the disturbance in the earth below. The beasts tunneled into the mountain themselves, burrowing deep and digging into the dwarves' own halls and cities. Dragon fire decimated the dwarves, and though many dragons fell, they took with them hundreds.

The dwarves lost city after city along the mountain range and poured, starving, into the deepest and most fortified capital city of Thengar. There they made their last stand, and there the dragons ignited a chamber of gas from the earth's bowels. The blast was the end of the dwarves, and the dwarven mountain kingdom was conquered, the last of the dwarves defeated. Many lived on to starve or die fighting along the mountain range, but only a handful escaped. Ky'Dren had led that group.

The tale ended the day they left, and Whill closed the book. He released Roakore and the dwarf king gasped for breath. He stood so fast that his chair skidded across the floor.

"How in the hells did he end up in Agora, and why ain't there any record o' this from his gospel? It don't make no sense. This be directly contrary to the scripture."

Whill stretched his sore muscles. Though he had speed-read the tome, it had still taken nearly an hour. "We do not know that this book is true. Perhaps the lore masters can help shed light on its authenticity."

"Shed light? I ain't wantin' no light shed on this... this...blasphemy. Be ye understandin' what this would do to me religion, to me culture? If this be true, everything we live for be a lie!"

"But it could be also seen as liberating," Whill offered, trying to see the bright side.

"Liberating?" Roakore spat.

"Yes. If this is indeed true, if Ky'Dren learned stone melding from the elves, and you can do the same because you are of his line, then that means that you can move not only stone, but anything. It means that any dwarf can learn the elven ways."

"I ain't for carin' to learn the elven ways!" Roakore yelled as he paced. "Didn't ye hear? The elves let the dragons wipe out me people."

"You said yourself we don't know if it is true," said Whill, at a loss.

Roakore would not be consoled; nothing Whill said calmed him down. The dwarf king grabbed the bottle from the table and headed for the door.

"Where are you going?" Whill asked, getting up.

"I need to think!" said Roakore and slammed the door behind him.

Whill could only look after his friend with concern in his heart.

CHAPTER THIRTY-FOUR

Homeland

Aurora instructed the elves to the harbor of the capital city of stone named Grethen Dar. As they neared the harbor Aurora first realized that these were not mere fisherman that escorted her, judging by the armor they soon donned and the weapons they carried. Azzeal informed her that indeed these were his druids, each a master of one or more school of Orna Catorna.

"They are fourteen in number, each able to transform into one of seven of your people's tribal animals."

"One of seven of my people's... They will think that I command the spirits of the seven?" Aurora began to shake her head. "No, I cannot make such a claim, it is not right."

"It will gain their favor quickly," said Azzeal. "And it is true is it not? Surely one with the tribes at heart has the favor of the spirits?"

"You are right," she decided. "You have thought this through haven't you?"

"I have tried." said Azzeal as the boat docked.

There was not a soul to be found in the harbor. The boat was tied off promptly and Aurora touched her native homeland for the first time in a long time. It was good to be home. But something felt wrong about the place. The rift loomed in the distance beyond the snow covered hill that led to Grethen Dar. The sense of evil was nearly palpable. It came as a strange scent upon the wind, a feeling of foreboding that left her cold in her furs and elven cloak.

Azzeal and his druids took to land and before Aurora's eyes they changed into the spirit animals of her people. Two there were each, bear, eagle, hawk, snow cat, fox, dragon, and finally her own tribe's timber wolf. The elves in animal form regarded Aurora with quiet anticipation. She looked upon them with joy in her heart.

"Stay nearby," she informed them. "I will call out the chief of the seven and when I give word, come forth."

The elves took to the forest at the foot of the hillside two by two and disappeared within. Azzeal remained at her side as he promised he would. They began up the hill but did not veer towards the city. Instead they traveled to the snowy field on the other side of the city to the south.

An hour later they reached the high bluff that marked the very fields upon which her father had fallen. Aurora stood upon the plains and took in the crisp air; it was a good day to die. Her sword was sheathed; upon her back she wore her shield. She looked to the dragon-lance and to Azzeal.

"It is time," she said to him. "Lend your magic to my voice."

Azzeal nodded and raised a hand before her. Aurora spoke the words that she had waited to say for years.

"Icethorn!" her voice boomed with Azzeal's enchantment. It echoed over the hills like rolling thunder. "I challenge you chieftain of the seven! Come and answer the challenge of Aurora Snowfell!"

Her resolve was strengthened by the sound of her own booming voice. A horn answered her challenge. It rang out in a long deep keening that was heard for miles. The horn announced to all that there had been a challenge. Another, deeper horn bellowed forth, this one in answer to the challenge. Aurora's heart leapt in anticipation of the coming battle.

From the direction of he rift opposite the city and harbor there came the thunderous pounding of horses. Then too the sound came from the city. Soon a ruckus approached them from all sides as barbarians both mounted and on foot migrated to the field to bear witness to the challenge. Whispers of elf and Aurora Snowfell began to circle them as the hour passed and hundreds arrived. She assumed the fourteen elves to be watching from the woods, for no cries had yet announced their discovery.

"Aurora!" her mother ran to her from the crowd. She looked to have aged greatly in Aurora's absence. Her mother reached her and threw herself at her with open arms. Aurora embraced her tearful mother and felt the strength still left in her old bones.

"Oh my brave daughter what have you done!" she asked through her tears.

"I shall have my revenge. Mother, it is alright, we will talk after I kill Icethorn," said Aurora gently pushing her away.

All heads turned as the screeching roar of a dragon echoed from the city. Aurora knew the cry of that dragon well; ever did it play in her dreams. It was the cry of Icethorn's dragon Czarra

"Be safely away mother," said Aurora as she gently pushed her and brought her shield to bear.

"I love you Aurora," cried her mother as she was pulled along by two men.

"No final words mother, I shall live to see this night."

Czarra came into view over the city and flew quickly to the field to circle high above. Icethorn came down swiftly and flew low over Aurora and Azzeal and the crowd. The dragon roared as they passed and even the toughest of the barbarians were forced to cover their ears. Czarra landed before Aurora with a great flapping of wings that kicked up a bitter-cold whirlwind of ice and snow.

The crowd of barbarians had reached the thousands, and Aurora realized that they must have already been gathered within the city, likely due to the looming threat of the rift that crackled with lightning far to the south. The seven tribes stretched out around the field in a circle giving the two fighters a wide berth. The biting wind coupled with the overcast sky gave the day a dreary feel, but Aurora felt not the cold. The felt only her rage; she saw only her enemy.

Icethorn sat high upon his saddle at the base of his dragon's neck. Czarra the black glared at Aurora as if she were food and took four quick steps that brought the beast to within feet of her. Aurora found her courage and held her ground. Icethorn would not allow the dragon to attack her without a formal acceptance of the challenge, it would be considered cowardly. For the same reason Aurora stayed her fingers from pressing the gem that would extract the lance and likely kill Czarra. Icethorn pulled back his mount as he stared at Azzeal. The leaf-clad elf stood defiantly before him.

"What is this?" Icethorn asked the crowd as his mount was turned in a circle. "My ears decieve and mine eyes lie! Did I not hear challenge given strong? Why do I see no warrior before me.?

"I stand before you blind coward. Aurora Snowfell, daughter of Wolfbane Snowfell of the Timberwolf Tribe. I claim my bloodright as my father's daughter. I challenge thee."

Icethorn gave a hearty laugh and his heavy knotted black locks whipped his bare back. He wore seven heavy plates of armor strapped to his body with thick knotted braids of leather. Above heavy boots upon each shin were two plates or armor, the left was adorned with the standard of bear tribe, the right bore the howling face of the timber wolf. The plate armor upon his thighs depicted the fox and snow cat tribes. Upon his shoulders were large pauldrons engraved with the hawk and eagle. Dragon tribe was left for his thick chestplate of steel. His fur cloak of many tails blew in the wind. He regarded Aurora with wicked eyes set close behind a braided beard. The warpaint upon his face matched the black of his dragon; its sharp lines highlighted his fierce features.

"Your bloodright as daughter!" Icethorn laughed and many of the gathered barbarians joined in. "Daughters have no bloodright to challenge their father's killer," said Icethorn.

"Nor do you have the right of claim as chief of the seven. When you took control of the tribes, you broke all bonds of rights and law. I challenge you Icethorn to the death. I have the spirits of the seven with me, and I will jot be denied."

On cue startled proclamations began to ring out and in many places the barbarians began to part. Icethorn looked angrily to see what the cause was. Soon a pair of bears emerged into the circle, followed by timberwolves and two huge foxes. To everyone's astonishment two great eagles and hawks swooped down to land behind

Aurora. Out came the snow cats and finally and to everyone's awe, a pair of shimmering dragons landed before dragon tribe.

The crowd broke into frenzy. Women pulled at their hair, elders fell to the ground before the animals. The tribes fell in worship of their respective spirit animals. The elves had played their part perfectly. Aurora thumbed the ruby and the lance extended once.

She took four purposeful steps towards Icethorn and brought her shield to bear. The chieftain laughed and waved her away.

"You are food for my pet daughter Snowfell. Czarra she is yours," he said stepping aside. The black dragon lurched forth and spat a thin line of fire. Aurora quickly brought up her shield and cocked back the dragonlance of Ashai. Her arm was bathed in dragonfire as it thrust forth and the pointed end shot through the air from the main shaft and impaled the dragon through the head.

The crowd gasped as Czarra lurched back from the blow and reeled to the side scattering fox tribe. Aurora screamed through the pain of her burns and charged the faltering dragon. It fell and pawed drunkenly at the lance buried in its head. Aurora leapt upon its fore leg and with a war cry buried her longsword under its jaw. Czarra gave a strangled roar and spasmed; then he moved no more. Aurora swooned from the pain and pulled her blade free. She ignored her charred wounds and turned to Icethorn and let out a roar of her own.

The chieftain regarded her with burning hatred. He unsheathed a seven-foot long sword with sawed edges, and also a great one-handed battleaxe. Icethorn clanged the blades together and pumped his legs into a charge. Aurora answered the call and sped leaping from the dragon towards her enemy. They came together with a clash of metal. Icethorn was the bigger of the two by far, but Aurora came down upon him from on high. She shield-bashed the giant barbarian as he swung up with his axe and sent it wide; the collision left them both standing on solid footing. With matching growls they met with swords high above their heads. In came the axe from the side; out wide again went the shield. Aurora struck with sword low and Icethorn drove her blade into the dirt. He swung his axe to distract from his intentions as he slipped inside her reach. Aurora knew his mind and twirled away behind the guard of her shield. Icethorn came on banging axe and then sword heavily against her shield. She struck from behind it straight out and drew first blood as she sliced his leg above the plate armor. Axe and sword came together in a blow that sent her tumbling across the grass. A sword landed upon her shield as she rolled and blocked. Icethorn hooked the shield with the curved blade of his axe and tore it from Aurora's grasp. The sword came down again and she was forced to block with her own. Towering above her Icethorn brought his axe down from the side. She brought her her sword down across herself and jabbed it into the ground to block. The axe hewn it in two and was turned in its flight. Aurora was hit hard in the head by the deflected axe and rolled blindly to her side. She got up quickly but stumbled as the world spun and her vision blurred. Icethorn kicked her in the chest and she landed hard on her back. She rolled over onto her abandoned dragonlance shaft.

Behind her, heavy footsteps followed by victorious laughter stalked towards her. She could just picture Icethorn raising his sword high over his head. She fumbled and clutched the dragonlance shaft and tucked it under her burnt arm so that it stuck out behind her. Through her blurred vision she saw a shadow loom and a sword raised high.

There was a coward at her back.

Aurora touched a gem upon the shaft and the lance doubled in size as a pointed end shot forth and hit with a thud. Aurora's vision had begun to clear, the world stopped spinning. The shadow before her dropped its sword behind it and reached for the shadow of the protruding dragonlance.

Aurora stumbled to her feet and the sights and sounds of the world came rushing back to her. Icethorn was raging like a bull as he slowly extracted the dragonlance from his chest. The man's eyes bulged and his mouth frothed with blood, but he kept pulling the lance through. Aurora took up Icethorn's axe and walked to stand before the impaled barbarian. She set a heavy foot on the shaft where it met the ground at a slant and Icethorn howled. He clawed at the thick dragonlance that had made a hole in his chest the size of a fist and cursed Aurora.

"You maggot with your elf magic, die, die, die squealing like your fa–"

The battle axe cut through his neck and sent the head flying in a spray of blood. The body remained frozen in place, propped up by the lance. Aurora took the head of the former chieftain and held it high.

"I am the chief of the seven. If any challenge my claim, come forth now!" she yelled and tossed the head of Icethorn. The elves, as spirit animals, stalked forth to create a ring around Aurora, the dragons, hawks, and eagles took to the sky and circled above her. The barbarians of the seven tribes began to chant the name of their new chief of the seven. The name Aurora Snowfell echoed over the snow covered hills, through the city and forest beyond. It even reached the ear of the lone dark elf that stood at the base of the storming rift.

CHAPTER THIRTY-FIVE
Meeting of the Masters

Roakore was nowhere to be found when Whill left his room that morning. He was greeted by the dwarves and especially by Lunara, but nothing was asked of him about Roakore, and Whill did not ask. Dwarves didn't get into other people's business, and for that Whill was grateful.

He left the mock mountain and made his way to the pyramid in which he was to meet with the masters. It had been a week since he had been given the books, and today he was expected to answer their quizzing. He smiled to himself as he went over books at random, seeing them perfectly in his mind. He could just imagine the looks he would get when he answered their questions.

Entering the pyramid, he found the masters seated as they had been before. But this time there were neither test items nor queen. Zerafin, however, was present. Present also were many of the elders he had seen before. Although he felt prepared for the task ahead, he still found himself nervous.

Whill strode forward into the meeting hall and stopped before the gathering. Crossing his arms, he bowed slightly and waited. The elves rose as one and returned the bow. The king remained standing while the others sat. Something in his eye reminded Whill that Zerafin did not approve of his and Roakore's running off into a portal.

"Now that we are all here, we may begin," he said dryly. "When last we met, you performed tests from each master. The masters would like to give their rating of your skill levels and ask what you have learned from the tomes."

"Am I allowed to sit whilst I answer?"

Zerafin blinked at him and stared; before he could respond, Angril of the Krundar arose.

"Make yourself a chair," he said, gesturing to the stone beneath Whill.

Whill looked at the stone and then at Angril. "You make a chair. The tests were last week, remember? I am the rightful King of Uthen-Arden, the kingdom that gave you this land. All I ask for is a godsdamned chair."

Whill could not believe the words that had come out of his mouth. He sounded just like the Other—his pained inflections, the sneer; he could almost hear the blood in his mouth. He looked wide-eyed at the elf master as everyone stared at him, some showing their thoughts and some not.

"Please," Whill muttered and looked at the ground. He tried not to think of the Other. The ground shifted below him and he turned to watch a smooth, curving chair grow out of the stone. He turned back to the Krundar master, who only bowed and took his own seat.

"Thank you," said Whill as he sat, not meeting Zerafin's eyes.

"The first of the masters, please. You have the hall," said the king, taking a seat.

Master Libratus of Arnarro stood and directed his attention to Whill. The blue tendrils upon his robe seemed to swirl around the sleeves of his lokata. "You, my friend, have baffled my understanding of the learning process. As I am sure many of my fellow masters will attest, you have abilities that no elf under one hundred years of age has. It may even be a new form of Orna Catorna that you are using, something yet unseen until now. While we must learn everything about the part of the body we are healing, you have not. While we must understand how the body heals itself, you do not. Yet you can." He waved a hand absently at the air. "My final evaluation is that I do not know. To me it seems a testament to the prophecy."

The elves stirred, both believers and nonbelievers of the prophecy. "I will speak no more of it." Libratus waved them away. "Did you read much of the art of healing?" he asked Whill.

"Yes, I found it quite interesting. I have always had an attraction to the art. I consider the power to heal the greatest of all gifts."

"Indeed." Libratus smiled with a raised chin. "And how far did you get?"

"I read the entire tome," Whill said with pride.

Libratus nodded slowly. "I see. Very well. What is the center bone of the human hand called?"

"In elven or Agoran speech?" Whill asked.

"Elven," Libratus replied, sounding intrigued.

"It is called the astellarden."

"And what is the tendon that runs above it from knuckle to wrist?" Libratus pressed.

"Minnetus," answered Whill.

Libratus looked to the ceiling in thought. "Quarts of blood in the elven body?"

"Five."

"Which god strand is responsible for the body's healing?"

"Number twenty-seven."

"How do healing stones work?"

"A frequency is given to the smoothed crystal that the body of the wounded responds to. This frequency is determined early in elven culture and shared with few. Usually healing stones are carried by those they are meant to heal. There are others as well, however, such as Krenolian rubies and Shadrol emeralds, which can be used on anything with the guidance of the wielder," Whill answered with a smile.

"Page seven hundred nine, paragraph six, third word in the first sentence," said Libratus with a scowl.

Whill grinned. "Blood."

Defeated, Libratus laughed to himself and clasped his hands before his chin. "Are we to assume that you can recite all of the tomes so?"

"Yes, I can see them all clearly," Whill confirmed.

There was a rustling of masters and elders as murmured discussion abounded.

"Is this a new ability?" asked Libratus.

"Well…yes, it is. I turned my mind-sight inward and enhanced the parts of my mind that control memory and learning."

Libratus nodded to himself, looking disappointed. Many of the elves seemed to share his sentiment. "You do know that this type of meddling is shunned by the elves of the sun?" he asked.

"I am not an elf," Whill reminded them. "I need to learn all that I can as quickly as possible if I am to face Eadon. Or do you all have a better plan?"

"These rules are set in place for a reason. Past abuses have dictated the necessity for such ways," said Libratus.

Whill rose from his chair and addressed them all. "I am done discussing elven rules. Does anyone have anything to offer in the form of help? Or are we to sit around talking about what I should and should not do?"

Zerafin rose from his chair with a scowl. "You should show more respect for this court."

"I have respect, my friend, but do the elves? Maybe Kellallea was right when she caused the elves to forget magic. What good has it done Agora? You have not shared your gifts with man nor dwarf; sickness still plagues the world. Life has not been made easier by your magic—it has become a nightmare. You are strangers to men and despised by most dwarves. Perhaps if you had shared your magic with Agora, we would now stand a better chance."

He turned as if to leave but whipped back on them. "Perhaps I should not be the one being tested here. Tomorrow I will strike a blow to Eadon's armies that he has never felt: tomorrow I wage war. If you would join me, then do so, but do not get in my way."

Whill turned from them all, went through the sunlit entrance, and never looked back.

Outside of the building he was met by a huge crowd of elves who had come to see him. He stopped before the blocked path and sighed with frustration. Next to him the Other looked at the crowd of groveling elves with disgust.

"And here we always thought the elves so mysterious and special. They act like groveling swine."

"Shut up," Whill told him. To the crowd he spoke for all to hear. "Here I am!" His voice boomed over them as he stretched his arms out wide. "The one named in prophecy. The one foretold to rid the world of Eadon. I am Whill of Agora, I am legend. I am prophecy and death. Look at me now and look no more. If you would heed my legend, then heed my word."

The city had grown dead quiet as Whill's words echoed throughout, enhanced by the sword at his hip. Everyone waited for the word of Whill of Agora; the prophecy's lore masters waited eagerly for his gospel. Maidens and males alike looked on in eager anticipation. Whill let them wait, let the tension build until he knew he had everyone's complete attention.

"I am not a weapon, I am a man, and I will not help those who do not help themselves. Decide if you will flee or fight, and do it soon, for I grow weary of those who would see me save them."

The crowd suddenly parted frantically as a white dragon landed before Whill. Upon its back sat Avriel. Whill cocked his head at the strange image of Avriel riding the dragon she had once possessed. He climbed the white dragon Zorriaz and Avriel smiled back at him before coaxing the dragon up. Zorriaz spread her magnificent wings and the crowd parted further. Her legs rippled with muscle as she leapt thirty feet into the air and began to slowly climb up and away from the temple. Looking back, Whill realized that many of the masters and elders had come out of the pyramid at some point in his speech and were now among the thousands who watched them sore over the city.

"I am going with you into the portal," Avriel said over the wind and in his mind at the same time.

"The portal likely leads to the horrors of the hells. It makes no sense for the princess of the elves to do such a thing. You will remain with your people," Whill argued without passion, as if that was simply the way it would be.

Avriel turned and gave him a furious look. "I will? You command me now?"

"No," he said, staring back at her. "I speak as the king of Uthen-Arden. A war zone is no place for someone so important to her people."

Zorriaz gave a screech and suddenly dove straight down. Whill was forced to cling to the saddle he and Avriel shared. The dragon leveled out and abruptly turned skyward as it beat its wings forward to land. Zorriaz came down on her hind feet and Avriel gave Whill a shove that sent him flailing from the saddle. He would have hit the ground hard had he not quickly slowed his fall. Avriel leapt from her dragon and came around the front to face Whill.

"So a battlefield is no place for women?"

"Avriel, I didn't say—"

"A princess of the elves should sit home and look pretty for her people and be gushed over all day?"

He laughed. "Now you are just making things up."

She shoved him. "But my brother the king, he should risk his life in battle? Is he not more important to his people? You are a king, yet you fight."

Avriel pushed until Whill's smile was gone. She shoved him again but he caught her wrists. Avriel pulled back but he held her firm. She tried to speak and he kissed her. Her protest became a whining moan as she pulled herself forward and their embrace sent them to the moss-covered stone below.

Zorriaz snorted as if annoyed, and when it was apparent the two would not part soon, she leapt and flew off. Avriel and Whill's kiss began slowly as they savored the moment they had both dreamt of. Soon it turned urgent and frantic as they both were driven mad with passion for one another. They rolled upon the moss between the raging falls and laughed between kisses. Avriel pushed Whill down and with a wry grin raised her hands. The vines along the rocky falls nearby climbed up and over them, forming a dome that let only small light inside.

CHAPTER THIRTY-SIX
Whill Rising

Later that night Whill ate dinner with the dwarves at the large table in the main hall of the mock mountain. Some fifty dwarves there were, along with Avriel, Lunara, and Tarren. The feast was had and pipes were lit, and soon talk turned to the possibility of portals within the dwarven kingdoms.

"How in the hells did the portal get inside me mountain twenty years ago? That's what I be wonderin'," said Roakore.

"Maybe the dark elves disguised themselves as dwarves or something," Tarren offered through a mouthful of food.

"It is possible," said Lunara. "No matter how they did it, it was done. Now the possibility exists that there may be more in the other mountain kingdoms."

Roakore nodded. "That's what I be thinkin'. I had me dwarves search every inch o' Ro'Sar, but no sign o' a portal was found. Word was sent for the other kings to do the same. When we left Ro'Sar, no word had come back by falcon."

"All I know for sure is that the longer we wait, the more time Eadon has to prepare. I am done waiting," said Whill.

"Hear, hear!" cheered Philo and drank down his beer. It seemed that the dwarf used any excuse to drink down a beer. He cheered just about everything anyone said.

Whill nudged Tarren and motioned for him to follow. The boy followed Whill to his room. Whill turned within the threshold and was about to speak when Tarren did.

"I know," said the lad. "Lunara will be watchin' over me while you are off fighting."

"Are you happy with the arrangement?" Whill asked.

Tarren scrunched up his face as if Whill were crazy. "Well, no, I would rather you didn't have to risk your life for everyone. But I don't mind bein' with Lunara. She is a good person."

"Indeed."

"Do you think you can stop him?" asked Tarren quietly.

Whill did not want to lie to the boy. "No," he answered truthfully, and Tarren bowed his head.

"But you have the sword of power. Can't you kill him with it?"

Whill shook his head. "It is complicated. The sword may actually be Eadon's, and if that is true, I cannot kill him with it. Elves cannot be killed by their own sword."

Tarren looked confused. "Can't you use the power in it to kill him?"

"I don't know," said Whill. "But one thing I do know is that I can use the sword against his armies, and I intend to. I will crush them all."

Tarren smiled up at him. He seemed convinced that Whill could do what he said. Tarren had to believe that Whill would be all right. It had worked before.

"Between Lunara and that Holdagozz dwarf, you will be safe," he said.

Tarren shrugged. "Yeah, I'll be fine."

Whill smiled and picked him up in a bear hug. "One day life will be normal again, Tarren."

The boy laughed, returning the hug. "No, it won't."

Whill put him down and Tarren looked up at him with a grin. "I am the ward of Whill of Agora, my best friend is the son of a dwarf king, and I have an elven godmother. Life will never be normal again," he said with a brave smile.

Whill could not help but laugh.

He did not sleep that night. He did not need to. The sword and the anticipation of what he might find on Fendora gave him all he needed to stay wide awake.

Whill left Avriel and the rest of them and quietly snuck out of the elf-made cave. He unsheathed Adromida and with a thought he willed himself up and into the sky. He flew steadily to the falls and landed upon one of the many outcroppings of rock that split the raging waters. The moon was a looming mass in the clear night sky. Only a few long clouds passed slowly, like whales in an ocean of stars. Moonbeams like rays of light piercing though water fell across the land and illuminated the already glowing city.

Whill dug into the memory of the tome of Gnenja and began practicing one of the many sword-fighting forms. The Koresnian method was first. Focusing on balance and defense, it was a valuable way to protect against attack, though in a tight spot it would not be useful, as it demanded space to move in. For an hour Whill went through the curving blocks and brilliant feints it offered. He could not believe how good it felt to work with the sword; it seemed to meld to his body so that he did not so much wield it as dance with it. Together he and the blade twirled and struck like a viper, only to leap seven feet landing in a crouch with a sidelong slash.

Far below, someone in the city noticed Whill there upon the falls silhouetted in the giant setting moon. Word spread quickly and elves came in droves. Soon the entire riverside was packed with elves mimicking Whill's forms. Anyone of the Gnenja discipline and even farmers and elves of the market came to watch Whill. But there, high above it all, Whill did not notice. He saw only the form, knew only his body and the blade. Across from him the Other had materialized, but Whill ignored him. The Other mimicked his every move flawlessly though he held no sword.

Long into the night Whill performed the forms. He put the Other out of his mind and began yet another form. This, the Derzarrian, focused upon nothing but offense. It was a powerful form of heavy strikes and sweeping slashes. The blade became a blur of singing death in his hand.

Morning came with the sun and the first of the beams hit Whill there high upon the falls. Below, upon the banks of the river where the sun had yet to shine, the elves looked up at their savior of legend, brilliant as the sunrise, and many believed.

Whill executed the forms flawlessly, twirling, spinning and leaping with a grace few humans could match. His body had been made whole again by the blade and the elven care. He was once again in his prime. He could hold impossible positions due to his strength and new-found skill. He could linger in a leap or come down like lightning if he chose.

After the sun had been in the sky for many hours, Whill finished the last routine, brought the blade to his face, and breathed deeply. He knew he had yet to understand fully the wealth of power within the blade. In truth he had barely scratched the surface of what he knew to be possible with it. He felt as though the sword could move mountains without noticing a depletion of power, and it scared him.

Whill sheathed his blade and found what seemed to be the entire city staring at him from below. Whill ran and leapt from the stone out and over the river. He fell slowly and traveled quickly across the water. He came down next to the dwarven living quarters and found them all outside, armor-clad and in formation. Elves there were too, and Whill marveled that half the city had armored and prepared overnight. Before him stood an army of elves, and he recognized all of the schools of magic represented there. All of the masters were present, as well as many of the elders. There were droves of druids in animal form, from bear to wolf and great cat. Zerafin split the crowd on horseback and rode to face Whill. He wore full elven plate armor of silver with gemmed buckles and straps, with large shoulder plates that glowed from behind the cracks with a blue brilliant light. Zerafin looked like a true elven king of legend, as had never been seen upon the shores of Agora.

"The elders, and the masters, and the elves of Cerushia have decided," said the king for all to hear. "You are worthy of legend, Whill of Agora, and we will fight alongside you to the ends of the earth if need be. For we shall be victorious in this fight, or we will die trying!" The elves and even the dwarves cheered agreement.

"It is good to know that I am not alone in this," Whill told the crowd. "I thank you."

"It has been decided that we will strike Fendora together, today," Zerafin announced.

Whill looked across the ocean of stoic elven faces. "I intended to infiltrate Fendora alone."

"There is no need for infiltration. We are attacking and taking the rock. It was lost to our cause long ago. It is now a desolate breeding ground for draggard and a dark-elf naval base, and it must be taken. It shall be the first of many offenses. We have already sent word to the dwarves of Helgar." Zerafin gestured to Roakore.

"Aye, laddie!" Roakore grunted. "I been in touch with the king o' Helgar. It seems the elves gifted the dwarf with a speaking stone a while ago. I don't know why he trusted the thing, bein' as suspicious as any dwarf about the elves. But I spoke to him while you were doin' your dance on the falls. It took an hour and many questions from both o' us before we believed it was each other, but it turned out to be a trustworthy trinket. I told the king we meant to take the island, and he agreed to it. It be in the interest o' the Helgar dwarves to take the island outpost. Already they fight to keep the eastern edge o' Uthen-Arden clear between mountain and sea. They fight for the beach even now."

"Yes, we will rendezvous with the dwarves upon the western coast, and from there we will wipe out the enemy," Zerafin said.

Whill wanted to scream with excitement. Finally something was happening! If he could get elves and dwarves to fight together for Fendora, he could do anything.

"To Fendora!" Whill screamed, pumping his fist.

"To Fendora!" the crowd bellowed.

CHAPTER
THIRTY-SEVEN
Kell-Torey Siege

It took the dragon-hawk a little less than two days to reach Kell-Torey. The beast did not stop for rest; if it needed any, Dirk assumed that it did so while gliding upon warm currents. Neither did it hunt. Dirk called the dragon-hawk Fyrfrost when he got tired of calling him dragon, and the name stuck.

When Kell-Torey came into view, Dirk sat up, alert, and gasped at what he saw. A dark storm hung over the city and a strange tear like a knife wound cut from the heavens to the earth. The rift wore lightning like a wreath, and within, stars could be seen dancing in darkened space. From the rift poured armies of draggard and massive dwargon, and draquon flew from the portal in droves. The city was under siege, and it was not going well for the Eldalonians.

Coming in from the north over the nearby lake, Dirk could make out massive siege weapons. Rams and catapults rolled out of the rift and already missiles were being hurled at the outer wall of the city. Three of Kell-Torey's outer walls had already been breached, and smoke billowed from three rings of the city.

"To the castle, Fyrfrost!"

The beast flew under the cover of its ever-changing wings, over the smoldering outskirts of the city. Many draquon circled the city, diving down at leisure and plucking scurrying people from the streets at will. They easily dodged the spears and harpoons, though Dirk noticed that a few soldiers had been successful at netting one of the beasts. As he flew silently overhead, he watched as they hacked and chopped at it in a rage.

Over rooftops and high walls the dragon-hawk came to the sealed castle grounds. Dirk steered Fyrfrost to a high tower and steadied the beast to circle.

"Look for me in the windows," Dirk told his mount and leapt to the tower. He threw his grappling hook and caught a small windowsill at the center of the tower. He swung and landed upon the tower's winding outer stairs. With a flick of Dirk's wrist the hook fell and wound quickly into his belt. He caught it and clipped it secure. In a crouch he surveyed the castle grounds from on high. Through his hood, night was like day, and he saw that nothing moved upon the rooftops or high walls. The courtyard below was busy with shuffling soldiers, but up here nothing stirred.

Dirk took from his pocket the timber-wolf trinket. He studied it for a moment, debating whether or not he should summon the spirit. He found himself scared that Chief might not return after the blow he had taken while still in physical form.

"Chief," he finally whispered, and held out the carving.

He grinned when the mist appeared and spiraled from the trinket. Arching up like a snake, the smoke shimmered and circled Dirk as it grew. Dirk felt Chief graze his back and turned to find the spirit wolf staring at him from only feet away.

"Before you get upset, hear me out," said Dirk holding up his hands defensively. Chief showed his teeth and his displeasure. "If I hurt you I am sorry, it was an accident. I thought you would have…gone ghost when the pillar fell. I meant you no harm."

Chief stared at Dirk for a long time and finally wagged his tail and took in their location. Dirk smiled and chanced a stroke of the wolf's back. "We have no time for stealth. It looks as though we are too late. Bigger things are going on here besides the assassination of a king. The entire city is under siege. There is some kind of rift in the valley below, no doubt leading to Drindellia and Eadon's legions. We go to find the king. Let no one stand in our way, human or dark elf."

Chief growled low in acknowledgement and followed Dirk silently into the castle. They slipped into a darkened room through the window, and Dirk saw it to be a small library. Chief became translucent and drifted through the wall. He remained in that form as he silently stalked to the door and out the hall.

Dirk waited by the door for Chief to return. When he drifted in, he looked at Dirk, pawed his nose, and looked to the door.

"Smell, stink...is it draggard?" Dirk asked. Chief shook his head and Dirk laughed quietly. "You're a smart one, eh, Chief? Well, then, let's kill ourselves some draggard."

Dirk opened the door silently, the enchantment in his gloves muting the hinges. To the left the torchlit hall led to a staircase and to the right there was a long hall and a bend. Dirk listened intently and his enchanted earrings complied.

Below, far below, came faint sounds of struggle—a scream, crashing wood, breaking glass. Dirk darted for the staircase with Chief at his side. They went down the winding staircase tower seven floors before coming to the main hall. Chief ran ahead of Dirk, sniffing the floor and the air around him. His hair stood straight along his spine and he whine-growled to Dirk.

"Show me the way," Dirk bade him and the wolf was off running down a hall. Dirk followed at a silent jog, noting the doors to his left and right. The arrangement and size of the open doorways suggested he was passing the main kitchens on his left. To the right he assumed the dining hall sat, its five service doors spanning a long section of hallway.

Farther into the keep, Dirk came to the armory. The mangled bodies of many soldiers littered the floor. There were a few dead draggard , but where there was one draggard body, there were five men. Chief went through a wall and Dirk followed, turning a corner at the end of the armory and coming to another stone hallway draped in shadow and dead. The sounds Dirk had heard before were no more. Nothing moved within the castle but him and Chief, it seemed.

Chief came to a painting at the end of the hall and clawed at the stone below it. Dirk touched the stone with his gloved hand and felt a small breeze through the sensitive gloves. He pushed on one of the bricks and the wall turned in upon itself. Chief took up the trail once more down a wide, winding staircase and Dirk's unease only intensified.

After what Dirk guessed to be three floors, they came to an opening littered with dead Eldalonian soldiers. At the opposite wall a large iron door had been blown out of its frame. Beyond lay a torchlit room. Chief began to growl at the doorway and he crouched low as if stalking his prey.

Chief charged into the room and disappeared from sight. Dirk followed cautiously and grimaced when he heard Chief's yelp and the crackling of lightning. He dove through the threshold into what had once been a siege shelter but was now destroyed and riddled with bodies. These were not soldiers, nor were they servants. Here was the tomb of the royals of the kingdom, their golden buttons and fine, bloodstained clothing giving them away.

Dirk ducked behind an overturned table after tossing three darts into the darkness. They hit with a bang and their light brightened the entire room. Chief growled and metal sang from its sheath. Dirk dared a look over the table and saw Krentz standing there in the light.

"Down, Chief, wait. I would have words with this one," he said, standing.

"I see you have a new pet, a spirit wolf. Very Dirk Blackthorn," said Krentz.

"What have you done?" Dirk asked, seeing the children among the fallen.

"What you could not," she answered quickly and took a step toward him. Dirk noticed something hanging in her grasp, a severed head. Upon its wide-eyed head sat a crown of gold.

"Then it is done," he whispered.

"It is done; my father's will is done. Whill is now the rightful heir to Eldalon, for after this night, none of his line lives."

"Now what?" Dirk asked, coming closer; he could almost reach out and touch her. The glow of his fire darts waned, and the light danced upon Krentz's tears.

"Now you let me pass," she answered in the voice he loved.

"Or?"

Krentz lifted her chin. "I cannot go against my father's will," she said with pain.

"Fight it!" he screamed.

"I will die!" she answered with a cry of pain from fighting the fealty spell and not attacking Dirk. She unsheathed her sword and slashed at him in a blur of movement. Dirk's dagger and short sword were out in an instant. He parried a slash and deflected a stab and together they danced their familiar fighting rhythm. They separated and held a sword's length between them.

"Let me pass," she begged.

"I cannot."

"Then kill me now, for I cannot!" Krentz bent in pain at the waist. "Or else let me pass, and forget me. Do not seek me out; do not come for me…I cannot…" she stammered and fell to her knees in pain at her defiance. She would be dead soon unless she fought her father's enemy.

Dirk sheathed his blade and looked at Chief. "There is another way." He looked back to his beloved and bent to kiss her quivering lips. "I love you," he whispered.

"I…" She shuddered as pain wracked her body.

"Now, Chief!" Dirk yelled, and the spirit wolf attacked and clamped on to Krentz's wrist. Her shields were down for Dirk and the wolf drew blood.

"Back to your realm, Chief," Dirk cried, desperately holding out the figurine and hoping against all hope that his plan would work. Chief began to dematerialize, and his contact with the dark elf brought her with him. Both elf and wolf turned to mist and smoke, which swirled up and into the trinket. Chief had brought Krentz to the spirit world through it. Dirk squeezed the timber-wolf figurine tightly and pocketed it, hoping that Krentz would survive.

He surveyed the dead nobility, numbering over a dozen. To his credit, the headless King Mathus held a sword in hand. Apparently he had gone down with a fight.

Dirk left the dead and went back to the roof the way he had come. From the tower window he surveyed the city beyond. There was no way to tell how long the siege had been going on, but by the looks of it the city had been surprised by the attack. The fact that three defensive walls had been compromised was not a testament to the length of the siege, but rather the efficiency of the dark elves. No army in the history of Eldalon had ever breached every wall—this would be a first. Knowing the relationship between Eldalon and the Ky'Dren dwarves, Dirk knew that they would rush to help as soon as they received word of Kell-Torey's plight, but help would come too late. Kell-Torey was doomed.

The squawk of the dragon-hawk told him that the beast had returned. It came into view as it flew toward Dirk. He leapt from the window and landed upon the large saddle. The dragon-hawk became camouflaged and together they flew out over the city once more. The draggard and dark-elf armies had taken the fourth wall already. Explosions of multicolored spells followed the soldiers as they retreated to the fifth wall. The sky was littered with draquon who had taken the fight to the inner defensive walls of the city. Many of the larger winged beasts carried dark elves who dropped down into the city and wreaked havoc.

Dirk circled the city, flying high above the swarms of draquon that stalked their prey. His dragon-hawk mount growled low in his throat. Dirk shared the sentiment. He had no stake in this fight, but seeing his fellow man being destroyed by the draggard hordes gave him no pleasure. Anger welled in him as he watched the city burn, one he knew well. The screams and cries of the desperate people of Kell-Torey rang out into the night, and he could not ignore them. The dragon-hawk veered into a descent, wanting to join the fray. It was all Dirk could do to rein it in.

"This is not our fight!" Dirk yelled against the wind, the smoke from the burning city choking him. The scent of burnt flesh rode on the smoke, and Dirk cursed to himself.

He looked to the portal and the still-marching armies pouring from it. "There is nothing but death here, dragon. If you want to hurt the dark elves, let us go to the portal. I have a plan."

The dragon-hawk immediately changed course and headed toward the rift a mile away. They flew over dark, seething armies of nightmarish beasts, some large enough to pull a catapult behind them. The war machines were like nothing Dirk had ever seen. One in particular would be suitable for his plan. He watched as a mammoth half-dragon, half-dwarf dwargon pulled back the lever and unleashed a boulder-sized projectile into the sky. It sailed over the outer walls and hit the city, taking out an entire building in a giant fireball.

The dragon-hawk flew the mile quickly, and the closer Dirk got to the portal, the more his dread grew. Through it was a starlit sky, like a lake turned upright. Dirk and his mount were dwarfed by the rift, which was twice as tall as Kell-Torey Castle's highest tower. It hummed and vibrated with chilling notes that turned Dirk's blood cold. For some reason the rift reminded him of a recurring nightmare in which he cowered under the head of a needle so large that it blackened the sky.

"There!" Dirk pointed to a war machine a hundred yards from the rift. "Fly me low over it."

Dirk unbuckled himself from Fyrfrost's saddle and crouched upon it. "You are a dragon, Fyrfrost, let's have a ring of fire around that machine!"

As if waiting to be unleashed, Fyrfrost roared and banked hard left. He circled wide of the war machine and unleashed his breath upon the draggard armies.

Dirk leapt from his mount as it connected the circle and banked over the war machine.

The assassin fell through the air and landed upon the dwargon that had been pulling the catapult. Before the beast could react, Dirk plunged his dagger, Krone, into its neck while landing upon its back. "Do you understand Agoran speech?" he demanded, twisting the dagger.

An unintelligible mumble was the beast's answer, but Dirk could hear confusion along with the fear and rage.

"Elvish, then," said Dirk in the elven tongue and got a positive groan. The heat from the fire was nearly more than Dirk could bear. Without his enchanted armor and cloak he would not have been able to stand it. The dwargon, however, seemed more afraid of the fire than hurt by it.

Three draggard that had been lucky enough to be close to the machine noticed Dirk, and like a pack of wolves they circled him and the dwargon. They looked curious as to why the beast had not killed him yet.

"Kill the draggard quickly and turn this machine around," said Dirk. He rode the dwargon with an arm around its thick neck and the other hand clutching the dagger. He braced himself for the fight and the dwargon made short work of the much smaller beasts. The dwargon then did as Dirk had ordered and turned the machine around. The circle of fire around them, at first twenty feet high, had burned down to ten. Over the circle flew many draquon, their hateful eyes boring into Dirk.

"Hurry up," Dirk said anxiously in Elvish. The beast redoubled its efforts and soon had the war machine turned toward the portal. Dirk counted the reserve bombs in a holding bin on the side of the catapult. Ten.

"Load this thing up and fire short!" Dirk ordered, and by the dagger the dwargon was forced to comply. He turned a wheel and secured a heavy rope around a lever. From the bin he lifted the large bomb with ease and dropped it into the basket.

"Fire!" Dirk yelled as a draquon swooped down toward him with reaching claws. The bomb flew through the air only a hundred feet and exploded with a ground-shaking boom. Draggard and dwargon alike flew in all directions near the portal.

"Duck!" Dirk warned, and as the beast did so the attacking draquon missed him by inches. Dirk leapt from the dwargon. "Fire them all at the base of the rift!"

The draquon circled Dirk within the slowly waning circle of fire. He unsheathed his short sword and opened his arms to the beasts. "Come on!" he challenged and the draquon answered. The beast dove at Dirk and a dart found its eye. The dart exploded on impact and the headless flying draggard fell into the flames.

The catapult fired again and Dirk watched the flaming boulder disappear into the portal. There was no vibration from the impact, but from the portal came fire and draggard bodies. He had stopped the dark-elf advancement for a time, but he had also gained the attention of the surrounding armies.

"Time to go, Fyrfrost!" Dirk yelled to the sky.

Two more draquon dove toward him as the lever clicked again and the huge stone of the catapult dropped, sending another bomb flying. Dirk engaged the nearest draquon as it landed and with a roar charged with its trident. Dirk dodged the strike of the ten-foot nightmare and darted under the weapon. As the draquon pulled back the weapon, it also struck with its spear-like tail. The tail struck like a snake and Dirk rolled to the left, letting the tail glide off his enchanted cloak. His boots carried him along so quickly that no sooner had the draquon missed with both trident and tail than it was slashed by a stinging blade across the back of the legs. Dirk stabbed the legs of the beast with both dagger and sword, and by the time he had passed, the beast had been forced to take to the sky.

Dirk leapt and did a half twist to face the retreating beast. He threw an explosive dart at its belly and dropped a smoke bomb at his feet. He barely was out of the way when another attacking draquon charged, flying blindly through the smoke. The retreating beast exploded, and the distraction and smoke was enough for Dirk to land a killing blow. With a quick and powerful blow to the back of the neck with his short sword,

Dirk severed his attacker's spinal cord. The draquon landed in a tumbling heap and rolled into the now-five-foot-wide flames.

"Fyrfrost!" Dirk cried, not caring if he attracted unwanted attention. He already had it. Scores of draggard and dwargon hissed and growled just beyond the flame. The catapult clicked and launched again, but the projectile exploded only twenty feet from it. Dirk saw a purple dark-elf spell hit the bomb, and then he saw no more.

CHAPTER THIRTY-EIGHT

Fendora

The elven army made for the northern coast of Elladrindellia along with the small dwarven force. Avriel stubbornly refused to stay behind, and she flew upon Zorriaz at the head of the group above her brother and his mounted elves. Regiments of elven armies joined them at the beach from both the east and west. Whill was awed by the hundreds of elven ships that waited offshore. Fleets there were with hundreds of warships and rammers, each manned by powerful elven masters.

Upon his elven horse, Whill gave Zerafin a look. "You did not gather this force overnight. You planned and set this into motion days ago."

"Yes," said Zerafin. "I have been planning this attack for a long time. Fendora is a prime target."

The elven armies poured onto the many battleships that would carry them to the beaches of Fendora. High above, Roakore circled with Silverwind. A strong breeze came up over the beach and high waves crashed steadily onto shore. Far to the north, a darkness of cloud gathered.

"They prepare for our arrival," Zerafin noted as he and Whill watched the armies load.

"Let them prepare. They cannot know what is coming for them," said Whill, hearing the voice of the Other and no longer caring.

Zerafin's gaze lingered on him as if he had sensed a change in Whill. "The elders and masters were impressed by you yesterday. Until then the vote had been split concerning your worth."

Zerafin watched his sister circle overhead upon Zorriaz. Whill laughed. "All I had to do was chastise the elders and masters."

"Elven culture is…polite. Oftentimes we use small lies to avoid confrontation. We do not often speak so directly to others, only those closest to us. Your straightforwardness gained their ears."

"Then this is the beginning of the end," said Whill, looking off to the north at the gathering darkness. A smile crept onto his face. "I would see light pierce the darkness."

"Then let us pierce it," said Zerafin.

The two rode to the harbor and boarded a warship. Whill had seen the design in books, but in life the ships looked much barer. There was neither harpoon nor cannon, no catapults or crossbows mounted to rail. Upon the elven warship, the only weapons were the elves.

The deck was flat and rose slightly toward the middle. Dotted along the smooth dark wood were large flat crystal circles. These were the power source behind the elven casters. The crystals held large amounts of stored energy, and it was a great honor among the elves to be chosen to harness that energy. These casters were chosen from the best of each school.

The ships cast off, and telepathically the captains steered the fleets out. Krundars upon every ship wove the wind into the fin-like sails and rushed the currents along beneath, and soon they were traveling faster than it seemed possible. The fleet cut through the waves with ease as they sped faster still. The concentration of air weavers and water weavers caused huge gusts and northerly swells that lifted them up and rushed them on toward Fendora.

The fleets made it to the island in two hours, and brought with them a tidal wave. As they approached the island the darkness grew, and the closer they got, the more dramatic the disturbance became. Now, sailing toward the island at breakneck speed, Whill could begin to make out a swirling storm of lightning and clouds of darkness. If it was a portal, it was quite unlike the one he had traveled through previously. If looked rather like a tear in reality, and through it a starry sky could be seen beyond the storm.

"It looks like the gate to the hells, laddie," Roakore yelled over the torrent as half of the ships veered left along the coast of Fendora and the other half went right. Behind them the ocean wave hit the coast with devastating effect. Orbs of pulsing light came alive under the flood, the shields of dark elves who had been lying in wait. Lightning crackled and struck one of the ships. A cascade of multicolored sparks shot into the air as the blast was deflected by the warship's shield. Spells suddenly began to pour from the left side of the island as Whill's ship and the rest of the fleet sped by. The water swelled beneath them once more as the Morenka water weavers strained to cause another wave. The island seemed to sink from Whill's perspective as the ships rose with the water. Quickly the water turned and they were falling and a wave shot out from beneath them and ravaged the coast. Anything within a few miles would be washed out.

Spells continued to rain down upon the shields of the fleet, but they held steady. Now high walls and castles could be seen on the island, where the water could not reach. The fleet barreled into the harbor, and he began to think that the elves meant to crash the coast. Here the rocks were few and the beaches stretching. Whill held firm the rail and waited for the collision. But it never came.

An order was shouted from every ship, and as one they slowed until they had all packed into the harbor. A horn blew and the elves stormed the beaches, running and leaping along the many boats to reach the shore. Whill and his group were the first upon the beach, and soon Roakore and Avriel landed as well.

Far inland there was a loud blast and a sudden silence. A strange sound echoed through the air for a long moment before a stone the size of a castle tower came shooting through the sky. It barreled down upon the center of the fleet, and many shouts of "Shields!" went up. Roakore lifted his hands to the sky and strain furled his brow as he pushed against it. Elven Ralliads too raised their hands to it and the stone began to slow. Whill stepped forward and lifted his right hand. The stone stopped dead and floated for a moment above them. The Ralliad nearby watched in awe and lowered their hands. Whill brought back his hand and the monolithic stone moved with it. He then heaved and it flew back the way it had come. None breathed as they waited and listened. The boom that erupted shook the ground beneath them and the elves cheered.

"Roakore, my friend. I would offer my strength to you and your men," Whill said, leaning in close to the king.

"And we would be acceptin'," he said with a grin.

Whill called up what he had learned from the tome about multiple spell targets. He scanned over the regiment of dwarves as elves rushed by. They looked to their king as they bounced impatiently on their toes. Whill built the spell in his mind and shot out his right hand before him. Painless blue lightning cracked the air and a snaking arc hit each dwarf in turn. There were alarmed shouts and protests but then a sudden quiet as the dwarves perceived the incredible energy they had just been given. They looked wide-eyed at Whill and to their king; it was painful for them to stand still.

"Charge!" Roakore bellowed, and the dwarves joined the elven charge up the beach and over the high bluff. Whill took to the sky and beheld the island. Sporadic clumps of forest speckled the mostly stone island. Tall, thick walls surrounded nearby castles and fortresses. Deeper inland he saw a huge dwarven force battling hundreds of draggard. Beyond them swirled the shadow rift. Whill was shocked when he looked to where the rift met the ground. Armies of draggard, dwargon, draquon, and unnamable beasts filed through. The lines of marching nightmares branched out like ant trails to the many harbors and their dark elf warships. Whill was horrified to think that this rift had been opened for a week or more. The seas would be swarmed by the fleets of dark-elf-led draggard armies. Whill had to close the portal.

That rift, how can it be closed? Whill asked Zerafin with his mind.

I do not know. This dark sorcery is beyond any of us. Eadon's greatest threat is that he has no boundaries; there are no limits to what he will do or create. He is heedless of the gods and nature. There was disdain in Zerafin's mental voice.

Whill flew over the charging elves and dwarves and headed toward the army of Elgar dwarves that was making slow progress toward the nearest castle. They bent under shield and used the scant cover to advance against torrents of flying stone and spells. The frontline of the assault pressed stubbornly against a thick draggard mass. Whill landed among the frontline dwarves and blasted a group of draggard away from them. He unsheathed his sword and slammed his fist to his chest. The Elgar dwarves cocked their heads and relaxed their arms as Whill turned, raised the sword, and pointed it at the advancing hordes. He opened himself to the sword and released massive amounts of energy through Adromida. Blinding, pure white light lit the day as if it had been dark. Everyone was forced to turn their eyes from the light as the sword hummed with a power that made the nearby dwarves' teeth chatter.

Then suddenly it was over. The dwarves turned slowly to see what had happened, and they gasped when they beheld a sea of stone beasts. Whill turned and saluted them once again. "Let's give 'em hell!" he shouted in Dwarvish, and the armies went berserk. They charged toward the castle in a rage as Whill flew on. Spells shot through the air and Whill dodged many. He reinforced his shield with the humming power of Adromida and the spells blew up on contact. He sent a massive fireball at the fortified door and the explosion shook the ground. The dwarves cheered and charged into the castle.

Soon Roakore's dwarves and the elves caught up and charged through the field of stone draggard, leaving them crumbling in their wake. Whill marveled at the array of spells that curved up and slammed into the draggard masses. The elves unleashed such a powerful assault that the dwarves were soon charging past the castle and into the main body of the dark-elf force.

In the distance the rift swirled with lightning and blackened clouds. A horn blew and many more answered the call as the dwarven and elven armies clashed with the dark elves and their hellish creations before the shadow of the rift.

Whill yelled to the elven healers to focus on the leading dwarf charge and they complied. The frontline dwarves plowed through the draggard and did not slow as the casters made up the sides of the phalanx, and rained down spells of fire and ice. The draggard were considered animals, and so the Zionars were free to use their gifts. They intruded the draggard minds and instilled numbing fear into their hearts. Many attempted to run, others clawed themselves to mutilation. Whill shivered when he saw what those like Ornarell could do.

Zerafin led the elven charge upon his white horse, hewing draggard with his blazing sword and screaming "For Drindellia!" with every kill. Soon shouts of "For Ro'Sar!" and "For Elgar!" rang out as the dwarves too joined in. Roakore and Silverwind were a devastating pair against the draggard and specifically the dwargon. Silverwind's talons easily pierced the thick, scaled hide of the draggard and crushed them like prey. Her razor-sharp beak sent heads rolling in the blink of an eye. Roakore rode her as if they were one. Those draggard that his axe did not reach, his stone bird did, and to devastating effect.

Helzendar and Philo and his fifty dwarves overtook a castle and routed the occupants, and draggard and dwargon alike fell from the castle walls to the stone below. In the wake of the elves and dwarves, the castles were left smoldering.

Whill flew high above the battlefield and studied the armies below. With his mind-sight he scanned the auras, looking for the dark elves. They had yet to show their faces.

"What if this is a trap?" asked the Other, who was suddenly floating there next to him.

Whill gave a start and cursed under his breath. "I don't care anymore. If Eadon is here, so be it; if he is not, I will destroy his entire army."

"You? What have you done?" the Other asked. "You read a few tomes and you are a master? I would show you things beyond your wildest dreams." He stared at Whill with a gleam in his eye. The darkness cast by the rift of the starlit sky on the other side made his sunken face the more haunting.

Whill convulsed and suddenly was not controlling his movements. He fought for control but was met with a mental assault of pain and dark, blood and chains. Whill fought through the visions but could not keep his focus. Fear became his only thought, pain his only emotion.

The Other flew Whill to land atop the hill that the armies had just taken. Below, a valley led to where the churning portal met the ground. Thousands of beasts and abominations had gathered to face them. Still there was no sign of dark elves.

Avriel landed next to Whill and a bloody-mouthed Zorriaz stared keenly at the portal as if hypnotized.

"They number in the tens of thousands; reinforcements join us from all sides of the island soon. Shall we hold our ground?" Avriel asked Whill and Zerafin, who came to stand next to Whill.

Silverwind gave a squawk and landed next to the dragon. Roakore gave the beast an uneasy glance and then looked at Whill.

"What's that, lad? You be injured," he asked, pointing at Whill's face. Blood trickled from his nose and ears, eyes and mouth. His armor was suddenly dirty and dented; cuts and scrapes covered his exposed flesh.

The Other did not answer but ignored them all. He strode to the highest point of the hill and opened his arms out wide. Whill fought within his mind for domination. He called to the blade and it answered, but as it answered him, the Other gained strength also. His fortress of pain intensified the more he fought, and he soon found himself writhing in mental agony. Whill was hit by the memory of the chains. He could feel the pain of the barbed chains being pulled through his arms from hand to shoulder, and there the spikes held them in place. Whill had hung from those chains for a month as rats slowly ate away at his feet. He screamed in agony but there was no one to hear but the Other, who smiled.

The Other bellowed into the stormy heavens before the rift, and the ancient elven words echoed across the island for miles. He unsheathed the blade Adromida and stabbed it to the heavens. Lightning exploded from it and parted the dark clouds above. Through the hole in the clouds sunlight poured and seemed to swirl around the blade. Again the Other bellowed in ancient Elvish, and the clouds above exploded and rain and fist-sized hail began to fall upon the draggard armies in and around the portal. The Other ended the long spell with a low guttural growl and everyone watched in awe as the very rain caught on fire, and the hail became streaking purple fireballs. The purple fire-rain fell upon the armies and burned through scale and hide, bone and tooth. The shrieks and screams of thousands of dying beasts filled the air and added to the chaotic tumult. The rift swirled and the wind blew the deadly fireballs across the land swiftly. Soon the entire valley below was aflame with dancing purple fire.

Trapped within his mind, Whill fought the memories and the crushing fear but to no avail. It was not until Avriel's hand upon his shoulder caused the Other to lose his concentration in her eyes. The spell ceased and Whill was suddenly able to mentally wrestle the Other for control of his body. He fell to a knee and panted as he stared out over the destruction the Other had wrought.

Cheers rang out as elves and dwarves alike celebrated the destruction of the armies. Rain soon put out the purple flames and smoldering bodies littering the valley for miles. Through the rift the draggard armies stopped marching and it became quiet.

Avriel, with her hand still upon Whill's shoulder, turned him to face her. Gone were the Other's scars and blood. She smiled at him with concern. "Are you all right? I could not contact you, there was a shadow... was it—"

"It is all right, I am fine." He suddenly noticed the entirety of the elven and dwarven armies watching him. "Let us bring the fight to them! To the rift!" he yelled above Avriel, and then gave her a long, fierce kiss that sent the dwarves into louder cheers.

The armies charged over the smoldering remains of the draggard armies down into the valley. Through the rift, all that could be seen were stars in a clear black sky. The wind near the rift blew at high speeds and made advancement hard. Dirt and debris flew around the mouth of the rift and the armies soon came to a halt before it. Whill walked a few steps closer and turned back to his friends.

Without a word, Whill summoned the courage and flew from the ground up and into the rift.

CHAPTER THIRTY-NINE

Chieftain of the Seven

None stood to challenge Aurora that day, and soon word had spread throughout all of Volnoss. Aurora Snowfell, the Chieftain of the Seven, had defeated Icethorn, and now called all warriors to the rift.

A camp had been made close to the rift that night, and by morning the warriors of the seven tribes began to file onto the Gretchnar Hills, where the mysterious portal had appeared only days ago. Any that had gone through the rift had not come back out, but that did not stop brave barbarian warriors from going through also.

Aurora met with the chiefs of the seven tribes and learned that the rift had appeared but nothing had yet come through. She told them to rouse their armies and have them there immediately. The chiefs complied and soon the vast stretching camps of the seven armies grew around the portal.

She looked out over her vast army on the fifth day and felt such pride that she was overwhelmed by tears. She was the chieftain of the seven, she had avenged her father, and she would lead her people to glory. Aurora was confident now that she was free of Eadon's curse.

Azzeal came to stand beside her as she surveyed her army from on high. Her tent had been set up on the highest bluff overlooking the rift. Through the portal could be seen bright stars against a background of dark. The stars shifted nearly unnoticed within the rift, whose crown of storm cloud and lightning never ceased to rage.

"Soon they will come forth from the rift, and you will be tested," said Azzeal at her side.

Aurora looked down at him and scowled. "I answer not to Eadon."

She expected Azzeal to once again argue the point, but he did not. Aurora had gotten to know the elf well enough to know that something was amiss. He had a look in his eyes she had not seen him wear. He seemed distance, as if a great burden weighed upon his mind.

"What is it?" she finally asked when he would not meet her gaze.

Azzeal jerked as if he had been roused from a trance. He met her eyes searching, and finally looked away.

"I am master of many schools of Orna Catorna. Others I have studied and have some skill in."

Aurora looked to him waiting, she began to feel as though she did not want to hear what came next, so heavy was the weight of his words.

"I have had a vision of the near future." he said with uncharacteristic intensity.

"Soon the rift will empty, and your debt shall be due," he explained.

"I die, is that it?" she asked with a raised chin. "So be it, my people will fight on in my stead. The dark elves shall not have Volnoss. I will die defying Eadon."

Azzeal shook his head gently with her every word. "Will you?" he asked, clearly angered by her words.

Aurora turned on him with anger of her own. "Yes! My life is forfiet; I have done what I came here to do. If my pledge of fealty remains then I shall die defying it."

"Even at the expense of your tribes?" Azzeal asked.

"What do you know?" she asked, tired of his riddles.

Azzeal would not meet her eyes. His haunted gaze looked beyond the army and rift below.

"I have never had much interest in the art of Aklenar. It is a difficult and dangerous practice. Many elves with the gift have gone mad trying to decipher the future. For once it is seen..." he looked to her and smiled weakly. "Remember this, if you side with Eadon, you will wish you had died instead."

Azzeal turned and was gone in a shower of falling feathers. Aurora heard his words again in her mind. What had he seen that had shaken him so? What would she do? Was she truly prepared to die and leave the fate of her people to the gods?

"Many ghosts haunt you this night," said a voice.

Aurora whipped her head and scoured the tent. From the large open window she could see the entire room. It held little place to hide. She wondered if she had imagined the voice when it came again.

"My master told me that you were a rare specimen, 'a beauty of the north to match the fire burning strong within her', he had said."

The ground at the center of the tent bulged and grew. Grass and dirt fell away leaving a dark figure standing before her. Aurora reached for her sword but an unseen force held it firm.

"That won't be necessary," said the figure.

Although it was an hour before sunset and even with the many candles alit in the tent, a shadow played around the figure leaving him cloaked in darkness. The voice was none she recognized.

"I am Zander, it is an honor to finally meet you... general." said Zander.

"General? If I am a general of yours release my sword arm."

Zander nodded curtly and Aurora felt the grip let up. As soon as she was free she unsheathed her blade and had it at the phantom's throat in a heartbeat.

"Who sent you?"

"You know who sent me."

"Why did you call me your general?"

"Because you are my general."

"Enough of the games!"

Zander turned to black smoke which swirled around Aurora and flew to a chair at her large table. He solidified sitting back easy with one leg over the other. The shadow had left him. Aurora stared across the room at a devilishly handsome dark elf with swirling dark red tattoos of intricate patterns and arching symbols. She shuddered with realization.

"Eadon," she whispered.

"My master, and yours as well," Zander smirked and his long pointed eyebrows lifted lightly his black bangs.

Zander indicated the chair opposite himself with a gloves finger set with a long curved metal talon. His arm and body alike were bound with twisted leather and black shining metal; over his shoulder and draped about him was a cloak of living shadow. A sapphire the size of a fist was set at the center of his chest, it pulsed faintly casting a light red aura about him. Aurora took the seat; she felt very small before the dark elf. Her vow of fealty to Eadon played out maddeningly in the back of her mind. She wanted to flee, flip the table and run, run far from here.

"So soon you have forgotten your vow?" Zender asked with a small scowl. "Do not tell Zander Miak that you stand conflicted."

Aurora could not speak, her head swam sickeningly. Her vow to Eadon blended with that cursed voice relentlessly singing "coward at your back".

Zander moved to speak low across the table as if conspiring. "Our master has the entire country in a choke hold. All of the rifts save this one have poured forth his magnificent armies. Mighty Eldalon has fallen, the dwarf mountains have been compromised, and as we speak Cyrushia falls. What is it that you ponder?"

Aurora failed to hide her shock in hearing of the fate of Agora. Where was Azzeal, why had he abandoned her? She remembered her words to the elf; her promise that she would die rather than join Eadon. But what of her people?

"It sounds as though there is no use for us. It sounds as though we have won," said Aurora trying to relay bored detachment. Zander's eyes told her that he was no fool.

"There is much to do. The dwarf mountains will take years to route. The barbarians will be glad to return to northern Ky'Dren will they not? T'was once yours was it not?' The horn of Eldalon as well; it shall fall upon your people to conquer and claim that as land."

Zander moved like a stalking cat around the table to kneel at her feet. "I see your heart Aurora, it is good that you are bound by honor. But where does your guilt and loyalty lie? Your people were murdered by humans and dwarves; tossed from Agora like animals and left to die on this frozen wasteland. The time for tears is past, now is time for justice."

Aurora listened to the dark elf enchanted. His words weaved a beautiful tapestry of reclamation and conquest, a return of her people's honor and homelands. A tear found her cheek and she knew why Azzeal had left. Another spilled down her opposite cheek and she knew what he had seen. Aurora put her hands to the dark elf's shoulders and she grinned. "Let us begin."

CHAPTER FORTY
The Lady and the Wolf

The explosion threw Dirk back into the catapult with so much force that he was knocked unconscious. Had the enchantments about his armor not absorbed the brunt of the blast, he would have been destroyed. What armor was left had been drained of power and was now no more than leather and metal.

His ears hammered and he could hear nothing of the world. In a daze he blinked at the smoldering world and knew he must be dreaming. There, standing between himself and the seething hordes, was Krentz. In one hand she held her blade and from the other she blasted draggard with spells. Her tight, sleek armor reflected the dancing flames around them with its seamless sheen; it looked as though she wore black ice.

He drifted in and out of dreams. In one he helplessly watched Krentz fight a dark elf. In another he watched as whirlwinds of smoke and ash flew up as a brilliant dragon with silver feathers landed and began ravishing monsters mercilessly. In his final dream Dirk watched the rift float by as if time had slowed. Beneath him Fyrfrost steadily beat his wings, and Krentz's sweet voice hushed him back into deep dreamless sleep.

He awoke in a field of tall golden wheat next to a thick forest. His armor was gone, and he wore nothing at all. Instantly he became alert to his surroundings. He crouched on all fours and peeked over the wheat to the dark forest. Sound came from within, a soft hummed song that was hauntingly familiar to him. He was drawn into the woods by the voice—by her voice.

Dirk followed Krentz's humming and came to a small clearing. There hanging from an oak tree were his underclothes. He pulled on his trousers and laced them up as he looked around at the apparent camp. He quickly realized the humming had stopped. He walked into the clearing, and through the trees on the other side came Krentz. The low morning sun shone through clouds, sending beams of light dancing through the clearing.

"This is real?" Dirk asked hopefully as he walked slowly toward Krentz and she to him.

"It is." She smiled.

"Before…that wasn't a dream?" he asked, coming closer.

"No." She laughed and hugged her lover.

Dirk took in the smell of her hair and knew it to be true. "But how?" he asked, backing his head and looking her over. "You defy the will of Eadon as we speak. How did you get out of the relic? Where are we?"

She kissed him for a long, soft moment. "It is over, my love. We are free."

"But how?" he insisted.

Krentz lowered her gaze and turned. She walked into the clearing and Dirk followed. Her right hand found her left arm and held it the way that she did when she had something she did not want to say. It was a nervous tic Dirk knew well. She led him to the middle of the clearing and turned to sit with him.

"When I went into the spirit world with the wolf... something happened that broke my vow of fealty. I must obey it no longer. We are free."

"What happened?" asked Dirk, squeezing her hand and hoping it was anything but what he guessed.

Krentz took a deep breath through her nose and smiled sympathetically. "I died."

Dirk swallowed hard and ran a hand through his hair as if wanting to tear it out.

"It is not your fault, it is not a bad thing, it was the only way," she told him urgently, but he was not convinced.

"How were you revived?" he asked, touching her warm flesh.

She turned her head to the side and moved away from him to stand. Turning to face him, she wore the same shy look she had the first time they had laid together.

"I wasn't," she said, rubbing her arm. He rose to come to her but she stepped back and held out a halting hand.

"Don't. I must show you."

Dirk nodded slowly and stood opposite her. Before his eyes she became translucent and turned to silver-gray smoke. Astonished, Dirk watched as the smoke snaked its way around him, causing him to turn with it. She took form once again before him but remained translucent.

"You are...?" Dirk struggled to speak past his sorrow. "You are a ghost? I have killed you?" he said with the heavy weight of guilt. He reached for her but his hand moved through her as if through air. The hairs on his arm stood up and he looked upon her painfully.

"You have freed me," she argued as she materialized and took his hands in hers. "Only through death could I be free of the curse. You have given me that, and I have come back to you." She gave him a smile he did not share.

"But your body...where...?"

"I do not know. When I went into the spirit world, my body...it changed. Now I am like the wolf. I am of the spirit world."

Dirk's tears threatened to fall and she pulled him onto a kiss. "I was prepared to die for you. This was the only way. Now we can be together. Now we are free."

"Krentz, I never meant for this—"

"There was no other way," she insisted.

"There is always another way. I meant to trap you within the relic until I had sought out help."

"Help from whom?"

"Whill. He is in possession of the ancient blade. I had hoped—"

"Even if he could help, would he? You betrayed his trust, and I am a dark elf. No help would have come from him. No help will come from anyone, you know that."

Dirk sighed and sat again upon the grass. He looked around curiously at the forest. "Where are we? What day is it?" he asked.

"Don't you recognize it? This is Eldon Island. You have slept a day and a night. You needed it—what have you been doing to yourself? You had nearly enough adrenaline and dragonroot in your system to kill you, and you have barely eaten." She lectured him as she always had.

She was back, they were together, and they were free. The realization hit Dirk like a brick and he smiled. He suddenly rushed forward to kiss Krentz and she met him with equal urgency. They clung to each other in the afternoon sun as the pressure of the last few weeks finally lifted like the weight of a mountain. They were not only free of Eadon, they were free from worry.

They talked for hours and Dirk ate. Roasted cronies, wild onions, roots, and nuts were their dinner, and it was the most delicious food he had ever eaten.

Dirk told Krentz about his race to Kell-Torey from the portal in Uthen-Arden nearly a week before. And she told him her tale. How she had been gifted great power by her father, power that he did not give often or to many. How she had tried to sneak away, had tried to run. But the more she moved against her father, even in thought, the more she was pained. She could not even move to kill herself, or be killed. She tried to explain that she had not chosen to kill the royals of Eldalon, that it had been impossible to disobey. Dirk knew she was pleading her innocence to herself as much to him.

"The children, the families...I can still see their faces, I can still hear their surprise. I was the harbinger of death to the innocent...I—"

"Stop," said Dirk with a hand to her shoulder. "You did nothing. You were used, you were merely a weapon. Is the sword capable of murder?" He lifted her chin and released it roughly. "Remember the code that you taught me? You have not broken it."

"I killed an entire family!" She suddenly erupted into tears.

Dirk held her and rocked her gently. The wind picked up and the smell of thunderstorm rain filled the air. He looked around at the blowing trees and suddenly to Krentz, making the connection.

"Shh, do not punish yourself. You know that you are innocent in this. If you have guilt, only then are your tears justified." He made her look at him. "Did you want to do it?"

"No!" she cried, giving him a stabbing look.

"Did you enjoy it?" he pressed.

"No!" she yelled again, now angry. Lightning flashed in the distance and a crackling boom of thunder soon followed.

"Then stop this childish behavior! Or do you mean to ravish the world?" he asked, gesturing to the storm growing around them.

She looked up and blinked as if just noticing the massing darkness. Her hand flew to her mouth in shock and her eyes went wide as she saw what she had caused.

"Your father's gifts were great," said Dirk, watching the dark clouds above slow as she calmed herself. "And your guilt is great also. You cannot live with a storm raging inside you. Shed your tears and bury it, and never look back."

"You are right," she said, sniffling and combing back her hair with her fingers. She laughed as she pulled herself together and stood, needing to walk. Dirk followed her to the field he had awakened in. The dark clouds had blown past and the clear sky whispered of twilight. Fyrfrost suddenly appeared, morphing from the color of the blue sky above. He furiously beat his wings to slow down and landed. He ruffled his feathers and dropped a doe at Dirk's feet.

"I take it you have met Fyrfrost," said Dirk.

"I have," she purred as the dragon-hawk offered his head for her to stroke. "He told me the name you gave him. He said you freed him from dark-elf twins."

"He told you?" Dirk mused. "He never talked to me."

"His thoughts, you fool man." She laughed. "I have met and spoken to Chief as well."

"What?" Dirk exclaimed. "Chief speaks? I don't believe it."

She laughed again. "He does."

"And what does a spirit wolf have to say?"

"He says that you are a great hunter, even though you are small." She grinned.

"Small?"

"Yes. It seems that he is from the barbarian island of Volnoss. There they grow to nine feet sometimes."

"Yes, I have met one recently," said Dirk, thinking of Aurora Snowfell with a smile.

They returned to camp and summoned the timber wolf to guard for the night. From Fyrfrost's saddle they gathered blankets and made their bed beneath the stars. Long into the night they talked and laughed.

It had been a long time since they lived so many peaceful years on Eldon Island. Dirk had spent many long years in search of Krentz, lonely years in which he had obsessively tracked any clue of her. In the end he had quite stumbled upon her in Del-Oradon.

Dirk held her close and listened to her soft breathing upon his chest. Finally he could rest.

CHAPTER FORTY-ONE

Strangers in a Strange Land

Whill flew through the rift to Drindellia and came out in the midst of a nightmare. The armies of draggard, draquon, and dwargon that marched toward the portal were innumerable. The landscape was littered with crystal monoliths that rose up into the sky, threatening to reach the heavens themselves. Out of the bases of the crystal towers dark hordes poured. With his mind-sight Whill was able to make out the life-forms within, and he was shocked to see the towers teeming with life.

Miles away and in every direction around him there were other rifts. Whill's dread grew as he counted eight others beside the one he had come through. The elves could only see six with Queen Araveal's looking glass, which meant that three of the rifts could not be seen from the air.

"The other rifts are within the mountains of the dwarves," said the Other, floating next to him.

Whill was too absorbed in the magnitude of the implications of what he said to be annoyed with his split personality. The dwarf mountains were being invaded; all of Agora was being invaded, on a scale that had never been seen.

"This horde will destroy the worlds of men, dwarves, and elves," said the Other cryptically as he floated around Whill, staring him down. "Give me control and we shall destroy them all."

Whill was tempted to give in, to let his other side take responsibility. But he did not trust the Other, which was to say that he did not trust himself. He knew that the more he let the Other lead, the more powerful that side of him would become. Whill was reminded of the fact that Eadon likely had tortured him only to create the Other, the side of Whill that would blindly strike, giving the dark elf lord what he wanted.

"No!" he said firmly. "You are not welcome here."

The Other's face twitched and his bloodshot eyes bore into Whill's. Below, the armies of draggard advancing through the rift were suddenly blown back by a multitude of massive explosions as the elves of the sun and the dwarves of both Ro'Sar and Helgar stormed through.

"Not welcome? In my own body?" the Other hissed. "You ungrateful cowa—"

"You were created for this very purpose, don't you see? You are a pawn in Eadon's game and nothing more!" screamed Whill.

"You know nothing of my creation; you are too weak to see. Without me you would have died in that dungeon," the Other snarled, his eyes and nose now bleeding profusely.

"If you want to help, get out of my way," Whill warned, unsheathing the ancient blade.

Roakore flew through the rift with Avriel and the armies of his allies behind him. He gave a war cry that was matched by the piercing cry of Silverwind as they came out on the other side. Roakore's gusto temporarily faltered as he laid eyes upon the largest gathering of creatures he had ever seen. He knew that indeed the rift led to Drindellia, where it seemed Eadon had been brewing an invading army. Strange crystal megaliths speckled the barren valley and glowed in the night. The king noticed the other rifts and rage burned within him.

Ahead Whill was floating in midair, the ancient blade in his right hand. Below, a barrage of spells and fireballs flew through the rift and hit the advancing draggard forces with devastating effect. Through the rift the allied armies charged. Roakore spurred Silverwind into a dive and joined into the fray. His hawk came down fast upon two draggard and with crushing claws lifted them into the air to fall down upon their kin. Roakore guided his stone bird off to the side of Silverwind, braining the seething draggard as they flew past.

A horn blew from somewhere within the legions and was answered by many more. From the hovering crystal monoliths came scores of winged draquon, and upon the backs of the largest were dark elf riders. Roakore veered left and flew over the elven forces.

"Hundreds o' draquon come from the east! To the air, elves, to arms!"

Avriel joined him and circled the Elladrindellian forces. She bellowed a call to arms in Elvish and dozens of Ralliad masters shifted into birds of prey and took to the air. Roakore and Avriel led the group of nearly fifty Ralliad shifters straight at the draquon forces. From below, spells shot into the sky from dozens of dark-elf casters. From behind the flying Ralliad group, counterspells blasted forth to intercept. Roakore squeezed the saddle horn and prepared for evasive maneuvers when the counterspells erupted in an explosion and shower of green and blue sparks. Below the flying elves the dark-elf spells hit the wall of combined energy of the sun-elf counterspells and were absorbed by the wide shield.

The first of the draquon reached the group and Roakore sang a dwarven war chant as he hacked at the passing beast. His axe tore the underbelly of one beast and sent it spinning out of control. Another came at him from the right, but Silverwind quickly banked and caught it in her crushing claws.

All around them the Ralliad elves engaged the charging beasts, and though the shape-shifting masters could make short work of the draquon, the beasts kept coming in droves. The Ralliad masters were able to cast in their animal forms, and where a talon or beak might not kill a draquon every time, their spells could. Broken draquon bodies and elf bodies' alike fell from the aerial battlefields and crashed upon the warring groups below.

Whill fought the Other for control but quickly found himself losing. Pain and depression, guilt and sorrow plagued his mind in a nefarious orchestra. And while the Other had six months of torturous memories at his disposal, Whill did not know how to attack his own ego. To him pleasure was pain and sorrow joy, and therefore Whill could only try and ward off the mental attack.

He screamed in rage and dove through the air at his doppelganger. Adromida streaked through the air, leaving a streak of blue light in its wake. The glowing blue sword was met by likewise glowing red chains. The chains wrapped themselves around the ancient blade several times, and with a maniacal grin the Other yanked the sword from his grasp.

Whill blacked out and found himself once again within the dungeons of Del'Oradon Castle. Burning chains held his arms high as his toes barely scraped against the floor below. The right side of his face was swollen and throbbing, his right eye useless or missing, he could not tell. He looked around at the familiar cell; the dank smell of the slimy walls reminded him of a sewer. The barred door before him offered nothing of the world but the distant cries and sobs of his fellow prisoners. His own maddening cries echoed in his memory as they had so often done within these subterranean chambers. Whill shivered with fear and pain as he watched shadows dance beyond the bars. Distant torchlight caused the phantom dark-elf torturer to loom upon the tunnel wall, and Whill heard himself whimper.

"This isn't real."

The shadow on the wall grew bigger.

"This isn't real."

A hooded figure came into view in the hall.

"This isn't real."

The cell doors flew open and the figure slowly crossed the space between them. His foul breath played on Whill's face and he turned from it. His torturer brought a dagger to bear upon Whill's stomach, and with a grin he shoved it in to the hilt.

Whill let out a cry of pain and shuddered. "This isn't real!"

✕

Avriel steered Zorriaz the White to bear upon Whill. She had tried to contact him mentally but was met by a wall of silence. Something was wrong. Whill hovered high above the land at the center of the aerial battle with arms outstretched. He shuddered violently and arched his back to the heavens as if in great pain. He looked as though he was caught in the throes of a Zionar battle, but she knew better.

As she circled him, trusting the dragon-hawk to fend off any attackers, she yelled his name into the wind. The power from her blade helped amplify her voice, but Whill did not respond. Instead he screamed in rage and threw his arms up toward the stars. From each of his wrists, barbed chains ripped out of his skin and shot outward five feet. Whill bowed his head and the chains fell to his side.

Avriel flew to hover before him and called his name again. "Whill!"

Slowly he raised his head and the bloodshot eyes of the Other fell upon her. The pain she saw in those eyes made hers tear in empathy. "I had thought you dead for so long…," he said in a hushed whisper of reverie.

Blood trickled down the chains as he reached a trembling hand to her face. Avriel smiled upon him sympathetically.

"I love you, Avriel," said the Other, barely containing his composure.

"I love you as well, Whill." She smiled and laid a soft hand upon his. "Come back to me," she said gently, hoping that, like before, it would help Whill to regain control.

Around them the battle raged. Spells and draquon alike flew at them, but none could penetrate the shield circle the Other had built around them. Tears of blood fell from Whill's dirty face.

"I have come back to you. It's me, Avriel, it is Whill. The man you knew, not this cowardly imposter. And it is I who shall wreak vengeance upon our enemies."

A large fireball exploded against the Other's shield in a shower of sparks. Debris sent a sun elf in bird form falling broken to the ground below. The Other released Avriel's hand and with a wicked smile summoned the power of Adromida. Avriel watched on as the bloody chains began to glow until they were too bright to look at. The Other left the shield floating around Avriel and with chains spinning joined the aerial battle.

The glowing chains cut through draggard bodies easily as the nearby elves gave Whill a wide berth. The Other sent butchered pieces of draquon raining down upon the legions below. A mounted dark elf screamed the name of Eadon and put every bit of stored energy it had into a spell meant for Whill. The writhing black tendril was intercepted by a glowing chain and absorbed instantly. The astonished dark elf reared its mount to retreat as the Other raised a hand and the dark elf shot to it until he was held firm in an iron grip.

"I will destroy you all," said the Other and sucked the very life out of the dark elf.

With a satisfied shudder he discarded the dried husk that had been the dark elf. Then he set his eyes upon the scores of draquon flying toward the allied armies. He flew well ahead of the battles of land and air, and with arms raised to the sky, he conjured a swirling ball of energy. From Adromida he let the energy flow into a dense ball of swirling light until it hummed with tension. With a scream of rage he sent the energy ball flying to the center of the circle of rifts, nearly two miles away. Any draquon that got in the path of the missile were disintegrated as it flew the distance in seconds.

The Other turned back toward the armies of his allies and with outstretched hands summoned a shield to encompass them all. Behind him the energy ball slammed into the ground and swallowed all sound. All heads turned to the spectacle as the Other's spell flashed and then disappeared. Sound returned to the world and a groan louder than shifting mountain rumbled through the ground for miles. A circle of darkness appeared where the energy ball had vanished, and everything nearby was pulled into it. Draggard and dwargon alike fought each other to get away as the black hole drew more and more beasts and dark elves alike into it. The nearby crystal monoliths too were pulled in and crumbled violently as they mashed with everything else being sucked into the small, dense black hole.

Suddenly the pulling stopped and again it was quiet, and then just as suddenly a deafening explosion ripped through the air as the black hole exploded and a shockwave tore across the land in every direction. Everything for miles was disintegrated as the shockwave and ensuing fireball obliterated any sign of the dark elves or their hellish creations. A mushroom-like cloud of fiery smoke and ash reached up until it flattened against the heavens as the shockwave and fireball rolled harmlessly over Whill's shield and around the allied armies.

Finally it was over, and a hot wind fell upon the faces of the allies as they stared at Whill in awe as he floated high above the desolation of his spell. The few dark elves who had managed to shield themselves from the blast wasted no time in fleeing. It was a while before anyone noticed that along with the dark-elf armies, the rifts had been destroyed as well.

The day had been won, but now the elven and dwarven armies of Agora were trapped many thousands of miles away in Drindellia. Quickly the cheers of both elves and dwarves were replaced by a foreboding at the realization of their plight. They had no way home.

THE END

Dear Reader,

Thank you for purchasing this book. I hope you have enjoyed the adventures of Whill of Agora. What started twelve years ago as a story for my children has turned into the Legends of Agora universe. I hope that interest in the series allows me to continue the story for a long time to come. If you like the books tell everyone you know on Facebook and Twitter and so on. Its fans like you that make all of this possible.

I would love to hear what you thought of the story, so please feel free to join in the conversation at www. whillofagora.com.

If you would like, feel free to leave a review of books one and two on Amazon.

I am a self-published author and do not have the luxury of a team of promoters at my disposal. You are my team, and I appreciate your efforts and support.

Thanks again, friends, for following Whill this far. I hope to go on many more adventures with you in the future.

I have recently published two children's books that I think you will find enjoyable. The Sock Gnome Chronicles follow the adventures and exploits of Billy Coatbutton. Billy is a sock gnome living within Sockefeller Castle; book one, *Billy Coatbutton and the Wheel of Destiny*, follows Billy as he attempts his first test of mastery to see if he will become a treasure hunter like his father.

Adults and children alike will enjoy this satirical romp into the lives of sock gnomes, while at the same time answering the age-old question, where *do* those missing socks go?

Thank you once again for your support,

With humble appreciation,
Michael James Ploof

29214892R00313

Made in the USA
Lexington, KY
19 January 2014